"How did it start?" I ⬛⬛⬛⬛⬛⬛⬛⬛⬛
suburbia, past all the ic⬛⬛⬛⬛⬛⬛⬛⬛
lawns and into yet anotl⬛⬛⬛⬛⬛⬛⬛⬛
houses and immaculate ⬛⬛⬛⬛⬛⬛⬛⬛

"I got a call from one Mrs. Rye in Bloodworth Commons," Ken said. "She said that she was afraid her daughter was making a very bad choice."

"Yes?" I wondered if Ken could have blown all this out of proportion. I'd grown up in deepest, whitest suburbia. A bad choice might mean that the poor girl wanted to wear her third-best jeans to the church picnic.

"Well, it appears that little Suzie Quinina Rye—not so little, since she's about seventeen—has fallen head over heels for a mysterious older man. I've heard through the grapevine that there were many cases of anemia and strange neck injuries in this area..."

I felt a shiver run up my spine and noted that the sun was setting. "So...there's a vampire on the loose?"

"Unless I'm mistaken, from what I can *feel*, it's a very old vampire who's been asleep for the last couple hundred years. And has never learned...eating manners."

"Oh," I said, and shivered again, quite sure he wasn't talking about using the right silverware.

He parked the car. "And this," he said, "is where the vampire lives." He waved his hand to a tiny enclosure bordered around by a Victorian iron fence with a plaque saying Historical Pioneer Cemetery.

I frowned at Ken. "How do you know?"

"Because last night I almost caught him," he said. "Oh."

"And he almost staked me."

—from "A Matter of Blood"

Fangs for the Mammaries

Edited by
Esther M. Friesner

A Baen Books Original

Baen Publishing Enterprises
P.O. Box 1403
Riverdale, NY 10471
www.baen.com

ISBN: 978-1-4391-3392-7

Cover art by Clyde Caldwell

First Baen paperback printing, October 2010

Distributed by Simon & Schuster
1230 Avenue of the Americas
New York, NY 10020

Pages by Joy Freeman (www.pagesbyjoy.com)
Printed in the United States of America

Additional Copyright Information

Contents

Because an anthology of funny stories about
vampires in Suburbia
cries out (or howls at the moon) for
an eminently suitable dedicatee,
it is with great respect, friendship,
and appreciation for innumerable vampire jokes
That we Undeadicate this book to
Marty Gear
a.k.a. "Vlad".
Fangs a lot.

Esther M. Friesner is the author of 35 novels and over 180 short stories and other works. She won the Nebula twice, as well as the Skylark and the Romantic Times award. Best known for creating and editing the wildly popular *Chicks in Chainmail* anthology series (Baen Books), recent publications include the young adult novels *Temping Fate*, *Nobody's Princess*, *Nobody's Prize*, and *Sphinx's Princess*. She lives in Connecticut with her husband, is the mother of two grown children, and harbors cats.

Introduction

Esther Friesner

Goot eeeevening. Velcome to my eeeentroduction.
Enter freely and—
SLAP!!!
Whew. Thanks. I needed that.

Welcome indeed to this, the third in our glamorous and high-paying literary *tour de force* exploring
the economic, sociological, and ecological impact of
witches, werewolves and vampires in that geographi-
cal subset of the world popularly known as Suburbia.
But before you step over the threshold to explore
the sanguinophagous delights within these pages, I'd
like to have a few moments of your time to lay some
cards on the table.

I feel that, given the fact that this book is devoted
to the carryings-on of vampires in the suburban milieu,
we really need to have a few ground rules in place
and understood before turning our attention to those
critters of the night who spend their days six feet
under said ground. (Figuratively speaking, of course.

For all I know, every last surburban vamp is spending the sunrise-to-sunset hours in the family rec room, comfortably snuggled away inside some sort of spiffy container purchased at the local IKEA.)

Case in point, my failed attempt at beginning this introduction. Campy *faux* Transylvanian is jangly enough to the innocent ear, but when the reader's eye must wrestle with that dreadfully twisted orthography, it becomes the realm of Cruel and Unusual Punishment.

And we don't want that. We love our readers. We cherish our readers. We want our readers to be happy. Or at least mollified. And face it, now there is a lot of stuff written about vampires—as well as *how* it's written—that leaves many a reader in a state of definite nonmollification.

Hence, the ground rules in effect for this Introduction, viz.:

1. I promise not to put on a really bad Bela Lugosi accent in print. I can't make the same promise for any of the other authors, however, nor can I extend said promise to any time you might happen to run into me at a party. Just be grateful for miniscule favors, move along, and be careful which parties you attend in future.

2. I promise not to make any of the far too easy puns that swarm around just about every mention of vampires—suburban or otherwise. This is an especially vile temptation under the present circumstances, seeing as how this is a book about vampires in

Suburbia. As I might have mentioned in the Introductions to previous anthologies, Suburbia has become a very easy target for the Hip, the Hot, the Artsy, and the Artsy-with-a-capital-F. Thus I promise not to yield to the urge to make vampire-slanted puns about how Suburbia bites, sucks, is dead, drains your blood, drives you batty, etc.

It is one thing to shoot fish in a barrel. It is another thing to bring flamethrowers into play against beached guppies.

Except I pretty much just did that, didn't I? Oops. Well, never mind. The thing about vampire puns—even specifically targeted *suburban* vampire puns—is that no matter how many I may choose to make outright or by sneaky-Pete allusion (as above), there are plenty of Gentle Readers out there who are already hastening to come up with oodles of their own "I can top that!" word-play.

Go for it.

Forbear from sharing them with me, but go for it. Meanwhile, back at the Introduction Rules...

3. I promise not to take any shots—cheap or otherwise—at any of the trendier media presentations of vampires in the suburbs. This includes movies, TV, and, of course, novels. My personal opinion (as distinct from my *im*personal opinion?) shall be kept to myself. The Internet is already burgeoning with plenty of folks who have taken issue with certain of the newer,

perhaps not *quite* traditional, staggeringly
popular versions of non-urban vamps. Let
the eloquence be theirs.

Again, just because the barrel is brimming with
trout and there's a Keen-O Destructinator Ray already
aimed, primed, and ready to rock 'n' roll, does not
mean I need to pull the trigger.

With our ground rules in place, let us proceed
with all due decorum.

It is a fairly obvious truth that vampires and the
suburbs are a match made in Heaven, or maybe Lev-
ittown. Vampires do very well indeed in your typical
suburban setting. Remember Dracula? He didn't run
into any real problems until he took his act on the road
and traveled to the Big City. Some might argue that he
originally dwelled in rural isolation, not amidst suburban sprawl, but it wasn't as isolated as all that. Even
though there was abundant forest and packs of wolves
running pooper-scooper free across his front lawn, there
were also plenty of villagers within a leathery-winged
flight of his H.Q. And truly, many a modern American
suburban community's nexus could be classified as a
village, population-wise. (Castle Dracula, the ultimate
gated community? *You* be the judge!)

Another thing about the suburbs is the selective
isolation. Everyone is so polite, so respectful of their
neighbors (in general) and their neighbors' right to
privacy (in particular). As long as your dog does not
do his business on your neighbors' lawn, your kids
do not make so much noise that your neighbors are
disturbed by it, and your grass is kept clipped enough
to fend off your neighbors' monitory mutterings about

how *some* people's laziness is going to send property values tumbling into the septic tank, you'll be left the hell alone.

Unless your neighbors happen to have kids who are selling gift wrap, magazine subscriptions, fertilizer, cookies, candy, or any of the other school-and-other-kidcentric-organizational-fundraising ploys. Then you might as well leave a bowl full of money on the front porch if you don't want all of that doorbell-ringing to drive you over the edge.

Oh, and leave town on October 31.

But these are only problems for mere mortals. Vampires who desire their suburban seclusion to remain untouched are admirably equipped to withstand all of the pint-sized sales assaults the neighborhood can dish out. For one thing, if the kiddies come around hawking their wares during the day, the vampire is comfortably nestled in his coffin, incommunicado. Have you ever checked out some of the better models of coffins? Thick walls, comfortable mattresses, and most of them have better soundproofing than a lot of recording studios. Little Emily and/or Jason can ring the doorbell 'til the Golden Labrador Retrievers come home and they won't disturb the smugly slumbering vamp within.

And should little Emily and/or Jason try their luck peddling their wares after sundown...Oh boy! Who says you have to stay in the city if you want good take-out meals delivered right to your door?

Yessiree, there's no one quite like a vampire for saying, "All of you kids get off of my lawn!" and putting some *teeth* into it.

If you prefer to maintain that the modern vampire's

one true venue is the city, go right ahead. It's a free country. But at the same time, do please keep an open mind for just a little longer; long enough to dip into the delectable tales that lie beyond this introduction. If you don't find yourself able to imagine a world where the creatures of the night mix and mingle with the children of the SUVs, be thankful that the authors whose words await your perusal could and did.

Will the stories you encounter in these pages convince you that vampires and the suburbs go together like wine and cheese, gin and tonic, desperation and housewives, love and pre-nups and marriage? Perhaps. Will they amuse you? I think so.

Enter freely and of your own will.

A P.S. Addendum From the Department of ~~Blame~~ Credit Where It Is Due:

Although as we all know, editor-writers such as y'r humble & obedient servant (That would be me) are bottomless founts of scintillating creativity, especially when it comes to titles (C'mon, don't tell me you weren't awesomely impressed the first time you saw my little debutante princess, *Chicks in Chainmail*, winking saucily at you from the bookstore shelf!), sometimes we need help.

No, not *professional* help! But help with precisely *les mots justes* for a title for the next anthology coming down the tracks. And it is not always because the old cerebral title factory has been closed for renovations (a.k.a. We're going to Vegas, baby!) but because the Management recognizes the fact that coming up with book titles of a certain sort can be a heck of a lot of fun. It is good to share the fun.

In the past, with the Chicks in Chainmail anthology series, Really *Upper* Management has run a contest to Name That Book, which resulted in *Did You Say "Chicks"?!* as the winner. Well, if it worked once, it was probably a good idea, and so Our Publisher (I can't keep typing "Really Upper Management," and the acronym, R.U.M. sends the wrong message, don't you agree?) ran a new contest to name *this* book.

We got some delightful entries. Although I was not the final judge for this contest—we can blame the R.U.M. for that—I did get to see them, and I must say, I was impressed. But in the end, there could be only one to seize the laurels, and that was the title presently gracing the front cover of the very volume you now hold in your hands, Gentle Reader.

So hats off, kudos, and an appropriate serving of ruffles and flourishes to the winner, Ellen Kaye-Cheveldayoff!

Our thanks to you, and your laurels are in the mail.

Jody Lynn Nye lists her main career activity as "spoiling cats." She lives northwest of Chicago with two of the above and her husband, author and packager Bill Fawcett. She has published more than thirty-five books, including six contemporary fantasies, four SF novels, four novels in collaboration with Anne McCaffrey, including *The Ship Who Won*; edited a humorous anthology about mothers, *Don't Forget Your Spacesuit, Dear!*; and written over a hundred short stories. Her latest books are *A Forthcoming Wizard* (Tor Books), and *Myth-Fortunes*, co-written with Robert Asprin (Wildside Books).

Overbite

Jody Lynn Nye

"Open wide, please."

Obediently, Delilah Stollergard leaned back in the big chair and opened her mouth. Dr. Russell leaned forward with a little light and a probe to check her braces. She felt pressure tighten around her left fang and the adjacent bicuspid and prepared to wince. It didn't hurt. She looked up at him thankfully as he went on adjusting the metal bands. With a snap, he attached new rubber bands, then stepped back, wiping his hands on a towel.

"How's that feel?" he asked.

Delilah ran her tongue around, feeling the unfamiliar protuberances that lined her mouth.

"Fine," she said. "How bad does it look?"

"Not bad at all, for a mouth full of metal," Dr. Russell said, his pale blue eyes twinkling. "Here, let me show you."

He reached for her file. From it, he took a fresh photocopy of a sketch of her that he had done the first

day. She always found photocopies fascinating, because
they were the closest she or any of her kind would
ever come to being photographed. He had a lot of
artistic talent as well as being a good dentist, because
the girl in the drawing looked alive and interesting.
He drew a couple of quick lines over the bared teeth.

"You're showing good progress here and here. I'm
still waiting for this gap to close. It will take a few
months. We can't rush things, but I promise you you
will have a beautiful smile when it's all over."

"Great," Delilah said, sighing with relief. She
glanced out the window. Color still streaked the sky
at the far horizon. "Thanks again for opening the
office early for me."

"I'm happy to, Delilah," he said, his round, pale
face beaming. "I think my son would disown me if
I wouldn't."

Delilah felt the veins in her cheeks tighten, the
vampire equivalent of a blush. "We just like walking
together, that's all."

"Don't tell him I said so, but it's very kind of you
to welcome him the way you have."

"We're used to newcomers," Delilah assured him.
"There are only a few night schools like ours across
the country."

He smiled at her. "Whatever your reason, thank
you. See you next week, dear."

"Bye now," Delilah said, and hastily jumped out
of the chair.

It wasn't kind of her to show Jim friendship. She
liked him a lot. He was really nice and funny. If only...

"Ready?" Jim asked, springing to his feet as she
came out into the waiting room. He was tall and

lanky, his hands and feet seemingly too large for his thin arms, his face a long oval. His eyes were red like the rest of her friends', but his hair was stark white. Except for that hair, he was really good-looking. He smiled, showing perfectly straight teeth and gleaming fangs. It seemed totally unjust that he, the orthodontist's son, would never have to wear braces.

"Yeah. We'd better hurry," Delilah said. "There's assembly instead of homeroom."

If only, she thought, as the two of them hurried out into the dark, he had been a vampire like her.

Jim fit into Elizabeth Bathory High School pretty well so far. He was athletic, friendly, and nice. He horsed around with the guys just like a normal teenager, but Delilah feared for his safety. Social vampirism required total honesty. Since they couldn't see themselves in mirrors or photographs, they relied upon one another for information about their appearance. From what she had experienced of human girls, her kind were a lot less vain. If you had a tag hanging out of the collar of your shirt or the back of your skirt was unzipped or toilet paper was trailing from your shoe, someone would tell you—okay, in high school they were more likely to yell it at you from across the room than take you aside and let you know privately, but the assumption was still there that they were as open with you as you were with them. It could be a matter of survival. To be deliberately dishonest to someone was wrong. If they couldn't depend upon one another, their fragile society could come apart. It had happened in other communities.

She thought it was ironic that Jim and his father had come to Bath, Ohio. They admired vampire culture and preferred it over their own. For his part, Dr. Russell had never pretended to be anything but a human who saw potential clientele where his colleagues feared to go. The community had accepted him and his son. The one lie that they had told—by omission—was that Jim was human, too. One in a million vampires were born to human parents; the genes went as far back as Neanderthals, and might have been the death of that branch of humankind as well. It wasn't out of the question that Dr. Russell and his late wife were carriers. Jim liked the taste of blood. As an albino, he abhorred sunlight. He was stronger and faster than the average teenager. He fully intended to make the change as soon as possible.

Delilah was contributing to that lie by letting it continue. The deception ate at her, but she liked the Russells too much to reveal it. Even her folks didn't know that she was seeing a non-vamp boy. They liked Jim. The secret was the one source of friction between her and Jim. She had told him he had to come out before he was found out. When humans were surprised or frightened by the unknown in their presence, they killed. Vampires did the same thing, with less hesitation. Delilah herself had killed—but only animals. Vampire parents knew that their children had to learn where fresh blood came from. Usually they all consumed commercially-farmed blood, from the same sources as meat that humans ate. Delilah was proud that her family used only organic, free-range blood that had been gathered cruelty-free, though she knew her ancestors had consumed every species but their own. Their blood was toxic to one another. But she was afraid of what her peaceful, live and let live family would do to a human who had insinuated himself into their presence unawares. They would consider it no more than self-defense. Most vamps were afraid of their day-living cousins, not without reason. So had she been, until the Russells had come along. She was surprised to learn how alike humans and vampires were. That was good *and* bad.

The principal, Countess Olga von Mettenmeier, three hundred years old if she was a day, strode out into the spotlight on the center of the stage before the impatient teenage crowd.

"Sit still!" she boomed, aiming an imperious finger at the floor. Her prominent jaw had a quivering bag of flesh under it like that of a bullfrog, the source of amusement to Delilah and her friends. The iron gray eyes, the same color as the countess's hair, peered around and seemed to bore into all of them at once. The students squirmed and sat still. "Good! We will not keep you long. Bathory High is hosting its annual science fair next month. I am looking forward to each of you presenting an experiment or a thought-provoking study. You find that funny, do you? Some day each of you will have reason to have learned to think. Consider this a practice session. We have invited the press. That means you will be constrained to behave yourselves more than you normally do. Anyone who causes trouble that makes it into a news report will fail the assignment. Is that clear?"

Jim and Mike Lippman did a painfully accurate pantomime of the principal that ceased abruptly when the fierce gaze fell on them. They froze.

"Very nice, gentlemen," she said, her eyes glowing red. "You can perform that again at the talent show.

But it will have no place at the science fair. Try to use your analytical faculties, not your taste for foolery. Dismissed!"

"How does she always see us?" Mike asked, plaintively, as the crowd rose around them.

"Because it's always you," Delilah said, clicking her tongue in disgust. She gathered up her books.

"I have a great idea for a study," Jim said, helping her. He glanced around, then lowered his voice. "Will you help me with the animations?"

"Sure," Delilah said.

"Hah!" crowed a voice behind them. "Russell can't do his own magic. You stunted dweeb! Carb-eater!" The owner of the voice was a boy with an almost feminine beauty, dark hair that contrasted strongly with his pale skin, wide brown eyes, and long eyelashes.

"Artiss, will you grow up?" Delilah asked, putting the most pity she could into her voice. Artiss Conrad had been her best friend when she was little. They had gone all the way through primary school and junior high, but Artiss was stupidly jealous of the attention she paid to Jim Russell. He was making it impossible to stay friends with him.

"I'm not the one who bleaches his hair!" Artiss sneered. Jim stepped forward to shove the other boy playfully, but Artiss slid out of his reach. He ran toward the glass doors of the auditorium, dissolved into fog, and went under them. On the other side, he rematerialized, and looped his hands through the handles. Jim reached the doors and tried to pull them open. He was strong, but Artiss was stronger. He made faces at them through the glass. Jim pounded on the windows. Artiss laughed wildly.

"Mr. Conrad!"

Principal von Mettenmeier strode up, slipped effortlessly into fog, which seeped between the closed doors. She took Artiss by the ear until he let go of the door.

"Ow! Ow! Ow!" he yelped.

"Now, go to class," the countess said, as the students poured out around them. "You are causing everyone else to be late, and I will not excuse you." Artiss gave Delilah a reproachful look, then transformed into a bat and flitted away, keeping near the ceiling. She was disgusted.

"It's all right, Mr. Russell," she said kindly. "Everyone grows into his or her powers at a different rate. But," she added with a fierce glare, "just make sure all the work is your own."

"It is! It will be!" Jim promised.

Von Mettenmeier nodded. "I trust you."

Delilah saw Jim cringe and felt her heart sink. That trust had been broken even before it was given.

The science teacher, Dr. Lemuel Travanti, had been a contemporary of Leonardo da Vinci, something that he never let his students forget.

"He tell me my thoughts are brilliant—brilliant!" Travanti insisted with a flamboyant Italian accent, pounding a fist on his desk. "So I expect you to listen to my lessons, and find your own brilliance, which is not so brilliant as mine, of course. This fair, it is a showcase for all of you, and it reflect on me, of course. So your work will be grand and glorious. I expect nothing less!"

Delilah groaned and buried her face in her hands. She had no ideas at all. Artiss waved his arm in the air.

"Will you have to approve our projects before we start them?" he asked.

"Of course, of course," Travanti said, nodding. "So, you start us off, Mr. Conrad? You have the good idea?"

"Yeah," he said, with a mean look in Jim's direction. His eyes glowed like rubies. "I want to do a comparison of the lies that humans tell, and the harm they have caused throughout history."

Delilah felt her heart stop for a moment. Did he know? Was he planning to reveal Jim's secret in the middle of the science fair? In front of everyone *and* a bunch of reporters? There'd be a bloodbath! She wanted to grab Jim by the arm and fly him out of the classroom. Jim's face paled even further than Delilah thought was possible. She reached out to touch his shoulder. He shook her hand off.

"This is science, not sociology," Travanti said dismissively. "You save that for if we have a history fair. And I do not want a project that is a direct insult to the father of a classmate, you understand? That does not make use of your brilliant mind, which, as I say, is not as great as mine, but has its own promise."

Artiss looked disappointed.

"You have got to let people know," Delilah said to Jim, as they walked home from school close to dawn. "You can't let him blow your secret like that. You could get killed!"

"I know," Jim said, miserably. "I wanted to wait out the school year before I told. I figured if people had a chance to get to know me, they'd like me enough so it doesn't matter."

He sounded even more glum a week later when she came in for her next tightening. His father, though, was over the moon.

"Countess von Mettenmeier called me in for a parent-teacher conference," Dr. Russell said, as he tightened her bands. "It's the first time I met her. A very impressive woman, isn't she?"

"Mmmf, mmf," Delilah replied around his fingers and dental instruments.

". . . I thought there was trouble, but it was marvelous news! They want to give Jim a certificate for academic excellence. It will be presented—along with the others, you know—at Awards Night next week. She wanted to make sure I would be there. Oh, I will. I wish his mother could have seen this."

"Mm mfm."

Dr. Russell beamed down at her. His blunt canines made her shudder just a little. "You're right, I am proud. He's so much smarter than his old man. I was afraid he would be overwhelmed by getting to know a new school, a new neighborhood, but he just slipped right into place. I put it down to knowing you, young lady."

His father's elation was Jim's depression. The tall boy sloped toward school, his long spine bent over like a laboratory assistant's. The heavy, overcast night seemed to match his mood.

"There is no way I can tell the truth now," Jim said, woefully. "I'll get double resentment from people if I do. For sure not until after the science fair."

That is, if Jim didn't have to run for his life before that.

"Let me see if Artiss really knows anything," Delilah said, hoping to keep his mood up. "You've been so careful up to now."

"If he thinks you're trying to shield me, he'll blow the whistle sooner," Jim said.

"I know. Just . . . let me go to lunch with him alone today? I'll see what I can find out."

"How come you didn't reply to my blog on Sketchbook?" Delilah asked Artiss. They had found a table near the glass wall of the yellow-painted cafeteria that looked out on the night garden. Bats flitted around the peonies that even this late in the year attracted ants and other insects they loved to eat. "I know you saw that new series on HBO. I wanted you to post what you thought."

"I turned it off during the first episode—dammit!" Artiss choked and looked down at the red splotches on his hands. "I hate these bleeping new serving packs," he said. "You sink your fangs into them, and they leak all over the place." He slammed the opaque white bubble onto the long cafeteria table. More blood seeped out of the dispenser holes.

"Those foil seals are just creepy," Delilah agreed. "I get a shock every time my braces touch them."

"Your *boyfriend* doesn't seem to be having any problems," Artiss said, with a pointed glance toward Jim, who was sitting with Mike. The two of them were laughing over something.

"Come on, Artiss," Delilah begged. "You're my best friend. I've known you since we were babies. Don't shut me out."

He put his tongue up and licked the blood off his left canine. Delilah noticed for the first time that his incisors were crooked. He needed Dr. Russell, but she was sure he would rather die than go for treatment to a despised human. "I didn't know you went for freaks."

"It's not what he looks like. It's what's inside him. He's nice and smart."

"Not so smart," Artiss said, smirking. "He blew that glamour lesson in magic class. He can't cast a spell for anything."

Delilah glared at him. "That was really mean of you." When the teacher stepped out of the room, Artiss had taken the opportunity to use his new skill to throw illusions on the hapless newcomer. Others had joined in the fun, surrounding him with monsters, falling furniture and fake walls. Jim was so dazed by the end that he had walked into a real wall trying to leave the room. Jim was at the top of the class academically, but it was all theory to him. One day, after he got someone to change him, he'd be great at magic, but not yet. Artiss used to be the top student in every class, until Jim came along. He was still the most talented, but losing his stardom obviously still stung him.

"It was just fun!" Artiss said. "If he needs to be wrapped in shrouds to stay safe, then he's not going to make it here. Let him and his creepy dad go back where they came from."

"They need to be here," Delilah said firmly. "You're not really going to do a project about human lies, are you?"

"No, I am going to make a study of all the massacres of vampires by humans over the course of history," Artiss said, bitterly. "What do you care?"

"You're just being ratty to Jim's father so it hurts Jim. I thought you were better than that."

"Maybe I'm not as superior as your freak," Artiss said. "Maybe I feel betrayed."

Delilah was shocked. "Betrayed? How? We never said anything about dating each other. Ever."

"Maybe I changed my mind," Artiss said, lowering his dark brows over his eyes. Delilah stared into the red glow, at a loss. How had she missed all the clues he must have been giving her? If Jim hadn't come along, would she ever have noticed?

"I'm sorry..."

A bell rang at the front of the lunchroom. Delilah looked up. The school nurse sat down at a table to the side with an insulated zippered case. Artiss got up and kicked his chair so it slammed against the table beside Delilah. He stalked up to join the line in front of the waiting nurse.

Like a lot of vampire youths, Artiss had a congenital disease that meant his hemoglobin couldn't absorb the donor oxygenators from the blood he consumed. It was like diabetes, from the readings Delilah had done in science class about humans. Artiss and her other friends with the disease could die in their teens from the condition. Jim and the others knew about it, because the sufferers had to line up several times daily for iron injections. Artiss knew that the others put up with his anger because they were worried about him, which made him angrier. No one liked pity. Artiss threatened them if they didn't stop treating him like *he* needed to be wrapped in shrouds, but they were decent people and couldn't help it.

She still wasn't sure what he knew about Jim. Artiss could still put a spin on his project that might make others start to ask questions about the Russells. Any revelation might evoke comparisons to Jim's father, and maybe someone would test the boy to see how much human he had in him. Which was a lot. One hundred percent, in fact.

Jim had been absolutely right about the notoriety that went with getting an academic certificate. He and three girls had been singled out for honors. The girls suffered the usual catty comments, which died down after another week, but Jim became the object of an undercover campaign of sabotage and malice.

"I'm worried about blowing my cover," Jim confessed. "The last one, Nerys Binarti, scooted into my locker disguised as a bat, then pretended I had enchanted her and locked her in there on purpose. Mr. Travanti gave me detention for Wednesday. I couldn't argue and say I was capable of twisting her mind like that. What if they want me to demonstrate? Dad and I will have to leave again." He made a face. "I don't want to go. It sucks to be the new guy all the time. People have been really nice about not staring at me here."

"Well, when you can turn into a dog, white hair is just no big deal," Delilah said. "Look, it would be better if you would just tell someone. *Now.* Is there a teacher you trust? What about Countess von Mettenmeier?"

"No!" Jim said, alarmed at the thought. "I want to get through this semester. I have to. They'll stop bugging me sooner or later."

"Not if Artiss is behind the harassment," Delilah said.

"Don't worry," Jim said confidently, shouldering his bag as they rounded the corner toward his father's office. "I'll deal with Artiss."

✧   ✧   ✧

Delilah read through the text on the standing board at Jim's table, which was in the second row on the broad auditorium stage. She read it through again, and shuddered. The magical animations that she had provided for him shimmered and danced in the center of the open space, repeating again and again. They showed the combined digestive and circulatory systems of a vampire. She followed the path of ingested blood. It went down the esophagus, then was absorbed through a membrane in the stomach lining that filtered it. The animation enlarged at that point to show the capillaries that fed the new blood into the vampire's own circulatory system. Platelets in vampiric ichor erased the DNA of the species from which the blood had come, leaving the cells functioning as they would in a healthy organism. Waste products were collected in the intestines and kidneys, but the model ended at the tabletop, discreetly above the parts of the body that showed their elimination. Down the sides of the standing display ran a series of images of distorted or unhealthy cells that prevented absorbtion of this nutrient or that. The top one was of disk-shaped cells that were bleached pink instead of a healthy red. She groaned.

"I can't believe you talked me into helping with this," she said.

"It wouldn't look good without special effects," Jim said. "And I can't do them. Yet." He gave her that hopeful look.

"No, and maybe never!" Delilah said. "Why did you do this? Artiss is going to be upset that you're airing his iron deficiency in public! Is this revenge for him picking on you?"

"No!" Jim said, his eyes widening in alarm until the whites around the red irises were exposed. "No, I've been doing some research. I think it might be possible to splice genes to prevent iron deficiency. When I go to medical school, hematology will be my special subject."

"You just want to drink the specimens," Artiss said, with a sour expression.

Delilah jumped.

"I didn't see you."

"Yeah, you never do anymore," Artiss said. He scanned Jim's display. "So the freak hits back, huh? I didn't know you had it in you." He turned his back on them and sauntered over three rows to where his table stood. Jim looked stricken.

"That wasn't what I meant to happen," he said.

"Do you want the good news or the bad news?" Delilah asked, after a moment of shock.

"Bad news," Jim said at once.

"He's pissed at you."

Jim made a face. "No kidding. There's good news?"

"Yes," Delilah said, tension in her neck easing for the first time in an entire month. "He doesn't know you're human. Did you hear what he just said about your hematology specimens?"

"Yeah!" Jim said, a smile easing across his long face, and his shoulders relaxed. "Whew! Now I can come out at a time when it'll do the least damage."

Delilah settled down to enjoy herself. Her project had been on bats, animals that she had always loved. The vampire bat was too obvious a choice, and besides, Bobbie MacKenzie was doing her paper about them. Instead, she had chosen Amazonian fruit bats to demonstrate echolocation, a trait that vampires used as well as their small mammalian counterparts. She had set up a miniature cylindrical sound chamber made of plexiglass with images of bats whisking around and between obstacles. Doing it with electronics was beyond her skill level, though she had recorded the shrieks of bats from the local zoo. The rest she had had to do with illusion magic. She had just enough talent to draw power to run her display and Jim's. He credited her on his paper, so there were no falsehoods here. She had fun watching the visiting reporters screw up their faces in pain at the sharp sounds coming from her display. The article that the school had put in the paper about the science fair had attracted loads of visitors. She hoped it would help make people think of the vampire community as friendly and welcoming. A human high school was only about six miles away, but it might have been on another planet. One with too much daylight.

"Smile!"

A flash of light exploded in Delilah's face. When her eyes cleared, a hand was holding a square of white up to her.

"Robin, what are you doing?" she asked.

Robin Feldman was in the year behind Delilah, but she mingled cheerfully with all the classes at Bathory.

"Kirlian photography," Robin said. "I'm taking pictures of everyone's aura. I'm going to post mine on Sketchbook. You can, too, if you want."

"Thanks," Delilah said, holding the little square as it darkened. She couldn't see features in the mass of colors that radiated outward from a silhouette in the center, but it was the closest thing to a real photo of herself that she had ever had. "It's awesome!"

"Yours is really pretty," Robin said, peering over her shoulder at it. "You should see some of the others. Here's Jim's." She held out a mass of rainbow color. "It's the strongest image I have been able to get. He must have a really powerful aura."

"Don't show Artiss," Delilah whispered. "He's in a bad mood."

"He already saw it," Robin said, apologetically. "Hecate, I hope that's not what they're fighting about."

Delilah followed Robin's gaze until she spotted the two boys. Jim was in front of Artiss's display, which was titled bravely, "Vampiric Superiority Against Overwhelming Enemy Numbers." Her friend's face was purple with fury. Jim's was uncharacteristically pink. Delilah made a beeline for them, weaving in between people. She had to make them back off before they started fighting. The principal had told them what would happen if they made a scene.

". . . Sticking it right in my face, right here!" Artiss snarled, his fangs glistening dangerously. Some of the adult strangers, almost all humans, backed away from them. "No, I do not want to be part of your ongoing study. I would be happy if you went back to your coffin and buried yourself for ten thousand years!"

"Look, we don't have to be enemies," Jim said. "I'd be grateful to have your input."

"Well, here's my input," Artiss snapped. He put his fingers up in a V-shape, and his voice took on the echo of power. "I call on the powers of darkness to cast you out. Let light and fire consume you!"

Jim recoiled, throwing his hands up before his eyes.

"Artiss!" Delilah shrieked. "Stop that!"

Artiss spun and thrust his forefinger to her nose.

"Don't you defend Mr. Perfect, here. He's not real, wanting to embrace his enemies."

"I'm not your enemy!" Jim protested. "Well, I...I don't want to be. I want you to accept me. Please!"

Artiss gave him a glare, but it melted off his face, leaving his faunlike features blank. As Delilah watched in horror, Artiss sank to the floor. She threw all the magic she knew at him to catch his head before it bounced off the stage boards.

"What happened?" Jim said, kneeling at Artiss's head. Other students were on their feet. "I didn't do anything to him!"

The faculty judges came toward them in an alarmed group. "What is wrong with Mr. Conrad?" demanded the countess.

"He's having an attack," Delilah said. "I bet he didn't eat lunch."

"Is his medication here?"

"He gets it from the nurse," Delilah said. She bent her head over Artiss's mouth. He panted in short breaths, only a few per minute.

"Someone, go!" ordered the principal. One of the elder students jumped up from his table, leaped into the air in bat shape, and flew out the door.

By then, the human reporters had taken one of two actions. The first and overwhelmingly larger group fled for the doors, bursting out into the night, many of them screaming. The second, smaller contingent were huddled, wide-eyed, at the side of the stage, the men with their arms protectively around the shoulders of the women, their cameras and recorders held out like weapons. Delilah wanted to run to them, to reassure them that they weren't in danger, but Artiss came first.

"Can't move," Artiss murmured. Delilah let out a little cry of relief.

"Lie still," she said. "They're getting your injection."

"He needs iron," Jim said. "I bet he hasn't had any all day. Look at the color of his skin. He's critical. He could die, Delilah."

"No!" she protested, cradling his head in her arms.

"Didn't eat. Too excited." He glared at Jim. "All your fault."

"It is, kind of," Jim said, grimly. He thrust a wrist into Artiss's face. "Bite me."

"What?" Delilah asked.

"Bad time for insults, freak," Artiss gasped. "You'd like that." Biting another vampire tore up their digestion for days. All other blood on earth was edible and safe, but not their own.

"Bite me," Jim insisted. He took a deep breath and let it out. "I'm human. Take my blood. Save your life."

Weak as he was, Artiss could still show scorned disbelief. "You are not a bleeping human."

Jim reached into his mouth and removed his fangs. To the horrified cries of the other students, he revealed his blunted canines. "I am so. These aren't real. My dad made them for me. Hurry. What have you got to lose? How long until you pass out?"

"Not long," Artiss said in a fading voice. His eyes rolled upward. Suddenly he reached out. With amazing strength, he grabbed Jim's arm and bit down on the other's wrist. Jim gasped. Delilah could tell it hurt like crazy. She had never been bitten by anything but her hamster. Artiss fed, the blood rolling down the sides of his face.

The pain was the least of Jim's worries, to judge by the others homing in on him.

"Mr. Russell, stand up," boomed the countess. Her eyes were aflame with fury.

"Not yet," Jim begged. "He needs more. I . . . I can stand it."

The countess pointed a finger, and Jim's chin rose in spite of himself. "Mr. Russell, what is the meaning of this? Are you trying to poison your classmate?"

"It's not poison," Jim said. "Countess, I told you a lie when I enrolled—just one. I'm everything else that it said on my transcripts. Only, I'm not a vampire. I'm a human."

Countess von Mettenmeier grabbed his shoulder and lifted him into the air. He dangled from her grip like a kitten in its mother's mouth. "Come with me, Mr. Russell." She turned and marched out of the auditorium. Jim's long legs kicked in the air.

"Jim!"

"No one else comes!" the principal boomed over her shoulder. The rest of the faculty advisors swarmed after her like a pack of wolves. Delilah sat down beside Artiss, stricken with fear. She had been afraid of this for months. He was going to die, or worse, get expelled.

"Damn him!" Artiss said. Delilah looked down at him. His face looked less pinched already. The purple faded from his cheeks. "Just when I was comfortable hating him."

"He couldn't let you die," Delilah said.

"But he's a bleeping *human*. Why wouldn't he? He's not one of us."

"Yes, he is," Delilah said fiercely. "He's *our* human. It's okay to be human, if you're like us. He couldn't help being born needing . . . needing food. He wants to make the change. He just can't yet, but he will."

"He won't live that long," Artiss said. "I've seen the countess mad before, but never like that. Hey, wait for me!"

Delilah ran for the door, changing to a bat as she ran. She took off. Artiss was wing to wing with her.

They resumed their normal shapes when they reached to the principal's office, and pounded on the door with both fists. The countess answered it herself and looked down her aristocratic nose upon both of them.

"What are you two doing here?"

"What's going to happen to Russell?" Artiss demanded.

"Go to the nurse, Mr. Conrad," the principal said. "You have been ill. This is a very serious matter."

"But you know his father's a human," Delilah said. "Can't you understand that he might want to keep his condition a secret?"

"Honesty is a vital trait in our culture, Miss Stollergard," the principal said, her eyebrows lifting incredulously. "Are you falling into the human way of thinking?"

"No! I mean, I understand why he did it. He wants to belong, Countess," Delilah pleaded. "Don't hurt him."

"Hurt him?" Countess von Mettenmeier echoed. "I have not hurt the boy. I brought him here for *his* protection. But he is answering questions. You must understand that his credibility has suffered a mortal blow. The community will not be pleased to have a liar in their presence."

"But he saved my life," Artiss said.

"Yes," the countess said, with a wintry little grin. "I agree, that does make him seem more than human. But we have to maintain a higher standard."

"Can we see him?" Delilah asked.

"No. An explanation has to be made before we loose him again upon the world. If we do. Go back to the fair. Go! Don't question me again."

Dr. Russell stood back from the chair and wiped the probe clean on a towel. "How does that feel?" he asked.

Artiss sat up, grimacing. "Like you scraped my gums off."

"That means I did an extra good job," the orthodontist said, beaming. He snapped rubber bands onto the new braces. "You know, if you were human, I'd have to pull out your canines to straighten your teeth."

"No!" Artiss glared. Then he realized that Dr. Russell was teasing him. Delilah, at his side, snickered. "But you don't have to with us."

"No, I'm pretty good at what I do," Jim's father said complacently. "You'll have a smile that's good for hundreds of years. See you next week, Artiss."

"Thanks," Artiss said, and struggled out of the deep chair. He gave Delilah a sheepish glance. "C'mon. We'd better fly if we want to get to school on time."

Delilah looked alarmed. "We can't. We'll leave Jim behind."

"It's a figure of speech!" Artiss said. He pushed out into the waiting room, where the pale-haired boy was waiting. "Come on. We've got practical magic today. You going to be as inept as you were yesterday?"

Jim smiled, and the false fangs clamped into place over his rounded canines gleamed. He didn't have to wear them any longer, not after the countess's stirring defense of him at assembly the week before, but he liked them, and Delilah preferred the way he looked in them. "Probably. What are you going to do about it?"

"Enjoy it," Artiss said. He marched out the door of the orthodontist office, his head high.

Delilah took Jim's arm. Together, they followed him into the clear night.

Dave Freer is a former ichthyologist/fisheries scientist turned SF/fantasy writer. He now has eleven books in print (the most recent—*Dragon's Ring*—came out last October) a number of which are co-authored with Mercedes Lackey and/or Eric Flint. He is also the author of about twenty other short stories, and a teens novel. He lives in Australia and he has learned a lot about teenagers from his sons, though very little about vampires. He does wonder why he is so anemic.

"If Music Be
the Food of Love…"

Dave Freer

"You have blood spots on your collar," she said, with nasty glee.

I sighed. Zara always delighted in pointing that sort of thing out. Being a vampire isn't easy. And then I had to put up with Zara as well. "And you have a zit on your nose," I said, peering down my own nose at her.

It had the desired effect. Frantic squinting. Feeling with long black fingernails. "Eugh, gross! It's not fair." She stomped off in her Doc Martens to go and apply more makeup. She's not very good at it. It's not easy when you can't use a mirror. It's harder when you're a teenager. Zara's been that way for three hundred years now and she's not got any better at being subject to teen hormones, or at applying makeup. Immortality has its downsides. Being a teenager forever is one of the worse possible ones. Having to live with one

forever is, however, the worst curse of being one of
the undead. And I had endless millennia of it ahead
of me. Zara is my daughter. And no, I didn't bite her.
Banish the thought! It's enough to make blood turn to
ashes in my mouth. I did help to hammer the stake
through Count Orlok's heart, though. It took Zara
nearly a century to forgive me for "ruining her life"
and "interfering." Actually, I'm still regularly accused
of the latter.

It's true, of course. But when did that ever stop
a father?

I changed my shirt. The blood was probably more
of an artifact from shaving without a mirror than a
soft white throat. I had a glass of wine and checked
my e-mail. I've done my best to move with the times.

Her favorite heavy metal CD played upstairs for
what I would swear was the third time. She'd gaged
the volume nicely. Enough to drive me mad, not
enough to get the neighbors to complain. I looked
at my watch. Again. Finally, although I knew it was
a mistake, yelled "Zara! We're going to be late." Yes,
I knew this was self-inflicted injury. I shouldn't have
made the zit comment.

No reply came from upstairs. Just more so-called
music. I tried again.

So...eventually I went up to deal with the Saturday night tantrum, one of my least favorite pastimes.

I still would have preferred that to finding a room
empty of anything but the sound of abused electric
guitars.

There was a note on her coffin.

"Don't even think about looking for me."

So I didn't think about it.

I just started doing it instead.

The window was open, so it was obvious how she'd gone.

I grimaced so hard that it hurt my fangs. I hate flying. And I hate being a cloud of bats (if there is one thing I despise above all other vampire misconceptions, it's the bizarre idea that vampires can transform into one bat. We're un-dead. Not un-massed. A single bat that weighed the same as I did would fly just like depleted uranium—only if fired by a tank. And no. We do not fly like Superman.) Shapeshifting is not comfortable and becoming multi-corporate means that my mind also gets split into many fragments. Bats—even ones with a bit of human mind, are not good at things like "Stay together and don't get eaten by owls." Although it can't kill them (there are few silver-beaked or even garlic salami munching owls out there), being regurgitated by an owl makes even death seem attractive.

But what else was I to do?

Well, I could have taken the car. But instead I discorporated into bat-fragments, left my clean white shirt with the rest of my clothes, and fluttered into the suburban night sky. Looking into the street-lit darkness at picket fences and neatly clipped lawns. Listening for ultrasonic squeaks from another cloud of bats. And trying to keep myself together. Some of the bats-parts kept getting distracted and flapping off to catch moths.

There were squeaks about, but unless Zara had been scattered—an owl can do that—she wasn't still flying about. Which left her, sixteen years old—well, three hundred and sixteen, but still looking sixteen—with no clothes, somewhere. A father still gets rather upset about this kind of thing, even after three hundred years. Even fathers whose daughters don't need a nice lead-lined coffin by morning would get worried.

I spiraled up higher, looking and listening for a clue. Instead I found a house party. To one pair of bat-sensitive ears, it was an assault. To seventy pairs, it was like having your brain pounded in a mortar with a pestle. And yes. I do know exactly what that feels like. People come up with bizarre ways to try to kill the undead.

The cloud of bats that was me still flew closer.

Anywhere quite so many people were screaming seemed worth investigating. And the couple beneath the laurel bushes didn't really need all their clothes right now, so I removed a pair of trousers, and a shirt, and, in my folly, a pair of shoes. No socks. People who have sex in socks are deluded about their contraceptive powers. Those two didn't notice bats laboring to fly off with the clothing into the deep shadows next to the wisteria trellis. The shoes were outsize and ridiculously pointy-toed. The pants needed a hand to keep them up, but they were less conspicuous than wondering into someone's party in a very pale white birthday suit.

I need not have bothered. There was loud music, but no people. That had the mark of my daughter about it. Empty rooms, signs of flight. Chairs tipped over, glasses scattered. Yes, Zara had been here.

So I shuffled on in the funny shoes. Towards the open door where the music was blasting from. To where my daughter was hanging adoringly over a console, a spotty youth, and an assembly of amplifiers, speakers, and turntables. A poster hung over the front of the console proclaimed that DJ Frank was for hire. By the looks of my idiotic daughter she was eager to do so. She had obviously acquired a skirt—or, at least a broad belt, and a blouse—from somewhere, and outsize jacket, so I didn't have to kill him immediately. Just relatively soon.

The two of them were so wrapped up in talking—in this noise—that they hadn't even noticed me.

I cleared my throat. That didn't work, so I decided to clear his instead. I lunged one-handed (the other was busy holding up the trousers).

"Daddy," shrieked Zara. "Don't you touch him."

I didn't, because one of the long toes of my borrowed shoes hooked in the rug. As I fell, I let go of the trousers to catch myself. The result was undignified and allowed spotty Frank the DJ to retreat.

"Man, are you some kind of weirdo?" he asked, as I pulled up my trousers, and stood up, sans one shoe. He was only human. No match for my strength and speed... if I dropped my trousers and kicked them off. Mind you, that could give most humans a remarkable turn of agility.

"It's only my father," said Zara crossly. "He always ruins everything."

I looked at the wreckage of what had been someone's lounge. It now had broken furniture and four unconscious people scattered around it. "I think you've beaten me to it. It's time we went home, young lady."

"Why?" she asked, hands on her hips, eyes narrow. "Why can't you just leave me alone?"

"Because, in the absence of your mother, I am supposed to look after you," I said, measuring distances with my eyes.

She stamped her foot. "Daddy, I really am old enough to look after myself."

The DJ looked at the empty room—well, empty except for the four unconscious men. "Dude, like, she's got a point. And this isn't the seventeenth century, you know."

"I know. They had better taste in music then. Look, display some common sense and run away. I don't want to hurt you, but very shortly I am going to have to."

He reached out and flicked a switch—at the same time as he flung a piece of black cloth ripped from the side of his console. He flung it—not at me, but at Zara. I had to cope with the ultraviolet strobe without that slight protection. I didn't do so very well. There is a reason for spending the daylight hours in a coffin, besides tradition.

When I woke up, the room was lit merely by ordinary incandescent bulbs, with no threats beyond a police officer who had eaten too much garlic in his chicken tikka pizza. It was an insult to good taste, but not enough to make me feel more than slightly bilious.

"Even if they are your trousers, sir, I still have to charge you with public indecency," said the officer to the fellow I'd last seen beneath the laurel bushes. He was still wearing his socks, but had acquired a fluorescent police waistcoat to inadequately wrap himself in.

I cowered back against the wall. "Don't let him hit me again, officer," I said weakly.

The cop took a firm grip on the large, red-faced owner of the trousers I was wearing. "It's all right, sir. We've got him under control."

"One of the other witnesses from that lot we found

running down the street said it was a young woman," said the second cop doubtfully.

I nodded, as the man in socks gargled with a response. "The two of them. Some kind of sexual frenzy. I came over to ask them to turn the music down. I didn't see all of it."

The officer nodded. A middle-aged man recovering consciousness was a more credible witness than a buck-naked youth with gelled hair. "Were you the citizen who called in to complain about the noise?"

I shook my head. "Must have been one of the other neighbors. I wish I had left it to you. If you could help me to the bathroom? I'm going to be sick." If there is one thing that years of vampirism have taught me, it's how to be a glib liar.

The poor fellow in socks had turned puce and was shouting incoherently and trying to get at me. So he got tazered. That worked for me. So did a solicitous cop helping me to my feet. "You're really pale, sir. Are you all right? An ambulance is on the way."

I was tempted. There is nothing quite like a blood transfusion for a vampire. But I had a daughter and DJ to pursue. So I settled for kneeling in front of the toilet and making suitable noises. The officer of the law stood and watched. I pointed at the little bathroom window. "There is someone out there. A woman."

He ran off, so I locked the door and discorporated into bat-forms. While he was eagerly beating the bushes—I suppose the idea of finding a woman in only socks was more interesting than watching someone puke—I fluttered off—just in time to see that indeed, he'd got lucky there, too. Now I knew where Zara had found her clothes. I just didn't know

where she'd gone. The cloud of us fluttered home
to go and try to approach this rationally. Bats think
they are rational, but they tend to be obsessed with
moths. It's easier to think in human form, and easier
to do this somewhere that you won't be arrested for
indecent exposure.

Besides, I needed to call the Van Hellsings and
tell them that we wouldn't be coming for dinner.
The old folk doted on Zara. It was a pity that they
didn't have any children of their own, after the tragic
death of their son. They'd been a bit more sensible
and fortunate with their money than I had. But that's
one downside of being immortal and finding that in
changing times one can no longer rely on peasant
rents. Pitchforks and flaming torches—the peasants
could still be relied on to provide those, but rents
were a thing of the past, which was why I had to
sell the old place and now teach medieval history in
the local community college. At night, of course. My
powerful hypnotic mind control was almost enough
to get some of the students to pass, as well as give
blood. I've been taking a series of correspondence
courses myself over the years. I put a reading light
in my coffin fifty years ago, and added a computer
terminal and keyboard about five years back. It beats
setting fire to your own coffin with a branch of candles.
I study. Surf the web. There's nothing much else to
do—it's that or daytime TV.

Back home, I dressed, listened to the music of
distant police sirens—a sweet sound if it is far away,
and googled DJ Frank. After a while I narrowed the
search terms. There are a lot of David John or Darren James Franks out there. But when I added music

and hire and locality—I got him. Well, I got a contact mobile number. Which wasn't being answered right now, and dawn was dangerously close. Real sunlight, not just ultraviolet strobe, was not something vampires throve on. But he had put a cloth over her ... so he must know something. He was also going to know something about angry fathers at this rate. The trouble was that this angry, worried father was shortly going to have to crawl into his nice lead-lined coffin with the grave soil of Carpathia, and I had no idea where to go to next. It was then that I had the bright idea of looking around Zara's room, where, as the sky turned bloody and the first commuters set off for work, I found her cell phone. I took it to my coffin with me. Yes, reading her text messages was prying. I try not to, but what was I to do? Call the police and report her missing? I could just imagine the interview: "How old is she, Sir?"

"Three hundred and sixteen and she usually sleeps in a pink plush-lined coffin, officer."

It was easier just to read the text messages. They all came from a number I recognised. I'd just tried dialling it. That made more sense than most of the language written there. "L8r" took me quite a while to work out, and I had been under the mistaken impression that "ur" was a city in ancient Sumer. But I had all day. It was plain that Zara hadn't dropped in on Frank by accident. Also it would seem, looking at the headlines online, that some youngster had even worse problems than Zara. A house party while his parents were away was not something he should have mentioned on a social networking site. It appeared that the revelers had done considerable damage. The police were looking for a neighbor who had witnessed it all . . . I never cease to be amazed by the talent of ordinary people to find logical rationalizations for the actions of the undead. It's very convenient.

I had a bit more to go on now. It was likely spotty Frank the DJ would know our landline number, and would not take calls from it.

So that evening, just after sundown, I went and left a bag of clothes just outside a conveniently empty house with a skylight, which was open enough for a bat. It's the kind of thing I have learned to notice over the years. I always had a few spots picked out in case we had to leave before the pitchforks and burning brands. Yes, even in suburbia. Trust me. A whiff of a vampire and suddenly they come out of the cellars and attics.

If there is one thing I like less than garlic it has to be motion detector burglar alarms with response companies.

I had to go through the whole process again, at a different house. But soon I was inside, dressed, and dialling "DJ Frank, a party anywhere." It rang.

"Frank Stine," he answered.

"Like, I was looking for DJ Frank," I said, trying to sound centuries younger than myself.

"That's me, dude. What can I do for you?"

"Well, like, I'm kinda looking after these crumblies' place while they're away. I got the keys so I can come in and feed the goldfish. And, like, I thought it would be a cool place for a party next Saturday. But they got no sound. I mean, can you believe it? So a friend said I should give you a call, see. I got some money for house-sitting . . ." I let my voice trail off.

"It's risky, dude. Cost you $150. And I take no responsibility for breakages."

"Oh, we won't break nothing," I said with convincing insincerity.

"I'll need cash up front," he said, showing remarkable wisdom.

"Okay. Um, can you come and collect it here. Like, I don't want my parents to know."

I gave him the address, and agreed a time. And set things up. Frank Stine wasn't going to get away this time. Once that was done, I settled down to wait. The owners of this place didn't have any vacu-packed whole blood in the fridge, so I made do with a glass of their Californian Pinot. The color is similar.

I had rigged a drop switch on the mains, and a simple arrangement with a jammed softball and a piece of string to make the door swing closed. In the good old days I would have had a faithful henchman to do the job. I missed the mad retainers of yesteryear, but short of employing illegals it was impossible to get good help these days. Also, as the Van Hellsings had found, besides the expense, a dishwashing machine is not quite so hard on old china.

He was on time. And, my keen hearing told me, not alone. He knocked.

"It's open," I called from where I waited in the kitchen. "I'm just fixing a sandwich." I watched him in the mirror in the hall. Of course, he looked alone in that. Holding hands with no one.

"It's DJ Frank," he said. "About that part..." The door clicked shut behind him and the lights went out. "Oh shi..." was as far as he got before I reached him. One of the minor compensations of being infected

with vampirism is being supernaturally strong and
fast. I grabbed him and instinctively bit.

Which was also where my plans went awry.

I nearly broke my canine on what my lips said was
a lump of steel. And it appeared, by the force that I
was flung away with, that Frank, too, was possessed of
superhuman strength. He tore the door right off its
hinges, and he and Zara were gone before I could sit up.

I left quietly, propping the door back in place. My
mind was somewhat confused—and not just because I
had hit the wall rather hard with my head. The SMS
record on Zara's phone only went back two hundred
messages—about a week for a teenager, it seemed.
How long had she known him?

And what was he? He had a reflection—he wasn't
a vampire, as I was. And what had I bitten? I decided
that I was going to need help. One hates to admit
family problems to others, but I had known Abraham
Van Hellsing for many years. His own family history
had not been untroubled.

The Van Hellsings have managed, in these degen-
erate times, with the encroachment of suburbia, to
retain some of gothic charm to their home. Money
helps, of course. Crenellations and rotting gables do
not come cheaply, although being adjacent to the
graveyard had kept property prices down.

I knocked. The knocker was a gift from a little
place in the Borgo Pass. I had given it to them. It
had a lovely hollow boom to it, due, I believe to an
electronic amplifier. He was a fine scientist, Abraham.
He was a doctor of science and literature as well as
medicine, much interested in galvanics and medicine.
His wife Elizabeth answered the door. The signs

of her madness—well, modern art (in my day we called it madness, and I am not sure that we weren't right)—were much about her on her paint-spattered smock. She smiled. "Vladislav. Abraham is up in his laboratory. It may cheer him up to see you."

Normally, we met over drinks. Very civilized. I had not been into the Doctor's laboratory for many years, back when he had still been hoping to find a cure. "I need his help," I said. "A family matter, you understand."

"Oh dear. I really do think you should let her do ballet if she wants to."

"I am afraid it is a bit more serious this time. She's run away."

Elizabeth pulled a face. "So awkward with our special needs. But a young gel needs space. Let me call Abraham."

It wasn't space that I thought Zara needed. But I waited until Abraham came down. I could immediately see that something was troubling him. His ginger hair was disordered and his blue eyes were a little wild. He still bowed and clicked his heels in the German manner. "Mein Gott, Count. Elizabeth tells me we have a similar problem."

I blinked. I knew that their only son had died. And vampires don't breed, or the world would be neck-deep in the undead. "I have been a fool, delving into the mysteries that no man is meant to understand."

I nodded and patted him sympathetically. "I tried to read *The Female Eunuch* myself once."

"I have not been that depraved," he said, slightly indignant. "No, I have been trying to bring forth life from dead tissue. And my creation has turned against me."

"What?"

He groaned and put his head in his hands. "Alas, it is true, my dear Vladislav. Elizabeth and I saw your Zara, and we desired the same."

The poor fellow had plainly gone mad, just like his wife. "What?" I was beginning to feel like a parrot, or one of DJ Frank's stuck records.

"We made ourselves a son. I have been working on tissue culture and galvanic re-animation for the last century or so. But I think the DNA I recovered from the grave was perhaps degraded. And I have been obliged to send Fritz out to fetch extra bits from the neighborhood." He waved at the graveyard. "Livers especially."

"And you have succeeded?"

"Ja." Abraham Van Hellsing sighed. "But I have over-reached myself and created a monster. Young Quincey does not like Bach."

"I can't say I like heavy metal either. But Zara, she does. She's still my daughter in spite of it."

Abraham nodded heavily. "Yes. But I spoke perhaps a little intemperately about techno-beat. It is not easy, you understand. And now he has rejected his creator. Gone off to loose that curse on mankind." He groaned. "I have tried to find him. His mother and I want him back. And now, my friend, you too are as afflicted as I am."

I smiled and patted his shoulders again. "One of the things I have discovered while teaching are these wonderful industrial ear plugs, intended for working with heavy machinery. It dulls the pain. And I think we can find our little runaways."

"There are half a million people in this city, and

I do not know what name he is using or how he is managing to earn a living."

"I do," I said cheerfully. "And while I think sixteen was considered just about on the shelf back in Carpathia, I have always felt it a little young for marriage. But I'll grant that Zara has been sixteen for so long that she must be just about be ready to be seventeen by now. She's had enough practice."

"What do you mean, Vladislav?" asked Elizabeth.

"I mean that if you don't bring your shotgun along, I will," I said cheerfully. "Unless you have some objection to an alliance between our houses."

He looked a little taken aback for a second. Then he smiled. "Not at all. So you mean . . . you think they are together?"

"Yes. I suspect your creation . . ."

"Our son!" he thundered.

"Your son is now calling himself Frank Stine. He's a DJ offering to provide music for parties," I explained.

Van Hellsing sighed. "How can you be sure? I mean the name . . . he is so sensitive about his origins."

"Not many other sons have a bolt through their necks," I said feeling my tooth. "We have his assumed name, we have his profession. We have a much better chance of finding him." I didn't add that perhaps "Frank" was easier to live with than "Quincey."

By pre-dawn we had paid visits to a number of people called Frank Steyn, Stein, and Stine. Many of them had suffered for the thoughtless name their parents had bestowed on them. None of them had been brought to life by powerful galvanic forces. We returned, despondent, to Van Hellsing's home.

"I cannot think where we could look, Vladislav,"

said Van Hellsing heavily. "We tried so hard. We gave him everything. Love. The computers. The sound system...electronic equipment. We gave life and voltage!"

"We even bought him the music he wanted," said Elizabeth, wringing her paint-stained hands.

"And have spent a fortune trying to adequately soundproof his rooms, as a result," said Van Hellsing sourly. "Although I would welcome the bass making the walls rattle again. At least I knew he was home then."

"I don't suppose you've looked there?"

"But there is no music," said Elizabeth.

"I know it seems unlikely, but let's have a look. And..." I said, "I think, given my experience of Zara's psychology, and my years of experience of raising a perpetual teen, we should pretend to object."

Van Hellsing—a man of vast intellect—nodded. "Let me just drop the steel shutters. I had them fitted in case of a sudden rash of pitchforks and torches and wooden stakes."

I wished I could afford that sort of thing these days. At the flick of a switch, cruel daylight was banished, as well the possibility of escape. We went down the passage to the room with the "private! keep out" sign.

Our little lovebirds, with headphones on and staring into each other's eyes, did not even hear us arrive.

I must say that Abraham Van Hellsing does thunder "I made you!" very well. Elizabeth's tears were a nice touch. I did the furious father to perfection. I've had a lot of practice. They stood together bravely, and explained how they were going to get enough money for a suburban crypt and laboratory of their own soon. We were suitably grumpy about it.

They make a very annoying, noisy young couple.

Julia S. Mandala has two published novels, *The Four Redheads: Apocalypse Now!* (with Linda L. Donahue, Rhonda Eudaly and Dusty Rainbolt), and *House of Doors*. Her works appear in *Witch Way to the Mall*, *The Four Redheads of the Apocalypse*, *Dracula's Lawyer*, *International House of Bubbas*, *Houston, We've Got Bubbas*, *Flush Fiction*, and *Best of the Bubbas*. She holds degrees in history and law, and is a copy editor, scuba diver, underwater photographer, costumer, and belly dancer.

Soccer Mom SmackDown

Julia S. Mandala

I pushed open the old refrigerator that served as my makeshift coffin. In the shadowy basement corner, my son Austin huddled in a ball. The scent of blood raised an instant alarm—and hunger.

"Austin, honey, are you all right?"

He raised his head and with my vampire-enhanced vision, I saw his swollen black eye and blood smeared across his nose. I wished I had time to feed before tending to him, but I'd simply have to exercise self-restraint. Sucking your own kid's blood is just bad parenting.

I gathered my son in my arms, trying not to breathe in the heady aroma of fresh blood. Filling my thoughts with the unappetizing image of garlic bread sprinkled with holy water, I asked, "Who did this?"

"Brandon," he said, his voice muffled against my shoulder.

"Brandon Caldwell?"

"No."

"Brandon McMichaels?"

"Brandon Sanchez," he said with a hint of impatience.

There were only fifteen Brandons in the fourth grade. Then again, there were ten Austins. I'd wanted to name my son something unusual, like John, but my husband Percy claimed the kid would get beat up. I supposed "Percy the Pussy" would know.

"Well, I'm going to pay Brandon's parents a little visit tonight," I said.

Austin drew back, his eyes round. "Mom, no!"

"Not *that* kind of visit. You know I don't feed off people." *Yet.* Bullies usually learned by example, and most parents of bullies saw nothing wrong with their precious child terrorizing another. If I heard the "boys will be boys" excuse, I was pretty sure vampires would be vampires.

"Talking to them will just make it worse," he said, wiping tears and smearing blood.

"You have a right to be safe at school—especially for the tuition that place charges."

After I cleaned up Austin and gave him an ice pack, I microwaved some blood liberated from the local blood bank. Amazing speed and other vampiric powers had *some* advantages, though they didn't make up for all that I'd lost.

While I sucked lukewarm blood from a plastic bag, my husband Percy wandered into the kitchen. His gaze locked on the bag and he didn't even try to hide his distaste.

"God, Louise, do you have to do that here?"

"It's the kitchen."

"I mean in the house. And especially over the sink.

The kids don't need to learn bad manners on top of everything else."

I counted to ten, something I'd been doing a lot lately. "Why didn't you clean Austin up and ice his eye?"

"He wanted his mom," Percy said with an accusatory stare.

"Ooh, good twist of the knife." My vampirism had put more than a little strain on our marriage. "*You're* the parent—"

"I had a brief due by six," Percy said. "Getting the firm to let me work from home was hard enough. If I don't meet deadlines, they'll fire me. Then we'll all be out in the street." His lip curled. "Well, *you'll* have your refrigerator."

"I'd have a coffin if you weren't so cheap." Money wasn't the problem, though. Over the past five years, Percy had found some pretty inventive excuses for not buying me a decent resting place; once he claimed to be waiting for the new models. "I'm surprised you haven't latched me in while I'm sleeping."

Percy's expression showed he'd considered it—more than casually. Counting to fifty—ten wasn't nearly enough—I headed to the bedroom I hadn't slept in for five years. I strapped a Kevlar vest over my T-shirt. The two decent vampires I'd met since being turned said that monster hunters staked first and asked questions never, so I took no chances when leaving the house. To further blend in, I sprayed on a fake tan every two weeks.

As I pulled on a black velour track suit, my six year old daughter Ashley scurried into the bedroom and watched with imploring eyes.

"What is it, Ash?" I asked.

"I promised not to tell," she said, practically dancing with the need to let the secret out.

"If it's about Austin getting beat up, then spill it." I folded my arms across my chest.

Ashley smirked. "Brandon Sanchez didn't beat up Austin. Madison did."

A girl? Geez, that sucked. Percy needed to give Austin some fighting lessons. Or, considering Percy's childhood history as a punching bag, maybe I'd be the better teacher. "Was it Madison Pak?"

Ashley shook her head and stuck her thumb in her mouth, a habit I couldn't get her to break.

"Madison Chang?"

"No, mommy," she said around her thumb. "Madison Smith."

Madison and her mother, Heather, moved to our neighborhood a month ago. As of the last "Mother's Night Out" (a tradition I instituted so I could keep up with school events), the other fourth grade moms had learned little about the Smiths. Madison's mother, Heather, had volunteered to coach the kids' co-ed soccer team, the Battle Hamsters—a name we'd thought the political correctness police couldn't fault. When the PC contingent claimed it was degrading to hamsters, though, I couldn't argue—given how badly most kids play soccer. But they had no better suggestions, so the name stuck.

Since it was my turn to bring snacks for tomorrow's game, I had a legitimate reason for seeing Heather. I checked the clock. Seven-thirty—not too late to go over.

I stopped at Kroger and picked up a tray of assorted cookies. That should cause a riot after the game as kids fought, whined, or screamed for their favorite kinds. Vindictive, I know, but I *was* a vampire—had been ever since that unfortunate late-night shopping event at Kohl's. Percy always said I'd kill for a bargain. But I never thought I'd *be* killed for one. The bitch took all my blood and my eighty percent off leather handbag—then had the nerve to act like giving me immortal life as a vampire made up for it.

I pulled into the Smith's circular drive and parked behind an SUV with a Battle Hamsters decal on the back—a hamster in a Viking helmet, a sword clutched in its little paws, superimposed over a soccer ball. A bumper sticker read, "Do you *really* want to tailgate a woman with PMS and a Glock?"

After I rang the bell, Heather Smith opened the door to the two-story stone-faced house. She wore her bleached-blond hair in a ponytail. Her large brown eyes gave her a fawn-like appearance, and her lips were full and pouty. She wore the exact same black velour track suit as mine—and looked better in it. *Bitch.*

"Heather? I'm Louise Sullivan," I said sweetly. We shook hands around the precariously balanced cookie tray.

For an uncomfortable moment, Heather stared into my eyes, then gave me a once over and shrugged. "Let me take those cookies," she said. "Oh, assorted. *Great.* Will you be at the game Saturday?"

"I have to work." Work. Yeah. While other moms cheered their kids on and sipped venti extra caramel, extra foam lattés, I'd be crammed in a fridge, drenched in SPF 50, with towels stuffed around the door so no stray light got in. Percy videotaped the games so we could watch them together later, but it was a sucky substitute. Unlike Ashley, Austin remembered a time when *I* coached his team and was room mother for his class. Sometimes I felt like such a crappy mom.

"You wanna come in for a Diet Coke or something?" Heather asked. "My ex took Madison to dinner, so I'm alone until nine."

"Sure." After seeing the bumper sticker, I wanted to get a sense of Heather's personality before broaching the Madison problem. Plus, an invitation into the house could prove useful later.

The perfectly decorated living room looked like a photo from *Martha Stewart Living*. I hated Heather even more.

She handed me a chilled can of Diet Coke. I forced down a sip. It tasted like rot and I'd probably have cramps later from imbibing non-blood, but I needed to make a good show. At least the soda was caffeine-free. The last thing anyone needed was a jittery bloodsucker.

"The divorce must be hard on Madison," I said. Perhaps Madison's bullying was a cry for attention. I wondered how a divorce would affect Ashley and Austin—not that divorce was really an option. I couldn't exactly go to court, so everything would be decided in Percy's favor, including custody. And I couldn't lose my kids.

"The divorce hasn't been easy," Heather said, "but it's better than the constant fighting that went on before. Marc just couldn't accept me for who I am."

I knew the feeling. "Dare I ask for a tour?"

"I warn you, the place is a mess."

The house was pristine, even Madison's room. A toy crossbow and assault rifle hung on wall pegs, and a clown punching bag stood in a corner below a *Rambo IV* poster. Just what you'd expect for a tomboy bully.

When we reached a closed door, Heather hesitated.

"Is that a closet holding family skeletons?" I asked. "Or is *that* the messy room?"

She grinned. "No, this room just freaks some people out."

"I'm pretty freak-proof."

The blueprints probably listed the room as a bedroom. It looked like a grownup version of Madison's play area. An edged scimitar, a bone-handled dagger, a battle axe and other assorted weapons hung on the walls. A heavy punching bag and a battered target dummy stood in opposite corners. Only the shop vac beside a chest of drawers looked out of place.

"That's quite an arsenal," I said. Fear—and possibly Diet Coke—knotted my gut. Of all the bad luck...

Heather skimmed her fingers across the dagger handle. "Collecting weapons is sort of my hobby."

"Do you know how to use them?"

"Oh, I play with them. You know—to keep in shape. It's *way* more fun than pilates." She opened the chest's top drawer and selected a wooden stake. "You know, you almost had me fooled with that cheap fake tan and drinking the pop."

"Aw, crap." Frantically, I shifted into mist form— something I'd only recently learned to do. The first time I accidentally went all "misty," it startled me so much I rained in my pants.

Heather grabbed the shop vac hose. "I have a Hoover, Louise, and I'm not afraid to use it!"

Unsure of the effects of being vacuumed, I rematerialized in "vampire mode"—fangs, black eyes, the whole nine yards. With vampire speed, I zipped downstairs. To my astonishment, Heather followed with super-speed almost as fast as mine. I lost a few seconds opening the deadbolt, then ran to the street.

"You're not getting away from me!" Heather shouted, her sneakers slapping the sidewalk as she ran like the Bionic Woman. I'd heard some monster hunters had "special powers." I supposed I was about to find out what that meant.

Turning to mist now might let me escape, but that would only delay the inevitable confrontation. I ran in the opposite direction from my house, not wanting to bring this trouble home. Percy would never let me hear the end of it. And *my* house really was a mess.

Wispy fog created halos around the streetlights. When I reached the park, Heather pursuing like a dog chasing a fox, I raced onto the soccer field, the flattest unpaved surface. Breathing hard, Heather stopped several paces away. I didn't need to breathe—one point in my favor.

"Heather, let me explain—"

A car roared up the street then screeched to a halt halfway on the sidewalk. Percy jumped out, leaving the door open and the engine running. He'd come to my rescue! He did still love me.

"Get away while you can!" he shouted.

After a moment, I realized he was talking to Heather. *Schmuck.*

Percy jumped between us. "You don't know what you're up against. My wife is a—"

"Vampire?" Heather said, then spun Percy around and held the stake to his throat.

I froze.

"Hey, I'm human!" he said.

"That buys you nothing, Renfield," Heather said, pressing until the stake made a dimple in his skin. "You're sheltering a killer."

"Oh, my God," Percy whispered. "Louise, tell me you didn't hurt Madison."

I choked on outrage. "What have I ever done that would make you think I'd harm a child? You used to trust me!"

"You used to be human!"

"Nice, Percy." I was starting to feel like no one appreciated my self-restraint. No wonder so many vampires went bad.

"Look, you two clearly have issues," Heather said. "But I don't really give a crap because none of that will matter once I've staked Louise."

Percy struggled against her hold, but her arm didn't budge.

"That's my wife," he said.

"Not anymore. Now she's just a blood-sucking killing machine."

"I've been a vampire for five years and never killed anyone." Although I did have a mental list of who would make my top ten if I ever turned to the dark side.

Heather's lip curled and even Percy looked doubtful.

"Christ, Percy, what do you think keeps me from feeding off the living?" I asked. "My love for our children, my love for you."

He stared at me blankly. Percy's name was rapidly climbing into the top ten.

"Don't believe her, Percy," Heather said. "She kills. They all do."

"*You're* the one threatening a human life," I said. "Let Percy go. Please."

She shook her head sharply, as though waking from a trance, then shoved Percy toward the street. "Leave before I change my mind."

Percy hovered uncertainly.

I jerked my chin toward the car. "Go home, Percy—"

Stake raised, Heather ran at me. The point slammed against my chest, right over the heart.

Her arm bounced back. Heather cried out and so did I. Despite the Kevlar vest, her strike would leave a spectacular bruise. The woman was as strong as she was fast—and had good aim. Too bad she couldn't teach the Battle Hamsters to kick with the same accuracy.

"Louise!" Percy stepped toward us, but Heather halted him with a threatening wave of the stake.

"I'm okay," I said.

"Yeah, about that." Heather rubbed her wrist. "What are you wearing under there—a brass bra?"

"Kevlar."

"Crap, I wondered when vamps would think of that." Heather shrugged and drew the bone-handled dagger I'd seen earlier. "I hate cutting off heads. It's just messy. And getting the bloodstains out—"

I raised an eyebrow. "You're gonna cut off my head with a dagger?"

"I'm gonna slit your throat and bleed you until you're too weak to move. *Then* I'll go home and get the axe."

"Mrs. Smith—Heather," Percy said, holding his palms out. "Stop. You can't—"

She lunged. As I dove away, the dagger slashed through my sleeve and nicked my arm. I swung my other arm and knocked her to the ground with a blow that would have broken bones of a normal mortal. The soccer field hadn't seen this much action since the Battle Hamsters played that epic game with the Mighty Moon Princesses that ended in a 0–0 tie.

"Why are you doing this?" I asked as thick black blood seeped from the cut.

"It's what I was born to do—kill monsters." Heather rose, dusting off grass. "You're evil. You feed off people like telemarketers feed off the stupid."

"I don't feed off humans! And *I* don't teach my children to be bullies!"

"What the heck do you mean by that?" Heather demanded.

"Your Madison beat up my son today."

"*What?*" Heather's arm went limp. If I'd wanted to, I could have torn her throat out. Instead, I told her what had happened.

"I don't understand," Heather said. "Madison talks about Austin all the time. She has a crush on him—at least I *think* it's your Austin she has a crush on."

"Helluva way to show it," Percy said.

Heather turned the dagger, watching the streetlight glint off steel. "Are you sure it wasn't Madison Pak?"

"Certain," I said.

"Where would Madison learn that it's okay to beat someone up?"

Percy and I stared pointedly at the dagger.

"Oh. Yeah. Right." Heather sank onto the bottom bleacher. "I've been trying to make the world safe for her. I never thought Madison would copy me like that."

"If you really want to do some good, why don't you go after the blood-sucking killing machine who made me?"

"Huh?"

I explained what happened that fateful night in Kohl's parking lot.

Heather's eyes blazed. "*And* your eighty percent off leather handbag? Oh, that bitch must die."

"By the way, not all vampires are evil," I said.

"That's . . . not what I was taught," Heather said. "But you could have killed me and you didn't."

"It isn't like I wanted this." I looked into Percy's eyes. "I'm trying to be the best wife and mother I can under the circumstances."

His gaze softened and he wrapped an arm around my waist. It had been a long time since he showed me any affection. I stopped trying after the time he said, "No, thanks, I'm not feeling like a necrophile tonight."

Heather rested her hand on my shoulder. "The city's putting lights on the soccer fields soon. Maybe we can get the Battle Hamsters scheduled for more night games."

My throat tightened at the unexpected onslaught of kindness. "Thanks."

Heather cocked her head. "Hey, you up for some payback, Louise? Vampires can sense their sires—you can lead us right to her."

"Can I carry the axe?" I asked.

"Sure."

"Okay, then." I pictured the vampire's porcelain cheekbones, her blood-coated lips, the black void of her eyes. A faint tug came from my right. I pointed. "She's that way."

"At the Golfsmith 'Moonlight Madness' sale?" Percy huffed. "That bitch must die."

"Count on it," Heather said.

I squeezed his hand. "Looks like I'll be home late, honey."

Percy kissed my cheek and didn't even flinch at its coolness. "I'll wait up."

After Percy drove off, Heather and I headed toward her house to gear up. Glancing sidelong at me, Heather started singing, roughly to the tune of the Notre Dame Fight Song, "Battle Hamsters, fight, fight, fight!"

I joined in. "Scurry with all your might, might, might! Stuff your cheeks with victory! And roll, Battle Hamsters, roll! Whoo!" We both raised a victory fist, then giggled.

"Wow, I haven't giggled in years," I said.

Heather put a hand on my back as we walked down the foggy street. "Louise, I think this is the beginning of a beautiful friendship."

Kevin Andrew Murphy has written a great deal of vampire fiction for White Wolf's World of Darkness and elsewhere, and now for one of his latest characters. "Tecate for Hecate" concludes the triptych begun in Esther Friesner's *Witch Way To The Mall?* with "Tacos for Tezcatlipoca" and continued with "Frijoles for Fenris" in *Strip Mauled*—but is defintely not the end of the magical misadventures of Bryce Pierponte, for whom the author has plans . . . Of course, those plans are mixed in with others, as Kevin is also doing work on the next volume of George R.R. Martin's Wild Cards series, *Fort Freak*, among other projects. Updates can be found on Kevin's website www.sff.net/people/Kevin.A.Murphy and the Deep Genre blog (www.deepgenre.com).

Tecate for Hecate

Kevin Andrew Murphy

When you could turn into smoke and slip through keyholes, you wouldn't think it would be particularly difficult to break into a blood bank. Then again, there was a reason why they called it "the Red Cross."

A white cross in a red heart made a potent ward, an ancient symbol against the undead, and as one of the not-exactly-living, Bryce was effectively blocked.

Fortunately, Bryce was not your average vampire, revenant, or blood-sucking ghost. He was a draug, one of the favored *Helleder* of the Norse goddess, Hel. Getting the favor of Hel was no mean feat (and thereby hung a tale, if not two), but suffice it to say, it involved being a magician with a near death experience that the Mistress of Niflheim had decided to make permanent, giving him an eternal gate pass to Sleet Cold, Her otherworldly manse—along with an insatiable hunger and an unslakable thirst. And while most of being a draug was a drag, it did come with a few perks. Being exceptionally strong was nice, even if not particularly useful at the moment and dirt common among the undead. Being able to grow to ten feet tall? Weirder, but neat, even if still not applicable to the task at hand. Being able to piece yourself back together after being ripped limb from limb? Surprisingly useful, especially if you'd spent the past few months living (so to speak) in the basement of a fraternity of rowdy collegiate werewolves. But keeping the rest of your magical abilities from life? A definite plus. At least if you'd started out as a magician, not that this was helping much at the moment. It was the first night of the dark of the moon, a perfect time for all sorts of interesting magic, and here Bryce found himself trying to break into a blood bank.

But any good magician, or even a reasonably competent wicked one, had more than one trick up his sleeve. Such as, for example, a familiar.

Of course, having a familiar was its own challenge.

"Do I look like a dog?" Matabor asked pointedly.

Bryce had to admit that Matabor did not. As a manticore cub, Matabor looked like a cross between a monkey and a kitten, with bat wings, a scorpion's stinger, and a triple-row of shark's teeth thrown in just for fun. But nowhere in the magical mishmash that made up his familiar was there anything slightly canine.

"I do not 'fetch,'" Matabor stressed. "I am a magician's familiar, a beast of legend, not some mere witch's puke to suck out blood and regurgitate it at her mistress's whim."

"It comes in plastic bags now."

Matabor's monkey eyes looked askance. Obviously modern convenience was not an improvement.

"Well, how am I supposed to get blood then?"

"Kill someone?" Bryce's familiar suggested. "I believe that still works, doesn't it?"

Bryce gritted his fangs. He was doing his best to be a good, or at least somewhat less harmful, undead person, but it was spring break and he no longer had the luxury of a house filled with extremely resilient regenerating lycanthropic frat boys who thought that brawling, biting, and turning into a wolf to lick someone's wounds was perfectly normal behavior. Of course, some of his bros at Gamma Rho Rho were starting to think Bryce was gay (untrue) or at least that he had some weird blood fetish (true, but not like they thought), so while they were away at the beach soaking up the vamp-killing rays, it was time for Bryce to pick up alternative methods.

Not that he knew what those were.

Bryce drove home before sunrise. Or, at least, to his dad's place, which counted as home for the break.

There seemed to be an unwritten rule, probably some underlying rule of magic, that when your parents wanted to have one of *those* talks, you couldn't avoid one short of being dead.

Even *undead* didn't cut it.

"Bryce, we need to talk," his dad said waiting, ironically, in the living room.

Bryce didn't need to talk. What Bryce needed to do was go to the undead room, also known as the basement, and crawl into the overcurtained trundle bed that passed for his crypt. But that's not what the phrase meant. "We do?"

His father nodded. "I know you're used to keeping your own hours, but since you've come back..."

Bryce knew he meant "from college" and not "from

the grave" but some explanation was needed. "Uh, I've just been going through, uh, stuff," he said lamely.

"*Bryce Arthur Pierponte,*" his father intoned, "I need you to level with me, so you are going to stay here and you are going to answer some questions *and you are going to answer them now.* Do you understand?"

Bryce froze. His father had used the dreaded Threefold Naming. It was usually bad enough when a parent used all three of a child's names, but with a magical being—such as, for example, a draug or bloodsucking ghost—the Three Names created a potent binding. Usually you also needed to have some of their blood and recite a few generations of ancestry for good measure, but this nicety was waived if the Threefold Naming was being done by a direct ancestor and blood relation. Such as, for example, your father.

"Yes, Father." Bryce had a natural knack for magic, stumbling into it once by saying just the right words. Now he knew where he got it. "What do you want to know, Father?"

"Don't you 'Father' me, Bryce. 'Dad' will do just fine. But answer me, honestly: Were you out buying drugs? Because I've been to college and—"

"No," Bryce broke in quickly, honestly.

"Then where were you all night?"

Bryce didn't want to say he'd been attempting to break into the blood bank. But he didn't have to say what he'd been doing. Just where: "The blood bank..."

His father swore and Bryce winced. This was another part of the drag of being a draug: Instead of being repelled by garlic or roses like the more common Romanian vampyr, he was repelled by repellant language. The blue streak his father proceeded to swear would usually have sent him screaming off into the night, but the Threefold Naming had also forced him to stay where he was, so instead, he was left a cowering wretch. "The blood bank, Bryce? The blood bank? I know I've been tapped out since the divorce—you can thank your mother for that—but if you needed money..." His father swore again and Bryce cringed. "Those damned vampires! You look like death warmed over. When did you last eat?"

"Two nights ago." That was when he'd bit Stewie goodbye.

Again the swearing. "Okay, I understand—new house, new refrigerator, nothing in it. But while we may be in the wilds of suburbia, we do at least have a twenty-four hour grocery." Dad took out his wallet, cursing softly as he fished out a twenty. "Did you get gas?"

"No."

Bryce cringed, then his father said, "Give me the keys." Bryce did, his dad replacing them with the cash. "The office is having me come in early again, and I've got a hell of a commute. But once you get some rest, *I'm ordering you* to walk to the store and find something to eat. And while you're at it, get some food for that poor mangy cat of yours." He gestured to Matabor and the cat illusion Bryce had masked his familiar with.

"Yes, Dad."

His father hugged him briefly. "Love you, son. I'll be back tonight."

With that, his father left, leaving Bryce with a few bare minutes to pack himself into the basement before dawn.

✧   ✧   ✧

Bryce had a hell of a commute as well, but a faster one. Everyone knew that the dead traveled quickly, and nothing is quicker than thought. With dawn, his had slipped into Niflheim.

In the heart of the misty realm of the Norse dead was Sleet Cold, the Hall of the goddess Hel. Bryce had been a part-time resident ever since he'd drunk from Her bowl, Hunger, and eaten with Her knife, Starvation. Sleet Cold was like an earlier incarnation of the Hotel California, but without the pink champagne or tacky seventies ceiling mirrors: Bryce could check out any time he liked, but he could never leave.

Not quite true, my honored guest, Hel corrected graciously, Her voice echoing inside his head. She was decked out in Her latest Cruella de Vil finery, a dalmatian-skin pantsuit with a matching pillbox hat. A lesser goddess could not have pulled it off, but it complemented Her complexion, white on one side, black on the other, bloodless pale and the bruised hue of a frozen corpse. *If you wish to leave Niflheim for Midgard on a more permanent basis than the arrangement we have now, I would be a poor hostess were I to not offer you the same bargain as the most honored of all my guests.* She gestured with Her one white hand to a man who was fairer still, His blond hair shining like a torch in the misty dimness of the hall.

He sat there, more beautiful than a hundred teen idols, more glamorous than a thousand Hollywood stars and starlets, and evidently more drunk than all of them combined. *Who's Thok?* He muttered, a horn of golden mead clutched in one perfect masculine hand. *Never heard of Thok...Never met Thok...*

Hel patted Him on the shoulder. *There, there, sweet Baldr. I'm certain that were Thok to have ever had the privilege of your acquaintance, she would have cried a river for your death. Even if all it would take to ransom you from my hall would be a single one of her tears.*

Baldr looked at Hel blearily. *I heard Thok doesn't even exist,* He said drunkenly. *I heard she was just your father in drag!*

My father? In drag? Perish the thought! Hel dimpled. *Loki may be guilty of countless crimes, but crossdressing? You must have him confused with Uncle Thor...*

Baldr chuckled. *Had to get that troll pretty drunk before he thought Thor was Freya...*

Bryce bit his tongue, not bringing up the origin story of Sleipnir. He watched as Hel gestured for Her maidservant to pour Her most honored guest more mead. The woman did, spilling it everywhere, but Baldr didn't seem to mind. He drained His horn then fell asleep in the freezing puddle on the table, slurring out, *Thok thuks...*

Hel turned to Bryce. *I offer you the same bargain I offered dear Baldr all those years ago: Were every creature in the nine worlds, the quick and the dead, to cry for your passing, then you could return. Indeed, as you are only half here in Niflheim, I would gladly accept half: the tears of the dead, the tears of the living, or any combination of half the tears of the worlds.*

"You are nothing if not gracious, Lady Hel."

She smiled a disturbing smile. *Care to play some chess? I do so love a good game...*

Bryce still wondered what Her chessboard was

called, what the pieces were made out of, but as with everything it Hel's hall, it was half black and half white.

Bryce nodded and chose white.

By the time the sun set and Bryce's consciousness returned to the world of the living and the vacationing undead, Lady Hel had beat him more times than he could count. His last match was taken over by the shade of Bobby Fischer, who had died in Iceland, so his presence in Sleet Cold made as much sense as anything metaphysical. Bryce hoped the legendary chessmaster would do a bit better, but he wouldn't bet on it.

Bryce was also starving, which was to say, more starving that usual. The baseline for any hungry ghost was hunger, but you could get around that so long as you occasionally fed.

Of course, there was also the matter of a magical binding and his father ordering him to go to the twenty-four hour supermarket and find something to eat. But what? The bag boy? The stock clerk? A couple checkers and late-night shoppers?

Thankfully, his father had ordered him to find *something* rather than *someone* and Bryce could turn into grave mist and back again. In rather short order, the meat locker had become a scene from "King Henry"—the Child Ballad as opposed to the fat guy with the multiple wives and the turkey drumstick. Though it was pretty close to that, too.

There was something cathartic in swelling up into a ten-foot-tall monstrous draug and noshing on sides of beef like they were Slim-Jims. Cathartic and somewhat disturbing. *More meat! More meat! More meat ya bring to me!* It wasn't quite the same as human—or, at least, werewolf—blood, but it still hit the spot, like filling up on a lot of empty calories.

Bryce didn't know where he put it all—conservation of mass was a concern of the natural world, not the supernatural—but he was at last picking his enormous teeth with a rib bone when he noticed an eyeball sitting on the floor in the corner.

It was not a mislaid cow eyeball. It was a human eyeball. A very pretty brown one, in fact, except for the fact that it was not in anyone's head and was staring at him.

It spun like a marble and rolled into a ventilation duct, the same ventilation duct Bryce had snuck in through himself in the form of mist. Bryce took the form of the Niflheim fog and followed, reforming on the other side. He watched as the eyeball rolled across the linoleum of the meat department and into the hand of one of the checkout clerks. She stood up, polished the orb briefly, and popped it back in its socket. She blinked and smiled. A very sharp-toothed smile. "Were you planning to pay for that?"

Bryce grinned weakly in return.

She rolled her eyes, independently for a moment which was truly disconcerting, but then they settled down and simply looked pretty again. Bryce sniffed. There was a smell of death about her. The same smell he had himself. "What are you?"

She laughed lightly. "I was about to ask you the same thing myself. You're obviously not an ordinary vampire." She sidled up to him, craning her neck, and Bryce realized he'd reformed a bit larger than his usual. He brought himself back under seven feet. "What are you?" she asked.

"I'm a draug. Scandinavian." She looked perplexed so Bryce explained: "A sort of Norse vampire. We do all sorts of magic, but we still drink blood. And eat stuff."

"You're not all into liver like those freaky Filipino vampires, are you?"

"The guys with the pop-off heads? Not particularly," Bryce said, failing to mention that he could take off his head if he really felt like it. "I just eat. A lot. But I'm not into liver."

She looked relieved. "I'm also not the usual sort of vampire. I am a lamia, from Libya," she stated proudly. "I can take out my eyes, as you saw. And rather than the usual bats, I can take the form of the python, the lioness, and the shark."

"Oh? I do wolves and jaguars."

She nodded then paused. "They have jaguars in Scandinavia?"

"It's a long story," said Bryce. "Could you show me where the cat food is? I do have money for that."

She did the disconcerting independent eyeroll thing again, but then took him by the arm. "Let me show you."

Her name was Anissa, and she'd been undead for a very short time—a very short time as the undead measured these things, which was twenty-three years. That was longer than Bryce had been alive, or undead, or even alive and undead put together.

"Then there was Hop Sing," Anissa recounted. "He was over three hundred years old, and one of those hopping vampires from China. Came over during the Gold Rush when they had all the Chinese working on the railroad. The hopping I could sort of get used to—it was kind of like a weird limp—but then someone spilled. a bag of rice on Aisle Five and, I kid you not, he had to stand there and count every last grain. It was like dating the vampire Rain Man or that guy from *Sesame Street*. It was over after that."

Bryce nodded. The Litany of the Previous Boyfriends was a ritual with a lot of girls on the first date, but with a lamia, it was to be expected. Bryce had remembered one other detail Anissa had failed to mention: The lamians were man-eaters, figuratively as well as literally. And Bryce realized he'd somehow become this one's latest catch.

"Then there was this Greek guy. Did you know that some Greek vampires bite noses? Freakiest thing." This said by a woman who could pop her eyes out and turn into an animal selectively. She was currently a giant python from the waist down, coiled halfway around him on the couch.

There was the sound of a car in the driveway. "About that," Bryce broke in. "That would be my dad. He doesn't know about the whole vampire thing."

She blinked. Or, at least, that's what he guessed it meant when the eyeballs on the coffee table bounced where she'd set them down the same way a regular girl might take off her glasses. "You're that young? Oh, I hadn't realized!" The note of pleasure in her voice made Bryce aware that he'd just been upgraded from *Nice Catch* to *Prize Catch*, but what he was more interested in was the fact that Anissa picked up her eyeballs and popped them back in her head and turned her snake tail back into legs and feet. He was so flustered by the sound of the key in the door that he almost forgot to change back from Super-Monster-

Basketball-Star–Size Bryce to regular under-six-foot Bryce. But he did, and that was what was important.

His dad came in, quickly noticing Bryce standing beside the couch, Anissa lounging on it, and put two and two together. "You're Anissa, aren't you?" Dad said. "You work at the supermarket. You have the night shift, right?"

The Rule of Three was strong, and while inviting a vampire into your house made you lose all power over them, there were ways to take it back. Such as, for example, a variant on the Threefold Naming.

"Why, yes," said the lamia, getting up from the couch. "I was just...helping Bryce home with his cat food."

"Meow," Matabor said from the kitchen on cue.

Dad turned to Bryce. "Did you get something to eat yourself?"

"He ate at the supermarket," Anissa explained. "He was...very hungry." She smiled conspiratorially at Bryce.

Dad nodded. "Good. I ate on the way."

"I should get going," Anissa said. "I need to finish my shift."

"Thanks," Dad said, opening the door for Anissa.

"You're welcome." She glanced back flirtatiously. "See you, Bryce."

Dad shut the door, looking to Bryce. It was a man-to-man look, but he didn't say anything more than, "I'm going to go to bed. Sorry for being such a poor host, but I've got another early day tomorrow."

"No problem, Dad."

Dad went upstairs, leaving Bryce the downstairs, the basement, and the trouble of being undead which was getting more troublesome by the minute.

He went down to his room, unzipping his backpack and getting out Master Seidel's formulary, the grimoire and magician's workbook that had started this whole adventure, along with finding his familiar. There was the section on *Immortality*, with Master Seidel's tart opinion about being undead: *A problem, not a solution.* Tell me about it!

Looking further, Bryce found the Lesser Bath of Hebe, Medea's invocation to the Greek goddess of youth. The ritual looked deceptively simple on the surface but, as Bryce knew from previous experience, it had all sorts of possibilities for complication if you made a few seemingly harmless substitutions. Then there was Medea's other spell, the Greater Bath of Hebe, a much more dangerous procedure, but one which could not only restore the aged to youth but the dead to life as well.

Bryce wasn't aged, but he was dead—or, at least, undead. Looking over Seidel's translation of Medea's original Greek, and translating a little of the Greek while he was at it—who knew that freshman Intro to the Classics could be so useful?—there was a bit of misnaming going on, since the Greater Bath of Hebe would more properly be translated as the Greater Bath of Hebe and Hecate, Hecate being the Grecian goddess of ghosts, witchcraft, and assorted necromancy who predated Hades as Ruler of the Underworld before getting a golden parachute into Her current position as Queen of the Night.

Well, he'd already met Tezcatlipoca, Fenris, and Hel. He wasn't being a proper magician if he didn't round things out and visit a few more gods and goddesses.

What's the worst that could happen?

❖   ❖   ❖

Hecate was analogous to the Roman Trivia, goddess of the crossroads, and a whole lot of the Greco-Roman pantheon was the same gods moving to new digs, getting different names and redecorating to suit the times.

Suburbia was more of the same if you just knew what to look for. The three-way intersection of Lady's Mantle Drive, Willow Tree Place, and Shadowdale Lane looked like something from any other subdivision, a sleepy three-way stop unlikely to get any traffic at the tail end of the witching hour. And even if you noted that this night was the second night of the dark of the moon, the true night of the new moon, the most propitious time to contact the Queen of the Night, you would not consider that spot terribly auspicious as a portal to the Underworld unless you thought about those names, the sacred herbs and trees, and how they might pertain to Hecate, aka Trivia of the Crossroads. Drawing a circle in the middle was also unnecessary, as there was already a convenient one set there, a dark moon forged from iron, mist curling slightly from the vents.

Placing the goddess's symbols was the first part: a key, a torch, and a serpent. Keys were easy, and a flashlight worked for a torch. And while finding a serpent might usually be a bit more difficult, Bryce had just met one.

"So I need to turn into a snake?" Anissa asked.

"It's the third symbol for the circle," Bryce said, chalking a triangle in the middle of the manhole cover. "You need to stand here."

"I've never done ritual magic," Anissa hissed silkily,

her lower half already coiling into a python's tail. "It makes an interesting second date. This something all draugs do?"

"A lot of them," Bryce said, but was only going from legend. He was the only draug he'd ever met, at least outside of Hel's Hall.

The traditional libations and offerings were a bit more troublesome. According to the *Iliad*, Hecate's sacrifice of choice was a Hecatomb, one hundred cattle slaughtered in honor of the goddess, then roasted and eaten by her followers with lots of singing and drinking.

Bryce had started the evening with a few sides of beef, so hopefully the current offering would suffice: the 100 x 100. It was from In-n-Out Burger's secret menu: a hundred beef patties and a hundred cheese slices stacked together into one ginormous burger, the closest suburbia came to a Hecatomb short of a Labor Day picnic. Plus a dozen baskets of fries.

The *Iliad* also listed barley and fermented beverages as traditional, but there wasn't an all-night barley takeout unless you counted beer, which Bryce thought should satisfy both. He had four cases of Tecate, chosen because the name rhymed with "Hecate," he was underage as well as undead (and Anissa had scored them), and, finally, because with his draug's allergy to dirty words, his options for drinking songs were severely limited. But he did know how to sing "Ninety-Nine Bottles of Beer on the Wall" in classical Latin.

The python coiled up alongside Matabor and watched as Bryce popped a bottle and began the invocation: *"Io Hecate!"* He poured the first taste onto the black iron circle, letting it pool, making it an even truer mirror of the dark moon above, the domain of Hecate. *"Nonaginta novem solum crapula parietis! Nonaginta novem solum crapula!"* Bryce watched the libations dribble down the holes into the Underworld below. *"Si unus illorum solum contingo cado..."* He swallowed a patty from the In-n-Out Hecatomb and a handful of fries, chasing it with the rest of the beer. *"Nonaginta duodeviginti solum crapula parietis!"*

Bryce popped another bottle and began the next verse. It sounded much more impressive and magical if you didn't understand the words. But counting out a sacrifice was old magic, and four cases of beer made for a pretty substantial altar to the gods even by frat house standards.

The trouble with suburbia was that it was hard to find a completely deserted crossroads even in the middle of the night. A car stopped at the stop sign. Then, the next moment, red and blue lights started flashing atop it.

Bryce may have been a magician's draug, but he was also a teenager and a college student and had no interest in getting arrested for underage public binge drinking, regardless of whether he could turn into mist and escape or not. He grabbed his key and the flashlight, scooped Anissa up onto one shoulder, then ripped off the manhole cover with one hand, tossing it aside like a Frisbee. He heard the crash as it smacked into the roof of someone's McMansion.

Sirens wailed as Bryce jumped down the sewer, falling down, down, down, Matabor fluttering on little bat wings around him and Anissa the lamia. It seemed like they fell for an eternity, or half of one, and Bryce realized somewhere in the descent that he was not reaching bottom and had just started another secret journey into the Underworld.

At last he touched down. It was very much like Niflheim, a realm of mist and smoke, except where Niflheim was cold as ice or sleet, Erebus was merely foggy and damp. At least Bryce hoped it was Erebus, rather than some deeper, darker region, such as Hades or Tartarus. It was also wetter, and he was standing in a puddle of water, leaking into his shoes.

He shone the flashlight around. The fog swirled and cleared a bit, and he saw that he was at the juncture of three tunnels, all alike. Well, almost all alike. The keystone of each arch had a symbol: the first, a key; the second, a torch; the third, a serpent.

Bryce didn't know if he was in an adventure game or a fairytale. Three paths. Three choices. Three symbols of knowledge. If this were a game, each of the paths would have some plot token he'd need to complete the quest. If it were a fairytale, two paths would lead to doom and only one would lead to some happy outcome. But since this was a secret magical mystical journey to supplicate the ancient Greco-Roman titaness of death, magic and the dark moon?

If it were, said an echoing voice in his head, *you might have brought all the libations you promised.*

"What?" said Bryce.

You sang of nine and ninety, yet I only see six and ninety here.

Bryce thought. Six and ninety. Ninety-six, exactly how many bottles there were in four cases of Tecate. Or any other beer for that matter.

And your Latin is atrocious, said the voice in his

skull. *However, points for attempting a Hecatomb. And bringing a lamian sibyl as your third token is done far less often than I might like.* The mist swirled and reformed and Bryce was looking at a tall, elegant woman flanked by six wolves. Her long titian hair was held up with a fine silver comb and She was garbed in a flowing gown, like midnight dusted with stars. In one hand, She held a Tecate. In another, a hamburger patty. And in a third, a basket of french fries. *These fried tubers are lovely. I started as an earth goddess. It would be nice if more supplicants thought to remember such trivia.*

Hecate/Trivia drank the beer, ate the burger, and nibbled the fries, all three at once. It wasn't so much a case of watching a three-headed six-armed goddess as watching three identical goddesses superimposed on each other, a triple-exposure of the divine.

At last She finished Her meal, tossing the scraps to Her wolves, who ran through one another as they snapped up the treats, superimposed in the same manner as their mistress. They at last settled down into two wolves, each of them occasionally having three heads. *And so,* the goddess(es) said, *how do you invoke us? Tender-Hearted Hecate? Bright-Coiffed Hecate? Night-Wandering Hecate?* The last three phrases were said all at once, each face of the goddess talking over the others. She reached out Her hands and collected Her tokens: the key, the flashlight, and Anissa the python.

This was a test, and Bryce realized the trial of the tunnels had merely taken another form. Then he remembered what his father had done earlier, the Threefold Naming: "I call upon Tender-Hearted Hecate, Bright-Coiffed Hecate, and Night-Wandering

Hecate—all three. How could I honor one face of the goddess and slight the others?"

It happens more often than not, said the goddess's first face, gesturing with Her key.

Those seeking illumination are often blind to it, said the second as She shone the flashlight in his eyes.

People are idiots, the last said simply, draping the snake about Her shoulders.

So then, said Trivia as one, *why have you sought us out?*

"I'm in a bit of a bind," Bryce said in the understatement of the year. "I'm undead. I'm caught between life and death, and while some of it's fun, most of it sucks."

That is unfortunate but true, said Tender-Hearted Hecate, the Key Holder.

Yet the same can be said of Life, remarked Bright-Coiffed Hecate, the Light Bringer.

And Death, finished Night-Wandering Hecate, She of the Serpent. *Consider yourself lucky. There are some hungry shades who bite noses.*

This wasn't the answer Bryce wanted to hear, though it was all very true. "But could You help me? Please?"

The goddess(es) cocked Her/Their head(s), considering.

The Light Bringer spoke first: *Lady Hel's realm is not our realm, but it is on the same level, and we **do** hear gossip.*

Your reputation is getting around, agreed the Key Holder. *But we hear good things!*

From wicked gods, finished She of the Serpent. *Lady Hel is quite taken with you, hence her gambit to keep you in her realm. But from what I've heard, she has offered you an out.*

"Half the tears of the world," Bryce said. "I'll have some trouble pulling that off."

The first offer is never the only offer, Bright-Coiffed Hecate pointed out.

Hades originally wanted Persephone for the whole year, said Tender-Hearted Hecate. *He settled for half.*

After Demeter went on strike, finished Night-Wandering Hecate. *That was politics more than anything.*

It's all politics, said Bright-Coiffed Hecate. *We gods use the laws of magic to our own ends, but are bound by them as well. Eating the food of the Underworld puts you in that Underworld god's power, but it is up to the god how long you stay.*

We could return you to mortal life, said Night-Wandering Hecate, *had you eaten the fruits of Tartarus while it was under our administration. And even with the current one, we have some influence due to our good friend Persephone. But Niflheim? Ten Hecatombs aren't worth an interplanar incident.*

Which is not to say that we won't help you, said Tender-Hearted Hecate, *because we can. We gods are bound by laws, even more so than mortals. We love games. And if you beat one of us in a game, you can ask for anything in our power. Anything at all.*

In Tartarus, we usually just roll the bones, said She of the Serpent.

The Light Bringer held the flashlight up to illuminate Her face. *But we are given to understand that Lady Hel has a passion for a game called chess...*

Beating Lady Hel at chess was easier said than done. Bryce could go to the goddess Athena and beg for a measure of Her wisdom, but given Athena's opinions of mortals who challenged the gods (and the fate of Arachne) this was an amazingly dumb idea. Bryce could likewise stop by the Well of Mimir en route to Niflheim and try to get a sip of wisdom, but the last person to do that successfully was Odin, the Allfather, who'd lost an eye in the process, and since Mimir himself was now dead and decapitated, this was again, a recipe for disaster.

Hecate's advice was far simpler: watch, learn, play, and lower your sights.

Lady Hel was a grandmaster of chessmasters, as one might expect of the half black/half white daughter of Loki. It was an honor to play against Her, and an even greater honor to not be checkmated in three moves. Bryce learned a great deal from the Lady of Niflheim.

Baldr, on the other hand, was the most beautiful of the Norse gods (excepting Freya, but that depended on your sexual preference). He was the most beloved of the Norse gods (not that it had done him much good). But He was not the most clever of all the Norse gods. Plus He'd spent His centuries in Sleet Cold drowning His sorrows in enough mead to souse Jormungandr, aka Lady Hel's other brother, the Midgard Serpent.

Even so, Baldr beat Bryce twice until Bryce followed more of Hecate's advice, keeping his eyes on the board, only the board, focusing on the game, and not allowing himself to be distracted by the god's beauty and magnificence. Bryce moved a black knight, exposing a bishop and springing the trap for the white king. "Checkmate."

There was silence in Sleet Cold after he said the word, and Lady Hel looked up from Her latest game with the shade of Bobby Fischer. She then looked at the board between Bryce and Baldr, the position of the pieces, black and white, and nodded with the finality of a chessmaster. *Well done.*

Baldr looked as well—at the board, at His drinking horn, then at the board again. *Well done indeed!* He laughed and clapped Bryce on the shoulder, and only the strength of the undead kept Bryce from being knocked off the bench. *Been a while since any mortal has bested me, if ever.* The sorrow then showed plain on His beautiful face. *You have made me laugh, and for a brief moment, I forgot. I would gladly grant you any boon it is in my power to grant, but I'm afraid since coming here, I'm a much poorer god than I was.*

Bryce steeled himself, remembering Hecate's advice, the thing to ask for: "I was told that on Your deathbed, O Baldr, Your father Odin came and whispered something in Your ear. This is something known only to You and Him, a great secret and a greater riddle, something skalds whisper of as an unknowable thing. Could I ask to hear this?"

Baldr turned paler than His usual snowy whiteness and was sober in an instant. *You could ask to know this thing,* He said gravely, *but it would be better for you if you did not.*

And, by the same token, you could ask that dear Baldr tell me this dear little secret, this small confidence shared only by him and the Allfather until now. Lady Hel stood, regal in an ermine cloak. *I would give much to know this small thing, clever Bryce, and your freedom from Niflheim would be but a start. Ask. Ask anything.*

She had said it. She had said the word Hecate had told him to watch for. "Then I accept Your bargain, Lady Hel, and in exchange for Baldr whispering to You His Father's confidence, I ask for one solitary trifle that is in Your power to grant: a single tear from the Giantess Thok," He stabbed the air with his finger, pointing to Baldr, *"for Him."*

For what may have been the first time in Her very long existence, Lady Hel blanched, Her black half changing to dark grey, her white as yellowed as old ivory. But then She recovered. *Clever. Very clever, little runeskald. Probably too clever for a mortal by half, even a draug. But Thok never cried for Baldr before. What makes you think she would do so now?*

"Because by now she is either a shade in Your domain and thus Yours to command, or because She is Someone Else who never truly was Thok, but is still in Your domain, and would do this one small thing because Her Daughter begged Her."

Lady Hel said nothing for a long while. *You had gained my friendship because you aided my brother, Fenris. Now you would gain my enmity while still spending half your hours in Sleet Cold, which can be a far less pleasant place than it has been for those who have drawn my ire.*

Bryce remembered Hecate's words. "Even so, I ask this. For Baldr."

Baldr stood, crossing to Lady Hel in two strides across the black and white tiles. *Checkmate, Loki's Daughter.* He caught Her by the shoulder and whispered something in Her one white ear, and for what was likely the second time in Her long existence, Lady Hel blanched. *But before you go to ask for my tear from Thok, there is something else. I recall you offered Bryce his freedom from your realm if half the world would give him their tears: half the living and half the dead or any combination thereof. Well, we now stand here in Niflheim and I ask all the shades,* "Will you cry? Will you cry for my friend Bryce!?"

There was a wailing then. A howling of voices and moaning and sobs and laughter and tears of joy. Drops like warm rain fell through the halls of Sleet Cold, melting the ice of the tables and chairs, rotting the tapestries of spun misery, the walls collapsing like a glacier calving into an ocean of tears and bearing Bryce away like a tidal wave...

Bryce awoke. He was cold, and his toe hurt. And there was something on his face.

He sat up, coughing, pulling the sheet from his face and taking great ragged breaths for the first time in months.

Someone screamed then someone swore and Bryce flinched, but only on reflex. "We've got a breather! Someone call ICU!"

Bryce looked around. He was in a morgue, next to a dead body, and the smell of blood in the air wasn't appetizing at all. He was alive.

"Calm down, sir," said the frantic coroner. "What's the last thing you remember?"

Bryce thought. There were a lot of things he remembered. Most of them wouldn't sound sane. "Um, falling down a sewer?"

"That's right. Don't worry. You had hypothermia. You were in shock. And your blood alcohol content is through the roof."

Bryce let them hook him up to all sorts of monitors and widgets and strange doctor contraptions and drifted off to sleep. Normal sleep for the first time in months.

Sleep was bizarre. Something about Hieronymous Bosch designing a Japanese game show with talking woodmice and an orchestra made of ukeleles and flugelhorns. In the middle of it, Anissa stepped through the Gate of Horn and told him not to mind all of this—it was just the Gate of Ivory working through its backlog and she'd talk to him when he woke up, something about him owing some ladies three beers for a game of Trivial Pursuit.

Bryce awoke again, finding himself in a hospital room. There was a flower arrangement, and his father, asleep in a chair. There was also a python who rose up and turned into a young woman. Anissa put her finger to her lips, gesturing Bryce to silence, then put her hand to his cheek. "You're alive..." she said softly, a flash of shark teeth in her mouth. "That was an extremely interesting second date..."

"What do you remember?" Bryce whispered.

"You drank a lot of beer and then jumped into the sewer. But you've come back to life. And you won't believe how intriguing and sexy that is." She paused. "And I had a dream about three women telling me that they wanted me to work for them as a lamian sibyl and you still owed them three beers."

"That and a lot more," said Bryce. "A lot more."

K.D. Wentworth has sold more than eighty pieces of short fiction to such markets as *Fantasy & Science Fiction*, *Alfred Hitchcock's Mystery Magazine*, *Realms of Fantasy*, *Weird Tales*, *Witch Way to the Mall*, and *Return to the Twilight Zone*. Four of her stories have been finalists for the Nebula Award for Short Fiction. Currently, she has seven novels in print, including *The Course of Empire*, written with Eric Flint and published by Baen. Her next book (also co-written with Eric Flint) is *Crucible of Empire*, published in March 2010. She serves as Coordinating Judge for the Writers of the Future Contest and lives in Tulsa with her husband and a combined total of one hundred sixty pounds of dog (Akita + Siberian "Hussy") and is working on another new novel with Flint. Website: www.kdwentworth.com.

Miss White-Hands's Class Goes Shopping

K.D. Wentworth

There was nothing like a fine April night for a field trip, thought Abigale White-Hands. Her young charges, five astonishingly lovely teenage Night girls, headed in a sedate line across school grounds to board the van. Starlight glittered overhead as though someone Up There had scattered fine rhinestones across the dark blue velvet sky.

She supposed a Day Person might have compared the stars to "diamonds," but teachers at Mistress Blandings' Academy for Discriminating Young Night Ladies did not receive a lavish salary. The work itself, educating today's Night youth so that they might slip into Day society unnoticed and serve their clans, was considered almost enough compensation by itself. Diamonds, though she quite admired them, were fearfully out of reach, and even rhinestones were a bit of a stretch.

"I'm hungry!" Preshea said, dropping to her knees by a daffodil bed, eyeing a wary squirrel interrupted in the act of digging up an acorn. She was of the Long-Legs Clan with their characteristic amber and red hair and brown eyes flecked with gold. The girl wore the Blandings black and red plaid school uniform with the unconscious grace of a young lioness.

"My word!" Abigale pulled the teenager to her feet. "Refined young Night People do not eat rodents unless in dire Need and certainly not in view of a public street!" She brushed off Preshea's grimy knees. "Whatever are you thinking?"

Off to one side, Edwina, Theodosia, and Zylphia all giggled. Rufina, the most timid, just stared.

"I'm thinking that I'm hungry!" Preshea twined a lock of red-amber hair about one finger and pouted, just as she'd been taught this quarter by that noted temptress herself, Sedelia Slim-Heels, in Blandings's acclaimed course *Human Seduction 101*. Not a bad effort for one so young, but the pout needed to be deeper, the eyes more hooded.

"You'll just have to wait," Abigale said and turned the girl around. "Rejoin the group, please, and do keep up! Come along, girls." Her back very straight, she led them to the school's small black van, which was waiting on the street.

The girls climbed in, chattering among themselves. Paolo, the driver, nodded at Abigale, giving her a feral grin. He was a Dark-Brow, a swarthy brute who often took on airs as though he was better than he should be, but a competent driver. Unfortunately, automobiles, with all their peculiar requirements and mechanical ailments, made her nervous and the school insisted she employ a driver for such outings. She sniffed. "Windsor Heights Rancho Estates Mall," she said.

The girls squealed. Abigale had not revealed their destination, just informed the class that there would be a *Life Skills* field trip that evening. She turned in the green vinyl seat. "You will behave like young ladies," she said severely. "Young *Night* Ladies. It is very important that you learn to handle yourselves amidst Day society. At all costs, you will avoid calling attention to yourselves. There will be no wandering off on your own, no flirting with Day boys, and absolutely no snacking."

They calmed somewhat, still whispering excitedly among themselves. Paolo put the van in gear, then drove through the suburbs that surrounded the school, past three bedroom houses with SUVs parked out front, tiny gardens studded with lawn gnomes, and the obligatory Yorkie or miniature poodle. Every dog they passed immediately howled, though cats sat on their haunches and just observed their passage with knowing amber or green eyes.

Night People and cats had always gotten along, she thought. Dogs belonged to the Day world.

The mall was open late tonight for its semiannual Moonlight Madness Sale, which gave them enough time to complete a session of lab work required for their *Life Skills* course. Night People must be able to move freely through Day society without attracting undue notice. Night children, who matured five times more slowly than their Day counterparts, often had trouble with this concept, which could be fatal for them personally as well as disastrous for the Night clans as a whole.

The Day world ignored them as long as they lived subtle lives. Humans preferred to think of vampires as nothing more than fictional and cinematic creations, and that suited the Night People. Being flamboyant and greedy served no one.

Paolo dropped them off at the south entrance, which was adjacent to the food court. "Return for us at 10:30," Abigale said. "If I need you before that, I will call on your cell phone."

He touched his hat, then drove away, smiling evilly. One of his fangs was chipped, hinting at a recent violent encounter. Disgusting. She had never liked him.

She looped the strap of her black purse over one shoulder, then herded the girls past the bustle of the food court and all those hungry humans. She stopped next to the Taco Youbeto counter and waited until the students met her eyes. "Now, we will inspect merchandise in a number of stores so that you may see for yourselves what young Day People are wearing this season. Your Clan-leaders have provided fifty dollars for each of you as a lab fee so that you may select one or more garments for yourself."

She passed out envelopes with the cash, then tapped a red pen against the cover of her notebook. "Remember: your acquisition's appropriateness will be reflected in your lab grade. You will also get points for—"

A short lumpish woman carrying a tiny apricot-colored poodle in her arms clacked past the group on high heels and the dog erupted into shrill, ear-splitting barks, struggling to free itself.

Startled, Theodosia, who was closest, hissed at the vile little beast. Her eyes, normally the blue flecked with brown of a Ruddy-Cheeks, flared red for a second. The woman cried out, then fled back outside the mall. At the Taco Youbeto counter, a security guard whirled around, bag in hand.

Abigale smiled at his witless, florid face, using the weight of her many Night years to soothe his suspicion. "Goodness," she said, projecting the *profound chill of winter snow* into her voice, "what was that all about?"

"I—" His mouth hung open.

Snow that blanketed everything, especially fear and curiosity, bringing deep cool calm. "I quite agree," she said as though they were having a sensible conversation.

"Miss White-Hands?" Rufina said at her shoulder.

Abigale did not look at her charge. The example of how to handle this sort of ruckus would be as valuable as anything else the girls would learn here tonight. "They should not allow dogs in the mall," she said, taking the man's black-uniformed arm as though they were old friends. She let the frost of her touch sink through his sleeve until he shivered convulsively. His sack of tacos dropped to the floor. "They're too unpredictable."

"I—" he tried again, but could get no further.

"Miss White-Hands!" Rufina sounded desperate, but then she was of the Willow-Neck Clan. They were lovely to look upon, with all that silken red-black hair, but tended to be melodramatic and flighty.

"Have a pleasant evening, officer," Abigale said, removing her hand and releasing the human back into the mall's currents of activity in the same fashion a human fisherman unhooked a trout and set it free to swim away. Then she turned to Rufina's diminutive form. "Never interrupt someone working an Enthrallment, child," she said sternly. "If I lose my focus, I have to start all over again and then it's much harder."

"P-please forgive me, Miss White-Hands," Rufina said. "I just thought you might like to know—" She swallowed hard. "They're—gone."

"Gone?" Abigale looked behind her, but saw only women towing reluctant wide-eyed toddlers by the hand and teenage boys slinking about in dreadful baggy pants that threatened to slide off their skinny hips at every step.

"They went—shopping, like you said," Rufina said. Her brows knit imploringly. "Can I go, too?"

"Certainly not!" Abigale's calm deserted her and suddenly the food court smelled of human blood and bone rather than tacos, corn dogs, and cheese fries. Though she had dined only three days ago, she felt abruptly ravenous. Nerves always allowed her tightly controlled Thirst to surface.

Four nubile Night girls loose in the mall without supervision! She had to corral them or there might be another instructor in her place at the Academy on the morrow and then it would take decades to find a new position. "Did you see where they went, child?"

Trembling, Rufina pointed right.

"Very well," she said, as a young father exuding the delightfully earthy fragrance of AB Negative pushed a camouflage-colored stroller past. Her visual field flooded with red. Breeding males were quite a nice vintage on the whole. That potent cocktail of hormones spiced the blood. Just a quick bite, the back of her mind suggested, a few seconds alone with him behind that enormous Buy One Get One Free display at the Drink Me nutritional supplements store, the tiniest nip and—

With a shudder, she turned away from the beguiling fantasy and focused her mind on the problem at hand. *Where* had they gone?

She extended her senses, listening for sounds that didn't belong in the low level babble of the mall. She heard quarreling voices, giggling, plastic sacks rustling, the rhythmic thump of athletic shoes against the tiled floors, the scritch of a custodian's broom. All perfectly ordinary.

Fuming, she peered into the Baths R Us shop, then U.R. Nickel's, followed by You Can't Make Me!, a fashionable store for 'tweens, featuring filmy blouses so low-cut, they were a Night Person's dream. No sign of her charges in their black and red plaid school uniforms. Rufina was trotting at Abigale's side, craning her head backward at such an extreme angle that she would soon have a cramp or run into someone. "Eyes forward, Rufina," she said crisply.

"Yes, Miss White-Hands," Rufina said, with such an air of dejection that Abigale knew full well the girl was regretting not having made her escape with the rest of the class.

A sudden shriek shrilled through the mall, rising from several storefronts away. Abigale oriented upon it. "My baby!" a woman was screaming. "What have you done!"

Babies were indeed succulent fare, their blood fresh and tangy, but rarely worth the uproar caused by imbibing from one. Abigale maneuvered grimly through the frightened crowd. Foolish, foolish, foolish! She would assign so many demerits, it would be two years before the young wretches saw the inside of another mall!

Security guards were converging upon Beaudelaire's, an inexpensive costume jewelry emporium catering to young people. Just inside, she found Preshea circling a screaming two year old child who had just evidently had her tiny ears pierced. The technician was dabbing the new holes with cotton while the tot's distraught mother attempted to soothe her.

"Preshea!" Abigale said.

The girl looked up, her eyes gone red, signaling her Thirst.

"Come here at once!" Abigale waited, head held high as Preshea edged through the crowd of onlookers. "What in the name of Darkness itself do you think you are doing?"

"Shopping," Preshea said as her eyes faded back to brown flecked with gold.

Abigale glanced at the child, which had now subsided into gurgling wails. "Yes, I can see that."

"No!" Preshea said. "I was going to buy some earrings, then—" She licked her lips.

"Get your ears pierced?" Abigale's toe tapped in its sensible black shoe. She took the girl by the arm and drew her back outside into the mall concourse. "And what do you think would happen when the holes immediately healed?"

Preshea's lovely young mouth made an O as the implications worked themselves out in her mind.

"Do you want to live in a moldy old crypt somewhere?" Abigale said. "Wear half-rotted winding sheets for clothes while you slip around in the night so no one can see you, and be reduced to hunting indigents, or do you want to be an accepted member of society, able to shop, attend parties, and join a suitable garden club?" Both Night girls just stared at her with wide eyes.

The young were so reckless! Abigale sighed and shouldered her black purse as though arming herself for battle. "We have to find the rest of the class. Do not even think of slipping away again!"

"Look, down there!" Rufina pointed over the rail to the lower level and Books Sandwiched In.

Abigale saw a table set up out front, stacked high with hardback books. A long line of people waited before it, among them the sylph-like form of—Theodosia. "Come along!" she snapped to Rufina and Preshea, then headed for the escalator.

Laughter filled the air as they approached and she could make out Theodosia's throaty young voice intertwined in conversation with a man's baritone.

"But—*vampires*!" Theodosia was saying. "You don't really believe they can turn into bats and fly, do you?" Her red *red* lips smiled as she leaned over the table so that her nose was mere inches from the man seated on the other side. He looked to be about thirty, with protuberant ears and a wretchedly bad haircut. His skin had gone almost pale enough for him to be one of Night's Children. The Blandings girl reached out and toyed with his ghastly green paisley tie. "That's so silly!"

He stared up into her face, mouth gone slack, eyes befuddled. "*Hot Nasty Thirst* is just a—a novel, miss, you know, fiction."

"And all that stuff about tearing people's throats out—really!" Theodosia said, and now she had climbed onto the table and was running her fingers through his rumpled brown hair. "Just think about it. If vampires did that, the corpses would just pile up and up and then the poor things would get caught all the time! Where's the sense in that?"

"You're taking up more than your turn!" the woman next in line complained. Fortyish, she looked like a sausage that had been stuffed into a glittering gold satin dress. "I want to get my copy signed, too, and I haven't got all night."

Theodosia turned and bared her fangs. The woman, along with the rest of the autograph line, gasped and fell back. A startled baby broke into piercing wails. Several mothers with strollers fled back down the mall. In their wake, an abandoned sippy cup rolled across the tile floor.

"Now," Theodosia said, turning back to the author, "about that nonsense with garlic and crosses—"

"Theodosia, come here this instant!" Abigale called as she hurried across the concourse.

The Night girl glanced over her lithesome shoulder and sighed. "Mr. Framington and I were just having the most interesting conversation about his new book." She licked her fangs and winked at the hapless author. "He's going to do a much better job on the next one, aren't you, Billy?" She sniffed at him as though taking in the bouquet of a flower.

Abigale circumvented the startled line of autograph seekers. "We have to go *now*!" She seized Theodosia's arm and pulled her off the autograph table. The pile of waiting volumes with their garish blood-drenched covers fell over.

"But—" Theodosia tried to regain her balance. "I wanted to get a book autographed."

Abigale resisted the urge to shake her wayward charge senseless, then hustled the three girls away from the bookstore and the indignant would-be customers. "What part of 'do not call attention to yourselves' do I need to explain?" she said as they walked briskly past the Bad Attitudes Shoe Emporium.

Theodosia glanced back over her shoulder. "But that book is totally stupid! He's getting it all wrong!"

"And how is that any of your concern?" Abigale answered as several teenaged girls clad in black leather pushed ahead of them and ran up the escalator, obviously in a hurry.

"It makes Day people think we're crude and vicious and stupid," Theodosia said. She turned as another girl jogged around their little group, this one tricked out in elbow-length black lace gloves and a jingling handcuff necklace. Theodosia's delicate fingers clenched. "Oh, cool! I want some of those gloves!"

"Not now," Abigale said, trying to hold a steady course through the thickening wave of shoppers who seemed suddenly to be mostly teenaged girls. "We have to find Edwina and Zylphia." There must be an extraordinary sale up ahead, she thought, watching teenagers surge up the escalator.

"But, Miss White-Hands, you said we could shop." Theodosia's voice was plaintive.

Squealing erupted from one of the stores on the upper level. Girls with cell phones pressed to their ears dodged past them, talking excitedly as they fought their way through the crowd.

The situation brought to mind fish swimming upstream to spawn. Sensing that the two remaining missing Night students might be found at the heart of so much commotion, Abigale persevered. Her nerves were strained, her throat parched as though it had been years since she'd fed, and the crowd smelled so warm and vibrant, it was all she could do to keep her mind on the serious business at hand as she followed the agitated humans up the escalator.

The sign above the source of all the excitement read Goth Topics. Girls were surging into the storefront, pushing and shoving, shrieking. Others were working their way out, triumphantly waving black leather pants over their heads, black boots, studded belts, black silk shirts, and corsets with their laces flying.

"Oh, I've always wanted one of those!" Preshea said as two girls danced past her, clutching black corsets. "How much do they cost?"

The teenager stopped for a second, her human face aglow. "Tonight everything is free!"

"Free?" Abigale seized the girl's wrist and projected *dark cool calm* at the giddy child. "Why would they give away store merchandise?"

"I—don't know," the girl said, blinking. She hugged the black leather corset to her meager chest with her other arm. "I was shopping the Buy One, Get One Half Off rack and then the manager climbed on a table and said everyone could take whatever they wanted. He said it was a special promotion just for tonight."

The young human smelled like O Positive, a common enough genetic variety but often quite satisfying. Abigale shuddered, trying to think of something else than how very hungry she was at this particular moment. She caught the girl's gaze with her own eyes and focused. *"Go home."*

Frightened, the child broke away, then disappeared

into the crowd. Abigale motioned to Theodosia, Rufina, and Preshea. "Girls, you will stay with me!"

She worked her way then into the store, as she passed, touching each human teenage girl who had evidently heard about the giveaway through cell phones and text messages, telling them all to *go home*. Some were able to shake off the suggestion, but more than half obeyed, looking dazed and disappointed.

Inside the store, she saw a lanky young man of twenty or so who needed a shave standing on a display table, watching with unblinking eyes of a human Enthralled as shrieking shoppers stripped the store of its mostly black wares. The youth had a pierced lip and nose, along with both eyebrows, and resembled, in her opinion, a pincushion. By his demeanor, he was obviously under someone's influence and she could just imagine who that was.

At his feet, Zylphia and Edwina were flinging merchandise to all comers. Their faces were flushed with the telltale blush that indicated they had recently fed.

Abigale shouldered through a last dense knot of teenagers struggling with one another over a rack of black vinyl miniskirts. "Girls!"

Zylphia turned. Her mouth dropped open as she met Abigale's steely gaze. Without looking, she groped behind her for Edwina, who was tossing pairs of black boots into the crowd with cheerful abandon.

"Stop this at once!" Abigale said, dodging teenagers with fishnet stockings looped around their supple young necks like scarves.

"We—" Zylphia said, and then apparently could think of nothing more to say.

"They—" Edwina was equally at a loss.

"We must get out of here at once!" Abigale said.

Zylphia snatched up a black shirt.

"Put that down!" Abigale snapped.

"But we're supposed to, like, shop," Zylphia said weakly.

Abigale pulled the offending garment from her charge's hands and held it up to the light. Composed of black mesh, it was as transparent as gauze. She shuddered. "Did you pay for it?"

Zylphia thrust her hands behind her back. "Um, no."

"Then," Abigale said acidly, "you have not engaged in normal human commerce as you were assigned."

"But Bruno said we could have whatever we wanted!" Edwina had to shout to make herself heard. She gestured up at the young man on the table who only stared vacantly into space. "Isn't he adorable? He's got twelve piercings!"

Someone had turned up the store's sound system and now the so-called shoppers were all dancing to a grinding beat while a recorded male voice chanted unmelodically about "dudes" and "dope," and "ice, baby." They had all seemingly lost their human minds.

Bruno's neck still looked pink where someone had apparently had her way with him, though the bite marks were already fading. It had been more than five minutes then. Abigale mentally recorded additional demerits to be filed against Edwina and Zylphia's accounts later. He would be fine—eventually—though on the morrow he would have trouble explaining his ill-advised agreement to give away the contents of the store.

"Come on!" she told the Blandings girls and elbowed her way out of the store. Blue-uniformed mall security guards had arrived, several riding on those odd little two-wheel carts. One by one, they were catching the dancing girls by the arm, pulling them out of the store, then stripping them of their booty.

"Don't lag!" Abigale called over her shoulder as she headed toward the I'm Not Listening! Boutique for Teens. It was deserted, she could see, most likely because no one was giving away merchandise inside. Once they got away from the crowd and that horrid deafening caterwaul that passed for music, she could call Paolo and have him pick them up at one of the mall entrances on the other side. This was such a fiasco, she did not know how she'd ever live it down. What would Headmistress Blandings, with her regal bearing and impeccable standards, say when she learned of this evening's shenanigans?

"Miss White-Hands!" Preshea cried.

She turned. One of the security guards had Edwina by the arm and was trying to take a chain link belt made of gleaming skulls from her. "Let me go!" Edwina cried, hanging onto her booty with all her strength, more than a match for the guard.

Her adversary was a paunchy, balding male, no taller than Abigale herself. His face was red with exertion. "Then show me a register receipt, missy!" he said.

"Give the officer the belt, Edwina," Abigale said severely.

Edwina put her hand on the guard's arm. *"It's— mine,"* she said in her best Enthralling voice.

The human stiffened. His hands opened and Edwina jerked the belt away triumphantly.

"My," he said, his voice gone oddly high, "aren't you a dazzling young thing!" His eyes were glazed, fixed now upon Edwina, and he seemed to have lost all awareness of the shopping riot in progress just a few feet away. He sank to his knees. "I think I need to—worship you."

"Hey, Tony!" one of the other guards called. "A little help over here!"

Edwina buckled the belt around her waist, then slipped her arm through Tony's and pulled him back onto his feet. "Isn't he cute?" she said.

Abigale drew Edwina away and touched Tony's cheek with her bare hand. *"Return to your work, officer,"* she said. "We were just leaving."

His mouth dropped open. "But—"

"Not another word," she said. "Off you go!"

Officer Tony stumbled toward the store. Three teenagers, all with spiky hair dyed a deep unnatural black, drew him into their dance. Another jumped onto one of the little guard carts and began doing wheelies around the crowded store.

Shaking her head, Abigale shooed the Blandings girls down the mall concourse before her. Outside, just above the grinding music, she could hear sirens. "Walk with your heads up as though you do not notice all this commotion," she said crisply. "Night People do not engage in human teenage histrionics."

Preshea sighed dramatically as four girls brushed past them, late to the riotous extravaganza. "This is so unfair!" she said, though she did not quite dare to meet Abigale's eyes. "I mean, when will we ever get another chance to go to a rave?"

"Rave?" Abigale's eyebrows quirked.

"It's a shopping rave, Miss White-Hands," Rufina said meekly. "You know, with dancing and music and rad clothes."

"And it's so totally cool!" Edwina said. She danced a few steps as they passed the In Your Face eyebrow threading kiosk. "And Bruno was freaking delicious!" She turned to Abigale. "Can't we go back—just for a little while?"

"No," Abigale said, "we cannot—"

Footsteps pounded down the tile behind them. Abigale turned and saw the security guard, Tony, running ponderously after them. She resumed walking. "Keep going, girls," she said, pushing Theodosia and Zylphia back into motion. "Take no notice."

"W-wait for me!" he huffed.

Abigale stopped, regarding him with distaste. "Officer," she said, "you have a job to do back there." She gestured firmly at the bouncing crowd of dancing girls back down the concourse.

"I quit!" He tossed his blue hat over the railing so that it sailed into the fountain below. "Just let me be with *her!*" Throwing his arms wide, he cast himself at Edwina's feet.

The little Raven-Hair minx looked up and grinned. "Can't I keep him, Miss White-Hands?"

"Don't be ridiculous," Abigale said, horrified. "Where would the silly creature sleep? What would you feed it? They need exercise, you know. You can't just shut them in the closet and put them out of your mind until you're feeling peckish."

"If she gets her own human, then I want one too!" Preshea said. "Fair's fair!"

The sirens were louder now. Abigale could see lights flashing red/blue red/blue through the outside doors just ahead. Her nerves were jumping and she was herself so very hungry from all the excitement that Security Guard Tony's scent brought to mind a brawny corsair from whom she had once imbibed in her wayward youth. The man's jowly neck was bared, sweaty, the pulse throbbing just beneath the skin, so very inviting...

But ladies did not dine in public, she told herself, and besides what kind of example would that be for the students? "No one is taking a human home," she said. *Not even me.*

A wave of police burst through the doors, waving nightsticks, hands on their holstered guns. Startled, the Blandings girls pressed back against a glass storefront as the police swept by. Abigale pulled the prostrate Tony to his feet. *"Go after them,"* she said. *"Provide assistance. They are counting upon you."*

He glanced at Edwina, who was pouting.

Abigale put both hands upon his face, turning his gaze back to her with all the weight of her many years. *"Go now!"*

"Yes, ma'am," he said, then saluted her and staggered toward the rave.

"Now, take that ridiculous belt off and leave it on the floor," Abigale told Edwina.

Edwina's slim fingers caressed the stainless steel skull buckle. "But—"

"The object of tonight's lab work was to shop," Abigale said. "To purchase, to exchange currency for goods as Day People do so that you can move freely among them when required." Her toe in its sensible shoe tapped on the tile. "Theft is an advanced lesson and not part of this quarter's curriculum."

One of the policemen was coming back. He was young and ginger-haired with a boyish crop of freckles scattered across his nose. "Drop it now, Edwina!" she said under her breath.

"Ma'am, we'd like to get your name as a witness," the officer said. He held a pen and notebook.

"Regina Foxworthy," Abigale said, then glared a giggling Theodosia into silence. The Foxworthy persona was one she used when she had to identify herself among Day People. She carried documentation to back it up. The students would all have to develop their own fake identities before they graduated from Blandings. "We have to go now, officer." She gestured at the girls who did not look in the least like demure students. "I have to get my charges away from this disgraceful exhibition of low mores."

"Indeed," he said, pen poised. "Their names?"

"They are all minors," she said, then her nose twitched. The man smelled—off. "It would not be proper to involve them in this nonsense."

"Not even if they started it?" he said with a wink. "At the moment, Bruno has quite a clear memory of their faces, hair, and uniforms, though I doubt it will last past dawn."

Zylphia gasped, and then the five of them did their best to look entirely innocent, with varying degrees of success. Behind Edwina's back, the purloined skull belt clinked onto the tile floor.

The policeman's merry blue eyes flashed orange for a second, then he displayed a grin that was decidedly more feral than any human should be able to manage. His ears became distinctly fuzzy. He was one of the Sharp-Toothed Folk, Abigale realized, Those Who Ran Under the Full Moon. Enthrallment would not work upon him.

"They may have provided a bit of the initial instigation," she said stiffly, "but they never meant for this to happen." She gestured at the gyrating teens who still filled the aisles of Goth Topics, struggling with each other over leather trousers and black high-heeled boots.

"What do you young ladies have to say for yourselves?" the officer said.

"We just wanted to have a bit of, you know, fun," Zylphia said. "We didn't mean any harm." A single bloody tear rolled down her perfect cheek.

Abigale realized the policeman was wearing a wedding ring. "Surely, officer, you have children of your own," she said with a hint of desperation, because she could not be certain of any such thing. "You can understand youthful indiscretion and lack of judgement."

He regarded her, his eyes gone a simmering orange again. Night People and Sharp-Toothed Folk had never been allies, down through all the ages in which both kinds had struggled to live unnoticed in human society. It might amuse him to embroil these foolish Night girls in a scandal that would cause their clans to disown them. Chin up, she waited, trying her best to look unruffled.

Finally, he rocked back on his heels and sighed. "Yeah, I do have kids," the officer said. "A boy and a girl, eight and five at the moment. They get into all kinds of scrapes, howling when they hear sirens and nipping at other kids' heels at school." He pulled a pad out of his pocket and scribbled. "This time I'll let your girls off with a warning." He scribbled, then tore two tickets off and handed one to Zylphia, the other to Edwina. "See that it's the last."

"Yes, sir!" Zylphia said, and Edwina was nodding vigorously.

He touched his blue cap, then waded back into the shopping fray, snagging corsets and trendy T-shirts as he went and cramming them under his arm.

"Now," Abigale said, "we simply must go!"

Chastened at last, the students followed her outside without another word into the fine spring air where she summoned their driver on her cell phone.

Once they were all settled aboard the van, the girls were oddly quiet—reflecting, Abigale hoped, upon the folly of their actions.

"You will all receive a failing grade for this night's assignment," she said as the bus eased over speed bumps in the mall parking lot, "with the exception of Rufina, who will be given a chance to make up the assignment."

The other four groaned.

"I don't know when I have been so appalled—"

"Miss White-Hands?" Theodosia said. She rose and worked her way up the aisle as the bus made a right hand turn onto the street. "We have a little something for you—a token—of our esteem—for the way you got us out of trouble back there."

Abigale sniffed, refusing to meet the child's eyes. Where had their so-called "esteem" been when four of them had slipped away to create chaos and make her look ridiculous?

Theodosia leaned closer, whispering in Abigale's ear. "I bought this with my lab money at You Can't Make Me! and we all think you'd look, well, really hot in it, Miss White-Hands." She dropped something into Abigale's lap, then retreated, head down, back to her seat.

Abigale's hands closed around something long and exquisitely soft. Feathers, she thought. Quite a lot of them. She took a better look. It was a sable feather boa. Without volition, her fingers stroked its silken length. She flashed back to her own wayward youth in Victorian London, a stage, several delectable politicians, their hot blood spiked with vodka and gin, sophisticated bars followed by utter dives, the shrill of police whistles ending with the cheerful eluding of the constabulary. In the depths of those wild nights, she had learned important lessons on how to take care of herself. Some things did have to be experienced rather than merely taught.

She looped the boa around her neck, her fingers lingering on the luscious feathers. "I suppose," she said without turning around, "I might consider awarding extra credit for several instances of moderately effective Enthrallment tonight."

Behind her, three of the Night girls whooped with joy.

And then that Dark-Brows wretch of a driver, Paolo, had the nerve to glance back at her over his shoulder and wink.

Sarah A. Hoyt's most recent novels are *Heart and Soul* from Bantam Spectra and—as Sarah D'Almeida—*Dying by the Sword*, from Prime Crime. Upcoming are *Darkship Thieves*, a space opera from Baen books, and *Dipped, Stripped, Dead* from Prime Crime (as Elise Hyatt). She lives in Colorado with four cats, two sons, and one husband who occupy her attention when she's not working her keyboard to death. She never meant to write a continuing series of short stories for these anthologies, but she'd guess when you name a character Nephilim Kentucky Jones III, you owe the poor thing something. So Ken Jones and Agnes Damon are back as their relationship—and their involvement in strange events—progresses in this story.

A Matter of Blood

Sarah A. Hoyt

"You know, he's probably a vampire," my sister Buffy said, turning away from the kitchen, where she'd been hanging a crystal at the window over the sink. Yes, her name really was Buffy and even though she was my older sister and had been born years before the name had acquired any connotation of vampire slayer, sis was clearly determined to make sure that nomenclature was destiny. Or something. "And don't snort at me," she said, before I realized I had snorted. "It's just like you to dismiss all matters of the spirit. You always were a hard one, Agnes."

I didn't tell her it was because I had grown up with nicknames such as Agony. Mom might have thought that calling me Agney made a good set with Buffy, but like the boy named Sue, I'd learned to fight before I could walk.

This time I snorted with intent and malice, and relished every snarly bit of it. As Buffy turned around to grace me with a horrified look from her limpid blue eyes—they were, too, just like her hair was the color of ripe wheat. Notwithstanding which, we'd reached our mid-twenties without my killing her—I said, clearly, "Ken is out in the sun all the time."

"With sunblock," she said. "He smells like coconut from ten feet away. Why would a man his color need sunblock?"

The man was Nephilim Kentucky Jones III, my boss, who, despite his name's evidence to the contrary, seemed like an eminently sensible man. And his color looked like it should be somewhere between espresso and whatever was darker than it, but it was strangely grayish and pale, as though he rubbed himself with chalk every morning. There was, of course, the possibility that he just used so much sunblock he was starting to fade. But whatever I thought of my boss's quirks—and there were a lot of them, considering he ran Nephilim Psychic Investigations—I wasn't about to admit them to Buffy. "He just has sensitive skin. That doesn't make him a vampire."

Buffy crossed her arms on her chest. And yes, nature had given her all the chest. "Next thing you know, you're going to tell me vampires don't exist!"

I didn't. I would have told her that six months ago, sure. But not since I'd found a job working for Ken. Yeah, yeah, so it wasn't the normal job path for your graduate from Classics Studies. Admittedly, some Roman incantations might have provided helpful background, except that Ken was more like to exorcize demonic apparitions with love poetry or—once, in the case of a very banal banshee—put them to sleep with *War and Peace*.

At any rate, in the time I'd worked for Ken, I'd learned that there were more things in heaven and

Earth than were dreamed of in anyone's philosophy, unless that person were a paranoid schizophrenic self-medicating with crack cocaine. I'd even seen a werewolf turn into a man and a man into a werewolf. And we won't even go into what happened when the local beautician visited the frog pond and decided to kiss the largest, wartiest of frogs. Let's just say they should be very happy that Ken was the sort of man who could, in fact, locate a kingdom the size of a suburban plot in the midst of the alphabet soup behind the former Iron Curtain. Because, otherwise, the Honorable Mirasco Ivan Alexiovich Albert Gustav Popov would have been up a pond without a crown.

That of course had led to a trip to Europe in the spring, where we'd gotten to visit some romantic castles because it was spring, which meant that we could actually glimpse the stones through a covering of ice. What with one thing and another, and both of us walking around sharing a single jacket of insulating material, Ken had informed me that his company did not, in fact, have any rule against employees dating. The announcement of this happy event had brought Buffy down on me to meet my prospective.

I frowned at her. "There might be vampires," I said. "But I've never met any."

"You're dating o—"

At that moment, the door to my two-bedroom apartment opened and Buffy shut up, as her mouth dropped open. Me, I just turned around to face my sweetie as he came in. Okay. I'm the first one to admit that Ken doesn't look like anything special. At least not with his clothes on—and that was something else I was never going to tell my sister. Naked, Ken looked like one of the nicer statues of antiquity. But that so absolutely was none of Buffy's business.

Dressed, Ken looked like a middle-aged black man, with his hair starting to recede and a bit of silver in his short, short hair. He could have been the group manager of a computer firm. Which he had, in fact, been before the last round of layoffs had propelled him into finding work in a less...orthodox profession.

At that moment he also looked tired and more than a bit worried. He had a shoulder bag on, and he stood there, swaying a little, as if he'd been up all night and most of the morning, since it was past eleven o'clock, and had been on his feet the entire time. He had a big blue bag hanging from his shoulder, and he blinked at me as if not absolutely sure who I was.

"Is everything all right?" I asked

He stared. "Uh. Everything. Fine. Garlic?"

I frowned at him, in turn. In our time together, even though he ate at my place and often spent the night, he hadn't ever gone so far as to ask for Italian food, much less just garlic. I sniffled the air, since my sister had been burning potpourri for two days straight, and at this point I didn't think I could smell garlic if someone shoved cloves up my nose—though from what I understood, that was a remedy against zombies, for the obvious reasons.

"Not that I know..." I said cautiously. I'd learned this was a good way to answer Ken when I had no idea in heaven what he was going on about.

He shook his head. There was a fine sheen of sweat on his brow. "No," he said, as though he were having trouble concentrating. "I wondered if you had any."

I swear I heard my sister gasp behind me, and

I wondered if Ken had somehow heard our previous conversation and decided to destroy her false assumptions. Because, look...it made no sense for him to ask me for garlic. I might live in Colorado now, but my family comes from the Midwest, where putting garlic in your food probably means you're a fast woman and destined for a life of perdition. Or at least for a life of hanging out with men who eat garlic. But one look at Ken's eyes was sufficient to tell me he was serious—and, after all, I was not only his girlfriend, but also his sole employee.

I turned back to the cabinet and searched desperately until I unearthed a little jar I'd bought, years ago, when I'd first moved out on my own. It had been part of a set of ten that were supposed to give me everything I needed in the kitchen. Of course, being a good girl, I hadn't finished it. Hell, I hadn't started it. "Garlic salt!" I told him in triumph.

He nodded grimly and extended his hand. "Will do." And he turned to head out the door.

"Wait," I said.

"Yes?"

"You...uh...you have...are you on a case?"

"Yes," he said.

Right. "Well, then," I said, self-consciously dusting my hands on my knees—not that they were dusty, because the apartment wasn't that bad, but because I was doing my best to shake the dust from my metaphorical sandals. "You need me."

I took two steps towards the door and realized Ken looked horrified. But then I noticed he was staring over my shoulder at my sister who—when I looked—was shaking her head at him.

"Never mind Buffy," I said. "She was born with a silver garlic clove in her mouth, or something."

"But . . . visiting," he said. "She's your sister. You want to . . . spend time . . ."

"Not above my job, I don't," I said decisively, because one more minute with Buffy the would-be slayer and I was going to go insane and probably turn into a bat, or at least a very batty person.

And like that, before I had time to do more than take another step towards the door, Buffy was putting something around my neck. For just a moment I thought she had lassoed me, but then I realized what she'd just hung around my neck was the pendant she'd been wearing—a silver cross. Well, at least, one of those self-consciously pseudo-Celtic crosses with a pearl in the center.

"Buffy!" I said. "Of all—"

But Ken was narrowing his eyes at me, as if he were trying to evaluate the effect of the cross on my ratty T-shirt and too-tight jeans. "No. Leave it be. If you're coming with me, it might be useful."

Minutes later, we were in the car and driving away from downtown and toward the suburbs. I looked over at Ken. He still looked like he'd spent the entire night awake, and possibly the night before that, too. I wouldn't know, since I'd been picking Buffy up at the airport, taking her to dinner, and showing her the local sights—which, in our case, consisted of a fiberglass fountain, in a park one block square. The fiberglass was of a man playing a tuba, and if you hit it at just the right time, you'd see his little purple dog come out and march with clockwork stiffness around the man. After which you'd go to the coffee shop around the corner to get a latté and biscotti to dampen your mad excitement, and then you were done with sightseeing in our fair city.

I tried to figure out how to ask Ken what the case was. It seemed a little odd that he should even attempt to resolve a case without me. Ever since our first case, in fighting a possessed grill, I'd been of great help to him. In that first case, he'd probably still be reading *War and Peace* to the grill if I hadn't found the backyard witch who had cursed it.

As it turned out, though, he spoke first—possibly because he'd traded in his ten-year-old cantankerous Volvo for a Kia of more recent vintage, which meant he didn't need to ride the gas quite so carefully to keep it from stalling. And he could think of other things. "Your sister," he said. "Does she have a problem with us?"

"Uh . . ." I shrugged. "Buffy has a problem with me. She's always had a problem with me since I was born. You see, she was five and already enrolled in an Ivy League kindergarten, and I came along and I spoiled her picture of the perfect princess."

He gave me a side long glance. "So it doesn't have anything to do with what I am?"

"No," I said. And answered a little more strongly than I meant to because—okay, yeah, it had occurred to me that was why Buffy was so hostile, but, damn it, one doesn't want to think of her own sister as racist—"It absolutely has nothing to do with race."

He chuckled and looked amused. "That's not what I said, hon. I asked if she had a problem with what I am." His hand waved around, meaning—I presumed—

the dumpy white car with the hand-lettered sign on the door reading "Nephilim Psychic Investigations."

"Nah," I said. "Or at least..." I shrugged and tried to inject levity into the situation. "She thinks you're a vampire." And in the next minute, as my beloved's hands clutched the wheel with a claw-like vise grip and he turned to look at me—all the while failing to drive around the curve of the road and climbing a sidewalk. "Look out!"

He recovered before he hit the cutesy mailbox with the dragon painted on it, and returned to the street. "Why—why would she think that?" he asked.

I shrugged. "Her name is Buffy," I said. "Like, you know, the vampire slayer on TV? She... My sister is very... media-oriented. Probably comes from being a weather woman for a TV station. Of course, she's in Florida, so I don't know how exciting that job can be. *And today, we shall also have beautiful sunshine.*"

He gave me a smile. "Well, they do get the occasional hurricane." For a moment he drove in silence, as if considering what to tell me, then sighed. "As it happens, the case I'm dealing with involves... well, I'm presuming it involves vampires."

"I see," I said. Amazing how far I'd come from the woman who had doubted that first grill could actually be possessed. "So... vampires do exist?"

He shrugged. "Yeah. I mean... most of—most of them are not, you know, like Dracula, with the cape and the evening attire... Not the real Dracula, of course. Mostly I've seen him in a chef's hat."

"What?" I asked. "The real Dracula? But—"

"He runs a vegetarian restaurant in Cincinnati. Does incredible things with tofu and red wine."

"Uh..."

Ken sighed. "See, the first thing you have to understand is that not all vampires are like in the books or movies. Heck, not even like in *Buffy*. Most vampires don't go around in the dark of night, sucking the blood of innocent victims. I mean, there's treatments for that, you know, and... well, most vampires are the salt of the Earth, really." He grinned, showing his slightly-sharper-than-normal teeth. "Though possibly not garlic salt."

"So..." I said, as I tried to wrap my mind around this. "You mean that vampires really exist and run restaurants?"

"And delis. And supermarkets. One of my very good friends a while back," he said, with the sort of pensive frown that denoted an old and cherished memory, "ran a convenience store. Very nice, you see, as he only worked at night. Which was good, because he was a pale blond."

In the back of my mind something not quite an alarm flickered, then vanished. No, never mind what he said about pale blonds, or the idea that perhaps he could withstand a little more sun because he had greater pigmentation. I was so not going down that path. After all... Ken was my boss and my boyfriend and I'd known him for six months. He'd never shown the slightest inclination to not drink... wine. Truth be told, he even drank my coffee, which, if it would not kill vampires, would at least make them gag.

"So, if the vampires aren't evil, what's this all about?" I pointed to the bag at my feet, into which the garlic salt had disappeared, and through the fabric of which I could see things resembling stakes poking out. Sharp stakes.

"I didn't say vampires aren't evil," he said, in a slow, patient voice. "They are like anyone else. Some are evil, some are bad... and some are just plain people."

"I take it it's not one of the plain people who's giving you issues?"

"Uh... no. I thought, you see, it was just a young and untrained one. Some teenager who just got turned..."

"How did it start?" I said, as I realized we'd driven far deeper into suburbia than we'd ever driven before, past all the identical houses with identical lawns and into yet another neighborhood of identical houses and immaculate lawns.

"I got a call from one Mrs. Rye in Bloodworth Commons." He waved his hand as we drove past a little plaque that read "Bloodworth Commons." "She said that she was afraid her daughter was making a very bad choice."

"Yes?" I wondered if Ken could have blown all this out of proportion. After all, I'd grown up in deepest, whitest suburbia. A bad choice might very well mean that the poor girl wanted to wear her third-best jeans to the church picnic.

"Well, it appears that little Suzie Quinina Rye—not so little, since she's about seventeen—has fallen head over heels for a mysterious older man."

"Right," I said, digesting that we were, in fact, rushing to the rescue of little Suzie Q. "But that doesn't mean he's a vampire."

"Well, no, it doesn't," he said, chewing on his lip. "But the thing is, you see, that... well, I have reason to believe..." He shook his head. "I've heard through the grapevine that there were many cases of anemia and strange neck injuries in this area..."

I felt a shiver run up my spine and noted that the sun was setting. "So...there's a vampire on the loose?"

"It's more than a vampire," he said. "Or at least more than any vampire. Unless I'm mistaken, from what I can *feel*, it's a very old vampire who's been asleep for the last couple hundred years. And has never learned...eating manners."

"Oh," I said, and shivered again, quite sure he wasn't talking about using the right silverware. "But still, even if there are injuries and...and anemia...I mean, no one has been killed, right? So what makes you think that the older man this girl is running away with is a vampire?"

Ken sighed. He turned abruptly into a side street that had fewer houses than the streets nearby. At the dim end of it, there was something that looked like a park. "I didn't. I spent the night before last at the library, looking up her genealogy. You see, some types of blood are more...well...have more flavor. And she has a weird middle name, which runs in the family. I hit, pardon me, pay dirt at about four in the morning. Quinina Rye died of consumption in Colorado in the late eighteen hundreds."

"Lots of people died of consumption in Colorado," I protested. "Lots of people came here to cure consumption. Sometimes it didn't work."

"Well," he said. "Yeah. But few people have a note made about them that she had puncture marks on her neck. And that the family had the undertaker cut off her head before they buried her."

"A vampire victim?" I said, still feeling like I should protest it.

He nodded and parked the car. "And this," he said, "is where the vampire lives."

He waved his hand to a tiny enclosure bordered around with a Victorian iron fence. It had a plaque saying "Historical Pioneer Cemetery" and it had at least a suburban plot's worth of room on either side of it.

I frowned at Ken. "How do you know?" Which was a stupid thing to ask of a man who had once tracked a wayward werewolf by smell alone.

"Because last night I almost caught him," he said.

"Oh."

"And he almost staked me."

"Stak—"

"A stake through the heart," Ken said, looking curiously flushed in the light of the sunset, "is fatal for anyone."

"Yeah," I said, which was something I'd learned. Just like silver bullets are fatal to everyone. Some means of killing supernatural creatures are just means of killing creatures.

We got out of the car, into the relatively chilly sunset. It was spring, but Ken was wearing his trademark long-sleeved T-shirt. Me, I was in ratty T-shirt and rattier jeans. And ever so gothic cross. Something was bothering me. "You went to the library at night?" I asked.

"The librarian is a vampire," he said. "Over in the old part of town. He's always willing to open for a friend."

"Oh." Again that odd little shiver, but I was not going to entertain the idea.

The gate to the little cemetery was chained shut, so Ken and I walked a little while around it, then climbed in over the fence—away from the eyes of law-abiding suburbanites. The cemetery was as I think cemeteries used to be before they started looking like weird parks with little cement plaques in the ground. There were tombstones and the occasional stone statue, and the stones had verses of the Bible, or sad things like "Mercy, my God." For some reason it gave one the same solid, time-honored feeling of castles or monuments—things with a tradition and an history.

As we walked past a grave, Ken pulled me away and pointed down, to where the path had corroded away underfoot, leaving a hole at the edge of the burial plot. I turned to him and started to say that I didn't wear heels and there was no need to be afraid I'd twist my ankle, but he put his finger to his lips and shook his head, and the urgent way in which he pointed gave me to understand that this was the place where our prey lay.

Ken enveloped my hand in his cool one—the consistently low temperature of his skin explaining why he always wore long sleeves, I guessed—and pulled me behind a vast oak tree facing the grave.

"And now?" I whispered.

"And now we wait," he said. "This kind of older vampire is like a nightclub hopper. He doesn't get up till after sunset."

I must have fallen asleep, because I woke up with the sound of wood knocking on wood and a voice speaking in a grandiloquent tone. For a moment I thought that Ken was reading the speeches of Lincoln to this particular vampire, but then I woke up further.

The voice was not Ken's, but a smooth, slightly higher voice, declaiming, "I assure you that you must let me forth, for tonight I claim the life willingly given to me. She vouchsafed that she is ready to die and die at my hand. Or, at the very least, at my fangs."

There was a further clatter of wood on wood, and then Ken saying, "You don't understand kids, do you? She's just a goth girl. She doesn't want to die any more than you do."

"But she hath assured me . . ."

"Desist," Ken said, his voice intercut by gasps for breath. "Desist and learn to live by the new rules, which say you don't take blood unwilling, and you don't feed from people. There are other ways in this modern age to get the necessary nutrients. They sell pills in certain stores and . . ."

"I will not submit to your emasculated age. A vampire is supposed to live in vein, or he's no vampire at all."

By this time I had got around the oak tree and had a good look at the fight—they were dueling each other with sharpened stakes, in the best style of sword-fighting movies. At least the sort of sword-fighting movies where one fights as if one means to survive to fight another day.

And what I'd suspected before I'd seen the fight itself became very clear to me. The vampire—wearing a suit of nineteenth century vintage—fought like someone just awakened, while Ken fought like someone very short on sleep.

As I watched, I saw the vampire stick his stake through Ken's arm. Ken screamed, and jumped back, pulling his arm free, but I knew I had to intervene.

The blue bag was at the root of the tree on the side where they were fighting. Clearly the vampire had managed to get to the stakes that Ken had left so conveniently lying about.

I reached into the bag and felt around, trying to get a stake myself and join in the fight. But my hand had no more than closed around a small round object, than I felt a hand close—in turn—on my shoulder and pull me up and almost off my feet.

"Oh, what a tasty little morsel," the old-fashioned voice said, sounding amused. "Did you perhaps not bring enough for all? Or do you not share?"

I started to swing my hand around to stake him, when I realized that what I was holding was not a sharp stick, but a small, round jar of garlic salt. Ah, well, when life hands you salt, make jerky. Or at least, salt the jerk.

I removed the lid quickly, with my teeth, then shook the garlic salt haphazardly upward.

As it turned out, he'd just opened his mouth in order to bring his fangs to my neck, when he got a mouthful of garlic instead.

His scream hadn't yet died down when Ken staked him through the heart.

"Why didn't you tell me?" I said, as we drove back. "Uh?"

I pointed at his sleeve, where the vampire had staked him through—and where no drop of blood showed.

"Would you believe that it missed me?"

"No," I said. "I heard it go in."

"Oh. Would you believe I had a condition..."

I found I was tapping the door of the car with my fingertips. "Don't make me spice you! Why didn't you tell me you were a vampire?"

"Spice...Oh! The garlic? I eat it. I have been desensitizing myself to it for—"

"Centuries."

"What? No. Agnes, I'm only forty-two. I was just unlucky, you know. Working nights as a programmer for a boss that, as it turned out, was a real blood-sucker. So when I was laid off, I thought I wanted to fight those evils people didn't quite know existed."

"Like possessed grills," I said. "And witches whose brooms won't fly right. And banshees in old college dorms and..."

"And vampires in the suburbs," he said.

"So, no loyalty to your own kind?"

He gave me an evaluating look, from beneath half-closed eyelids. "They're not my own kind," he said. "Just people with the same odd eating disorder. There are support groups...but it turns out you can get a pack of specialized vitamins at Partial Foods that takes care of the craving for blood and the need to take human hemoglobin."

"So you don't actually suck people's necks?"

"No! Nor...nor suck their blood in any other way." He sounded horrified. As horrified as he'd sounded once when I asked him if he killed people. The weird shiver that had run up and down my spine all night had vanished. Okay, so he was a vampire. Big deal. He was still Ken, my boss and my friend. "I just... it's just a weird eating disorder. And sun allergy. I don't actually...I wouldn't know how to..."

I touched his knee. "It's all right," I said. "I believe

you. You've told me more incredible things that turned out to be true, so I have no reason to doubt you."

He gave me a wobbly smile, and for just a moment, I thought he was going to go all noble and altruistic and tell me he could no longer go on with me now I knew he was a monster or something of that ilk. Which would have resulted in my beating him about the face and head with what remained of the stakes.

But what he did instead was pull to the curb, next to someone's manicured lawn, and take me in his arms—not troubled at all by the silver cross around my neck.

"Ah, Agnes," he said. "I may not suck blood, but I'll always be a sucker for you."

And then he kissed me. And his fangs—if they were that—didn't bother me at all.

Let my blonde sister dream of hunting a vampire. I'd already caught mine.

Ask her neighbors in the suburb of Dallas, TX, where she lives, and they'll tell you **Lee Martindale** is a quiet, somewhat reclusive housewife. But, like the characters in this volume, looks can be—and are—deceiving. She's a short story slinger whose work has appeared in numerous anthologies, including *Turn the Other Chick*, *Catopolis*, *Lowport*, three volumes of the Sword & Sorceress series, *Witch Way to the Mall*, and *Warrior Wisewoman 2*. She also edited the ground-breaking anthology *Such a Pretty Face*. When not slinging fiction, Lee is a Named Bard, Lifetime Active Member of SFWA, a fencing member of the SFWA Musketeers, a member of the SCA, and a frequent guest at science fiction and fantasy conventions. She and her husband George live in Plano, TX, where she keeps friends and fans in the loop at www.HarpHaven.net.

Sarah Bailey and the Texas Beauty Queen

Lee Martindale

Sarah Bailey was fairly sure the woman sitting across the desk from her wasn't human.

It wasn't that her face was as smooth and planed as the expanse of wooden surface between them. That could be chalked up to a good plastic surgeon, of which the Dallas Metroplex had more, per capita, than any place outside of Los Angeles. It wasn't that her hair was perfectly coiffed and expertly colored to a radiant golden blond, or that her make-up was so deftly applied that it was nearly impossible to see the trowel-marks. This was Texas, after all. And it wasn't that she kept office hours that didn't begin until after sunset. As she'd explained it, her typical, very high-end clients were busy professionals, and it made sense to set her hours to cater to theirs.

It wasn't even that she looked at Sarah like a hungry predator looked at a goat staked out in its path.

Jennifer Shick Haggard was a real estate agent, and "hungry predator" was in the job description.

What started Sarah's antenna twitching were the walls of Jennifer's office. The last time she'd dealt with someone selling real estate—and, granted, that had been a while—his office had been decorated with framed "Agent Of the Month" awards, membership certificates in various fraternal and service organizations, and letters of appreciation from various high-profile individuals. The walls of Jennifer's office were covered in shrines to popularity and youthful beauty.

Each shadowbox held a tiara, a beauty contest winner's sash, and a photo of Jennifer wearing the displayed finery and flanked by other smiling, similarly-dressed young women. Oddly enough, the sashes were mounted in such a way that the year didn't show, but that was something Sarah was willing to chalk up to vanity. If the hairstyles and gowns in the photos were any indication, the celebrated triumphs had taken place longer ago than Jennifer might want to admit and worked hard to hide. Sarah was fairly sure there hadn't been enough farmland in Collin County to warrant a "Miss Cotton Boll" pageant for at least thirty years.

Jennifer's voice pulled Sarah's eyes back to the woman across the desk. "I am so glad you chose me to find your new home," she gushed.

"You came highly recommended," Sarah replied. It was true. Jennifer's name had been on every list of recommendations, had often been the only name given, and her references practically glowed in the dark. "Don't take this the wrong way, but I just wish your services weren't needed."

"No offense taken, I assure you. Change is difficult, especially when that change isn't your own idea and you've lived in the same home for . . ." Jennifer glanced at the file in front of her. "Good grief, twenty years!"

"Twenty-two, actually."

And would happily have lived there another twenty-two, had a letter from the city not arrived informing Sarah that her snug little house and lovely old neighborhood were slated to be knocked flat and scoured from the face of the earth. Of course, it hadn't been couched in quite those terms. There were phrases like "keeping our community vibrant and vital" and "reaping untold benefits for our citizens from new commercial and residential opportunities." It bragged that the vote of the city council had been unanimous, and that no one had appeared at public hearings to provide a discouraging word. Not surprising, since the letter was the first she—and, she was willing to bet, her neighbors—had heard of either public hearings or the matter being under discussion at all.

The letter went on to say that the developer's representatives would be contacting her with a generous buy-out offer, and that Sarah was heartily encouraged to join with her forward-thinking neighbors in accepting it. In the unthinkable event that a less than cooperative response was considered, Sarah was advised that exercise of eminent domain was not only possible, but likely. The letter did not say, but it didn't take much research to find out, that the company developing the project was owned by two sitting city councilmen.

Resistance was well and truly futile. And it sucked.

"Forty years ago," Jennifer continued, "that section of land was pasture, populated by cows. City fathers and community developers saw so much more. They saw growth and progress. Soon they were building custom homes that drew the cream of comfortably affluent trendsetters, looking for prestigious addresses, all the way from Dallas. Some of them even became city leaders and pillars of this community themselves."

Jennifer paused, smiling as if remembering that period of time first-hand. Her gaze returned to the here and now, and her face took on a look of regret. "But, over time, the neighborhood declined, while newer, trendier developments sprang up farther and farther north." A smile returned to the precisely-defined lips. "And now, that area will become a source of pride again, a mixed-use mecca of boutiques, restaurants, a sports complex, elite exercise facilities, and million-dollar condos." Jennifer's eyes glowed, and for a split second, Sarah could have sworn it was in the literal sense. "It's very exciting. The suburban cycle of life!"

"The Discovery Channel should do a documentary," Sarah commented drily. "But, in the meantime, I need to find a new place to live."

"Yes, you do," came the affable response, "and quickly, too. Those bulldozers will roll in seventy-two days, and you certainly don't want to be in the way." Jennifer chuckled as if the thought amused her, then began flipping through the file. "Now, let's see..."

Sarah took a sheet of paper out of the folder in her lap and slid it across the polished wood. "I've made a list of my requirements. Things I want—and don't want—in a new place."

"And I'm sure it will be very helpful," Jennifer said, as she tucked the sheet into the file without even glancing at it. "Now, you've accepted the tendered offer, and a very generous offer it was, too. Seventy-five percent of appraised value is far more than is customary in these cases. Which means you'll be able to easily handle the down payment, closing costs, and my fee. Did I mention I've agreed to discount my customary six percent by half for you and your neighbors? Financing won't be a problem, regardless of your credit, since I have a close professional relationship with a number of mortgage brokers. All that's left is for you to sign a ninety-day exclusive representation agreement and we can start finding your dream home."

A few minutes later, Sarah left the office and walked to her car. She'd been told that there would likely be properties to look at within the next few evenings, and that if she required anything during the day, Jennifer's assistant, Benjamin Renfield, would be delighted to help her.

She couldn't be sure, but she got the distinct feeling that two pairs of eyes, one dull and complacent, the other sharp and hungry, watched her every step.

Professional movers and crews comprised of family members and volunteers began appearing almost immediately. The elderly couples who lived on either side of Sarah, and the aging widow who lived directly behind her, were first to leave, having bought into the big retirement village a few miles away. A family with a teenage son and tween daughter decided to upgrade to a bigger, newer house, despite worries about making the higher mortgage payment; the school district they were moving into boasted a middle school with superlative ratings and a high school with a division-winning football team. The two bachelor roommates from down the block—they'd been "bachelor roommates" back when Sarah moved in—threw a fine barbeque for the neighborhood, at which they announced they'd bought a condo in Oak Lawn and were opening a leather bar. The "next few evenings" turned into a week, but finally Sarah got a call from Renfield. Jennifer had an exciting property to show Sarah and would meet her at the office at dusk.

From the moment Sarah climbed into the passenger seat of Jennifer's late-model SUV, the blond woman kept up a running monologue liberally sprinkled with phrases like "hot new development" and "prime investment opportunity." Sarah remained silent as the agent chattered on about it being "right next to great new schools" and it not surprising her if "the next premier shopping mall went in just down the street." Sarah decided to refrain from reminding the agent that "proximity to schools or shopping malls" headed the segment on undesirable conditions on her list of requirements.

Only once did she make a comment, after they'd been driving north for what seemed like forever. "I was really hoping to buy a house in Texas, not go all the way to Oklahoma."

"Interesting," was her next comment, as Jennifer turned off the highway and onto a barely-cured concrete street.

"As you can see," the agent continued, driving through sepia-colored lighting toward the only structure visible in the area, "now is the absolutely perfect time to nail down one of these gems. You'll be able to select all your interior colors—carpet, paint, counter materials, even the cabinetry. *And* you'll be able to custom-select appliances and fixtures. Landscaping, too ... within the guidelines of the homeowners' association, of course. I can't use the word 'guarantee,'" and her voice dropped to a conspiratorial level and tone, "but it wouldn't surprise me if your finished house didn't appraise at significantly higher than the purchase price."

"Homeowners' association," Sarah said evenly.

"The strongest in the Dallas–Fort Worth area," came Jennifer's cheerful reply. "When Stonebend Estates is completed, it will be *the* showplace gated community in the state. Possibly the whole country. Buying in now is the best possible decision you could make."

Sarah looked around. Aside from a three-story Cape Coddish thing perched precariously atop an obviously artificial hill, the surrounding terrain looked like nothing so much as a war zone. Bare-scraped prairie, except for the aforementioned artificial hill, onto which a few concrete slabs had been poured. On one such slab, a metal framework rose in the barest suggestion that a house would stand there someday. Heavy construction equipment sat here and there, parked for the night.

"This doesn't look like anything's going to be ready for occupancy very soon," Sarah remarked.

"Seven months for the houses currently under contract," Jennifer answered. "Buy in by the end of the week, and you can have your new house between nine months and a year from date of actual closing."

Sarah took one more look around. "My needs are a bit more immediate than that. Did you have anything else for me to look at this evening?"

"I'm afraid not. Be patient."

Only after Sarah got home did she realize that there had been a slight, satisfied smile on Jennifer's face during the ride back and that, a couple of times, Sarah had glanced over to see the other woman delicately licking her lips.

Over the course of the next month, more of Sarah's neighbors moved away. Sarah, however, was no closer to doing the same, although it wasn't for lack of effort. During that month, Jennifer took her to no fewer than thirty different locations, each no closer to what the real estate agent insisted on calling Sarah's "wish list" than the last.

At least there was variety. On one end of the spectrum, there were condominiums, some converted apartment complexes, some custom-built enclaves, and all carrying asking prices that worked out to multiple dollars per cubic inch. They also all carried mandatory annual contributions to "communal maintenance" that equaled half a year's mortgage, and despotic "community standards" rules. "You'd think," Sarah commented, while viewing one such listing, "that much money would buy some garage space, some storage, and somewhere for visitors to park."

The other end of the spectrum measured in the tens of thousands of square feet and levels of luxury that bordered on the obscene. One, done entirely in pink from the stone of the pseudo-British manor house exterior to every surface, hard and soft, of the interior, went well beyond the border and straight to the heartland.

Even those weren't as bad as the properties available in neighborhoods built or being built to be "green." The houses were so tiny, spare, and pricey, the people living next door and across the street, who showed up to disapprove of Jennifer's vehicle almost before it stopped, so egregiously smug about their eco-warrior "neighborhood values," that Sarah had a headache before they finally got away. Although, she thought later, the chorused whine of wind turbines on every roof might have been a contributing factor.

It would have been maddening even without heavy equipment idling, figuratively speaking, just down the street, but the added pressure of impending homelessness upped Sarah's frustration level by many orders of magnitude. Jennifer, on the other hand, remained consistently cheerful. At every completely-off-the-mark property, during each time-wasting trip, she was unflaggingly enthusiastic and encouraging. The more stressed Sarah became, the more Jennifer seemed to thrive. Either that, or she was using a different shade of bronzer over her foundation.

Then came the evening, at the beginning of the sixth week, that frustration turned to slow-blooming hope. It began when Jennifer turned the SUV into a neighborhood where the streets were lined with thirty-year-old oaks, and the lawns were well-established and appeared to be cared for by proud—but not to the point of obsession—homeowners. It blossomed as the two women walked through the property. There were four bedrooms instead of the three Sarah wanted, and the backyard was slightly smaller than the one she was leaving behind. But the roof was only a year old, and the asking price was less than ten percent higher than her stated limit. Sarah crossed her fingers, told Jennifer to make an offer, and enjoyed the full flower of optimism.

For all but the last few minutes of the forty-eight

hour reply window of the offer. That's when Jennifer called, her voice oozing regret. "I am so very sorry. One of my other clients made a slighter higher offer today, and the seller, understandably enough, decided to take that one. But don't worry, several new listings came in today and..."

"Excuse me, Jennifer. Is it common practice for a real estate agent to show the same property to two clients?"

There was something that sounded like a chuckle on the line. "I do it all the time."

"And do you share information about pending offers between them?"

Several seconds of silence was followed by a very chilly tone. "That would be unethical."

"And that wasn't an answer," Sarah replied bluntly.

"Sarah, I understand that you're disappointed, anxious, and maybe even a bit angry," Jennifer began, "but that is no reason to insult me by impugning my professionalism. If there weren't an agreement in place, I'd be of half a mind to..."

"Believe me," Sarah cut in, "I am in way more than 'half a mind' to consider that agreement breached. Especially since, in my experience, people who flare up righteously indignant on so little provocation are usually indignant over being found out. So let's just call it even and wish each other a good life."

"Wait!"

"Yes?"

"This is so embarrassing. I can assure you...I swear to you...that I did not tell anyone but the seller's agent the amount of your bid. But," Jennifer paused, then continued with what sounded like shame, "your offer form may have been lying on my desk while I was meeting with that other client. I only stepped out long enough to sign some papers at Benjamin's desk."

A long moment followed, during which neither woman spoke. The only sounds across the phone lines were Sarah's anger-tamping controlled breathing and something from Jennifer's end that sounded a bit like someone tasting something particularly palate-pleasing.

"So you're saying," Sarah said after a while, "it was carelessness, not deliberate manipulation." Sarah wasn't sure, but the high-frequency line noise she suddenly heard sounded almost like someone hissing.

"Carelessness, pure and simple," came the reply after a short pause. "For which I am really, truly sorry. I promise you it will not happen again."

"It wouldn't, I'm sure. But, frankly, there doesn't seem much point to 'again.' You've had weeks, you've dragged me all over the county and into some of the neighboring ones, and to date, there's been exactly one that even came close. Unless I want to move twice, which I don't, and spend some very uncomfortable months in an apartment, which I *really* don't, a property needs to be found by day after tomorrow, an offer accepted by the end of the week, and closing completed by the end of next week."

"And it can. Several new listings came in just this afternoon, and one of them is almost exactly what you're looking for. Please, let me redeem myself and show it to you tomorrow evening."

"I already have an appointment tomorrow night, to see a house being sold directly by the owners."

"Oh, you shouldn't go that route, it's . . ." Jennifer stopped herself and changed tactics. "Please. All I'm asking is that you give me this one last chance. It's perfect for you. And if it's not, we'll terminate that representation agreement free and clear. But I really want you to see this one."

Sarah took a deep breath while she considered the idea. "Very well. One last property, either way. I'll meet you at your office at eight P.M."

Sarah cocked her head and regarded the vehicle pulling up into Jennifer's reserved parking spot: something tiny, powder blue, and ancient. "Isn't it adorable?" Jennifer squealed as she bounced up from the driver's seat.

"Uh ... yeah. What is it?"

"This," the real estate agent beamed proudly, "is a 1974 Chevy Vega Notchback LX. Four-on-the-floor manual transmission, sports steering wheel, twin-barrel carburetor, and a blast to drive."

"It looks ... really well cared for," Sarah said, looking in the window.

"Oh, she is. She was one of my prizes as Miss Cotton Boll, a big reason I entered that pageant, in fact. In a way, this car led to the win that led to all my good fortune, so she's had nothing but tender loving care ever since." Well-manicured fingers trailed lovingly across the sloped hood. "She's my lucky charm. And since I just know the property we're going to see will be lucky for both of us, I thought we'd go there in her instead of the SUV."

"Ohhh ... kay." Sarah carefully levered herself into the tight environs of the passenger seat, recalling an equally-small Toyota Corolla she'd owned for a number of years. She did have to admit, as they turned onto the street, that the Vega was peppier than she expected.

They'd been driving long enough that Sarah had tuned out Jennifer's familiar chatter about "prime investment opportunity." One word pulled her attention back to the blonde. "Oops."

"Something wrong?"

"Nothing that can't be fixed pretty quickly," Jennifer replied cheerfully. "One of my baby's few faults is that her engine overheats now and then. It means she's either low on coolant or low on oil, and my mechanic insists I check both the minute it happens. Something about engine fires, carburetor fires, something like that. This won't take a minute." She turned the car out of traffic and onto the first unoccupied street they came to: the entrance to Stonebend Estates. They pulled to a stop in front of the model home, and Jennifer got out and raised the hood.

Sarah also got out, giving her shoulders and knees a break from their previously folded position. As she stretched, she looked around. There had definitely been work done in the weeks since she'd been there. At least three houses now looked like houses, and two more had been framed. Several truckloads of what was apparently being labeled "topsoil" these days had been dumped into what would someday be those houses' front yards. And the model home and two of the units nearest completion now sported two trees each in their front yards, if one were generous in calling entirely-unsuitable-for-the-climate saplings, no taller than the average Great Dane and still in the throes of transplant shock, "trees."

"Low on coolant *and* oil," Jennifer trilled. "I've got both in the trunk. We'll be off to see your new house before you know it."

"No problem," Sarah called back as she heard the sounds of the trunk being opened. "Better safe than stranded." She continued to look at the construction as automotive-related sounds continued behind her.

The sudden sound of a shoe scraping on concrete close behind her caused her to start turning. Too late, apparently, as arms wrapped around her, trapping her own against her sides and pulling her against the body behind her before she was lifted into the air. "What the . . ." she shrieked, kicking both heels backward as hard as she could. Both connected with one kneecap each, hard enough that they should have had some effect. Effect did not occur.

Sarah's captor carried her toward where Jennifer leaned back against the car in front of the open hood, smiling in much the same way as she'd smiled in the beauty queen photos back in her office. "Thank you, Benjamin," she said, as her assistant placed the struggling woman on her feet. Any thought Sarah had of making a break for it when he released her died as his hands moved to her upper arms and held hard enough to leave bruises.

"What the devil do you people think you're doing?" she shouted straight into Jennifer's grill of perfectly-capped teeth. "And where the hell did *he* come from?"

"The trunk," Jennifer replied.

Sarah turned her head and regarded the other end of the small blue vehicle. "How? I've owned roomier purses!"

"Mr. Renfield is remarkably adaptable for a mortal," Jennifer replied, smiling indulgently.

"Thank you, mistress."

Sarah rolled her eyes in disgust. "Okay, one more

time. Will someone please tell me what this nonsense is all about?"

"In a moment," Jennifer replied as the smooth skin of her forehead split and something that looked like a cluster of calamari tentacles appeared, writhing in Sarah's direction. "Mmmm. Delicious," she sighed, closing her eyes and licking her red-painted lips. At the same time, the tentacles turned from grayish-white to pink. Or at least that's what it looked like, adjusting for the color of the halogen street lights.

"Let me take a wild stab at it," Sarah interrupted. "You're some kind of vampire. You feed off emotions, and Bennie here is your somewhat-human thrall."

Jennifer opened her eyes and chuckled. "I thought it would be a nice touch the minute I saw the name on his resume. To my happy surprise, he came with both the perfect name and excellent skills. Even with the . . . side effects . . . of serving me, he still maintains the website and types a hundred words a minute."

"Thank you, mistress."

"Shut up, Benjamin."

"Yes, mistress."

Jennifer threw a hard look at her assistant, then looked at Sarah with a slight smile. "Someone like you, someone less perfect, doesn't care about getting old. But I did. I was beautiful! I had the pageant wins to prove it! I had this!" She patted the powder blue front quarter panel lovingly. "No one in North Texas won more pageants or had more titles than I did. But there's a upper age limit for competitors, and I hit it. My life was over. The only thing left for me was to get married and find a good dermatologist."

"Poor you," Sarah snorted.

"I married Clyde, the most successful real estate guy in the county. I had the best dermatologist, and the best plastic surgeon, in the whole state. And," Jennifer's eyes gleamed with the memory, "before I got so old that neither of them could save me, I found a lover who made it possible to never have to worry about getting old again."

"You took a vampire lover who killed you," Sarah translated.

"Not killed," Jennifer corrected, "transformed. Armand explained it all to me and gave me a choice. I would be eternally beautiful by feeding on . . . yuck . . . blood, or I could feed on human emotions. My meals die either way, but feeding on emotions is so much less messy."

"All you had to do was let him murder you and stick a squid in your forehead. Classy."

"Oh, it was very romantic," Jennifer sighed, momentarily lost in memory. "Soft spring night, a full moon, parked in my baby next to the hay field that was going to be Clyde's next big money-making subdivision. The Hollywood Strings on the radio playing 'Theme From a Summer Place.' And Armand's sexy accent telling me how I would be the most beautiful woman around for years and years and years to come. Clyde was my first feeding, when I told him about Armand, and my first kill."

A manicured hand reached up and stroked Sarah's cheek. "And you're my next."

"Thanks, Jennifer, but you're not my type."

Jennifer chuckled again. "But you're mine, and that's really all that matters. I knew the first time you came into the office that you were going to be a feast. The situation alone promised that. Anger at how the city was putting you out of your home, anxiety over the deadline, tasty little bits of hope every time I called and said I had something for you to look at. Yum."

"And you deliberately showing me properties that weren't even close to what I was looking for."

"To borrow a phrase from the teenagers," Jennifer laughed, "duh. If you got cold feet, broke down, and bought one of them, I won financially. If you didn't and kept getting more angry and more desperate as the deadline approached, I'd feed, over and over again. You, my dear Sarah, weren't just a feast. You've been a banquet. Unfortunately, a banquet that's coming to an end, this being our last outing and all. But you know what ends a banquet, don't you?"

"Brandy and cigars on the veranda?" Sarah quipped.

"Dessert. Rich, elegant dessert. I thought, for a while, I'd offer you eternal life; make you what I am and bring you into the business. But I decided against that."

There was a deep rumbling from behind Sarah's head. "But, mistress, you promised to change *me* next. You promised when I became your servant."

"Shut up, Benjamin."

"Yes, mistress." The rumbling, Sarah noticed, quieted but did not stop.

"Now, where was I . . . oh, yes. I decided against turning you. You're much too stubborn now to be anything other than a threat to me after you transformed. You'd be competition, and I can't have that."

"So you're going to kill me. Drain off what's left of my emotions and kill me. Then what? Dig a hole in the middle of where they're pouring a new pad tomorrow, shove my lifeless body into it, backfill the hole, and wait for progress to finish hiding the evidence?"

"Almost right," Jennifer answered with another broad smile. "Drain off what's left of your emotions, dig a hole in the middle of that pad form right over there where they're pouring concrete tomorrow, shove your still-conscious-but-completely-paralyzed body into it, backfill the hole, and feed off your last deliciously terrified thoughts at being buried alive."

"I stand corrected. Just tell me one thing first," Sarah continued, watching Jennifer's forehead tentacles writhe in anticipation of what was coming. "That house we were supposed to be seeing tonight, the one that was supposedly perfect. Was that real or just something you made up to get me to meet you tonight?"

"There you go, impugning my ethics again. It's quite real, it really was listed with me today, and it meets ninety-five percent of your silly little wish list. You'd have loved it. Ask Benjamin; he talked to the owners and took all the information."

"I will. Thanks," Sarah replied before starting to struggle. As she expected, Benjamin wrapped his arms around her again. His new hold gave her the leverage she needed for the one desperate, go-down-fighting move she could think of. Hanging from Benjamin's arms, she curled up and lashed out with both feet, striking Jennifer hard in her silicone-augmented chest and knocking her right off her Prada high-heeled pumps, under the open hood, and flat across the engine compartment.

The force of Jennifer's landing knocked the brace holding the hood up out of its slot, and the hood slammed down, slicing none too neatly, but very effectively, through Jennifer's delicate neck. Which was, apparently, the trigger for several things to start happening at once.

Benjamin's hold went slack, dropping Sarah flat onto her backside. Benjamin himself went slack, folding into a fetal position on the concrete while making noises that reminded Sarah of a cow separated from her calf. Jennifer's head, with Jennifer's squid, landed on the street with a sound reminiscent of a coconut falling off a display stand at the market—only squishier—and both started shrieking, the combination sounding like a fire station's tornado siren. Jennifer's body started dissolving into malodorous shiny brown goo. And the powder blue paint job of the Vega started disappearing, replaced by rapidly growing splotches of rust.

Sarah scrambled to her feet and around to the other side of the car, grabbed the head by its carefully-coiffed hair, and tossed it into the trunk, slamming the lid down as hard as its rapidly rusting condition would let her. Some time between being picked up and having the trunk lid slammed on it, both head and squid stopped screaming as they joined the rest of the body in goohood.

Benjamin still lay, curled up and moaning pitifully, on the pavement. Sarah grabbed him by the back of his starched collar and dragged him to the curb, onto which she collapsed. For the next ten minutes, she kept one eye on him and one on the Vega as it joined the vast majority of its brethren in a long-delayed rusty demise. It was a bit like watching a time-lapse sequence sped up: the sub-compact turned reddish-brown, folding and collapsing in on itself as structural integrity became a thing of the past. The non-ferrous components—rubber tires, hoses, and gaskets, aluminum wiring, bumpers, and engine block—bubbled and dissolved in caustic contact with the ooze that had once been Jennifer Shick Haggard's body, until all that was left was a pile of powder roughly the size of a German shepherd. And then, even that was gone, scattered by a hot, dry, Texas August evening breeze.

"Ms. Bailey, are you okay?" The voice was none too steady, but at least it had more life than the dull, flat tone of before.

"A little shaky, but otherwise fine," she replied. "How about you? Do you remember what happened?"

Benjamin levered himself into a sitting position and swept his gaze across the now-vacant street. "Yeah," he said, turning to meet Sarah's eyes. "I remember everything." The mix of emotions swirling in his wasn't the most pleasant to see, but at least he had some to mix. Benjamin was young, and the young are resilient. "I guess we're stranded."

Sarah laughed. "Only for as long as it takes a friend of mine to get here," she replied, pulling a phone out of her shoulder bag, hitting a button, and putting it to her ear. Less than a minute later, she put the phone away and smiled at the young man. "Which will be somewhere between five and ten minutes."

"Thank you, mistr—Ms. Bailey." Benjamin shook his head and smiled sheepishly toward Sarah. "Sorry about that. One gets in the habit."

"It's okay." The two continued to recover in companionable silence until the lights of a vehicle approached. After introductions, and a promise to tell him the whole story "soon," they climbed into Will's truck.

David D. Levine is a lifelong SF reader whose midlife crisis was to take a sabbatical from his high-tech job to attend Clarion West in 2000. It seems to have worked. He made his first professional sale in 2001, won the Writers of the Future Contest in 2002, was nominated for the John W. Campbell award in 2003, was nominated for the Hugo Award and the Campbell again in 2004, and won a Hugo in 2006 (Best Short Story, for "Tk'Tk'Tk"). His "Titanium Mike Saves the Day" was nominated for a Nebula Award in 2008, and a collection of his short stories, *Space Magic*, is available from Wheatland Press (www.wheatlandpress.com). He lives in Portland, Oregon with his wife, Kate Yule, with whom he edits the fanzine *Bento*, and their website is at www.BentoPress.com.

Family Matters

David D. Levine

Seconds after the bell rang, ending the last class of the day, the long second-floor corridor clattered with slamming locker doors, the squeak of wet moon boots on linoleum, and the bird-like chatter of high school students. Orange sunlight slanted across the Celebrate America posters on the walls, their reds and blues already faded, though the Bicentennial had been only three months earlier.

"I think they're just trying to come up with some excuse for their sorry record this season," the girl at the next locker said as Julian Greene dialed in the combination on his lock. She wasn't talking to him. Julian knew the other freshmen considered him standoffish, but with his increasing responsibilities in the coven he found he had less and less in common with his classmates anyway.

"My brother's on the team," the girl's friend replied, eyes wide, clutching her books to her chest, "and he swears it's true. Five players all came down with anemia in the same week."

"But anemia isn't contagious! Isn't it?"

"It isn't supposed to be..."

Julian dropped his books in his locker and hauled out his heavy raincoat with the jingling buckles. He stuffed himself into it as quickly as he could, the other departing students jostling past him, then flung his backpack over one shoulder and hustled down the stairs two at a time. He had to talk to Daciana before she went home.

Daciana Niculescu's locker was at the other end of the first floor. She was a junior, but as new to the school as Julian—newer, even, because she hadn't gone to grade school and middle school with some of these same kids the way he had. And, like the thin and bookish Julian, she was an outsider, her pale complexion and peculiar vowels marking her as different. She was just closing her locker when Julian caught up to her.

"Hey," he panted.

"Hello," she replied, eyes wary.

"You wanna..." Julian paused, swallowed. This wasn't a date, he told himself. It was serious coven business. But it was still hard. "You wanna stop for hot chocolate on the way home? I need to talk to you about...some stuff."

"Okeh." That was how it came out, *okeh* instead of *okay*. Julian wondered if that was how they said it in Romania, or if that was just how it sounded in English with her accent.

The two of them headed out the door and down the stairs to the sidewalk, Julian flipping up his hood and Daciana putting on her sunglasses and popping open a big black umbrella. Even on a gloomy overcast day, Daciana always wore sunglasses outside.

They stopped at the ice cream shop on Olive Street, still open though devoid of customers—no one had wanted Valley Forge Fudge or Yankee Doodle Strudel back in July, and those Bicentennial flavors were even less popular in the depths of October. Julian got a couple of hot chocolates from the counter, and brought them to where Daciana sat at one of the little tables. She smiled her thanks, displaying prominent canine teeth.

Daciana and her family were vampires, refugees from the Ceauşescu regime's secret crackdown on all sorts of supernatural creatures in Romania. Every coven in America was helping vampire immigrant families get settled, and Julian's coven had two: Daciana's family here in Lakeshore, and another in the nearby suburb of Alewife Bay. Julian's mother had taken on assisting Daciana's family as a special project.

Real vampires weren't nearly as fearsome as the legends suggested. True, Daciana was pale and sensitive to sunlight, and there was the turning into a bat thing. But she had never shown any desire for human blood—though she always ordered her burgers at the youth center extra-rare—and she reflected in a mirror like anyone else. "How else could I do my make-up?" she'd joked, though Julian had thought that she didn't look like she needed make-up.

Before speaking, Julian sketched a sigil on the tabletop with his finger and muttered an incantation: Hermes's Secrecy, which would prevent any eavesdropper from hearing anything but an indistinct mumble. "You've probably heard about the football team," he said after the spell had taken effect.

"I have." Daciana took a sip, trying to act nonchalant,

but Julian noticed that her hand trembled as she raised the cup to her carmine-red lips. "But you know me. I would not—ah, how do you say . . . hurt a fly."

Julian swirled the chocolate in his cup. "I'm afraid the coven is going to want proof."

"But how can I prove I *didn't* do something?"

"Athena's Inspection."

Daciana took a sudden breath. Athena's Inspection was a powerful spell that could reveal the truth of anyone's statements, even their innermost thoughts. It was a difficult, painful, and disruptive spell to undergo, and could even do permanent damage. "Why just me?" she asked. "There must be other suspects."

Julian shook his head. "Your family are the only vampires in Lakeshore, and Mom's been spending so much time with your parents that there's no way they could've done it. But you . . ."

Suddenly Daciana reached across the small table and took both of Julian's hands in hers. "You have to believe me," she said.

Julian started at the sudden contact, but part of him thrilled at the touch of her soft, cool hands. "I do believe you. But I'm sure you understand there's some concern that you've gone rogue. For the security of the coven, and the safety of the lay community, we have to be sure."

"We are good people, Julian. Not monsters." Daciana looked down, still holding Julian's hands. "I thought we had left this . . . this persecution, behind."

"It's not persecution." But Julian knew that some members of the coven harbored deep suspicions of the Niculescus . . . as much because they were Communists as because they were vampires. Mrs. Birk, the head of the coven's Discipline and Security Committee, was particularly unhappy at their presence in the community. If she were the one to administer Athena's Inspection, it would not be done gently.

"Please, Julian." Daciana looked up again, her pale gray eyes brimming with tears. "I have already been through so much. If I were to be . . . laid open . . . by that spell, I do not know if I would survive. You have to convince them to leave us alone."

Julian swallowed. "I . . . I don't know what I can do, but I'll try." He placed her hands gently around the paper cup in front of her. "Have some chocolate. It'll help calm your nerves."

She dropped her gaze to the cup and raised it to her lips. "Thank you, Julian," she whispered, then drank. Julian watched her pale throat pulse as she swallowed the hot chocolate. He'd never seen anything so delicate.

They talked for an hour after that, and eventually he got her calmed down enough to leave the ice cream shop, but she insisted he accompany her to her house. "My parents would be so worried if they knew I was under suspicion," she said as they arrived at her driveway. "Please don't tell them."

"I won't."

"Thank you." And then she gave him a sudden kiss on the cheek and ran inside.

Julian stood on the sidewalk for a long time, rubbing with his fingers the spot where she'd kissed him.

"Julian!" his mother called. "Phone for you!"

Julian closed his grimoire, pleased for the interruption to his unending studies. High school had brought a dramatic escalation in his lay homework, and when he was done with that he needed to do some research on vampires so that he could best present Daciana's case to the Discipline and Security Committee meeting on Saturday afternoon.

"Hello?"

"Hey, Julian! Remember me? Liz?"

"Of course I remember you. I never forget a redhead." Even though she was a lay person, a year younger, and lived in Alewife Bay, Liz was his best friend, and she'd helped him out so many times he'd had to let her in on some coven secrets... not that he'd told his mother about that little detail. "I know it's been a week or two since we've hung out together..."

"More like a month and a half, guy."

Had it really been that long? Julian thought about it, realized she was right, and sighed. "High school sucks, Liz. Every one of my teachers thinks she's the only one giving homework, and that's not to mention... family business." Liz would understand that he couldn't be more specific than that on the phone, with his mother probably listening from the next room.

"My spies at Lakeshore High tell me that's not the only thing taking up your time. Seems you've been hanging out with a cute foreign exchange student." Liz was trying to sound flip, but beneath that joviality, Julian heard a real hurt.

"It's not like that! It's just more family business. And she's not an exchange student, she's, like, a refugee. My family's helping her family get settled."

"Okay." She didn't sound convinced. "Well, anyway. Wanna come over tomorrow after school? I can show you my tennis trophy." Unlike the bookish Julian, Liz was a natural athlete—not only was she a tennis star, she had a mean fastball, and had set a school record for javelin.

"All right. See you then!"

Daciana came up to Julian the next day in the hall, as he made his way to his locker, and asked him about something that had come up in English that day. They were in the same English class, even though she was two years older, but the expression of concern on her face seemed way out of line with the difficulty of the subject, even for her. After a while Julian realized what was really going on: she was worried about the upcoming committee meeting, and trying to distract herself by focusing on her schoolwork. But the hall was noisy and people kept bumping into them. "Come with me," she said. "I know a good place to study."

Julian followed her down the hall to the auditorium. It was locked at this hour, but Daciana was in the Drama Club and had a key. She made her way unerringly through the darkened backstage area, stepping over ropes and pieces of scenery that threatened to trip Julian up, and he reflected that a vampire's night vision would be a very good thing for a drama jock to have. At the top of a clanging metal staircase they found a steel fire door. Daciana used her key again, then waited until the door had closed behind them before turning on the light.

"Whoa." Julian turned in place. "It's like Ali Baba's cave in here." A gigantic moose head hung cockeyed on one cinderblock wall, between a bar sign and an amateurish portrait in an ornate gilded frame; a staircase with an extravagant bannister stood by itself, connecting nothing to nothing; a whole dining room set was made of papier mâché rocks.

"This is the prop room." Daciana plopped down on a paisley loveseat, raising a cloud of dust, and patted the cushion next to her. "I come here during my study period."

Julian's heart pounded as he settled in beside her; he told himself it was because of the stairs they'd just climbed.

They talked about participles and prepositions, and about the difference between the conditional and the subjunctive, and about their lives. Daciana's uncle Stefan had managed to obtain exit visas for his family and Daciana's, but at the last minute had given his own visa to Daciana's cousin Adrian, choosing to stay in Romania to help the rest of their extended family to escape. "Family is very important to my people," she explained, laying a hand on Julian's knee. "Even if you don't like them, they are still family."

"It can be like that here, too," Julian said, thinking about his parents. Sometimes it seemed that they were completely dedicated to making his life miserable, but he knew it was because they wanted only the best for him. He yawned and looked at his watch.

It was a quarter after ten. In the evening.

"Oh shit!" Julian jumped up from the loveseat, staring around, realizing that the prop room had no windows and no clocks . . . at least, no clocks that showed the correct time. "It's gotten way, way late."

Daciana looked at Julian's watch. *"Oh, la naiba!* My parents will stake me!"

"Mine, too." Julian stuffed himself into his coat as quickly as he could.

They raced through the school's darkened hallways, then ran down rain-slick streets toward their houses. But just as they reached Daciana's house, she stopped Julian with a hand on his shoulder.

"I was going to fly in my bedroom window," she panted, pointing, "but Papa must have closed it against the rain."

"Can't you just walk in the front door and take your lumps?" That was what Julian was planning to do.

Daciana's eyes went wide, and she shook her head. "You don't know my Papa. But if I can just slip inside somehow without being seen, in the morning I can say I got in earlier than I did and he'll believe me."

They tiptoed all around the house, but all the windows were closed.

"I'm doomed," Daciana moaned.

"No, wait," Julian said. "What's that window frame made of? Wood or aluminum?"

"Wood, I think."

Julian thought a moment. "Do you have a pencil?"

Daciana gave Julian a baffled look, but reached into her pocket. "I have a pen . . ."

"No, it has to be made of wood."

They both dug in their backpacks. Julian's was no help; he always used a mechanical pencil. "Here's a popsicle stick," Daciana said. "Will that do?"

"Maybe."

Julian closed one eye and held the popsicle stick up, horizontal at arm's length, so it matched the lower sill of Daciana's window in his vision. Then he spoke the words of Herne's Equivalence, blinking against the rain, feeling the stick grow heavy and warm in his hand. As soon as the spell was complete, he pushed the stick upward against resistance.

Twenty feet overhead, the window slid open an inch and a half. Julian strained, but that was all he could achieve. "Is that enough?" he gasped.

"More than enough," Daciana said. "But now you have to swear not to tell *anyone* we stayed out together so late. If word ever gets back to Papa, he'll stake me for sure!"

"I swear I won't tell," Julian said, and to show he was serious he sealed it with an oath to the Goddess.

"Thank you so much, Julian!"

And then she kissed him. A real kiss, on the lips. Her lips were cool and soft and wonderful, and Julian forgot the rain and the darkness and the fact that his parents were going to kill him as soon as he got home.

Then, a moment and an eternity later, Daciana pulled away and, with one last smile that showed off her canines, she dissolved into darkness. A sudden flittering of wings flapped upwards from where she had stood, ending with a small dark shape squeezing through the slightly opened window. Immediately thereafter, Daciana's face appeared in the window, waving and blowing kisses.

Stunned, Julian waved back, then sauntered through the rain to his own house, whistling "Silly Love Songs" by Paul McCartney and Wings.

His mother yelled at him for two solid hours and doubled his chores for the next month.

He didn't care.

The next morning, Julian's still-dreamy mood was ruined by two pieces of paper on the kitchen table.

One was a phone message in his father's handwriting: "Fri 7 P.M. Liz called. Very upset. CALL HER." The other was the sports section of the local newspaper, whose headline screamed "LAKESHORE QUARTER-BACK COLLAPSES."

It turned out that the quarterback of the Lakeshore High football team had stumbled home at ten the previous night, mumbling incoherently about some kind of attack after leaving practice, and had promptly collapsed on his own front stoop. He'd been admitted to the hospital with the same inexplicable "sudden-onset normocytic anemia" as other members of the team.

Toward the end of the story, one sentence chilled Julian's blood: "'I don't know what it is,' Coach Piaskoski said. 'At this point, I'll believe anything... even vampires.'" In the twentieth century, lay people's desire for a rational, comprehensible world could usually be counted on to protect the coven if something unusual leaked out. But sufficient evidence of paranormal activity could sometimes break through that veneer of rationality. That was how witch hunts got started.

"Morning, sleepyhead," his father said, entering the kitchen and pouring himself another cup of coffee. "You know, your mother and I were really worried about you last night. And your friend Elizabeth was just furious."

"I'm sorry, Dad. I won't let it happen again."

Julian's father peered over his glasses. "Is there... something going on, son? That your mother and I should know about?"

"No, Dad. I was helping a friend with some English homework and we lost track of the time." Which was true, mostly. "Have you seen this?" Julian pointed to the sports page.

"Mmm-hmm." Julian's father held an imaginary envelope to his forehead. "Karnac predicts a very interesting Discipline and Security Committee meeting this afternoon."

Julian's spirits sank still further, if such a thing were possible. "Yeah."

"You're our man on the scene, son. Are you fully prepared to present your report?"

"Uh . . . I still have a little research to do." In fact, he hadn't gotten to it at all. After Liz had called on Friday night, he'd gotten distracted and never returned to his studies.

"Better get cracking, then. The meeting starts at two."

Julian looked at the clock on the wall. It was already after ten. "Wow. Okay." He wolfed down a bowl of Count Chocula—the irony was not lost on him—and went to the locked cupboard in his room that held his grimoires and reference books.

Under most circumstances, vampires were normal, productive members of society; their fearsome reputation was mostly a matter of myth and legend. But sometimes a vampire went rogue, preying on humans like a hungry wolf. Rogue behavior was rare and not well understood, but it was beyond the individual vampire's control and most likely to happen shortly after puberty. And whatever caused rogue behavior also conferred a powerful hypnotic ability, which could allow rogues to go undetected for months or years.

Suddenly the doorbell rang, jerking Julian from his studies. It was Mrs. Birk, her high-pitched screech clearly audible even from the other end of the house. "Grim times, Mrs. Greene," she said to Julian's mother. "Grim times."

Soon Julian was standing in the rec room, presenting his report to Mrs. Birk and the other members of the committee. "There are rumors and suspicions," he said, "but so far I've seen no evidence anyone at the high school truly believes the football players' anemia is caused by vampires."

Julian's mother frowned at him, lowering her head like a bull getting ready to charge. "*Any*one, Julian? What about you?"

Julian lowered his eyes. "I . . . I don't know, Mom. I haven't found any other explanation. But I'm sure it isn't Daciana."

Mrs. Birk sat up straighter, glaring at Julian over her hatchet-like nose, and set her teacup down in its saucer with a precise little *clink*. "Your opinions are noted, Master Greene, but this committee deals in facts."

Julian's mind whirled. He knew that Daciana wasn't responsible for last night's attack on the quarterback, because they'd been together at the time. But he couldn't say anything—he'd given his word and sealed it with an oath.

Mrs. Birk's glare was still focused on Julian. "Have you anything else to add, Master Greene?"

Julian swallowed. "No, ma'am."

"Well then, thank you for your report. You are dismissed."

Naturally he went only as far as the top of the basement steps. Equally naturally, as soon as he rounded the corner the committee's discussions turned into an impenetrable mumble, thanks to Hermes's Secrecy.

Julian sighed. All he could do now was wait.

After staring fruitlessly at his homework, emptying the dishwasher, and pacing back and forth for half an hour, Julian suddenly remembered that he'd never called Liz back. He cursed and ran to the phone.

"Hey, Liz," he said when she came to the phone. "It's, uh, it's me." Silence. "You know ... Julian?"

"Who?" That single word was colder than a bus stop in February.

"Look, Liz, I'm sorry I forgot we were going to hang out. I was, uh, helping a friend with some English homework."

But unlike Julian's father, Liz was a kid and knew that kids didn't ever actually help each other with homework. "You were with your new Romanian friend, weren't you?"

Julian froze. He could never lie to Liz, but he'd sworn an oath ...

Liz lost patience with waiting for a response. "Thought so. Well listen, mister big high-schooler, I've got a new friend of my own!"

"What?"

"He's a sophomore at Alewife Bay High, and he's much cooler than you. He's got a leather jacket and everything. So, you know, next time you call maybe I'll be the one who's too busy to call back."

Before he could formulate a coherent response, he heard footsteps coming up from the rec room. Oh, shit. "I'm really really sorry," he blurted out at top speed, "but I gotta go I'll call you back soon okay bye." He ran to the living room and ducked behind the stereo cabinet, where he could see and hear into the foyer but not be seen.

His parents' faces, and those of most of the other committee members, were grim, but Mrs. Birk's harsh, sharp face was set in something resembling a determined smile. As soon as the door shut behind her back, Julian's father shook his head and sighed. "Did you *have* to vote to authorize Athena's Inspection?" Julian muffled a gasp. "According to Julian, Daciana said she couldn't take it."

"I know she *said* that," Julian's mother replied. "But she's young and resilient. She'll recover eventually." She put a hand on his father's elbow. "We had to do it, Michael. Lives are on the line, and the security of the coven."

"I know. But I don't have to like it."

Julian trembled in the darkness behind the stereo. This was all *his* fault! And now it was up to him to fix it.

As soon as Julian's parents went back downstairs to clean up the rec room, he dashed across the kitchen and into his bedroom. There he grabbed his backpack, scrawled a quick note to his parents, and headed out the door.

He hated leaving without telling them where he was going, but he didn't have a moment to spare. Mrs. Birk would probably head straight for Daciana's house as soon as she'd prepared the materials for Athena's Inspection.

Daciana's father was a big man with a heavy moustache and short, thick, hairy hands that looked like they could strangle a full-grown buffalo. "Ah, Julian," he said, after Julian had introduced himself. "Daciana tells us so much about you."

"Ah." Julian swallowed, and managed a weak smile. "Nothing bad, I hope?"

The moustache crinkled in reply. "She says you are very nice boy."

"Um. Thank you."

"I go get her now, okeh?"

Julian waited, hands bunched in trembling fists in his coat pockets, until Daciana appeared in the living room. As soon as she saw his face, her eyes widened. "We need to talk privately," he whispered. She called something to her parents in Romanian, then got her coat.

He explained the situation as they walked quickly down the block. "It would help a lot if you would let me rescind my oath and tell Mrs. Birk that you and I were together at the time of last night's attack."

Daciana bit her lip and turned her face away. "You put me between two stools, Julian. If I don't let you tell, your Mrs. Birk will torture me for information. If I do let you tell, Papa will find out, and then..." She shuddered.

"Athena's Inspection isn't torture. And surely your father will understand..."

Daciana stopped and faced Julian, her eyes two points of dark heat in the cold drizzle. "Don't presume to know what I and my family will feel and do, *străin*." Whatever that last word meant, it wasn't a compliment.

"Okay, okay!" Julian backed off, hands raised. "In that case...we'll...we'll have to hide you somewhere. Just for a day or two, until I can find some way to convince the coven to call off the inquest." He thought for a moment. "I have a friend in Alewife Bay. A lay person, but a really good friend." Daciana raised a skeptical eyebrow. "No, really, it's okay. She's helped

me before with coven business. We can trust her not
to turn us in."

He hoped.

Julian waited on Daciana's porch while she sneaked
back into the house for a few clothes and toiletries.
But as they headed for the bus stop, they saw Mrs.
Birk's car coming down the street . . . and, even worse,
she saw them, pulling her car to the curb and opening
the door. "Run!" Julian yelled. He grabbed Daciana's
hand and ducked between two houses.

"She's not as innocent as she seems, Master Greene!"
Mrs. Birk called after their retreating footsteps. "She is
a rogue vampire! Your will is not your own!"

Julian found his steps hesitating at that last, but
shook his head and kept running. "This way!" he said,
and they ran across someone's back yard, through a
gap in a hedge, up a driveway, and then the wrong
way down a one-way street. "She's too old to catch
us on foot," he gasped, "and we can go where her
car can't."

Julian and Daciana hustled across Lakeshore, cutting through yards and parks, ducking into the library
and out the back door. Finally they came to a halt
on Lake Drive, which followed the shore of the lake
all the way north to Alewife Bay and beyond. Julian
checked his watch. "Five minutes," he panted, and
for once the bus was right on time.

The bus ride to Liz's house took forty-five minutes
and Julian spent the entire time in silence, thinking
of all the ways this could go wrong. Mrs. Birk might
manage to track them to Alewife Bay. Liz might tell
Julian to go jump in the lake, after the way he'd been
treating her lately. And then there was the point that

Mrs. Birk had raised. Rogue vampires were indeed said to have powerful hypnotic powers. Could Julian trust his own memory of what had happened on Friday evening?

That he could maybe do something about. Once they got settled somewhere.

Julian's heart pounded as they walked up Liz's front walk, and not just from all the running he'd done in the last few hours. Not only had he treated Liz badly, he hadn't even called ahead. She might be out with her new friend the high school sophomore.

But when he rang the doorbell and asked for Liz, her mother only asked them to wait in the parlor. And when Liz came out, she didn't start off by spitting in his face. That was something, anyway.

"Liz, uh, this is Daciana."

"Oh really," Liz said, folding her arms across her chest.

"We've, uh, kind of got a problem," he continued, not knowing what else to say. "You know that Daciana's a, kind of a, a, refugee? And, uh, some bad guys from her old home country are after her. We need a place to hide her for a day or two. Life or death. Can you help?" It sounded lame even to Julian but it was the best story he'd been able to come up with.

Liz glared at Daciana, who glared right back. "Well..." Liz said, "I suppose you can stay in the wreck room. That's W-R-E-C-K."

The "wreck room" looked like it had once been a nice place, maybe right after World War II. But now the paneling was peeling off the walls, the carpet was damp and moldy, and it was half-filled with boxes of old *National Geographics* and broken furniture. "No one will find you here," Liz said, plumping down on a spavined couch. "Mom thought it was pretty grody when we first moved in, and it's only gone downhill since."

"Thank you for your ... hospitality," Daciana said, lowering herself warily onto a rickety-looking chair.

"The pleasure's all mine." Then Liz leaned down, looking serious. "So tell me about these bad guys from the old country. Adrian's been acting all weird lately and I'm wondering if that's why."

"Adrian?" Daciana and Julian said in unison.

"Yeah, Adrian." Liz seemed nonplussed by their reaction. "He's that guy I told you about, Julian—the one with the leather jacket. He's a Romanian refugee too."

"He's my cousin," Daciana said, and Julian noticed that when she said "cousin," her mouth looked like she was sucking on something really sour.

"What do you mean, 'acting weird'?" Julian asked.

"Vanishing for days at a time. Refusing to answer questions. Getting all shifty. Is he in danger, too?"

Something went *click* in Julian's head, and he swallowed hard. "Actually, from what you've said, I'm afraid that Adrian may be one of those ... those bad guys from the old country himself."

Liz folded her arms on her chest again. "You're just jealous."

Julian grabbed Liz by the shoulders. "I am dead serious, Liz. If he's what I think he is ... you could be in mortal danger."

Liz's eyes went wide; Julian had never grabbed her like that before. "Jeez Louise. Do you think we should call the cops?"

Julian and Daciana shouted in unison, *"No!"*

They looked at each other, unsure how to proceed, until Daciana whispered "It's . . . it's a family matter." She looked stricken. "Adrian . . . he is my cousin, but we are . . . not friends. Back in Romania . . ." She gave out a low, animal moan and ducked her head between her legs, the fingers tangled in her hair taut as whips. "He courted me. I spurned him. He tried to . . . force himself on me. I resisted." At that she brought her head up, and the smile on her face was a horrible thing. "I did . . . damage. Neither of us has ever told anyone about that night, and he's never tried to touch me again, but he's hated me ever since." She put her head in her hands again. "When my Uncle Stefan gave up his exit visa for Adrian, I cried for three days. Everyone thought it was because I loved my uncle."

Julian reached out a hand to touch Daciana's trembling shoulder, then drew it back. "Okay. As long as we're being honest here . . . Liz, here's the deal. Daciana and Adrian are both . . . vampires."

Liz paled, but said nothing, and Julian was proud of her. She and he had already dealt with dark forces, werewolves, and even the Horned God together, so vampires weren't too impossible for her to believe.

"Most vampires are good people," Julian continued, "but I think Adrian's gone rogue." He quickly outlined what that meant. "If we bring the lay police into a situation like this . . . Goddess alone knows what will happen."

"So . . . so what are we gonna do?" Liz said, looking back and forth between Julian and Daciana. "If he's as dangerous as all that?"

Julian closed his eyes. "Let me think a minute."

Half an hour ago, when he'd thought Daciana might be the rogue, he'd been planning to cast Apollo's Clear

Sight on himself; that spell was proof against most forms of hypnosis or persuasion. Under its protection, Julian should be able to slip through Adrian's defenses and subdue him with Morpheus's Draught.

But if Adrian really were a rogue vampire, he'd be willing to kill to protect his secret. Julian would have to make sure Adrian didn't realize his powers weren't working before Julian could knock him out. But Apollo's Clear Sight wasn't a subtle spell... Adrian would notice its effects on Julian from a mile away.

A plan came together in Julian's mind, but it would need all three of them to work. "Liz, do you think Adrian would meet with you tonight if you asked?"

"Uh...yeah, unless he's vanished again."

"Okay," he said. "Here's what we'll do. Liz, you call Adrian and ask him to meet you outside the Alewife Bay Mall at—" He glanced at his watch. "—ten o'clock. But when he gets there he'll find me, not you. He'll use his hypnotic powers on me..."

"Wait..." Daciana said, and at the same time Liz said "Hypnotic *powers*?"

Julian held up one finger. "You guys are both going to have to trust me. Adrian will have to hypnotize me because I'm going to threaten to expose him. I'll cast a spell on Daciana that will protect her from his powers, but I can't do the same for myself, because if I do he'll know we're on to him. While he's busy hypnotizing me, Daciana will sneak up behind him and douse him with Morpheus's Draught. Once he's asleep, we'll tie him up, then take him to Mrs. Birk."

Liz and Daciana both stared, blinking, at Julian. Finally Liz spoke. "That is the dumbest plan I've ever heard from you, and that's saying a lot."

"You got a better idea?"

"Why not just call this Mrs. Birk and tell her you know where the real rogue is?"

"She wouldn't believe me...she thinks I'm Daciana's thrall."

Liz just shook her head. "At least let me come with you. I was a Girl Scout and I'm sure I can tie him up securely."

One of Julian's many tensions melted away...he had been afraid Liz wouldn't even want to call Adrian. "If you insist."

"I do insist. But I still think you're crazy."

Daciana took Julian's hands in her own, so soft and cool. "It should be me who takes the risk, not you. He is my cousin, after all."

Julian squeezed Daciana's hands, then released them. "No. If Adrian hates you all that much, he'll try to do more than just hypnotize you. I'd never forgive myself if anything happened to you."

Liz glanced at the clock on the wall. "It's getting late. If we're going to do this insane thing we'd better do it now. I'll go call Adrian."

Julian excused himself to Daciana and followed Liz up the stairs. As soon as she heard his footsteps behind her, she turned and stared down at him. He stopped, unsure how to proceed. "Liz...look, I know I've been a terrible friend lately, and I apologize. But even so, I know I can trust you with my life. That's something I don't have with Daciana." Liz's face hadn't relaxed. "Are we still friends?"

There was an awkward silence. "Yeah," Liz said at last. "Now let's do this thing before I lose my nerve."

❖   ❖   ❖

Julian, Liz, and Daciana huddled in the bushes near the mall entrance, peering through the shrubbery at Adrian, who waited on the sidewalk in front of the mall entrance. Taller, more muscular, and, yes, cooler than Julian, he looked calm and confident and ready for anything. The full moon overhead silvered the wrinkled shoulders of his black leather jacket.

"Okay," Julian whispered. "You've got the Morpheus's Draught?"

Liz and Daciana each held up a small bottle—one Gee Your Hair Smells Terrific, the other Love's Baby Soft. Each contained a few ounces of the sleeping elixir Julian had mixed up in Liz's bathroom sink, using hazel and valerian from his backpack.

"Great. Now close your eyes and hold still." He laid a hand lightly on each girl's head and muttered the incantation for Apollo's Clear Sight. Even though Julian was not the subject of the spell, for a moment everything suddenly became crisper and sharper.

"Whoa," Liz whispered. "This is *awesome.*"

"It'll last about forty-five minutes. Also, if you think back, you'll be able to remember anything that Adrian hypnotized you into forgetting."

Liz's eyebrows pinched together for a few seconds. "You sure? Nothing's coming to me."

That puzzled Julian, but Adrian was glancing at his watch and pacing back and forth. "Okay, we need to move."

Daciana put a hand on Julian's shoulder. "Be careful."

"Thanks."

Julian slipped sideways through the bushes, then emerged behind Adrian, well away from where Liz and Daciana still hid. "Yo!" he called.

Adrian whirled, a picture of inhuman grace and strength. "What are *you* doing here?" His voice was deep and his eyes were dark and soulful beneath brooding brows. He was definitely cooler than Julian.

"I know you've gone rogue." Julian's voice caught a little at the end of that sentence, but he soldiered on. "I know you're responsible for the attacks on the football players in Lakeshore. And I'm going to stop you."

At that, Adrian laughed aloud. "You?" Then in one fluid movement he stepped forward and grabbed Julian's arms, drawing them sharply together behind Julian's back. Julian gasped in pain as Adrian doubled him over with the full strength of a young male vampire. "Little boy," he whispered in Julian's ear, "you have no idea what you are dealing with." Julian struggled ineffectually in Adrian's grasp, the vampire's breath cold on his neck.

Suddenly Adrian whipped Julian around with a painful wrench, to see Liz and Daciana just emerging from the bushes. He must have heard the tiny sound of leaves rustling. The two girls were at least fifty feet away—much too far to throw the small amount of potion in their bottles.

"Daciana," Adrian said. He made the name a curse.

Daciana responded with a vehement speech in Romanian, which just made Adrian laugh again. Meanwhile, Julian noticed Liz inching to one side, moving toward a position where Adrian couldn't see her and Daciana at the same time. But before she'd moved three feet, Adrian gave Julian a harsh jerk to face Liz and yelled "Stop!"

Liz stopped.

"Listen, clever girl," Adrian said. "You take one

more step—either of you—and the little boy dies."
He emphasized his statement by shifting both of
Julian's forearms into one powerful hand, gripping
the back of Julian's head with the other. "Maybe I
kill him anyway."

"You won't get away with it," Daciana said.

"Oh, my lovely cousin," Adrian sneered, "why
should *I* attack a boy from Lakeshore?"

Suddenly Julian understood what was really happening and why Adrian had not used his hypnotic
powers. He didn't have any! "You aren't a rogue at
all! This is all just a big frame-up on Daciana!"

"So clever for such a stupid boy." Adrian pulled
Julian's head back, baring his neck and making him
cry out. "The football players were only the beginning. Your murder will be the final bit of evidence
that drives the stake into Daciana's rogue heart." He
bent his head down, his teeth pricking Julian's neck...

And suddenly something smashed into the side of
Adrian's head. Immediately he collapsed, dropping
Julian to the sidewalk and landing on top of him with
an impact that drove the breath from Julian's lungs.
Adrian groaned and held his head, the blood seeping
between his fingers appearing black in the moonlight.
Julian tried to scramble out from beneath Adrian's
body, but he was pinned.

And then came a sickening sweet smell: hazel, and
valerian, and Love's Baby Soft...

When Julian came to, he found himself lying on a
bench with Liz looking down at him. "Wha...?" he
managed. "What happened?"

"I beaned Adrian with a rock," she said, and grinned
broadly. "From sixty feet away. Greatest pitch of my

whole career and I can't tell anyone about it. Then, before he could shake it off, Daciana ran up and dosed both of you with the sleeping potion."

"Where is he now?"

"Tied up in the back seat of my car, Master Greene," came a new voice. Julian looked up to see Mrs. Birk approaching from the parking lot.

"When did *you* get here?" Julian said.

"Just in time to hear Miss Niculescu's cousin implicate himself. He will be subjected to Athena's Inspection, and the full truth will be revealed." She frowned at Julian. "You didn't do a very good job of covering your tracks, young man."

"I'll try to do better next time."

After the situation had been explained to Mrs. Birk—and she wasn't happy about Liz being involved, not happy at all, but she agreed that, under the circumstances, the breach in secrecy would have to be forgiven—she took Daciana aside to grill her about Adrian. While they talked, Julian and Liz sat together on the bench.

"She was very brave back there," Liz said, gesturing with her chin to Daciana. "I can see why you like her."

"Yeah," Julian admitted. "But . . . Liz, even if I . . . if I like another girl, you're still my best friend. Nothing's gonna change that."

Liz gave him a serious look. "Promise?"

"Cross my heart and hope to die."

Side by side, they watched the full moon rise over the mall.

Hildy Silverman is the publisher of *Space and Time*, a four-decade-old magazine featuring fantasy, horror, and science fiction. She is also the author of several works of short fiction, the most recent of which includes: "The Darren" (2009, *Witch Way to the Mall?*, Friesner, ed.), "Uddereek" (2010, *Bad-Ass Fairies 3: In All Their Glory*, Ackley-McPhail, ed.), "Off-the-Wagon Dragon" (2010, *Dragon's Lure*, multiple ed.), and "The Vampire Escalator of the Passaic Promenade" (2010, *New Blood*, Thomas, ed.). She is a member of the literary programming committee for the Philadelphia Science Fiction Society and vice president of the Garden State Horror Writers. In the "real" world, she is a freelance writer who develops corporate training and marketing communications materials.

Sappy Meals

Hildy Silverman

SUPERIOR COURT OF NEW JERSEY
DOCKET NO. V-0523-09
TOWNSHIP OF PISCATAWAY
     v.
DRAVYN, LORD FREDERIC, ET AL
PRELIMINARY HEARING

What do you think we are, anyway?

I mean, really, Your Honor. Do you hold the spider accountable for the pesky mosquito that threw itself into her web? Would you prosecute the wolf for the kitten that wandered into his mouth? Does punishment await the knife-wielding maniac into whose woods teenagers wander to have extra-marital sex and smoke hashish?

Oh. The last one—really?

Please forgive my ignorance, Your Honor. I have only lived in New Jersey ninety years. Practically right off the boat, as you fine mortal folks say. Heh. Heh-heh.

Yes, Your Honor, of course, back to the matter that brings us together today.

The first one...yes, thank you, Mr. Assistant District Attorney—Quinton, is it? Fine, then, Mr. Quinton, I know she had a name.

Maria Susan Nadolski showed up at Colin's house on August the second of this year.

Yes, Your Honor, a mere day after the premiere of *Night Delight*.

No, I'm certain the timing wasn't coincidental.

Anyway, she rapped on his door and, like any reasonable citizen of Piscataway, he answered. If I may, I will refer to the statement of events Colin provided to me before he was grounded. *Ahem.*

"Hello," Colin said. "Are you lost?"

Maria Susan stared back at him. He states her eyes were alight. "I was."

"Um, okay." Colin shook his head. "You shouldn't be in this part of town after sundown. That is a violation of curfew."

"Shh." She pressed her black-lacquered fingertips against his lips. "Rules don't apply to us."

Colin stared at her. "Which rules? The Accords that say you can't come into our neighborhood after dark? Or the ones that say I can't drink you with a bendy straw if you do?"

She smiled at him. Took his hand and placed it on her, er, over her heart. "I've seen you at Quick Chek. I've seen the way you look at me."

"Oh, really." He leaned against his doorway. He notes that he smiled, but with his lips together, as is considered polite.

She nodded. Coyly, I'm sure. "I used to think it was creepy." Colin's smile faded at this. "But now, I know. I understand."

"Hm. Do you."

"Yes." She caressed his cheek. He mentions that her hand jerked back at the coldness of his flesh, but even this did not dissuade her. Rather, she gave her appendage a little shake and rubbed his sleeve instead. "You could sense that I'm not like the others. I've never fit in with them, never been one of the herd."

Colin choked back a laugh at this. "Really? Really. Okay, then."

She went on, oblivious to his amusement. "They don't understand me, because my soul is old and yet looks out at the world through the eyes of a young girl." She then gestured to indicate her still-ripening body.

Um. At this point Colin says he may have licked his lips, although that isn't terribly relevant, now is it?

"Why don't you ever say hi to me?" Maria Susan asked. "All you do is grunt after I pay for my Pop-Tarts."

"Well," Colin explained, "we only feed at night. Kind of like an eternal Ramadan." As you can plainly hear, Colin's a bright boy; quite worldly and a strong believer in diversity.

Well, it *is* relevant, Mr. Quinton. We teach our young to be accepting of other races, cultures, beliefs, and definitions of life. Would that your people were as open-minded.

My apologies, Your Honor. I'll get to the point.

It wasn't long before Maria Susan was toe-to-toe with Colin on the porch of his house, her arms wrapped around his waist, her cheek all but burrowing its way into his chest. "We are meant to be, Colin. We are soulmates, fated to walk this world together, forever. Don't you understand?"

He looked down at her, tried to extricate himself from her iron embrace. He notes here that he wished the threshold barrier that bars unwanted entry by our kind into your domiciles worked both ways.

Alas, though he retreated into the foyer of his simple, ranch-style home, Maria Susan remained firmly attached, and thus came with him. "This is going to end badly," he said. "You really should go."

"How can I go?" She gazed up into his eyes. "I will die without your love!"

By now, Colin's fangs must have been burning, poor boy. He said, "Look, you're only, what? Fifteen?"

"Sixteen and three quarters," she said, nuzzling his chest.

"Well, I may have stopped aging around twenty-two, but I'm closer to ninety-five in human years. You see the problem."

"My soul's all old!" she insisted. "And it wants to be joined to yours. Love me, Colin, and nothing else will matter."

"It'll matter to my *pater sanguis*," he said.

I must interject here, in order to remind this court of the impossibility of such a relationship as Maria Susan Nadolski had in mind, between mortal teeny-bopper and ninety-five-year-old vampire. I mean, really, what would they even have to talk about? How prom fashions have changed over the course of eight centuries? Politics? The ridiculousness of the concept should be obvious to anyone with firing neurons.

Alas, it was not to this poor, *dear* girl. She obviously wasn't the sharpest stake in the . . . er, I mean, she was clearly deluded by recent popular fiction.

Colin, on the other hand, has always been one of my most dutiful offspring, Your Honor. He . . .

One hundred fifty-six. No, forgive me. One hundred fifty-seven. I don't see how that is relevant, Mr. Quinton.

No, I don't think that is an excessive number of offspring. I have walked this Earth for three centuries. Your people have females spitting out dozens of pups at a go.

Okay, eight.

Fine; children, then. Pups, kits, children—they're all the same thing, Mr. Quinton.

Oh, so because yours are spawned by intercourse and ours through blood conversion, there's a difference? I don't think I like what you are implying, Mr. Quinton.

Forgive me, Your Honor. They are both biological imperatives in the end, are they not? To say one method is "normal" implies a slight that . . .

Quite so. Thank you, Your Honor. Unless the *esteemed* A.D.A. has an objection, I shall briefly describe the outcome of Colin and Maria Susan Nadolski's unfortunate encounter.

At this point, Colin says Maria Susan arched her neck and pointed at it, er, pointedly. She may as well have shaken a baby under the nose of a werewolf.

What, '*ew*?' Please, Your Honor, I thought the audiences at these proceedings were supposed to remain silent during testimony?

Anyway, Colin states that his fangs descended of their own accord, not out of any intended malice. After all, Your Honor, could you stop yourself from salivating at an offering of flawlessly-seared filet mignon?

The poor, flustered boy appropriately and thoughtfully warned, "If you don't get out of here, now, you're never going to leave."

And would you like to know Maria Susan Nadolski's response to Colin's last, desperate stab at restraint? To coo, "I never want to leave. I will stay with you eternally, my beloved. I understand you."

I rest my case, er, initial testimony.

What? No, that's all that is relevant, from what my *filius sanguis* told me.

No, I did not leave out the part where Colin *pounced upon and devoured* her, Mr. Quinton. Really, Your Honor, my opponent is being unnecessarily inflammatory.

Well, *I* would say that she gave clear consent and Colin accepted her terms.

Yes, I know the age of informed consent in New Jersey is eighteen, but there are extenuating circumstances—may I cite the precedent of *Smith v. Dragovic*? I quote, *If the ingestee gave clear consent, it is not the responsibility of the ingestor to confirm his/her true age, or the psychological or emotional state of the ingestee prior to ingestion. Furthermore...*

Yes, Your Honor. Of course you do not need me to—my apologies. I merely meant to clarify for the sake of the court...the rest of the court, not you.

Certainly. Yes, Your Honor.

I have no doubt that her parents are distraught, Mr.

Quinton. This is why my people made such generous donations to the Maria Susan Nadolski Memorial Fund in recent days. If you consider the amount of money her family will save on a graduation party, college, a wedding or two, gifts for grandchildren, why, they will come out quite ahead of the game. In this economy that is . . . what? *What?*

If I survive unto eternity, I'll never understand your priorities.

Mr. Quinton, thank you. That rather snide comment dovetails nicely with the second part of my testimony.

In the past months, my people have been absolutely inundated by doe-eyed proselytizers touting the joys of interspecies unions; knocking on our doors, going on about souls and mating and undying love, and blah, blah, blah. It has gone beyond being a nuisance and straight into harassment.

Your Honor, under the circumstances, my people have exercised marvelous restraint.

What is so funny, Mr. Quinton?

Yes, I do call only five "restraint." If an entire platoon of Happy Meals marched up to your front stoop, poured ketchup over themselves, and laid there awaiting your pleasure, I doubt only five of your kind would fall off their dietary wagons.

The other two females were eighteen and twenty-one, Your Honor.

Yes, again, clear consent was offered on multiple occasions, rather publicly, before their terms were accepted. I have depositions right here, along with copies of their birth certificates from City Hall. There you go.

The males? Well, one claimed to be twenty-one,

but was clearly quite a bit older. I mean, we aren't always great judges of the actual ages of your kind—to be honest, Your Honor, you all look rather alike in that regard. But, come on, this one had gray at his temples, his hairline had retreated to the thirty-eighth parallel, and his eyes had more crow's lines around them than a cornfield. Heh. Heh-heh.

No, Your Honor. None of this is a laughing matter. Quite right.

Yes, Mr. Quinton, the fourth boy is with us now. In fact, he's here today. Casanove, would you please stand up so the judge can see you?

Handsome, isn't he?

Yes, Your Honor, Vladimir thought so, too.

He is Casanove by choice, Mr. Quinton. I am aware he was born Shlomo Berkowitz.

Your Honor, is it a crime now for one to change one's name? I sincerely doubt that Casanove is the first Shlomo Berkowitz to...

Yes, Your Honor. He has filed for a legal name change. We have great respect for the laws of this land.

There is no need to smirk, Mr. Quinton.

Why Casanove and not the others, Your Honor? Well, I can only repeat what my children told me, but—and this is a bit awkward—the others were simply not of great interest to my offspring beyond the immediate. What is that saying—*why marry the cow if you can get the milk for free?* Well, just substitute blood for milk, and...

How is that offensive?

My apologies, Your Honor.

Anyway, Vladimir and Casanove developed a relationship, Your Honor. Yes, Casanove may have initially been motivated by that damnable *Night Delight* film, but they quickly moved beyond that silliness. Casanove actually courted Vladimir, brought him flowers, invited him out dancing, and really got to know Vladimir-the-person, rather than the mere romanticized avatar. Just look at them, Your Honor. Their bond is palpable.

Yes, Mr. Quinton, the parents again. What is this *Kaddish*? I'm not familiar with the term.

Oh. Technically, they are not wrong; he *is* dead by your definition.

Well, I don't really see how compensation is owed, as no actual funeral expenses were incurred.

Very well, Mr. Quinton. I will meet with Mr. Berkowitz personally once this hearing is ended . . . although dowries should traditionally be paid by the *bride's* family to the *groom's*.

Ah, yes, Your Honor. The last disappearance.

Diana Thornheart called herself a huntress.

Yes, Your Honor, her terminology, not ours. We actually do have a term for those who pursue us, the ones who like to call themselves slayers or hunters or inquisitors, what have you.

We call them "fair game," Mr. Quinton.

In any case, the last bit of unpleasantness involved Diana Thornheart and myself.

She first approached me as I left work.

I am a marketing manager with AT&T.

Yes, I am lucky to still be employed in this economy, Mr. Quinton. It also doesn't hurt that I bring a couple of centuries of work experience to the table.

Anyway, it was well before nightfall, and so a fairly safe time of day for an interspecies chat. I will refer to my official statement, if it pleases the court?

❖   ❖   ❖

"Excuse me, Lord Dravyn," said Diana. "Do you have a minute?"

I paused. "I suppose. You have me at a disadvantage, Miss...?"

"Thornheart." She looked at me with hard, cold eyes. "Diana Thornheart." A dramatic pause, as she obviously expected me to recognize her name and react.

I searched my memory but found no recollection of her. "Are you the SEO project manager? Because I'll tell you what I told Joe, we need that database completed before..."

"I don't work here!" Her dark brown eyes narrowed. "Fine, if you want to play, we'll play."

I shook my head, puzzled by her hostility. "Is there a problem?"

"Hm. Is there. Let's see." She held up her left hand and folded down one finger. "One, Maria Susan Nadolski." Another finger went down. "Gina Perelli." Another finger bent. "John Wayne Earl."

"Are you some sort of police officer, Miss Thornheart?" I asked.

She grabbed the front of my shirt. Rumpled the silk tie I'd recently gotten back from the dry cleaners. "It's Ms. Thornheart," she hissed in my face, "and I am much worse news to you than the police, Lord Dravyn."

"Actually, I just go by Fred..."

"Don't waste your vampiric charms on me," she snarled. "I'm immune."

"Is vampiric even a word...?"

"Listen!" She gave me another shake. A button popped off my shirt. "I know what you and your dirty little coven along Wyckoff Drive have been up to. It ends tonight. Do you understand me, Lord Dravyn?"

Now, Your Honor, at this point I knew I was dealing with a madwoman. And a poorly informed one at that. I mean, really, who doesn't know that "covens" are for witches, just as "packs" are for werewolves? We are organized much more logically, according to bloodlines.

Plus, she was rumpling the Brooks Brothers collar of the progenitor of the local bloodline. I ask the court, is that the act of a sane person? I think not. Anyway, to continue...

I plucked her hands from my shirt. She snatched them away, reached behind her, and thrust her hand down the back of her over-tight black leather pants. I wondered if she might have something wedged uncomfortably in her nether regions. As it turned out, she did.

After another moment or two of fumbling, she withdrew a slender piece of wood, sharpened to a fine point.

Now, Your Honor, if someone accosted you in the parking lot and then drew a deadly weapon, what would your response have been? Well, mine was quite measured and restrained, given the circumstances.

"There is no need to threaten me, Ms. Thornheart," I said. "I assure you, I have grounded those responsible for violating the Jersey Accords. They won't be dug up again for five years, minimum. Except for Vladimir, of course, but that situation is entirely different."

"You are the master of the local coven," she blithered. "Therefore, you are to be held responsible for their actions. You may not have heard of me, personally—though I doubt it—but you certainly know my make."

"Ford or Toyota?" I hoped a small, well-timed joke might lighten the mood. It did not.

She twirled the stake. It wobbled and nearly fell to the ground. She caught it with her other hand and frowned at it for embarrassing her. "I am a huntress of the night." She said it as though it meant something.

"Oh-kay." I backed away toward the safety of my Prius.

She followed me to my car. I frantically jabbed the automatic entry button on the door until the locks disengaged. "Ah, so you are familiar with hunters, aren't you?" She gave me a half-grin. "Then you know that I will not allow you to hurt another innocent human."

"If you want your innocent humans to stay safe, I suggest you tell the mayor to enforce the curfew for your young people," I said. "Better yet, how about you tell parents to keep their children from scarfing down pap like *Night Delight*? How's that for a novel solution? Parents actually taking responsibility for the viewing habits of the fruit of their loins?"

By this time, I had tossed my laptop case into the back of my car and slid into the driver's seat. Escape was nigh.

She thrust her stake between my knees.

"Hey!" I said.

"Remember my warning, Lord Dravyn. I know where you live." She hesitated. "Reside. Whatever. Mark my words, if one more young person disappears, I will visit you there."

"Lovely. I'll have tea on. Now, if you would kindly extricate your pointy stick from my bucket seat?"

She looked at me quite oddly. Licked her upper lip. Then she did something completely inappropriate.

She bent her head awkwardly, grabbed my chin with her free hand, and kissed me. Hard. On the lips.

Mr. Quinton, object as much as you like. That is what happened and how it happened.

I agree it doesn't make any sense. But sense had little to do with Diana Thornheart that day, nor she with it.

If I may continue?

I folded my lips into my mouth, in a vain attempt to escape her kiss. Finally, she let go and pulled at her stake. Unfortunately, what I am sure she intended to be a dramatic exit was foiled by the stake becoming tangled in a spring in my seat, so she couldn't pull it free. She jerked and twisted, but it remained stuck between my thighs.

"Allow me," I snapped. I reached down and plucked the stake free. It left a ragged hole in the material. I handed the stake to her and gave her a light tap that pushed her out of my car and a few stumbling feet away.

She waggled the stake at me as I slammed my door and pressed the ignition. "This changes nothing!" she called.

"Might I suggest professional help?" I said. Then I drove home.

I have the bill for the cost of repairing my car seat here, Your Honor.

Move on to that night? Of course.

It was after Shlomo . . . Casanove, apologies, dear boy. It was after Casanove's blood conversion. We held the usual "Welcome to the Bloodline" celebration at

The Palace—it's an Indian temple, but the Patel family rents it out quite reasonably—and I was strolling home around three A.M.

Without warning, someone dropped out of a tree behind me. I heard a brief scream and a *whoomph* of impact as someone belly-flopped onto the Tepes's lawn, rolled a couple of times, and fetched up at my feet.

Before I could determine more than that it was a female stuffed into black leather, she grabbed my ankles and reared back with her full weight. I landed on my knees and hands, scraping them rather nastily.

I twisted around and found myself nose-to-nose once again with Diana Thornheart. "Are you mad?" I demanded. "What do you think you're doing, launching yourself out of stately oaks at innocent passersby!"

"I warned you, Lord Dravyn." She staggered to her feet, loomed over me. "Shlomo Berkowitz has been missing for three days. He, and the others, shall be avenged."

This visit, she brandished both her silly little stake and a short sword.

Yes, a sword, I kid you not.

I don't know, Mr. Quinton. I assume she picked it up at one of those medieval shops in New Hope, or some such place. If I may go on?

She was holding the sword wrong. That got me to thinking.

"Listen, Ms. Thornheart—Diana." I held out my hands, fingers splayed wide, and sprang to my feet. "There is no need for unpleasantness. The young man you seek has merely converted, and I assure you, one hundred percent by choice. And, as I told you, my *progenies sanguis*—er, blood children, have been firmly admonished against accepting any more gifts, no matter how willing or eager. Why, they've turned away at least seven more little *Night Delight* fanatics in the last week alone."

"Not good enough." She waved the sword about and I winced as she nearly cut her own throat. "The only way to keep our children safe is to remove the head of the snake, and that would be you, my lord."

I took a step back. "Please. Diana—may I call you Diana? I appreciate your concerns, but this is not the way to go about it. There are laws that all of us must observe. I'm scheduled to appear in court next month to answer for the errors of my people. By the same token, you can't just sweep into our neighborhood and sling threats and pointy objects about willy-nilly." I studied her carefully. "I do like your outfit, though."

She adopted what I think was supposed to be a martial arts stance of some sort. At the same time, she blushed and the corners of her lips twitched. "You and I are going to waltz tonight, my lord," she said, but her tone was less hard-edged than before. "For one of us, it will be his *Swan Lake*."

I cringed again. "I think you mean 'swan song.' Who is writing your dialogue?"

She tilted her head to one side. "What do you mean?"

"Diana, please." I folded my arms. "I confess I am not terribly current on pop pseudo-vampire culture, but allow me to take a wild guess.

"There is a character that hunts my kind. She's a loner, fated to fight the minions of darkness, yet at the same time, she is tempted by the seductive appeal of the danger they represent. And then she battles the king of their kind, but surprise! He saves her life from even worse predators and she sees him in a whole new light. They fight and flirt and are drawn together and torn apart until the stirring climax when their attraction can no longer be denied and, against all odds and reason and logic, they come together in a union that is at last blessed by both their peoples as pure and inevitable and fated to be. Oh, and along the way, some relative of hers is killed, he is injured, and she nurses him back to health, yadda-yadda."

No, I don't ever run out of breath, Mr. Quinton. Quite sensitive of you to comment, considering you know full well *I don't breathe.*

Anyway.

Diana just stared at me. Finally, she said, "I don't watch movies." She let her arms drop limply to her sides, stake and sword dangling. "I don't even own a television."

I cocked an eyebrow at her.

She let out a puff of resignation. "So you've read *The Night Hunters* series?" I looked at her blankly. "By Sherri A.L. Binghead?" I shook my head. "Wow. Well, it kind of goes like that. Yeah." She straightened her shoulders and stared into my eyes. A little of her former fierceness returned. "They inspired me to the defense of my kind against predators like you."

"Wonderful." I mock-applauded. "You are not a teenager, Diana. If you were, such fanciful 'inspiration' could be written off to youth and foolishness. You are close to the middle of your life. That only leaves a few possibilities for your behavior." I held up my hand, fingers folded down. I raised one. "Insanity." I raised another. "Stupidity." One more. "Suicidal tendencies."

She closed her eyes. When she opened them again, they shone in the moonlight with unshed tears. Her voice thin, low, she said, "Is this the part where you rip out my throat, then have a hearty laugh over the remains of the dopey chick who pretended to be something more than she was?"

I sighed and brushed a leaf out of her hair. She shivered at my touch, but didn't try to slash or puncture me in any way.

"Diana," I said, "you are a lovely example of your kind. Whatever delusion in which you've been indulging, it isn't too late to leave it behind and live a normal life. Find yourself a mate, produce some chubby pups, buy a nice ranch off Stelton Road—prices are way down right now."

She grimaced. "Been there. Done that." She held up her left hand, showed me the tan line where a wedding band used to be. "It didn't work out well."

"Oh." I was out of helpful suggestions, so I offered the only comfort I could. "I'm not going to eat you."

She gave me a wry smile. "That's very understanding of you."

"Would you like that cup of tea I offered?" I pointed up the street to my house.

"Really?"

"Why not?" I shrugged. "Perhaps you and I can have a talk like two sensible representatives of our respective peoples, figure out a way to solve both our problems without resorting to summary execution." I nodded at her weapons.

She sighed. Nodded. "Maybe we can, Lord Dravyn."

"Call me Frederic," I said.

❖   ❖   ❖

What? No, that is all that is relevant, Your Honor. We went back to my house, had a lovely chat over a pot of green tea—well, she had tea, I had lamb's blood.

Again with the *ew*-ing?

Your Honor, Mr. Quinton. Neighbors. Fellow citizens, I submit to you that this is the problem in a nutshell. You only know us by reputation, not by our *selves*. We exist in the same city, work at the same businesses, walk the same streets, yet our interactions go no deeper than passing acquaintanceship. Everything you think you know about my kind comes from storybooks, television programs, and goofy movies. You don't know *us*.

Yes, Mr. Quinton. Your point is well taken. We only know you as walking sources of nourishment—from the *past*; don't get hysterical, people! Other than those who offer themselves up, all that is ancient history.

We can do better, all of us.

Diana Thornheart is quite well, Your Honor. In fact, she should be here by...ah. Diana? Thank you for coming.

As you can plainly see, she is unchanged. Her heart still pumps, her lungs yet breathe. You'll find nary a fang-mark on her creamy white skin.

No, Mr. Quinton, we are not together, not in the crass sense you imply, anyway. She and I *are* partners of a sort, though. We are in the process of forming a joint neighborhood watch.

You see, Diana has spent the last three weeks in an immersion program, Your Honor. She has lived in three different homes owned by all ages of my kind—ancient, recent, middle-lived—and from them learned about our history, our culture, our habits.

She has become a friend, not to our kind, but to the individuals who have hosted her. She knows us as Serena and Vladimir, Oscar and Rowan. And yes, as Frederic, *pater sanguis* of the Piscataway bloodline and Marketing Manager at AT&T.

And she and I have a proposition for you. An exchange program, if you will, one in which a few of your people are hosted by us while a few of ours spend time with you.

No, Your Honor, age does not matter. I totally understand the unwillingness to send your young ones to us for an extended visit. However, I give you my word there will be no more unfortunate misunderstandings of the nature that took Maria Susan and the others. By the same token, I expect no more groupies or hunters to wander over uninvited to Wyckoff Drive.

So, can we put all this unpleasantness behind us, Your Honor? Mr. Quinton?

Can't we all just get along?

Fruit of the Vein

Lucienne Diver

"Relax, Margo, no one's going to know you're drinking O-Neg and not cabernet or merlot or whatever."

I tried not to roll my eyes at my best gal pal. I'd been doing it way too much lately, and was at risk of becoming world-weary and cynical. Two hundred-plus years of life will do that to a girl. But you're only as young as you feel. Today I didn't feel much above a century. Tops.

"That's not what's got me in a tizzy—" I answered.

"You keep saying things like 'tizzy' and *that's* going to give you away."

"Can I finish a sentence?"

"Who's stopping you?"

This time the eye roll just got away from me.

"It's two things. One, this whirlwind courtship of Jason's. No one has even met this new girl. And whatever happened to the last one? Gwen, I think her name was. She seemed...nice."

"Since when are you so invested in Jason's love

life? Anyway, that's the whole point of an engagement party, so everyone can get to know each other."

"Really? I thought it was just an excuse to wring gifts out of your coworkers."

Lori sighed like *she* was the elder statesman. "Oh, like this is a new concept? What did they call it in your day? A betrothal feast? A handfasting?"

"Bite me," I answered.

"Sorry, dear, I believe that's a little more your field." Her gaze suddenly slid past me and locked on something or someone else. I could hear her heartbeat rev. "Now me, I'd like a taste of *that* vintage, wouldn't you?"

I followed her gaze and froze, glass halfway to my lips. *Oh no, he didn't.*

Jason and Tanya, who had yet to make their appearance, were having their party at a vineyard way out on the North Fork of Long Island, where even New York City's extensive transit system couldn't reach. I'd had to carpool with Lori to get here. There was no way dipshit...uh, *Daniel*, was just here moonlighting as a sommelier because his private investigation business was having a slow month. Which meant that either he was stalking me or he was here on a case. Since he'd virtually dropped out of contact after our fifth date, I was betting on the latter.

"Margo," Lori said, voice all concern. "Earth to Margo. You look like you've seen a ghost."

"Not yet," I answered, forcing myself to snap out of it. "But he may be soon," I added under my breath.

She heard me anyway. "Ooh," she cooed, "you have a history with handsome? I want to know all the gory details. Start with the important stuff—measurements, identifying characteristics..."

Lori was an assistant medical examiner, but get her into a cocktail dress and you'd never know it. Well, almost never.

"Give me a minute," I told her. I made it a statement, because if it sounded like a suggestion, Lori took it that way and did whatever the hell she wanted to in the first place.

"Okay, but don't think I'm going to forget this."

Hell no. Mind like a steel trap, that was our Lori.

I took my drink with me because I didn't dare freak out the plebs by setting it down on a passing tray. It would be just my luck someone would pluck it up to examine the color and talk about its legs. The tasting would be a rude awakening. I almost reconsidered for the entertainment value alone.

I stood just behind Daniel as he offered the choice of a riesling or a chard to two young ladies who were almost wearing their dresses. One was missing a sleeve and looked about to topple out of that side of her blindingly white gown, and the other's red dress had a demure Mandarin collar and a correspondingly high hemline to make up for it. In fact, her backside was very nearly the main attraction. I couldn't imagine how she could bend over, let alone sit.

They had to be from the bride-to-be's side, because Jason, Lori, and I all worked together—Lori slabbed 'em, Jason nabbed 'em, and I blabbed 'em—and I would have recognized the women if they were with major crimes or anyone related to it. Okay, so *blabbed 'em* was probably pushing the rhyme a little far. Probably I shouldn't try to be clever. I should leave that to the criminals I profiled. Being an inhuman lie detector had its perks. The vampire super-acuity let me hear hearts race and breath speed up. I could smell sour sweat and, most useful of all, stare unnervingly without blinking. The interview value of a good stare was not to be underestimated. It was the perps who, like me, didn't blink or sweat that were the most truly dangerous.

I cleared my throat, loudly, and Daniel spun around, ready to offer me some fruit of the vine when he saw that it was me. The man was good. He didn't betray by so much as an eye blink that he knew me from Adam. Or Eve.

"Madame," he said, turning to me with one of those professionally cheerful yet distancing smiles. "May I offer you a semi-dry riesling or a wonderful Long Island chardonnay with hints of vanilla and pear?"

He might have been offering white, but I was seeing red.

"Madame? Not mademoiselle or señorita or Fraulein?" I asked, my voice rising unintentionally.

The two young ladies moved off, wisely sensing that elsewhere was the best place to be.

More quietly, I asked, "What the hell are you doing here?"

"It's *madame* because you're spoken for," he said, his smile heating considerably, "and I'm on a case."

"Big words for a guy who vanished after a little heavy necking. I've moved on. And what case?"

"Moved on? Is he here?" he asked, looking around with a glint in his eye that said he already knew the answer. Damn him. It was that piratical look in his impossibly blue eyes that had gotten to me to begin with. "I'd like to meet him."

"No, you wouldn't. *What case?*"

"Serial killer. Looks like anyway. Men all dying in the ... er ... saddle, if you know what I mean. Bodies left slack, denuded. Five so far. None of their *dates* sticking around for the police or the EMTs."

"Why haven't I heard about this? Major case would be involved if there were any evidence of foul play."

"That's the thing. It's mostly been ruled natural causes. Heart attack. Friends describe each of the men's partners differently. There's been no reason for the police to connect the dots."

"Then how did you get involved? How do you know there's a connection? And what the hell does any of that have to do with you disappearing off the face of the earth and turning up here?"

A man and a woman dressed way more conservatively than Daniel's last two takers came up and offered their glasses for a refill, each choosing the chardonnay, the most popular wine in the world, though I'd much preferred the riesling when I'd been able to enjoy it. Now I only got the occasional taste off someone else's lips, which made me think of *Daniel's* lips, which made me want to go right back to the party and forget about cases and killers for the night. Find a flirtation. Maybe tap into some fresh fruit of the vein topped off with a well aged varietal.

Unfortunately, curiosity had always been my downfall. The couple moved on, and Daniel answered. "The sister of one of the men—she works in an emergency room. She'd seen one of the other victims come in and thought that maybe her brother's death wasn't just a freak thing."

"She wanted someone to blame for his death," I said.

"Maybe, but both men had been young, healthy—
one a runner, the other a lifter. Sex shouldn't have
been too strenuous for either of them. When I dug
around, there were others, same pattern. The weight
lifter you could maybe chock up to steroids, but the
others...There was too little cause, too much coin-
cidence to be natural."

Damn, this was way more interesting than small
talk with strangers.

"And you're *here tonight* because?" I asked.

He looked left and right to be sure no one was
terribly close by. "Because the bride-to-be is one of
my prime suspects."

"She knew all the men?"

"At least one. And she didn't exist beyond three
months ago."

A gaggle of folks came up to Daniel right then,
leaving me standing apart, slightly shell-shocked.

Surely, Jason would have checked out his fiancée, I
thought. But I didn't think it with confidence. When
I'd been young and stupid, going off with the rake
my society sponsor had warned me about, I hadn't
considered my reputation. I surely hadn't considered
that I might wind up allergic to sunlight and with a
sudden taste for blood. Not that I was complaining.
The marquis and I had had a good run. We kept in
touch. I *could* have had a date to the party if I'd
wanted one. If the marquis wasn't an entire continent
away. But we'd barely seen each other in almost a
century. That ship had sailed, and I'd had plenty of
time to get zen about men and going about in public
without an escort.

Speak of the devil. Jason, the man of the hour,

made his way toward us with the most absurdly beautiful woman I'd ever seen in tow. She had a mass of shampoo-commercial-perfect hair—deep chestnut mostly, but the party lights strung up along the porch railing and climbing like vines along the decorative trellises sparked glints of red and gold as well. Combined with an upturned nose, green cat's eyes, and Julia Roberts's full lips, she was stunning. And to top it all off, she had class. Her model-thin body was encased in a simple pale green sheath that did justice to her eyes and clung in all the right places and none of the wrong ones. If I'd been another kind of woman, I might have hated her on sight.

If I'd been a sensitive, I might have been able to tell just by her proximity whether she was a Legendary, but contrary to Hollywood convention, I wouldn't even know another *vamp* on sight if it weren't for the lack of heartbeat. There was no tingle or zing on meeting. There was, however, the possibility of sensing an old soul. It was all in the eyes—unless they were being lit from within by incandescent joy. Bliss was the great leveler.

Daniel leaned in to me. "You've got her beat, hands down." His breath was hot and heavenly on my ear.

I tried to quash my smile. "Liar," I said, out of the corner of my mouth.

And then Jason and Tanya were upon us, smiling like they'd won the lottery. That inner light in Tanya's eyes was searing, and the megawatt smile Jason was sporting could power all of Long Island for a week. For that alone, I hoped Tanya was on the up and up.

Their joy was almost infectious, and I had no problem smiling back as Jason made the introduction.

Tanya had a heartbeat. That much I could tell. It was pounding, but that could be chalked up to excitement. And she was radiating heat. I could practically bask in the glow. Jason couldn't seem to keep his hands off her—around her waist when she was by his side, trailing down her back as she leaned in to kiss me on both cheeks in the European way, though her voice, when she spoke, was unaccented.

"Margo, I've heard so much about you!" Tanya gushed. "Jason says you're just amazing."

There was no jealousy at all in her voice, and I didn't know quite how to respond. I was much better equipped to handle deception than sincerity. It required so much less tact.

"And he told me—okay, I have to be honest—next to nothing." I smiled to ease the sting. "How did you two meet? What do you do? How on earth do you get tall, blond, and sardonic here to smile?"

"Start at the beginning, go on until the end, and then stop?" she asked disingenuously.

I gave a short laugh. "Exactly."

Tanya turned to Jason, sliding both palms up his chest to his shoulders. "Darling, you know, we really should make a speech. Otherwise, we're going to be answering these questions all night."

Jason circled her waist with his hands and actually nuzzled her tiny nose with his more prominent one. It was a good thing he was able to meet her more than halfway. Otherwise, he'd have been mashing her face.

Darling? Nose nuzzling? Daniel and I exchanged a look. I wasn't sure it was suspicious, but it was borderline nauseating.

"Yes, dear," he answered, kissing the tip of her nose.

"Chat more later?" Tanya asked as she pulled him away to find a soap box or something for their speech.

"Absolutely." I smiled, trying to match her perk for perk. "We haven't actually chatted at all," I said to myself when she was gone.

Daniel looked about to say something when a scream from behind us split the night. We both raced for the stairs back up to the tasting room, dropping our blood and wine on the first table we passed.

Inside, a crowd had gathered. When I pushed to the front, bulling through with a shout out to my police credentials, I saw one of the underdressed debs—the one in red—collapsed on the floor, sobbing hysterically. Her friend, standing nearby, was a little better off.

"—in the coat room. Like... like a mummy. All drained and dry and, like, *dead*."

"Margo," Lori called me from a door near the entrance to the tasting room, off to the left of the crowd, "you're going to want to see this."

I excused myself from the hysterical girls and followed Lori's beckoning hand to the coat room, which was only barely used tonight. You never quite knew about New York in mid-September, but the night was as unseasonably warm as the day had been. There weren't many who'd taken advantage of the unchecked cloak room to leave behind shawls and light jackets just as easily hung on the backs of chairs, but whoever'd left the body hadn't been counting on the camouflage of coats. The man-mummy had been tucked under the counter, in a place usually reserved for bags and luggage.

The body faced us now, parchment skin peeled back from the teeth in a death's head grin.

"You move him?" I asked Lori.

"Not me. Not before crime scene photos and techs. One of the girls shook him, thinking he was just some guy who'd had too much to drink and was sleeping it off. She was going to call him a cab."

"I'm here," Jason said, peering into the room. "I've already called it in to the locals. Chaney and Alvarez are doing crowd control. What've we got?"

Lori and I exchanged a look and stepped aside for him.

"Damn," he said. "Damn, damn, damn," he added, closing the cloak room door behind him to block out any looky-loos. "That's what I get for being efficient."

"Come again?" I asked, looking to Lori to see if she had any idea what he was talking about.

She looked as baffled as I felt, and when I swung my gaze back to Jason, it wasn't to the hardened detective that I expected to see, the down-to-business, no-nonsense face he usually showed the world. It was the fiancé whose special day had just been trashed. There was about him a sense of . . . not quite panic or desperation, but something close to them.

"Look," he said, spearing first my gaze and then Lori's, "the local cops are already on the way. We have to solve this before they get here."

His heart was beating a million miles a minute, his brow was furrowed, and his jaw fully involved, tense. He was sending out stress vibes on all frequencies.

"Why?" I asked warily.

He focused on me then. "Because of Tanya. She's . . . not entirely human. Her identity will never hold up to a full scale investigation."

He *knew*. He knew and was ready to marry her. To *cover* for her. Sure, he knew about me. Most on the force did. Once "fiction" made us mainstream, there was no real reason for us vamps to stay hidden, but just like with witches and psychics, who'd been out in the open a lot longer, most people failed to really believe unless they'd had direct contact. It was amazing how much people could rationalize away if they wanted to. Which made me wonder what exactly Tanya was running from with her new identity. If she was a Legendary, it might only be the immortal problem of having to become someone new every few decades to explain our lack of aging, which some chose to do rather than live openly, exposing themselves to both skeptics and zealots, but it could also be something a lot more sinister.

"Jason, if she's a *killer*—" Lori started, her voice falling on the last word, like she couldn't believe she was saying it.

"Not a murderer," he said in disgust. "A succubus. It's a completely different thing."

We both stared at him in shock.

"Jason," I said, calmly, evenly, so as not to spook him, "a succubus drains their victims . . . just like this guy's been drained. It's what they do."

"She. Didn't. Do. It," he nearly spat, fists rising before he stopped himself, forced them down again. "She couldn't have. She hasn't left my side."

"Not even to use the powder room?" I asked.

"Not even," he agreed.

I gave him my unblinking stare, and he gave it right back to me. I could tell he believed what he was saying, but succubae were rumored to be able to change their forms to become the sexual ideal of each of their victims. If it was true, Tanya could easily have been any of the women spotted with Daniel's previous victims. For all I knew, she could even cloud men's minds. Succubae had never really been in my social circle or special field of study.

"I think there's someone you need to talk to," I told him, stepping for the door, forcing him to decide whether to give way or stand between me and Tanya... and possibly the truth. He moved.

"Fine. Lori, will you stay and guard the body? Do a preliminary examination?"

She looked hard at Jason and even harder at me, knowing she was missing something. Not thrilled to be left out. "As best I can without touching anything," she agreed.

Jason gave a terse nod and stepped out of the room with me.

A crowd instantly formed around us, a babble of questions—*Who is it? What happened? Did someone die?*

I caught sight of some white knight slipping away with the shaken girls, heading toward the door, and had to nip that in the bud.

"Excuse me," I called, loudly enough to be heard over the mob, who all fell silent around us to look where I was looking. "The police may have questions. No one should leave until they arrive."

That started a whole new flurry of questions at top volume. Red-dress's face turned, if possible, even paler than it had when she'd discovered the body, but she didn't protest as Detective Chaney herded her back to the others.

"Please, if you'll all have a seat outside," Jason added, "I'm sure the wine stewards would be glad to offer everyone a good, stiff drink."

Tanya was suddenly plastered to Jason's side, white showing all around her eyes. "What is it?" she asked.

I looked for Daniel and with a jerk of my head indicated a small office behind the tasting bar, which was probably locked. At least for now.

"Maybe we should talk in here," I said, leading the way.

Sure enough, the knob of the office door only made a quarter-turn before sticking tight. I gave it a good, sharp twist and suddenly it was no longer a problem.

Jason gave me a hard look, the cop in him coming out at last. Sure, assumed identities were fine, but just try a little breaking and entering...

"What's going on?" Tanya demanded, as soon as we had the door shut.

"You tell us," Daniel said, dropping his sommelier smile and almost immediately seeming to take on a rougher edge.

"Who is this guy?" Jason asked, fists clenching again until Tanya turned Bambi-sized eyes on him.

"I don't understand," she said, voice raising a near octave. "Someone's dead? What does that have to do with me?"

Jason caught her hands in his and looked deeply into Tanya's eyes. "He's been sucked dry."

Impossibly, her eyes widened. "But who? Who's been sucked dry and why—?" She gasped. "They know?" She turned to Daniel and me, raking us with her guileless green eyes. "But I don't need to. You don't understand. I'm a—"

"Therapist," Jason cut in, "dealing with sexual dysfunction. She gets everything she needs from her job. There's no reason she'd kill, especially not here, now."

Tanya looked at him accusingly, and I was betting Jason was speaking in code for sex therapist, someone who helped out with intimacy and other issues by making direct contact with her clients. It was perfectly legitimate, licensed, in some cases even covered by insurance. I had no idea he was such a prude. Still, he was a prude who made sense. There was no percentage in her having done the deed.

"Think about it," Jason said, that desperation back in his voice. "Do the profile. Who would have the most to gain by murdering the man? And why leave him where he was sure to be found? He would have been easy enough to hide. There are rows and rows of vines, plenty of places to bury a body."

I looked at Daniel. "It's your tale. Jason, this is Daniel Chase, PI. Daniel, this is Detective Jason Prentiss, but you knew that. Talk amongst yourselves."

Because I needed to think. I looked away from Tanya's Tinkerbell eyes, imploring me to believe her, rescue her. She'd be disappointed to find out just how much the damsel in distress thing played on my nerves.

First, we had to find out who the victim was. If he was an ex-boyfriend of Tanya's, bent on disrupting the festivities . . . well, that would make it all amazingly easy. Point the finger right at Tanya. Though it wouldn't explain the rash of other dead guys. If I assumed for a second that Jason was right and that she was innocent, where did that leave us? With a whole party full of suspects. This was clearly the work of a succubus . . . or maybe an incubus, their male counterpart. There was no reason to be discriminatory. And since they could change their appearances . . . it could be anybody. Oh joy, oh rapture.

"Jason, did you recognize the victim?" I asked when Daniel wound down, leaving the two lovebirds stunned.

"No," he said. "No, I don't think so."

"Okay, then, next step. You dig up a guest list while I take Tanya for a peek. Unless Lori has taken to picking pockets while we were gone."

"I don't have a master list here," he answered. "It's not like we were checking people at the door."

"Wonderful."

Tanya clung to his arm all the way to the cloak room, where Jason gave a knock with his knuckles to alert Lori we were coming in. Tanya barely glanced into the room when she jerked back into the hallway and her eyes filled with tears.

"It's one of my patients," she said, her voice breaking. "Martin Gorensky. I don't know how he got here."

It was easier to fake vocal cues than body language. She might have had eons to perfect the art, for all I knew, but I didn't see anything that made a liar out of her.

"Someone's framing you then?" I asked, only half as skeptical as I had been. "Who? Do you have any enemies? Disgruntled clients? Ex-boyfriends? Girlfriends?"

She was shaking her head vehemently. "No one that I can think of."

"What about you?" I asked, turning on Jason. "Anyone you've locked up out on bail or gunning for you? Pissed off ex-girlfriends? It seems like—" I shot Tanya a look. "—only last week you were going out with Gwen—"

I'd been going to ask how she'd taken the break up when the lady in white started as Alverez shuffled her and her friend out into the courtyard. I'd seen it out of the corner of my eye, and when I looked at her more fully, she didn't look back. She was, in fact, very pointedly keeping her gaze straight ahead, but I wasn't buying it.

She didn't look like Gwen. She was at least three inches shorter and a cup-size larger if the strain on her dress was any indication. I'd only met Gwen a couple of times. She was no Tanya, but... now that I thought about it, they had certain physical traits in common, like those rare green eyes. But something didn't add up. If succubae took on the look of a man's physical ideal, and Jason had been unlucky enough to fall for *two* of them, wouldn't they have been identical?

"You!" I called to the woman in white. "I'd like a word."

She *bolted.*

If she'd come back this way—toward the exit and the parking lot, Chaney or Alvarez could have nabbed her, but she ran toward the veranda off the tasting room, toward all the other guests.

Cursing, I kicked off my heels and took off after her. So much for blending. Guests gasped as I rushed past them, little more than a blur and a breeze. I caught the white wench's arm just as she hurdled a man with his leg propped on the chair from another table.

We went down in a puppy pile, and I heard something snap. Bone—I knew the sound. Probably the leg.

The man howled, and the white wench fought like a cornered cat, but finally she subsided into sobs.

The tears burned like acid. Or maybe I was just being dramatic. I pulled back, still with a hold on her arm to ease our weight off the downed man, who might have had a shiner starting to go with his busted leg. And a split lip on top of that.

"That *bitch*," she spat. "*Cheater*. Cheater!" she called, louder.

"Who?" I asked, though I had a pretty good idea.

People were pressing in all around us now, some helping the man and others rubbernecking. Apparently, there was a doctor in the house. But I focused entirely on the lady in grass-stained white. I needed her to confess before someone stole the moment away.

She looked up at me with tear-bright eyes. "You know her as Tanya."

"What about her?" I used a touch of the famous vamp mesmerism to keep her focused on me. Just that and no more. I played it fair and square. Anything else was a slippery slope that lead to vigilantism.

"She *cheated*. It was a competition—to get a man to love us first for our minds. No powers. No shifting. No nothing. She *cheated*."

She fought my hold then, looking around wildly, zeroing in on Jason, who stood just behind and a head above the first row of onlookers. She locked on him like a laser-sight, making him an audience of one. "You have no idea at all. None."

Before us all, she shifted, became Tanya, but as Mattel might make her—exaggerated curves, a miniscule waist, cheekbones that would cut glass. "I could be her. I could be anyone."

"Stop!" Tanya's voice cracked the night like a whip as she stepped forward. "Do you hate to lose that much? That you'd kill a man? Did you plan to frame me? Yes, I *cheated*. The stakes were too high to lose."

She looked back and caught Jason's eye, and I knew I hadn't mistaken the earlier bliss and its uncomfortable purity. "I love him."

There were *aws* from all around, but the three dead-center of the tragedy paid them no attention.

"I saw him first," the white wench spat. "He's mine."

"Over my dead body," Tanya answered.

Gwen or *whoever* lurched out of my grasp while I was distracted by sugar shock. I reached to grab her, but she'd locked on to Tanya with the strength of a kracken and was delivering a kiss just as deadly.

The audience gasped again. One man hooted. Another took a picture with his camera phone of the lip-locked look-alikes in a battle to drain or be drained. To him it just looked like lady love.

I snapped out a mental lash, hitting Gwen's off-switch, sending her nighty-night, and she slumped to the ground, sliding down Tanya's body in a way none of the men ... or even some of the women ... would ever forget.

In the distance, we heard sirens.

I caught Jason's eye over Tanya's shoulder, and he mouthed, "Thank you."

It seemed hours before Gwen, still unconscious, was carted away, all the statements were taken and the crime scene had become a mess of print powder and crime tape. I hoped I'd have the chance to interview her—satisfy my infernal curiosity about the whys and wherefores of her other victims. It could be that Jason's rejection had sent her on a spree or that she was using others to store up mojo to bring him back to her side, but what mattered right then was that Daniel was sitting next to me at one of the abandoned tables, a bottle of late harvest riesling and a single glass in front of him.

"I suddenly seem to have time on my hands again," he said, that glint back in his eyes. "You wouldn't happen to know how I can spend it?"

"You've probably got a report to type, an invoice to mail, another case awaiting your attention. Don't let me keep you," I answered, enjoying the breeze, knowing deep down that he wasn't going anywhere.

"Margo." Daniel took my hand and looked deep into my eyes. I blinked. "I just needed to catch my breath. You're—"

"Amazing? Beautiful? Magnificent?" The marquis had called me all of those things.

"Kind of a hardass," he said with a laugh.

I smiled, thinking that was a far more personal compliment.

"You're never going to cut me any slack. You're not easy to be with, but you're worth it. I've decided I like the challenge."

I was about to refute him when he leaned in and kissed me. Hard.

I finally got a taste of my riesling. And it truly was the nectar of the gods.

Daniel M. Hoyt's short fiction has appeared in several leading magazines and anthologies since his first publication in *Analog*, most recently in *Strip Mauled* (Baen), *Witch Way to the Mall* (Baen), *Something Magic This Way Comes* (DAW), *Transhuman* (Baen), and *Space Pirates* (Flying Pen Press). After tangling with the suburban witches of Costwold Acres (aka Cauldron Acres) in "The FairWitch Project" (*Witch Way to the Mall*), Dan was shocked to find werewolves living in a nearby neighborhood, where this story takes place. (He has no doubt vampires are lurking about in yet another neighborhood!) In his own neighborhood, Dan coerces computer demons to do his bidding and writes short stories, edits anthologies (*Better Off Undead* and *Fate Fantastic*), and works on his second novel while marketing his first. Catch up with him at www.danielmhoyt.com.

Stick or Treat

Daniel M. Hoyt

"Stick or treat!" a half-dozen priests, Van Helsings, and Buffys shouted in unison as I opened the front door. Crisp night air stung my nostrils and I shivered. I saw the dark shapes of the marauders' parents clumped at the end of the walk, their eyes blazing through the shadows, staring at me hungrily.

Ignoring the creepy parents, I screwed up my courage and feigned fear and surprise at seeing the little array of sharpened stakes and shiny crosses brandished at my midsection and thrust the bowl of Halloween candy forward, weakly pleading, "Take what you want, you fiends!"

One misguided little Buffy waved a carrot at me menacingly and eyed my bare forearm with an uncomfortable level of interest before snatching a handful of gummy bloodworms and scampering off, giggling.

I closed the door and nervously turned to my hostess. "Thank you so much, Jan, for having us over tonight. My Billy hasn't made any new friends since you moved out here to Black Forest. Poor thing is so withdrawn these days. It's been hard for him with no friends like your Van and no father figure since—"

I bit off the rest of the sentence. My ex had his place, and it wasn't here, it wasn't now—it wasn't with me in any way. Not anymore.

Jan Pyre-Bat blushed a deep red, in stark contrast to her normally pasty-white complexion. A hungry, vaguely threatening look—like the parents had—flashed in her pale blue eyes, but fled just as quickly. She licked her lips. "I'm glad to have you both, Jenny." She looked toward the living room, crowded to overflowing with miniature decorations—coffins, blood spatters, cobwebs, even a full-size Dracula that hissed dramatically, then calmly stated, "I vant to suck yore *blod!*" every few minutes. Bathed in moonlight through the floor-to-ceiling picture window, our fifth-grade sons helped each other into their costumes.

Billy's Darth Vader costume was simple enough to don, but Van kept tripping on the hem of his floor-length, black leather cape every time he bent over to pick up his officially-licensed Van Helsing crossbow. Billy sighed and snatched up a measure of his friend's cape. Van grabbed the crossbow and beamed. "Ready, Mom!"

Jan's husband, Stan, strode into the front hall. "Ah, blood pancakes for breakfast! Nothing better." He glanced at me nervously. "I'm off to work, Jan. You okay dealing with the kids alone?"

Smiling broadly, revealing pasty-white teeth with razor-sharp canines gleaming in the moonlight, Jan said, "Jenny's here to help me; don't worry."

Glancing at me again, Stan shrugged and turned

to the living room, calling, "Hey, boys! Want a ride to the Aickmans'? Mike said he'll walk you back from there with the Newblood twins." Mr. Pyre-Bat cocked his head quizzically when he saw my son's Darth Vader costume, but he said nothing.

Van squealed. "I hear Mike Aickman's dad, Robert, gives out full-size Snickers! Let's go!" Billy chased him out the door, speculating about the size of their bounties to come. A cat toy skittered toward the door with them. Stan Pyre-Bat punted the toy out of the way and followed, dancing through the next band of costumed little undead hunters rushing up the walk.

After they'd left, I turned to Jan, following her to a La-Z-Boy in the living room. A slightly metallic odor wafted from Dracula as I dropped into the buttery-soft leather recliner. "I'm so sorry about the costume. I didn't realize you were so . . . tightly themed out here."

She laughed and sank into the loveseat opposite me. "It's fine. How could you have known?"

My cheeks on fire, I looked away, embarrassed. "Well, ever since Billy told us you were . . . you know—"

"Vampires," Jan said flatly.

"Yes," I said, forcing myself to raise my eyes to meet Jan's penetrating gaze. "That. Anyway, I've always thought of myself of open-minded, and after that incident out in Costwold Acres—or is it Cauldron Acres now, officially?—when it came out that Black Forest was a big neighborhood of—"

"Vampires?"

"Yes." I'd been meaning to broach the vampire subject for a while, but this was not coming out the way I'd hoped, especially with Jan's ice-blue eyes burning in my mind. I sounded like an idiot. "I promised myself that if I ever met one of them, I wouldn't let my prejudices get the better of me, and—"

"And then you found out that your son's best friend of nearly five years was a vampire?"

"Yes," I said almost in a whisper and tore my gaze from Jan.

"I appreciate the effort, Jenny. Really, I do. I know this is hard for you. But try to understand how hard it was for *us*, living among mortals for so long, hiding our true selves. When we found out about *this* neighborhood—full of *our* kind—well, you can see why we felt we had to move as soon as possible."

I'd been kicking myself for not seeing the signs earlier. Van Pyre-Bat always wore a big, floppy hat to school and Billy complained about his best friend's obsession with getting greased up with sunscreen before every recess. But they got along so well, and Billy really wasn't socially...skilled, so I tried not to find fault in their friendship.

The doorbell's ring split the awkward silence, and we both hopped up to offer treats. On the way to the door, I casually grabbed a cardigan to cover up my bare arms. It was probably best *not* to test what little willpower the grade-school vamps had developed.

"I vant to suck yore *blod!*" Dracula announced as I opened the door.

The usual crowd of parents milled around at the sidewalk, but there were more of them this time, and they looked...hungrier. Glad that the treats were dispensed quickly, I flicked the door closed and we stood at the door, both of us staring away from each other.

After a few moments, Jan spoke first. "There really are a *lot* of Van Helsings, aren't there?"

"There *are!*" I said and twisted my head toward my hostess. "I guess it makes sense. I mean, we dress up as monsters and witches, right? Things that scare us?"

"Ooh," Jan said, crouching slightly and wiggling her fingers in front of her in mock menace, "people with sticks, that's so scary!"

We both burst out laughing and headed back to the comfort of the moonlit living room. I plopped into the recliner. "I'm so sorry if I made you uncomfortable."

"Don't mention it," Jan said, shaking her head, causing her limp black hair to fan around her shoulders. "I'm sure the time-shifted life out here is confusing and uncomfortable for *you*. We sleep all day and work and go to school during the night. For us, this is the time for the early classes. Halloween on a school night still means Van has after-midnight classes."

I nodded. "It seems a little strange to have the entire community structured like that, but I understand, given your ... condition."

"Oh, let's not do *this* again," Jan said, scooting forward to the edge of the loveseat, clearly annoyed. "Vampire. Go ahead and say the word. It won't kill you." Jan paused at my horror-struck expression. "And *I* won't kill you, either!" she said, smirking.

"V-vampire," I whispered, tentatively. I wasn't absolutely sure I believed her.

"Trust me, I know how you're feeling," Jan said. "Stan didn't tell me he was a vampire until I was four months gone with Van. He explained that all of our children would be vamps, but I had to *choose* it if I wanted it."

"You weren't *always* a vampire?"

"Oh, no!" Jan said with a wide grin that exposed

her sharp fangs. "We all marry into it, so to speak. I don't fully understand the biology involved, but basically vampire *women* can't conceive."

"Did you get... um, changed... right after Van was born?"

"No, it was years later. Frankly, I was scared when Stan told me about the vampire thing. I almost left him. Then I realized how difficult it would be to raise a vampire alone without knowing anything about them, so I decided to give Stan the chance to prove himself as a father. In time I came to view it as just another alternate lifestyle. By the time Van was in first grade and I found my first gray hairs, I practically begged Stan to turn me." Jan giggled and settled back in the loveseat.

"And now you're living in a full-blown vampire neighborhood," I summed up. "Quite a change from your childhood, I'd imagine."

Jan grinned again, flashing her pearly sharps. "At least I don't have to hunt for SPF 1600 sunscreen at WalMart anymore!"

A score of vampire-vanquishing mobs later, the hungry, desperate look crept back into Jan's face amidst increasingly more tortured conversations in the living room.

"Does it seem to you," I asked, "that the crowd of parents is getting larger as the night goes on?"

"Perhaps. It's a close-knit community, and you're a stranger here. Word spreads. They probably just want to meet you."

I grimaced, thinking of those hungry, burning gazes. "They sure *look* like they want to... um, you *did* say 'meet'?"

Jan smirked again and stood up. "Feeling like a little lunch?"

"Excuse me?"

"The kids will be home soon, and Van will need to go to school right afterward. I thought I'd make them some lunch. Blood sausage okay with you?"

Blood *what*? I swallowed bile and cleared my throat. "We just had dinner before we came," I lied. "But thanks for the offer."

"Oh, right," Jan called over her shoulder as she pushed open the kitchen door. She paused in the open doorway. "Since we moved to the Forest, I keep forgetting that *mortal* kids go to school during the day." She cocked her head. "Perhaps you'd like to take a stroll through the cemetery after Van goes to class?"

"Cemetery? I don't remember seeing one on the way here."

Smiling, Jan said, "It's out back. Everyone in the Forest has one. They're really just like your gardens— you grow flowers in it, you weed it, you bury your dead hamsters in it—it's just that *our* focus is on the gravestones. I'll show you later." She disappeared into the kitchen.

The doorbell rang.

"I'll get it," I yelled, and ran off to the door, clutching my cardigan close. Bracing myself for the onslaught of kiddie vamp killers, I yanked open the door and shoved the candy bowl without looking up.

"That's not what I'm here for," said a man in a guttural growl.

I looked up into five pairs of adult male eyes glowing in the moonlight. Young, but clearly adult; I figured the pack of them for early twenties. And they all looked famished. My heart seized in my chest and I backed away in terror, trying to breathe. I half expected my life to flash before my eyes, but it didn't. Instead, I saw them lurch toward me in slow motion, like the homeless people at the soup kitchen where I volunteered every Wednesday.

I stepped on the errant cat toy and lost my balance, crashing to the floor. The crack of an end table accompanied my descent, and I found myself hugging the cold marble floor with a bleeding palm.

"Back off, Phil!" Jan screamed over me and tugged on my arm. "She's my *guest*, and you will *not* snack on my guest!"

With her help, I was upright in seconds, a damp dishcloth shoved into my palm. Backing into the living room, I pressed the rag against my wound and hid behind Jan's protective stance.

A short blond man with a misshapen nose and a chin too large for his thin face lunged for Jan's feet. She squeaked and jumped back just as his face hit the floor where I'd fallen.

He licked my spilled blood, moaning.

Jan harrumphed. "Really, Jerry? And you wonder why you can't find a woman who will have you?" She tsk-tsk'd and shook her head, then turned back to me. "I ask you, Jenny, would you have someone with those manners?"

"Um . . . no," I said truthfully.

"*Some* men forget that they can't get away with this behavior *before* they attract a mate." She raised her voice. "What's the old saying, Phil? First comes what?"

Jerry moaned again and licked the last of my blood from the marble.

"'First comes love, then comes marriage,'" Phil mumbled, his head still hanging dejectedly, "'next come babies, and *then* you turn her.'"

"That's right. Did you get that, Jerry?"

Jerry scrambled to his feet and retreated to the doorway. "Yes, ma'am."

"You're done here," Jan said firmly.

All five of them nodded and slipped away amid mumbling apologies.

Closing the door gently, Jan turned to me and slouched against the door.

"That was amazing!"

"Not really," she sighed. "I was their high school health teacher about five years ago. They haven't yet forgotten how to respect me."

I stumbled toward the powder room between the living room and the kitchen. "I need to dress this wound."

"I'm sorry," Jan said quickly, "but around here we don't try to *stop* blood from flowing. We don't have a first-aid kit. You'll just have to hold the rag against it."

Continuing on to the powder room, I nodded. "Let me at least rinse the cloth, then. The cut didn't look too bad; it'll probably stop bleeding in a few minutes."

"While you're doing that, I'll clean up Jerry's drool. Yuck!"

"A big guy tried to *eat* me!" Billy yelled immediately after bursting through Jan's front door. I was still in the powder room, wringing the warm washcloth dry enough to use as a compress.

"Did not!" Van yelled back. "He tried to *suck* you! But I stopped him."

Two other voices said in unison, "*We* stopped him, too!" I guessed it was the Newblood twins.

"No way! It was Big Mike that stopped him," Billy insisted.

"I helped!"

The arguing quartet continued past my open door without noticing me and clamored into the kitchen. After a few seconds, I thought I heard an appreciative sigh behind me. I spun, startled.

He leaned against the flowered wallpaper in the hallway, next to a vase of black roses, his leather-coated arms folded across his chest and his right leg propped against the wall. He had the most amazing eyes, nearly colorless with a hint of jade, and his smile lit up the powder room.

I didn't see any fangs. My heart skipped a beat and a tingle crept into my belly.

He extended a hand. "Mike Aickman. Family friend."

"Jenny Virginia, *older* family friend." I took his warm hand and shook it, reluctant to release his baby-soft skin.

He laughed lightly, still holding my hand. "I wouldn't say *that*. You can't be more than—what?—twenty-five?"

Cheeks flushing hot, I looked away. "Oh, stop. *You're* twenty-five, not *me!*"

He put his free hand on my shoulder, leaned close and whispered, "*Thirty*-five." His breath was cold—probably from the chilly night air—but it was somehow sexy combined with the light caress of his fingers down my arm before grasping my unresisting free hand.

We stood close in the hallway for a minute or two, both hands in his, fingers interlocked. His cold breath cooled the exposed skin from my plunging neckline, and my legs felt gelatinous.

"Shall we . . . sit down," I said, seductively, deliberately, and led him to the living room. We snuggled into the loveseat together and stared into each other's eyes.

"I vant to suck yore *blod*!" Dracula announced.

"Mike?" Jan said, stepping into the room at that moment. "I see you've met Jenny?"

"I have," he breathed.

Still captured by his gaze, I said, "Oh, yes. He has."

"Did he mention he's a vampire?" Jan said drily.

"Vampire?" I said in a fog, before the word sunk in. I shook myself, figuratively, and instinctively leaned away from the gorgeous man.

Mike smiled his brilliant smile, and I watched his fangs lengthen slightly. "Sorry. I thought you knew."

"You can turn off the charm now," said Jan hastily.

I stared at Mike, but made no move to get away from him. He seemed tame enough. Also, he smelled really good, like he'd been rolling around in lilacs and baby powder. Something twinged deep inside me.

One thing was certain; Jerry could take lessons from this man. Vampire. Whatever. Two minutes ago I was pretty sure I would have followed him to the ends of the earth. Or at least the cemetery. Whatever he had was *powerful*. For the first time, I understood how vampires managed to seduce women before turning them. This one, at least, understood the concept of romance.

"Jenny?"

Considering my wet noodle of an ex-husband, I wasn't sure I'd turn down Mike even now. I wondered if he'd go for a "no turning" rule in our relationship?

"Jenny?"

Oh, Mike, where were *you* fifteen years ago?

"Jenny?" Jan sure was insistent. "If you're done fantasizing about your brood of little vamps, could you get the door? I need to stop the screaming in the kitchen."

With a great effort of willpower, I wrenched myself from Mike's magnetic presence and launched myself at the front door, still clutching the wet rag against my now-healed wound.

Phil's gang grinned evilly from the open doorway, blood dripping from their enlongated fangs. I screamed, stepped back, and threw the bloody washrag at Jerry.

He snatched it from the air and sucked it hungrily.

A wall of black leather obscured my view, bringing with it a waft of baby powder that made my legs rubbery again. "Mine," Mike said simply and closed the door on their gapes.

Spinning to me, he grasped my elbows and nudged me back to the loveseat, sitting me down gently, alone.

"Are you going to be all right, Jenny? I should be at work already, but I can stay if you want me to." His clear eyes betrayed genuine concern.

Patting the seat next to me, I scooted over a bit. "I want."

Mike smiled and eased next to me, close. He held my hand.

Instinctively, I jerked away at its iciness.

"Sorry," he said, and pulled a chemical hand warmer from his coat pocket. After activating it and holding it tightly for a couple minutes, he put it away and gently took my hand again.

His hand was warm, like before.

"A little trick we use while courting," he said, apologetically. "'Cold hands, cold heart,' you know. People *believe* that."

I could imagine. "What do you do for a living?"

"High-tech stuff."

I tried to hide my shock. "Really?" I said, my voice breaking a little.

"There's more of us than you'd think. Nobody thinks twice about a programmer who sleeps until dinnertime and works all night. How do you think the consulting field got so big in the early '90s? A vampire here, a vampire there; next thing you know, banking, mortgages, and tech are being run by us."

"Makes sense," I admitted.

"I vant to suck yore *blod!*" Dracula clarified, in case I hadn't caught the irony.

I giggled uncontrollably, and somehow ended up in Mike's arms, kissing him. My tongue lightly explored his fangs and I drew back, horrified at my own brazenness.

"Honestly!" Jan said, blowing out her breath, which she'd clearly been holding for some time.

How long had she been there, watching us?

"Can't I leave you two alone for just a few minutes?" Jan shook her head maternally and stared at me, wagging her schoolteacher finger. "And you, a mother with your son in the kitchen. You should be ashamed of yourself."

I was, actually. Jumping to my feet, I smoothed down my skirt and called out, "Billy! Time to go home." I needed to leave now, before I did something I'd truly regret.

Mike looked disappointed, but he smiled anyway. "Good night," he whispered.

"I vant to suck yore *blod!*" Dracula pleaded.

"Can you do it without turning me?" I couldn't believe I was asking this question. Lately, I'd been doing a lot of things I couldn't believe—like making love in the middle of the school day to a man I'd known for only a few months.

Mike breathed and nodded, his mouth moving but no sound coming out. Who knew you could render a vampire breathless?

"Do it!" I said, gasping. I lay back in my bed, sweat from our lovemaking gluing me to the red satin sheets. "Do it," I breathed, as a wave of lava heat washed over me.

His fangs stung momentarily as they penetrated my shoulder, a few inches from my throbbing neck, then my veins went cold for a second as he drew in my blood.

And then it was over. No worse than giving blood at the Red Cross.

He licked my wounds slowly, seductively, while my blood clotted. It took some time, but I was in no hurry. Each stroke of his tongue renewed my ecstasy, threatening to take me over the brink.

"Stick or treat!" shouted a gang of second-graders I recognized from the grade school in Billy's new school system in Black Forest. The crisp night air enveloped me like a blanket. I drew in a deep breath of the lilacs from the cemetery garden near my front porch and smiled. The perennial vamp slayers and hunters shoved their sticks and crosses at my four-months-pregnant belly.

Laughing, I offered my bowl of treats. "Treats, then. Where's your carrot this year, Millie?"

A slightly chubby girl with long, curly blond hair awkwardly pushed up her Buffy mask. "Mommy let me have a stick this year!" she said proudly, and re-applied her Buffy face, crookedly. "Stick or treat!" she repeated.

"I vant to suck yore *blod*," Dracula threatened behind me. Millie squealed and grabbed a handful of pixy stix before running off, still squealing.

Closing the door, I giggled and patted Dracula. It was Jan's housewarming gift for me and Mike, and it was the perfect welcome for my new life—at least, for now. One day, after we'd had a dozen cold-blooded, adorable little vampire kids, maybe I'd let Mike turn me—but not yet.

Billy bounded in from the living room, wearing his best friend's old Van Helsing costume. "I retooled the crossbow so it takes *real* stakes! Van says I can keep it."

Mike trailed my son, followed by his sexy baby powder scent. Mike raised his eyebrows and jerked his head toward Billy. "Promise not to use it on *me*, okay?" He raised his hands in surrender as Billy whirled on him.

"I don't have real sticks *tonight*, silly! I don't want to hurt my friends." He looked down, ashamed. "Okay, I have *one*."

"Billy!"

"It's just in case I see that meanie, Jerry! I'll stake him for you, Mom."

How sweet! "My little vampire slayer," I cooed as he went out the door with my darling Mike for his first Halloween in his new neighborhood. So confident now, and full of life. I thought it would be hard for him, one of the few humans attending middle school at night with all those vamps, but they seemed to take it in stride, and Billy was happier than he'd ever been in our old human neighborhood. What a difference Mike had made in his life.

Alone in my new house, I waited patiently for the next round of costumed vigilantes for the living to arrive at my door. At least this year I had nothing to fear from Phil's gang—not with Mike around. And I had every intention of *keeping* Mike around.

Once you go Drac, you never go back.

Selina Rosen's stories have appeared in several magazines and anthologies. Some of her fourteen published novels include *Queen of Denial, Chains of Freedom, Strange Robby, Fire & Ice, Bad Lands* (with Laura J. Underwood), and *Sword Masters*. She owns Yard Dog Press and created their Bubbas of the Apocalypse universe.

Food Quart

Selina Rosen

"Well, it took longer than I thought it would," I said with a sigh.

"What took longer?" Walt asked impatiently. He was my boss and normally a nice, easy-going guy, but I was being purposefully evasive and right then neither he nor the officer seemed very happy with my answers. Of course, I wasn't terribly worried about their happiness. I'd had a sweet deal going and it was over.

"Just took longer than I thought it would is all." I shrugged. I've gotten really good at being vague—lots of practice.

"What did?" Walt looked like he was about five seconds from pulling his own hair out.

"No, dammit," Officer Dumbass said, pounding his fist into the table right in front of me. "I asked you a question. Don't change the subject."

No, Dumbass wasn't his real name, but I don't really remember his name or anything else about him, except that from the moment I saw his fat, doughnut-munching face, the word "dumbass" just popped into my head and stayed there.

I guess he thought I had been quiet way too long, or maybe he was just angry because his table pounding hadn't gotten even the slightest of reactions from me, so he did it again, harder and closer to me.

"Answer my question!"

"Which one?"

His eyes narrowed to slits and I could hear his heart rate and the pattern of his breathing change. "Why aren't you on the cameras?" His words came out like a hiss, like he thought if he opened his mouth too wide he might say something he didn't mean to.

"On the cameras?" I asked, as if I didn't understand the question, though at that point I have to tell the truth I was doing it more to upset the dumbass than anything else. I've been caught plenty of times and I knew I'd been caught again.

"On the film in the cameras. Why is there no footage of you making your rounds?"

"Yep, it took longer than I thought it would," I said again.

Officer Dumbass let out a groan that sounded a whole lot like a scream and he just started pacing back and forth like a caged animal.

"Mark," Walt said, with a calm I could tell he wasn't feeling. I turned to face him. "Look, I've got no problem with your work. God knows you're the best damned security guard we've got here. Never called in late, never called in sick, you haven't missed a single day in three years, but . . . Well, your time cards are always punched and I have no doubt that you're doing your job, but the officer has a point. Why aren't you on any of the surveillance tapes?"

Now, I'm pretty good at the game, and the truth is I probably could have kept them going for hours till they were ready to kill me and themselves, but by then I was just bored with the game. I wanted to get it over with and go and pack so that I could move.

"I don't show up on the tape because I'm a vampire," I said.

They both just looked at me and then they started to laugh. They kept laughing till Walt saw I wasn't laughing and then he stopped abruptly. Officer Dumbass sort of laughed to himself for a minute before realizing that it wasn't funny anymore.

"Seriously, Mark, quit dicking around," Walt said. "Now, this kid is dead. He died in the mall on your watch. Didn't you see anything? Hear anything? It looked like he just flipped out and then fell..."

"...but the coroner said he died of exsanguination, yet there is no blood anywhere. Yeah, I know," I finished for him. "Look... he wasn't a kid; he was scum. I would have gotten him outside and no one would have been the wiser, but he figured out what I was and he came in the mall to hunt for me."

"What utter crap!" Officer Dumbass said. "I don't have time for this. A confession is a confession, even if it's a crazy guy's confession. How about I just clamp your happy ass in handcuffs and cart you down to the station? See how funny you think all this is then."

My lips curled into a smile. "Why don't you just do that then?"

"All right, you!" He grabbed hold of my wrist and I easily threw him across the room so that he smacked the wall and fell down. He drew his gun as he stood up. I smiled again and his hand started to shake.

"Seriously, dude, do you really want to play this out?"

"How?" was all Walt got out.

"I told you. I'm a vampire," I said.

Walt sat down across from me. "Why?"

"Why what?" I asked.

"That's it! This guy's just a crazy. I've got a murder to investigate and you're wasting my time." Officer Dumbass holstered his gun and nearly ran out of the room. For a minute it looked like Walt might run after him, but he stayed there. He looked at me, obviously confused by the officer's reaction.

"He knows what I am now. No one wants to tangle with a creature of the night. He just wants to get as far away from me as he can so that he can start to unbelieve what he knows is true, so that he can sleep at night and walk into the shadows without feeling them come alive. It's a kind of sanity preservation thing."

"Why?" Walt asked again. I really didn't get his question, and he must have known it from the expression on my face because he added, "Why would you choose to be the night security guard at a mall?"

I nodded and admitted it was a good question. "Most people figure . . . you have supernatural powers, you can just do whatever you like. Live the rich high life. But here's the truth—when you have to sleep all day and you drink human blood for sustenance, there just aren't a lot of jobs you can do. Not a lot of people who want you around. You get turned—and it doesn't happen much because vampires don't like a lot of competition for the food supply—and for a minute you're all *I'm immortal, I can do anything!* But you find out real fast that just isn't the case. No more tanning on the beach, your favorite Italian restaurant is right out, and money still doesn't fall from the sky into your pockets.

"Now, I suppose you think I could just target rich people's houses, eat them, and steal all their stuff, but you know as well as I do that you can suck the life's blood from a dozen homeless guys and no one will even notice, but you eat one rich guy and every cop in town will be looking for you. Of course, you're spending their money and pawning their stuff and eventually you're going to get caught. True, you can probably get away, but then where are you? Right back where you started with no money and no place to live. Quite frankly, it sucks.

"And I don't care how much you think you'd just cling to the shadows and enjoy the nights alone and sleep in a crypt during the day. You do that for a few weeks and all you want is a good hot bath and a soft bed. Think about it. A security guard, a rent-a-cop at a mall—it's perfect. I walked all over this place from 8 P.M. to 6 A.M. I got to see normal people doing normal things and bask in humanity and no one noticed me—not to really look at me—because, face it, a big guy with a gun and a badge just intimidates the hell out of most people, so they try not to make eye contact. Except for the creeps. They just have to screw with me and that's how I know who the troublemakers are and then...Well it's just about getting rid of them, isn't it?

"Believe it or not I'm a nice guy, Walt. I don't like to feed on the blood of the innocent. Working here...I don't have to tell you, you know what happens. People move out of the city to the suburbs to get away from the scum and then what always happens? The scum starts to bleed out of the city, too. A couple of kids who were on the edge of a street gang in the big city get moved out here because their parents want to keep them out of the gangs. They bring their thuggy little brats out here and then before you know it they're recruiting all the little preppy idiots to start their own street gang. You can't get away from it; there is no safe place for people to raise their kids anymore.

"When I first started working here three years ago, this mall had become a safe harbor for a gang of teenaged idiot children and dope dealers, so decent people were reluctant to even come and shop.

"I hunted out the troublemakers and no one thought anything of it because it was my job. The bad apples? Well with few exceptions they're the ones that stay till the last minute then hang at the doors and dare me to make them leave. They are almost too easy to kill."

I smiled then, and I guess it was the first time Walt had really taken notice of my teeth, because he cringed. They're the same teeth I've always had.

"I'd follow them outside, grab them—usually in one of the loading docks—I'd drink all their blood then stuff them in a half dozen heavy-duty trash bags and sling them in the dumpster. Like I said, it took longer than I thought it would. Usually a bag busts and someone finds a body way before now."

"You . . . you've done this before in other towns?"

"Sure, it's a perfect job for a vampire. I've been here longer than anywhere else. This is a real bummer. I mean I really like it here; it's just so handy. I live in the apartment complex right across the parking lot so I can walk to work, which makes my carbon footprint smaller..."

"Wait wait wait! You worry about living green?"

"Why wouldn't I! Geez, you humans are going to live eighty years, a hundred tops. Most of you don't care what you do to the earth or yourselves. Me? I'm going to live forever; I need the world to stay in one piece. I need humans."

Walt swallowed hard. "For companionship?"

I smiled. "Whatever helps you sleep at night, Walt."

"How many people have you killed in my mall?" he asked.

"In the mall? Only the one."

"How many?" he demanded, as if he still held any of the cards.

I shrugged. I hadn't really kept count. It's not like I have to eat every day, and the more I eat at one time, the longer I can go between feedings.

"I don't know—a couple of dozen give or take."

"You blood-sucking fiend!"

"Ah, now you're just trying to hurt my feelings. Look...I only killed people who needed killing. People who, quite frankly, any decent person would want to kill, but they wouldn't or couldn't. I used to be human, too. I know what rage lies in even the meekest human heart. Always having to walk away, turn the other cheek, it's enough to make a man insane. You just suffer one fool after another in an endless progression of swallowing your pride and there is never a thing, not one thing you can do about it, because if good people defend themselves against the scum by doing the only thing that works—which is killing them—then they're punished. I can do whatever the hell I like. Some guy cuts in front of me in line, I eat him, and I don't mean in a pleasant, sexual way, either."

"You're trying to justify mass murder."

"Is it working?" I asked with a smile. As vampires go, I'm not much for the brooding, quiet stuff.

"What happened last night?"

I nodded. He wanted to know about the idiot in the pants with the crotch that hung to his knees. "I caught him and a buddy screwing with a couple of teeny-bopper girls and I told them to move on. They started taunting me. You know, calling me names, threatening me, telling me I wouldn't be so big if I didn't have a gun. See . . . that's always what happens with the little punks, I know exactly what I'm dealing with but they don't have a clue. Or, he didn't till I ordered them to leave. As we were walking out, he was watching himself in the mirrored glass on the front of Facson's Shoes. I guess that's when he noticed I didn't have a reflection. I knew the moment it happened because he turned to look at me and then turned back to look at my lack of reflection. You know, just back and forth and back and forth, each time the mask of fear on his face becoming even greater. Finally I bared my teeth at him and said, 'Still think I need my gun?'

"Well, I figured I'd lost that meal. I mean, few people who figure out what I am really want to tangle with me. Of course, his problem was he was with his friend and his friend didn't believe him, so he had to come back to try to prove what I was. I really have no idea what he planned to do. Stupid little pecker head didn't even have a stake.

"He had hidden in a clothing rack in one of the

trendy clothing stores with names that rhyme with tap or O'Zook. You know, the ones that think they're so different, yet all look exactly the same. They sell torn jeans that have been washed in rocks for more money than some of these kids' parents make in a week, and slap bottle caps on seat belts and call them 'accessories.' I guess he thought it would be easy to get out of the grated front gate on the store. It wasn't, and I found him in about three seconds, just trapped there like an animal in a cage waiting to be my dinner.

"He cried and ran to the back of the store, looking for a way out as I took my key and opened the grate. I slung it up in one movement and he screamed like a little girl, then went running out. I let him get past me. I could have grabbed him easily, but sometimes I like to play with my food before I eat it."

Walt made a face and I shrugged and went on.

"Besides, I really didn't want to kill him in the mall. It wasn't part of the plan. He screamed a lot. He even tried to make a call on his phone, but he got scared and dropped it. A real douche, this guy. I opened an exterior door and tried to get him to run out it, but he was just too stupid to live, so I finally gave up and just killed him and ate him, and then . . . Well, I knew his death had been caught on film, so I just left him there." I shrugged. "I had a good run here, didn't I? I mean, think about it—three years ago when I took this job, you told me yourself that if we couldn't do something about getting the gangs and the dealers out of the mall, it wouldn't be open much longer. You don't have that problem anymore, do you? Remember what it was like before?"

"Why...I don't understand how that many people could go missing and no one would notice. No manhunts, no broadcasts on the TV, no posters all over town, nothing." Walt seemed more confused than anything else.

"Come on, most of them were gangbangers and/or drug dealers. They wind up dead or skip town without telling anyone all the time. Most of the people who noticed they were missing were probably glad they were gone. Look." I stood up. "I've only got about four hours of darkness left and I need to pack and get to a motel before sunup." I took off my badge and my gun and handed them to him. "Thanks for the opportunity, Walt. It's been nice working for you."

He just nodded and said nothing as I left.

When I got to my apartment, opened the door, walked in and saw all my stuff, a wave of sadness washed over me. I had really started to think of this place as home. I'd even bought furniture and books and—God help me—video games. Now I was going to have to leave all my stuff and run off into the night with a suitcase full of clothes. I'd have to start all over someplace else.

I grabbed a couple of bags and just started gathering up my clothes and anything else I could lay my hands on and stuffed them unceremoniously inside. I closed them, with their lids bulging, then grabbed my car keys and headed for the door.

I was so lost in my own thoughts and sudden grief that when the knock came, I actually jumped—and, let's face it, I'm the scariest thing I know. I walked to the door, looked out the peep hole and saw it was Walt, alone. I thought he had to either be the bravest guy I'd ever known, or the stupidest. I put down my bags and opened the door.

"What's up?"

"Can I come in?" I nodded and he walked in. "Can I sit down?"

"Yes, of course." I motioned towards my recliner, which had me thinking of how I might be able to get it into my car. I loved that chair.

"Look, as soon as you left...Well, I got to thinking about what you said about the mall before you started working for us. I have to tell you something." He swallowed hard. "You know, before you applied for the night guard position, before my promotion to head of security, I had your job. I couldn't do anything about what was going on in there. The cops...Well, they have to see it or it didn't happen. One night as I was getting ready to lock up, three big guys..."

Well, of course it was big guys, because no one ever says they were attacked by three tiny—or even moderate-sized—guys, or a big guy and two little guys.

"...run up, force the door open, run back inside, and proceed to kick my ass. My gun never cleared leather. They beat the crap out of me and then they just took off. They didn't even take my gun. They didn't take anything from the stores. They didn't even vandalize the place. It was just an act of senseless violence and they were laughing the whole time. I got to my feet and ran out after them, pulling my gun, and just for a second I wanted to shoot them in their backs, but then I thought about how I'd explain it and...Well, just like you said—I'd be in trouble. There would be no explanation for why I shot them in the backs. It was just a bit of fun for them and I was never really the same again ever."

"No offense, Walt, but is this going someplace? Because I really need to hit the road."

"Why?"

He was big on that question that night.

"Because I don't want the cops sniffing around and I need to be inside again before the sun comes up..."

"They don't have any evidence. Do you think Officer Dumbass is going to run to the precinct and tell everyone that you're a vampire? I burned those tapes. He was in such a hurry to get out of there that he forgot to take them with him, and you know he's not going to want to admit that he had evidence and lost it. You can stay. It will just be our little secret, yours and mine. You like it here; I like the place since you've been here. So we have a deal?"

I nodded happily, because the whole time he'd been talking I'd just kept thinking about all the stuff I'd worked for that I was going to have to leave behind. You get attached to things. It may seem stupid, but I like my furniture and my pictures. I like having someplace to call home, and an actual routine.

Walt stood up then and headed for the door. When his hand grabbed the handle, he turned. "I just want to ask you one small favor."

"Anything."

"Don't eat in the food court, okay? I eat there and it would just be gross."

Susan Sizemore lives in the Midwest and writes an awful lot of vampire stories—including the *New York Times* bestselling Primes series and urban fantasy Laws of the Blood series. You can visit her website at http://susansizemore.com.

Dazed and Confused

Susan Sizemore

"Just bring me a cup of coffee and nobody gets hurt."

Oscar winced at the tone of voice of the woman in the next room. Why had his mate asked him to drop by her workplace if he had to listen to this?

He glanced past his wife's shoulder at the pink curtain separating them from the angry mortal. "Why do they always speak so loudly?" he asked Myna.

Myna shrugged. It made the pink enamel hoops of her earrings sway. Oscar didn't like that his pale, raven-haired beloved wore so many pastels these days, but he understood. He was wearing a yellow polo shirt himself. And khaki pants. His grandparents would roll in their graves—if they weren't currently organizing something called a Koffin Klatch fundraiser for the Resurrectionist Church the whole bloodline had recently joined.

Times were—well, what they were. One changed with them or moldered in a box, lying on the soil of one's homeland, probably in a stinky old basement or in your kids' garage.

He was drawn from his reverie when Myna passed a hand in front of his face. "You're brooding on the good old days, aren't you?"

Oscar knew what she was going to say next, so he said it for her. "There were no good old days—only the fear of being hunted down and killed." Myna didn't like him to mention that at least back then they could do some hunting and killing themselves. "I hate being civilized," he muttered.

"You always say that when you're trying to get out of something."

She put her hands on her sensuously curved hips. He couldn't help but smile longingly. His mate always made his fangs ache.

"I really need your help this evening, Oscar." She jerked a thumb toward the curtain that separated the office from the spa. "The hard cases always show up on the nightshift," she said.

To punctuate this, the mortal in the other room spoke loudly again. "I know my husband spent a small fortune for this whole mind/body healing ritual thing, but I like my mind and body just the way they are—caffeinated and grumpy."

"I've got to go." Myna shook her head. "The wrist restraints aren't going to hold her much longer. They're on a timer, after all."

People liked to play at being subdued by vampires, but that's all it was these days—play.

"I can't leave until my last client does," Myna went on. "And Cecile needs someone to accompany her."

"It's my night off!" Oscar complained.

"We agreed to raise our offspring together. The Nightshade Girls' rules are that first year members always have to be accompanied by a parent."

"It's a neighborhood candy sale," Oscar sulked. "What could hurt her? She's a vampire."

"Let me out of here!" the mortal in the spa shouted.

Myna pointed him to the door. "Go. Take care of our child." Then she was gone with the speed of a blink, leaving him staring and the curtain swaying in her wake.

"Damn," Oscar muttered, and accepted that his will must be subsumed by the greater good of kin and kind when all he'd wanted was to throw back a bloodbrew or two with some buddies at Underground, the new chain supernaturals' bar at the mall.

"I don't see how you can call it disrupting when all we did was express our opinions."

The mayor glared up from his desk at Charlie Hewson. "You were screaming like maniacs."

Rachel put a calming hand on Charlie's tense arm. "We were a bit emphatic, dear. You have to concede that much." Charlie didn't like to concede anything when he knew he was in the right, which was why she had to take on the task of being the voice of reason.

"It was a public meeting." Charlie glared back at the mayor. "You had no business having us dragged into your office."

"I could have had you dragged off to jail. But I'm your brother, and—"

"Freedom of speech is guaranteed—"

"Brandishing stakes and torches—"

"It was a flashlight," Rachel put in.

"It's still an expression of hostile intent and a

flagrant violation of the new hate crimes and civil rights statutes." The mayor stood and made soothing, patting motions with his hands. "Now, I know you wouldn't really kill a vampire, Charlie."

"Oh, yeah?" Charlie sneered. "Are you a vampire lover?"

"Vampires are voters, too, Charlie."

"Are you forgetting that a vampire bit our mother?"

"Our mother ran off to live with a vampire of her own free will. They've been together for twenty years."

"They always send Christmas cards," Rachel said.

"Which I burn," Charlie growled.

Actually, he always handed them to her to burn, but she'd been saving them in a box in case he ever decided he wanted to reconcile with his mother. Not that she didn't agree with Charlie that vampires were a deeply evil menace, but family was important.

"The point is, you shouldn't have forced us to leave the city council meeting just as we were making our point," Rachel spoke up. "Which is that our city cannot afford to add any more all-night programs to our schools. And don't point out that voting vampires pay taxes, too, Reginald," she admonished her brother-in-law the mayor. "It's bad enough that all of the sports programs have gone to evening-only schedules. Now you're proposing to send our children to school at night! We say let the vampires be home-schooled if they—"

"Death to all vampires!" Charlie spoke up.

"That would be best," Rachel agreed. "But since that isn't likely to happen—"

"We have the right to express our opinion in a public forum!" Charlie shouted.

"You do," the mayor agreed. "But not until you go

home and dump your junk. Come back wearing a tie, little brother, and I'll let you complain as much as you want. I mean it," he added before Charlie could protest.

He pouted instead. "Fine," he finally said.

It still took a bit of tugging and cajoling for Rachel to get him outside.

"We can't go home yet, sire!" Cecile complained.

He'd suggested it after yet another door had been slammed in his little girl's face. They were now standing at a street corner just outside the glow of an overhead light. He hated seeing her looking so forlorn.

"Call me daddy," he reminded her. "Aren't you tired, sweetheart?" he cajoled.

"It's only eight o'clock," she pointed out.

"Don't you have homework to—"

"I won't get my first batwing badge if I don't sell all my candy!" her voice rose into the night.

"Well, then, I'll buy them from you."

"That's against the rules! We have to obey the rules, si—daddy!"

She started to cry, blood-red tears staining her pretty pale cheeks. Oscar knelt beside his fragile darling and held her close. He hated the way the mortals in the neighborhood had rejected and hurt his little night-blooming flower. He hated that his own words hurt and disappointed her.

"Of course we have to obey the rules, Cecile," he told her. "I don't know what made me say such a stupid thing." He dried her tears and gave her a hug. When he straightened, he took her hand. "Let's try the houses on the next block, I'm sure you'll make some sales further up the street."

Oh, yes, we will be selling some candy soon. Beware my wrath, pitiful mortals! Oscar thought as they went on their way, hand in hand. He almost laughed, but loud expressions of "BWAAA-AAA-AAA" tended to give away the presence of evil intentions. And he wasn't going to upset his little Cecile.

"Look at that," Charlie said when they came out of the house after changing clothes.

Rachel ignored the outrage in his voice while she locked the door, then she turned to him. He was pointing at the house next door. She moved to the side of the porch to get a better view.

"Vampires," she whispered after a moment. "Two of them. Why are they talking to Mrs. Donovan?"

The Donovans were quiet about it, but Rachel knew they didn't approve of vampires settling in town any more than she and Charlie did. They and the Donavans had traded information about the garlicked communities springing up in the sun belt, not that any of them could afford that sort of exclusive real estate in the current economy.

Rachel gasped as she saw a vampire take Mrs. Donovan's hand.

"Come on, we have to help her!"

Charlie leaped over the side bannister, barely missing the rose bushes beneath, and sprinted toward the house next door. His tie flapped in the breeze as he ran. Rachel stayed where she was for a moment, not sure if she'd be more concerned about her husband or the flowers if he'd come down on the bushes. But the dear, thoughtless, fanatical man was trying to save humanity and she loved him for that.

"Oh, Charlie," she said, with an indulgent smile, and followed him on the hunt for vampires.

Oscar continued to look deeply into the stunned woman's eyes while Cecile fidgeted beside him.

"The lady said a bad word to me," his child whimpered.

He patted Cecile's head while continuing to hold the woman's gaze. "She didn't mean it. Apologize to the little girl."

"I'm sorry I called you a parasite."

"Do you want to buy candy?" Cecile asked.

"You want to buy a lot of candy," Oscar said. Soothingly. Firmly. Insistently.

"I want to buy a—"

"Stop it, you parasites! I know what you're doing, mind rapist!"

Oscar knew that voice—Crazy Charlie. Every vampire, ogre, and werewolf in the county knew Crazy Charlie. Most had restraining orders against him and his wife. At this moment, Oscar wished he did. He sighed.

"I'm not a parasite!" Cecile wailed as Oscar turned toward the insane man running toward them. "I came out of mommy's tummy!"

"You came out of somebody's tummy," Mrs. Donovan muttered from her doorway. "Like in those *Alien* movies."

"We reproduce a bit differently," Oscar said in the neutral, reasonable tone he'd taken classes in mastering. Besides, they only used assisted suicide volunteers and condemned criminals these day. Vampire reproduction was regulated, it was all perfectly legal, and at least the hosts died in ecstasy.

"What do you want, Charlie?" he demanded as the man came storming up to them.

Oscar was relieved to see that the man was dressed decently instead of wearing one of his T-shirts with crude, inflammatory slogans like *My Species Right or Wrong!* Cecile was already upset enough without having to be exposed to more mortal prejudice.

"Stop bespelling that woman!" Crazy Charlie shouted. "And get your little monster away from her!"

Cecile hissed at the furious intruder, but since her adult fangs hadn't come out, her reaction was brave but unimpressive.

"Hush, darling, daddy will take care of this," Oscar said. He carefully made sure Cecile was standing behind him. "I haven't been bespelling anyone," Oscar told Charlie. "I am a law-abiding citizen. Unlike yourself."

At least bespelling wasn't the term vampires used for projecting their will. And he'd only been bending the law a little. For his child's sake. He was a modern vampire who firmly believed that subverting anyone's will was wrong. Convenient, but wrong.

Crazy Charlie's wife came running up and put her arm around the other woman. "What did he do to you? Have you been—violated?"

"Will you two stop this ridiculous drama?" Oscar demanded. "Are you ever going to leave your respectable neighbors alone? Can't we live together in—"

"Living is the operative term," Crazy Charlie interrupted. "As in, we're alive and you're a corrupted semblance of living flesh."

"You've had a lot of practice saying things like that, haven't you?"

"You can't distract me with sarcasm, monster."

"Or with mind games," the wife spoke up proudly. "Charlie's immune."

Oscar managed not to point out that one needed a mind in order for it to be played with. "I have heard that about you," he said instead. He stuck his hand out toward Crazy Charlie. "Let us shake and be friends."

Crazy Charlie drew back as though Oscar had mentioned neck biting in a thick Hungarian accent. Oscar had never tasted human blood in his life. No matter what his parents said about the delight of it, he was sticking with cow blood, thank you very much.

"I know what you were doing and I'll have the supernatural squad on you for it. You can't get away with it. Everyone knows I can detect when your kind uses mind tricks. I've turned in others."

"That is true," Oscar conceded.

"Don't patronize me."

Damn it, there was no civilized way of dealing with the man!

Oscar turned to Mrs. Donovan instead. "Will you please reassure Craz—um—Charlie that all is well."

"She's fine." It was Charlie's wife that spoke up. The women had been whispering to each other while Crazy Charlie made a scene. "They were only trying to sell her candy, Charlie."

"Only, Rachel? Only?"

"I want my mommy!" Cecile added to the shouting.

"We really need to get back to the meeting," Rachel said.

"Too late for that now. It'll be over before we get there." Charlie glared at Oscar. "I can't even blame you for that. My brother tricked me to push his pro-monster agenda through the city council without any opposition."

Cecile kept crying, calling for Myna, and tugging on Oscar's pants leg.

"My daughter wants to go home," he told the humans. So did he. He took Cecile by the hand. "Let's go, darling."

When he started to walk away, Charlie blocked his way. "You're not going anywhere, mind rapist. You're mine now."

"I beg your pardon?"

The human fought his revulsion and stepped close to Oscar. His voice was low and threatening. "Do you want me to report you to the cops? You want to protect your family, don't you?"

"I was only selling the woman candy!" Oscar regretted the words instantly. It was as good as an admission.

Crazy Charlie's smile was frightening, the look in his eyes insane enough to scare a vampire. "You're mine," he repeated.

Oscar gulped. This monstrous human was right. One little mistake could destroy his family, the life they enjoyed, protected under the law. The acceptance his whole kind was slowly building in the community. He could only nod in defeat.

Cecile tugged on his hand. "Daddy!"

"Rachel!" Crazy Charlie barked at his wife. "Take this—child—to her home."

If Oscar had spoken in that tone to Myna, he'd get his throat ripped out, but the human woman meekly answered, "If you want me to, dear."

The man didn't reply, as he was already talking to someone on his cellular telephone. "Get over to my house right now, Reginald. I know you're the mayor. That's the point. There's someone I need you to talk to. To change your opinion on the school schedule changes, that's why..."

"Go with the lady," Oscar said when the woman took Cecile's hand. He didn't want to let his child go, but he had to stay here to protect her.

Rachel paused in the kitchen doorway and stared. "Oh, it's still here."

The creature gave her an unhappy look. "Believe me, I don't want to be."

It had been bad enough walking beside the young monster home, but the last thing she'd ever expected was to have a vampire in her house when she returned. Sitting at her kitchen table. Holding one of her coffee mugs. She'd throw it out as soon as the vampire left. Maybe she'd throw out everything in the room. At least she'd call in a cleaning service to give her house a thorough going-over. With holy water. And Charlie had better not complain at the expense, since he was the one who'd brought a filthy monster into their home.

Still, she almost felt a pang of sympathy at the sad look on the vampire's face, and in the defeated slump of his shoulders. Its. Remember that it only mimics humanity. Still...

"Charlie, what have you been up to?" she demanded.

Her annoyance at her husband faded as soon as he looked at her, his eyes shining, a triumphant smile on his lips. Seeing him just made her heart melt. Which made it very hard for her to remember what their couples counselor kept telling her about asserting herself more—theirs was supposed to be a partnership and not a fan club for Charlie.

"Reginald just left. He agrees with us about school policies now," Charlie said. He gestured at the vampire. "Our friend here—"

"Friend?" Rachel questioned, thoroughly shocked that he could use the term so easily. "Charlie, really—"

"—used its persuasive powers to convince him that even vampires hate the idea of night classes for their little monsters. They can just keep their school books in their dank and dusty coffins with 'em."

"My daughter's coffin is pale blue and decorated in posters of her favorite pop singer—but I do agree about the benefits of home schooling."

Rachel heard everything Charlie and the vampire said, but she remained fixated. "Friend? What do you mean by calling a vampire *friend*?"

"Servant, then," Charlie answered.

"Slave," the vampire complained.

"We should have talked about this before you invited it into our home. You know we're supposed to communicate more."

"Why are you bringing up that couples counseling crap now?"

"You do that too?" the vampire asked Charlie. "Our counselor has us use whips on each other. We've worked out several problems that way. But I don't suppose humans—"

Its voice trailed off as Rachel and Charlie concentrated on each other.

"We have a wonderful opportunity here," Charlie told her. "It'll do anything I tell it to," Charlie bragged. "If it doesn't, I'll turn it in for attacking Mrs. Donovan."

She put her hands on her hips. "Do you really mean *we*, Charlie?"

"What is the matter with you, woman?"

"You gave me an order tonight and I obeyed it without thinking. Well, I'm thinking about it now and we need to discuss your high-handed behavior."

"What order?"

"You don't even remember, do you?"

"Taking my daughter home," the vampire said. "Thank you for that, by the way."

Charlie turned to the vampire. "Do you have to put up with this from your wife?"

"Of course." It sighed. "She has the same mental powers as I have."

"This whole fashion about going to counseling is crazy. How'd we get talked into it?"

"The city council supported a media campaign to convince everyone that it would benefit everyone in our newly-mixed community. You were drunk when you interrupted the meeting and your brother talked you into volunteering to counseling with your wife."

Charlie rubbed his jaw. "Oh, yeah, I remember. Sort of."

"Charles, will you pay attention to me?" Rachel demanded.

But he didn't. "We're going to have to do something about that the next time we talk to my brother," he told his new vampire friend.

"Charlie, you can't make it use mental powers on the mayor again. I'm not sure changing his mind on schooling was ethical."

"Ethics don't come into it," Charlie said. "I'm working for the greater good."

"Not my kind's good," the vampire muttered.

Charlie rubbed his jaw and yawned. "I need to think of how to use Oscar next."

"Stop giving it a name, Charlie."

"Or at least give me a better name than Oscar," the monster said. "I don't know what my parents were thinking."

The vampire's amiable chatter was really making her nervous. It was probably why she was so cross with dear Charlie. Not only was the vampire acting like a person, Charlie was starting to treat him like one. "Will you make that thing leave?"

His response was. "Rachel, honey, make us some coffee."

Rachel glanced at the clock on the microwave. "I don't think that's a good idea, *honey*." She didn't think he detected her sarcasm as it wasn't something she normally did. She appealed to his sense of responsibility. "We have to be at work in a few hours."

"I'm not going to work—I'm going to rule the world!"

The vampire's outraged expression raked her husband, as did hers. Charlie just sat there looking smug.

She wasn't going to put up with this nonsense. "Make your own coffee, your highness. I'm going to bed. And I'm making a counseling appointment for us first thing in the morning."

"Oh, no." Charlie shook his head. Then he rubbed his jaw thoughtfully and looked from her to the vampire and back again. "You really don't understand, sweetheart, but you will. I love you and this is for your own good. Our own good."

"What are you talking about, Charlie?"

He gestured to the vampire. "Do your stuff, Oscar."

The vampire stood. "As you wish—master."

Rachel was about to point out that it didn't need to be sarcastic since Charlie was immune, or need to use that silly movie vampire accent...then all she could see was the vampire's eyes.

Beautiful. Deep. Wise eyes.

He was the sort of person one naturally listened to.

Please make us a pot of coffee, lovely one. His voice caressed her. *You know you want to obey your husband in all things.*

I do. But our counselor says...

I feel the need to submit in your mind. That is your true nature. Don't you want to follow your true nature? Forget the conventions of suburban life and live as you wish?

Well, yes, she told the lovely creature as she moved the kitchen counter.

Follow your heart then.

Rachel watched her hand reach toward the coffee maker. For Charlie's sake. Her heart sang. *Thank you,* she told the creature.

Call me Oscar, the sweet voice inside her advised gently.

Of course. Thank you for the help.

When the coffee was brewing, she stepped back and looked complacently at her dear husband. "Anything else?" she asked.

"Good work," Charlie said to Oscar.

"May I go now?" Oscar asked.

Charlie waved toward the back door. "Why not. We'll talk soon."

"No doubt."

Oscar gave a polite little bow. Rachel almost giggled

at the incongruity of formal gesture combined with the vampire's casual shirt and khakis. He glanced her way, expectantly.

"Good night," she heard herself say. Well, the guy wasn't all that bad. "And bring your daughter around tomorrow night," she added. "I'd like to buy some of her candy."

"Hey!" Charlie complained.

"All things have their price," Oscar told him. "Your wish is my command, but my kid has a quota to make. Fair deal?"

"Fair deal," Charlie agreed grudgingly. When the vampire was gone he turned to her, his eyes bright with lust. "Never mind the coffee, do you still have that French maid outfit you wore last Halloween?"

"Oh, yes!" she cooed, and ran to the bedroom to change.

Robin Wayne Bailey is the author of numerous novels, including the Dragonkin series, the Frost series, and the Brothers of the Dragon trilogy, among others. His 1998 novel, *Swords Against the Shadowland*, which featured Fritz Leiber's Fafhrd and Gray Mouser, has just been republished by Dark Horse Books. His many short stories have appeared in many magazines and anthologies, and he received a Nebula Award nomination for his story, "The Children's Crusade." A former president of the Science Fiction & Fantasy Writers of America, he lives in Kansas City, Missouri. Visit his website at www.robinwaynebailey.net.

Trampire

Robin Wayne Bailey

She had legs like the horns of a Texas steer, long and
smooth as ivory, cool and round and well-shaped, and
wide apart, and she wore her red hair piled so high
on her head it threatened to set off the sprinkler
system. Even in the bar's gloomy darkness, with wisps
and clouds of cigarette smoke flirting with the shifting
shadows to the strains of soft taped jazz, her green
eyes shone with mystery and amusement.

I recognized Maggie Cummings at once. Her movies held places of honor on the shelves of my shabby
apartment, classic titles like *Saddle Tramp*, *Naked Ninja
Vixens*, *Maggie After Midnight*, and my favorite, *Legs in
the Air, Sucker!* I'd watched them all so many times I
could recite the mono-syllabic dialogue with one hand.

Someone tapped me on the shoulder. "Stop staring
through the curtains, Rufus! You're on!"

Lemon Denton was the owner of the Blue Room.
"Blind" Lemon Denton they'd called him during his
own days on the jazz/blues scene. He'd never really

been blind. He'd just liked the big dark glasses. Lemon was a little black man with a perpetual pucker where his mouth once had been, the fate of so many trumpet players. He pointed to the stage and thrust my guitar at me.

I snatched the guitar, a shiny Martin D15 acoustic dreadnought, from his unworthy hands. "Not much of an audience tonight," I muttered.

"Well, you're not much of a musician," he shot back. Professional jealousy. Lemon was old-school blues. I was a younger, hipper cat. He turned his back without another word and returned to his bar. I took a moment for a deep breath and a little visualization, but mostly I was visualizing Maggie Cummings and a scene from one of her videos. With a shrug, I hugged my guitar and stepped out onto the small stage.

A single spotlight shot through the dark, hitting me like a punch between the eyes. "Mother fu...!" I thought I heard Lemon chuckle from the back of the bar, the old bastard. Dazzled, I groped my way to the stool at the stage's edge and positioned a pair of microphones. That stool fit my ass with an intimacy that scared me sometimes. Like the seat of a bicycle after a fifty-mile ride, it *knew* me in ways the Bible never approved of.

I balanced the Martin on my thigh, draped my right arm over its curvaceous mahogany body, and played my long black fingers over its sleek neck. Pretty quick I began to sweat, and not just from the heat of the spotlight. Music had a way of stirring a man's hormones, and I had to get laid soon or bust.

Closing my eyes, I touched the strings, and prepared to strike a warm-up chord.

A soft voice made me look up. Maggie Cummings was no longer sitting at the booth where I'd first spotted her. She stood at the foot of the stage with a glass of red wine in one hand and lips that looked like an invitation to the Policemen's Ball, which was also the title of one of her videos.

"I heard you sang a good song," she murmured just loud enough to hear. "I heard you had a style."

There she stood, so close I could've leaned down and touched her, but if I had my mama would've risen up from the grave and slapped my hand. "So you came down to see me and listen for a while," I responded, trying to be cool. "Yeah, I know that song, too." To demonstrate, I picked out a few notes of "Killing Me Softly." It wasn't really my kind of song, and a sharp, harsh *twang* followed the last note.

"Fuck," I said. "My g-string broke!"

"That happens to me a lot, too," she said, raising her glass with a wink and a smile. She changed the subject. "Don't you have a band?"

I held up my left hand. "Had one," I answered. "Threw it away when my last wife left." I grinned and fished in my pocket for the package of extra strings I carried onstage. "I'm a one-man show."

"Sweet," Maggie Cummings answered. "I'm a one-man woman."

Her videos said otherwise, but who was I to quibble with a come-on like that? I stripped the broken string off the guitar and began setting the new one in place. With a look back over her shoulder, she turned and headed for the bar. She walked like a cat, but her hips moved like a force eight earthquake, and the Transamerica Tower was shaking in my pants.

Tuning up again, I picked a few notes experimentally, and then strummed a B-A-D chord progression for pure orneriness. When I looked up, Maggie Cummings was no longer at the bar, but her wine glass was still there, mostly full. An older, respectable-looking couple walked through the door, looked around and took a booth at the back. Lemon glared and made a gesture to get the show started as he hurried to their table.

My head churned with thoughts of pretty Maggie. Had she walked out without me noticing? I couldn't remember my prepared playlist, yet suddenly my hands began to roam over the guitar, gently at first, but then harder and harder as I drew volume and power from the Martin. At last I recognized what I was playing—Little Milton's blues classic, "Woman You Got a Spell on Me."

The room became a blur as I leaned into the microphone and belted the lyrics. My fingers found chords I didn't know I knew; the strings vibrated at my touch. I beat my foot on the floor and squeezed my eyes shut. Maggie Cummings danced in my brain and on the insides of my eyelids.

Then the song ended, and I flowed right into another. "Baby, take me deep where it counts!" I sang, and "Red Hot Voodoo Mama!" I shook my head without missing a beat, opened my eyes and gazed around. The older respectable lady was laying back in the booth with her blouse open wider than a church door on Sunday, and her respectable man was preaching the sermon with his right hand. Lemon was grinning and keeping time with his fist on the bar. A half-dozen people had drifted in, and the place was rapidly filling with smoke again.

"Rock me, baby, like my back ain't got no bone!" Another handful of people wandered in and found seats. A pair of suited black cats found bar stools; a blue-haired punk and his pink-haired girlie grabbed a booth. Some lonely looking businessmen seated themselves at a table.

Then Maggie Cummings strode through the thickening blue smoke like something spectral, with another wineglass in her hand. Right up to the edge of the stage she came and took a chair from one of the tables. Smiling her biggest straight-to-video smile, she sat down right in front of me. It was the best Sharon Stone impression I ever saw in my life, and suddenly I was suffering for my art.

I let rip with one more song, "I'm built for comfort!" I'd never performed it before because it was a woman's song, but the audience erupted in applause, whistles and whoops as I climbed down off my stool to take a break. I'd never gotten that kind of reaction from a crowd before, and man, it felt good!

Lemon was waiting in the wings. "Cat, where you pullin' that shit up from? I'll book you every damn night! You never sang like that before!"

I grinned and thought of Maggie in the front row as I settled the Martin into its guitar case. "I got me some inspiration," was all I said. "Shouldn't you be watching the bar?"

Lemon leered and jabbed a finger against my chest. "Well, your inspiration has decided to watch the bar for me, and she's selling drinks faster than I ever could. That woman's got some fine pork chops on her and no fat to trim!"

Further proof that "Blind" Lemon wasn't blind,

but I didn't tell him so. I made my way past him and down the narrow corridor to the tiny closet that laughingly passed for my dressing room. Taped to the door I found a napkin upon which Lemon had drawn a star and written my name. I guess I was flattered, but when I stepped inside and flipped on the light the room was still full of brooms and mop buckets and stacked up cartons of beer and liquor.

Squeezed between the cartons, though, was an old army cot where I sometimes slept if I drank too much after a show. Next to that was a cheap full-length mirror over which I'd hung a fresh shirt. I liked to change sometimes during breaks.

At the foot of the cot near the mirror was a bottle of Jack Daniels. Unscrewing the cap, I sat down and took a long swig, and when I put the bottle down, Maggie Cummings was standing inside the door. Startled, I spit a spray of whiskey halfway across the room.

"Baby," she said with a mixture of sympathy and amusement. "Between the sweating and the spitting, you're leaking water like a Dutch dike."

Embarrassed, I pushed the bottle under the cot and wiped my lips and nose. "I ain't Dutch," I answered, "and I sure as hell ain't gay." I looked up at her again, squinting against the room's single bare bulb. The light shimmered around her red hair, turning it to strange fire. "How you move so quiet, woman? And what the hell you doing here, anyway? You're a star, and the Blue Room ain't nothing but a dive!"

Maggie Cummings straddled my knees and sat down. With only the slightest of frowns, she began to unbutton my sweat-drenched shirt and push it off my shoulders. "I just needed to get away for a while," she answered. "I'm a little too much in demand right now. Some pushy fans were getting under my skin. I got in a cab and told the driver to take me to the last place anyone would look for me."

Now this wasn't fair. With my shirt pushed halfway down my arms, I couldn't move my hands at all. She was playing it cool as ice, but I was generating heat like a rocket on the launch pad just before take-off, and brother I was about to take off. Bending sideways, she grabbed the Jack Daniels and held it to my lips.

I swallowed, and she screwed the cap back on. "Ain't you going to have a drink?"

Maggie Cummings ran one hand through my hair, then jerked my head back sharply. Her face came closer, all video smiles, sexy and full of promise. Then I saw the sharp points of her incisors. The long sharp points. "I think I will," she said. "Thanks for offering."

She bit me. I felt the sting of her fangs, the slight brush of her tongue, which was rough and surprisingly cat-like.

"Well, what do you think?" she asked a moment later. A tiny trace of blood graced her lips.

I frowned and thought. "Kind of reminded me of my very first time. Over quick, but I was only fifteen."

Maggie threw back her head and laughed, and I turned my head to glance at the mirror. It reflected her blouse and her skirt and her spiky little high heel shoes, but of Maggie herself—nothing.

"I knew there was something special about you, Rufus Washington, the minute I saw you." She ran her hands over the wiry hairs on my chest, and Cape Canaveral started rolling out another rocket with a really big payload. "Want to do it again?" she asked.

"Uh-huh," I nodded, wishing I could free my hands. "Just don't put none of your vampire venom in, or whatever it is. I'm not ready to be *that* special."

She leaned close again, moved my head way back, and ran a slim, manicured finger along the vein that popped out. "Right here," she whispered, and I groaned a little with anticipation as she bit me. I felt her tongue once, maybe twice, on my skin, and then it was over again, quick like the last time. Too quick. I wanted more.

"Later, sugar bear," she said, teasing me with her touch and her smile. "If you really want to. But you've got another set to play and a roomful of fans waiting for you." She pulled me up off the cot, helped me out of my damp shirt, and wiped me off with it. I looked in the mirror as I reached for my clean shirt and touched my throat. "Do I need a band-aid?"

She spun me around, rose up on tiptoe and kissed me like a normal woman, so long and deep my tonsils started slam dancing. My knees turned to jelly, and I broke out in a sweat all over again. I take it back—no normal woman ever kissed me like that.

Then, stepping back, she smoothed her skirt and patted her hair into place. "You are one tasty man," she said. "I think I've got a part for you in my next picture."

I caught my breath, barely able to focus. "I got a part for you, too," I replied, reaching for her. Vampire, porn star, I didn't care what she was. I was in love!

Someone knocked. "Get your ass out here, Rufus!" Lemon called through the door; then he cracked it open an inch. "Lot of people out here waitin' for your special entertainment."

Maggie helped me into the clean shirt, standing so close I could smell my own blood on her lips. "I was hoping for some special entertainment, myself," I grumbled as she fastened the buttons and adjusted my collar. I felt like a fool, though, and a little kid, because even as I said it, I knew I'd just had the most special thing in my life—twice.

Maggie slapped my ass and pushed me toward the door. "You go kill 'em, sugar," she said. "Knock 'em dead." Then she added with a wink, "Just a figure of speech."

I started my next set, playing in a daze. My fingers ran up and down the frets, moving on automatic, as I flowed from one song to the next. In the white glare of the lone spotlight, the strings seemed to sparkle, and the notes poured from the mahogany soundboard with the power of a full blues quartet. The guitar was there, and the bass seemed to be there in the low chords, and the beat, too.

And my voice was there, blending right in with that guitar. Damn, I never sounded so good before, hot and cool and whiskey-voiced, whatever the songs required, softer than a baby's ass sometimes or rough as jagged steel, all the classics, like "Mister Big Thang" and "Do Me on the Back Side" and a lot more.

Blind Lemon was drumming on the bar, popping open beer bottles and setting up drinks as fast as he could pour them. A couple was swing dancing between the tables. The punks were banging their heads like they were at a metal concert while other people shifted around, moving in and out of the smoke and the spotlight like frantic shadows.

The old couple was doing all right, too. Oblivious

to the rest of the crowd, Mama was practically on her back right there in the booth, and Daddy was rounding third base and making straight for home like a major leaguer. Nobody cared.

And right there in the front of it all, with everything going on around her like she was the center of the whole fucking universe, Maggie Cummings sat smiling with an untouched glass of red wine and her green eyes glued on me like she didn't see anybody else. Sometimes she'd touch the hem of that leather skirt or shift those long legs, and I'd just forget where I was.

I was in love. The realization hit me like a beer bottle right between the eyes. I mean it splashed over me and ran down my face like cold, sudsy foam, right down my neck, under my shirt and past my belt into the place where it tickled and surprised the most. *Love!* It just made me want to jump up and shout!

"You took a bite outta my heart, baby!" I sang to her, and "Don't let the sun come up, cause I'm goin' down tonight!" Classic blues numbers both, I swear, even if I'd never played them before.

The whole joint was jumping, and I sang right through my next break. Maggie called my name, and the rest of the crowd picked it up like a chant as they clapped their hands together on the beats. The suited black cats abandoned their barstools, whipped off their jackets, and jumped up on the stage to back me up with some of the tightest harmonies I ever heard. At the bar in back, Lemon reached under the counter for the trumpet that had lain hidden there for years. He blew a few riffs, blending right in with the Martin, then began to rock out like the pro he once had been.

There was never a night like it in the Blue Room. The energy in that place threatened to blow the walls out, and I started crying just from sheer exuberant joy. I'd died and gone to musical heaven. I sang a note and held it, pouring everything I had into the long vibrato, drawing it out to its aching conclusion and letting it go. The final guitar chord, an unfettered arpeggio, stung the air like whip lashes. My hand froze on the strings. I stared at the upturned expectant faces, listened to the roar of their adulation, breathless and, for the first time all night, uncertain where to go next.

The entire room fell silent. I drew a deep breath and started to strum a chord just to buy time. But before I touched the strings again, before anyone could break that silence, a high sweet *a cappella* voice rose from the edge of the stage. Maggie stood up slowly like a woman in pain, holding on to the table for balance, tears streaming down her made-up face, mascara running in dark streaks as she looked up at me.

"I can't make you love me," she sang with a slow shake of her head. She was saying goodbye, and I could feel whatever magic was in that room, draining away. But I didn't want her to go, and I told her on the strings, making that guitar whimper and beg as it began to pick out the notes. Lemon felt it, too, as he added his own softly yearning accompaniment. The back-up cats got in on it, too, echoing Maggie, turning her words into a harmonic round. The audience drank it all in. Grabbing for someone, anyone in the dark, they swayed side by side in the smoke and shadow and then began to sing the chorus, too.

I reached down and took Maggie's hand, pulled her up on the stage to my side and nodded toward a microphone. I didn't understand what she was feeling right at that moment, what drove her to sing like that, but whatever it was, it was deep and old and beyond consolation. I stopped playing. Lemon took my cue. So did the back-up. As the song neared its natural end, Maggie carried it home in stark *a cappella* style once again.

When it was over, she looked at me with moist emerald eyes full of hurt, and I squeezed her hand. Choking out words through a tight, forced smile, she laid her head on my shoulder. "Who says I've got no soul?"

A loud disturbance at the bar interrupted my response. A bottle crashed; someone screamed; a table fell over. Drinks spilled and glasses broke as a dozen uniformed men and women charged into the already crowded bar, brandishing badges and weapons. At first, I thought they were police. The Blue Room was being raided!

But then, amid all the pushing and shoving, I noticed their uniforms were not police uniforms at all, but some gaudy kind of militaristic outfits, and they weren't waving weapons. They were waving Bibles!

A lean and rangy-faced old man with almost no hair on his head and eyebrows like a buzzard, reached the stage, leaped up and shoved me out of the way. I stumbled back, mindful of my guitar and Maggie. But Maggie was nowhere to be seen. A voice roared into the microphone, causing an ear-splitting feedback. "This is a Citizens' Action!" the old man shouted.

"And this is a Smith & Wesson!" Lemon answered

from the bar as he raised the pistol he kept under the register.

A half-dozen guns came up and trained on Lemon with hammers cocked back. The Bible-thumpers had come armed. One of them reached over the bar, wagged a finger under Lemon's nose and took his weapon.

"*Be prepared*, sayeth the Lord!" the old man cried into the microphone as he drew out his own gun.

"That's the goddamn Boy Scouts," I growled as I set the Martin aside. I drew myself up and puffed out my chest. "Now you scrawny little white puke, unless you want me to turn you upside down by your ankles and pluck out the last feather you got left, get the fuck off my stage and out of here."

He turned the gun my way. "My name is Fred Werthem, founder and president of the National Association for Morality through Biblical Law and Action."

"NAMBLA?" I glared at him. "You're telling me you're the president of NAMBLA?"

"We're suing for the trademark!" he snapped defensively. He waved the gun around in his right hand and the Bible in his left and shouted into the microphone again. "Now, you sinners and blasphemers, just settle down and zip it up!"

The not-so-respectable old man in the back booth stood up and adjusted his pants with an open show of contempt, and his contempt was not just open, but in plain sight. Sitting down again, he placed a protective arm around his wife.

"We're here to shut down this den of iniquity and to make a citizens' arrest. You're sheltering a harlot and a tramp that goes by the name of Maggie Cummings. You may have seen some of her movies—I know I have—and they're degrading and disgusting. They corrupt the mortal soul and drill holes in the very fabric of society."

"Hey, Fred, which one's your favorite?" I asked as I looked around. *Where was Maggie?*

"Legs in the Air, Sucker!" he answered too quickly, forgetting to turn away from the microphone.

As if on command, the table of businessmen, now thoroughly drunk, pitched back and threw their legs up over their heads. Half the bar joined in, moaning and grunting and groaning as if they were all having the orgasms of their lives.

"Mine, too," I told Fred. I still couldn't see Maggie anywhere, and I wondered if she'd escaped.

"Knock it off! Stop that!" Fred raged, red-faced with embarrassment as he pointed his gun at the businessmen. "You perverts! You're all in violation of Leviticus, chapter . . . something or other!"

My mind raced, and I remembered something Maggie had said earlier, something about pushy fans getting under her skin and needing to get away. She'd meant these guys! Just how much did they know about her? "You and your merry little band of Keystone Creeps have been following Maggie, haven't you?" I accused angrily.

"Of course!" Fred snapped. "We've trained for a long time for an opportunity like this. When we saw the announcement that the Queen of Straight to Video was visiting our fair and beloved city we knew it was a sign that now was the time to stand up for decency!" He gestured to his gang of wannabe terrorists. "Get to work, troops. We know she's here someplace!"

Lemon moved before I did. He didn't have his

gun, but his trumpet was still at hand. Snatching it up, he puffed up his cheeks and blew a powerful blast right into the ears of the two nearest fanatics. Dozens of people clapped hands over their ears, and Lemon swung his instrument with all his strength.

It was the distraction everyone needed. The bar erupted as the Blue Room's customers leaped at the Fred Werthem's followers. Bottles flew, then chairs. Tables crashed and overturned. Without thinking, I jumped on Werthem, knocking the gun from his hand as I tackled him. My teeth locked on his neck.

Somehow, he found the strength to push me off. Wide-eyed, he pressed a hand to his bloody wound. "You . . . you bit me!"

I wiped the back of my hand over my mouth and noted the red smear and the coppery taste of blood in the back of my throat. "Yeah, I'm kind of surprised myself." I ran my tongue over the tips of my teeth. Everything seemed normal.

Lemon blew his trumpet again. The bent and dented instrument made a harsh, horrible screech, but it was still plenty loud. He waded through the battling mob, wrecking eardrums right and left, collecting pistols and shoving them into his pockets and waistband. Lemon laughed like a crazy man until someone beaned him with a Bible and he sank to his knees.

Fred and I looked at each other. We each grabbed one of the microphone stands, but as my opponent drew back to swing, the pink-haired punk girlie took out his legs in a flying tackle. At almost the same time, someone flung a barstool. Noting its trajectory, I made a desperate dive to save the Martin, and with

the guitar wrapped in one arm, slid off the end of
the stage. Unfortunately, the microphone stand came
with me, and I got up with my instrument safe only
to trip over the heavy base. The Martin howled in
despair as it banged on the floor.

Chaos reigned in the Blue Room. Two of Worthem's
wingnut troops, showing their true colors, fled out
into the street. My big black back-up singers chased
after them and dragged them kicking and screaming
back into the bar. The middle-aged gentleman at the
back booth, packing a surprising punch, got up and
positioned himself to block the door against any other
attempt to escape, while his wife, now in possession
of Lemon's trumpet, demonstrated her own musical
skill, blowing "When the Saints Go Marching In" with
hip-swinging gusto on the top of her table.

I'd seen a lot of bar fights in my time, but this
was the strangest. In fact, the entire night had been
flat-out strange and dream-like. Maybe I was just deep
in the Jack Daniels and stretched out on the cot in
the broom closet in the grip of the bourbon. Maybe
Maggie Cummings had never been here at all. Maybe
there'd never been an audience, and I'd never been
a star even for a night. Maybe the throbbing in my
head was all booze-induced.

Oh, Lord, I want to be in that number...

The entire bar froze, and everyone fell quiet again,
so quiet that I heard the hammer cock on the gun at
the back of my head. Crazy Mama stopped blowing
her horn. Lemon, on his feet again, checked a punch
to someone's chin. The blue-haired punk boy broke
off an embrace with one of Worthem's female troops.

"Now for the last time, you sinners!" Fred Worthem

called out in a shaking voice. "Where is the tramp! Where is she?"

No one answered, nor even seemed to breathe.

Then, a small black shaped fluttered in the glare of the single spotlight, and for a moment, Fred Worthem and I stood illuminated like two characters in Bob Kane's famous bat-signal.

After a moment, the shape in the spotlight changed. Maggie Cummings, gloriously steamy in her bare nakedness, red hair shimmering like fire and green eyes glowing, floated straight down through that brilliant beam to the edge of the stage. Worthem's gaze locked with hers, and he gave a little girlie scream as she bared her fangs with a hiss.

Fred Worthem, founder and president, moralist and gun-toting would-be radical domestic terrorist, dropped his weapon—and fainted.

I nudged the gun away with my toe. "Bumbler," I said.

Maggie frowned. "Is it my breasts," she asked, sounding worried. "Am I sagging? After all, I'm almost a hundred and fifty."

As glad as I was to see her, I had my own worries. Putting fingers to my lips, I stretched my mouth as wide as I could. "Are my teeth normal? I bit him, and it was kind of gross."

Maggie rose up on tiptoe and kissed me. "You're fine, sugar bear. More than fine." She picked up someone's suit jacket and slipped it on. Somehow, she managed to look even more naked with it on.

I grabbed her as people began to shift around the room. I wasn't interested in them right then. "Where did you go, Maggie? I thought you were gonna leave me."

She gave a shy smile, something I'd never seen in her videos. "I thought about it," she answered, looking down. "But I hung around." She pointed toward the ceiling.

"I'm in love with an old bat," I said.

Maggie jabbed me in the gut. Then she pressed against me. "Ours would be a mixed marriage."

I touched my neck where she'd bitten me twice. I knew what I wanted. "It wouldn't have to be."

Her eyes widened. "You mean . . . ? Are you sure?"

"I can never get my act together before sundown anyway," I said. "And I could still keep playing here for a while, at least. I might be undead, but I still have career ambitions."

She kissed me again. "We're both natural performers!"

"Well, why don't you both perform your asses down here and answer a few questions," Lemon called from the middle of the bar. The other patrons were busy tying up the wannabe terrorists with lengths of rope, duct tape, and anything else from the bar's storage room. "Particularly what we're supposed to do with all the ambulatory refuse."

I looked down at Worthem, who was still unconscious. I almost felt sorry for him, just not sorry enough. Poor man looked like he could use a drink, though. All his followers did. "When you got 'em tied up," I suggested, "break open a case of *Jack*. Feed 'em plenty of that—pour it down 'em if you have to—and they won't remember anything. Whiskey hangovers are the purest kind of justice."

Lemon frowned. "What about the cops? Should I call 'em?"

I shrugged and put my arm around Maggie as someone handed her her shoes. I didn't want to risk any of us being taken to jail for questioning—or, worse, locked up. Maggie wouldn't look good in morning light. I wondered, though, about the customers who had fought for us. What if one of them talked?

The blue-haired punk kid walked up with a pen and a napkin, his pink-haired girlfriend in tow. "We were wondering," he said nervously, "could we have your autographs?"

"Now pack up that guitar, and you two get outta here," Lemon insisted when we'd signed the napkin and handed it back. "I got cleanup and a new trumpet to think about, and you got things to do. Man, this has been the best night ever!"

"We'll help," the old couple offered.

"We'll all help."

Maggie and I left arm in arm and started down the sidewalk. Though it was still dark, I gazed up at the sky once, remembering the sunrise and wondering if I'd ever see it again. With a star like Maggie at my side, it didn't seem to matter. She seemed happy, too.

"You like walkin' around like that, don't you?" I teased as I listened to the click, click, click of her high heels.

She tugged at the lapels of the suit jacket, which gaped open across her breasts and hid nothing.

I stopped in the soft glow of a streetlight, looked at her for a long moment, drinking in her beauty, but also glimpsing a strange innocence that I'd never noticed in any of her films. I set my guitar case down and kissed her then, long and deep, savoring the cool taste of her, knowing that I'd found something unique.

And when she kissed me back, her fangs brushed ever so delicately over my throat, not penetrating, but with a tantalizing promise of that.

"Tramp," I whispered.

She answered in my ear. "Prude."

"Tramp."

She patted her hair. "You love it."

Sarah Zettel is author of fourteen science fiction and fantasy novels. She is also contributing author and project manager for the online fiction site Book View Cafe (www.bookviewcafe.com). In her free time, she chases her son, learns the fiddle, gardens infrequently, and considers sleeping sometime in the near future.

Vampless

Sarah Zettel

Sunday

Sometimes I think I'm the only girl in tenth grade who doesn't have a vampire.

I mean, okay, Johanna Prescott doesn't, but she's soooo busy with her AP physics that she probably wouldn't know a vampire if one, you know, bit her. And Stephanie Gibbs doesn't, but she's president of the Vampstinance society and spends all her time trying to get girls to give up their vamps.

As *if*.

I mean, I've *heard* it, okay? Like my mom *ever* shuts up about it. "Marcia, having a gorgeous immortal (Hannah says never, ever call them Undead. It's a total insult) swear eternal love for you does not make you a better person. What makes you special is what's inside!" Blah, blah, blah.

But if nobody can see what makes me special because it's all inside, what's the *point*?

The point is that my mom's got wolfsbane growing in with the roses and a crucifix superglued to every window in the house. I don't even want to *talk* about where she's got the holy water stashed and I have to be in by four-thirty from October to March.

I'm doomed to spend high school vampless.

Monday

OMG! Hannah's got a vamp. She told me yesterday at lunch. She was wearing this totally cute blue turtleneck that she got at Forever 21 (which is *the* place for vamp-worthy clothes), but she wouldn't show me the marks. She says she didn't let him bite her yet. She says you shouldn't on the first encounter (you don't *date* a vamp. That's completely for daytime boys.) and after that you should just let them have the wrist, 'cause on the neck is for after the eternal love declaration and maybe after they've fought another vamp for you.

Anyway. Details: His name is Damien. He's a Russian vamp from the Rasputinov clan, which is cool beyond belief. Hannah says it's the second or third oldest of the big clans. He says he's over a hundred, and that he got vamped during the Russian Revolution when the Bolsheviks stormed the Russian court and rounded up the Czar's family. He was one of the bodyguards for Princess Anastasia and he'll never forgive himself for not being able to protect her. He's got blond hair and blue eyes and he's really, really tall.

I am soooooo jealous I could scream.

Tuesday

So, I asked Hannah how she encountered Damien. We were at Friendly's Ice Cream ('cause it's the only place you can walk to and her mom won't let her drive yet either and if Trenton, Michigan's got a bus, it died of loneliness). We'd just sat down with our mochaccinos and I asked and she got this *huge* goofy grin on her face.

She leans in real close and she says, "I went out as a hunter."

"A what?" I hate sounding stupid, but she was making *no* sense.

Which gives her an excuse to look all smug. "A hunter. You know, a vamp killer. The good vamps—you know, the ones who are looking to go with daytime girls, not just hook up and drain—think hunters are total hotties. It's not just what you look like with a vamp, you know." Cue the superior look and tossing the hair back so everybody can see she's wearing a turtleneck (purple) to cover up the bite marks she hasn't got yet.

"How would I know?" I say it around this big lump of whipped cream. "Mom's got me totally quarantined."

Hannah shakes her head in deep sympathy and slurps mochaccino. "She has got to get with the program. Anyway. If you want to get a really good vamp, you've got to show them you're brave. So the best way is to get yourself a wooden stake and a completely hot outfit and go out like you're hunting. And I was down by Preston's Market..."

"You went down *there*? After dark?" Putting it

out for a vamp is one thing, but Preston's is down next to this closed down factory that used to make car parts or something. Down where the junkies and the gangbangers and other losers hang. Down there something truly uglifing could really happen.

But again, I get the "duh" eyeballs from Hannah. "Well, *yeah*. What was I supposed to do, hang around here all night? Like a vamp is ever going to fly over *our* street."

"Tell me about it." Our street used to be a field or something. It's got two kinds of houses on it; the colonial and the split level. If you go two blocks over, you get two other kinds: the split level and the colonial. They run in straight lines, block, after block, after block. The trees are skinny saplings and if you don't have a car you can't even get to the mall or the movies or anything. My folks moved us here because supposedly it's got good schools.

I wouldn't know. What I do know about Trenton is it's *beyond* boring. Is it any wonder all the girls are trying to get vamps? It's not only totally cool, it's just about the only thing there is to do around here.

"So, anyway, I'm down by Preston's," Hannah says, "And pretty soon I see *him*."

Him. Damien. She says his eyes shine in the dark when he looks at her and *everything*. "And he comes out of the shadows and he's all 'You shouldn't be out here alone,' and I go, 'I'm not scared.' And he goes, 'You should be, little girl.' And I go, 'I'm ready for anything,' and I show him my stake."

"You show him your *stake*?"

"Duh! You've got to show them, or they're going to think you're just some stupid kid who doesn't know what they're doing. Anyway, I show him my stake and he gets this hungry look on his face..."

I slurp more mochaccino. "I thought they all looked like that."

"Not that kind of hungry." Her eyes go all misty and she gives this big sigh. "Heart-hungry. *Soul-*hungry. And he said he'd better walk with me, and I said he'd better not try anything, and he said he wouldn't and..."

"And did he...?" I crook my fingers and stab down.

She knows exactly what I'm talking about and she shakes her head "Nope. Just walked me home. He said he'd never met anybody like me before. Not for a hundred years. He said I look like *her.*"

"Who!" I'm done trying to keep my cool.

"*Her.* Anastasia! Like maybe I'm her reincarnation or something..."

Whoa, I'm thinking. *This is so totally huge.* "Did he say that?"

"No! Of course not! But like, what if I was? What if we've got an actual Destiny?" She says it in this excited whisper, like she didn't want to believe it, because she wanted it so much.

The *only* thing better than having a vamp is having a Destiny. Not everybody does. Most people (even the ones whose moms let them out of the house) just kind of stumble around and have to make the best out of whatever they can find. But if you've got a Destiny, that's it. You don't even have to *try* anymore because it's *going* to happen. It's going to work out. It *has* to.

Wednesday

Hannah wants me to meet Damien. She says since
I'm her complete BFF I should. Besides, she says if
she's got a Destiny, she's not going to be around much
longer, and she doesn't want to leave me vampless
when Damien takes her out of here.

I almost started crying. I felt like such a complete
baby, but what am I going to do if I haven't got a
best friend *or* a vamp?

I've *got* to get out of the house.

Thursday

I finally figured out how to get out of the house.

The irony is that it was Stephanie Gibbs who gave
me the idea. I got to school and there was Stephanie
out front trying to pass out these totally lame leaflets
about how the Vampstinance clubs of Wayne County
are doing this Vamp Free Night march and rally. I'm
ready to shove the thing back at her when I realize
this is *it*. If I tell Mom that I'm joining Vampstinance
and I'm going to the rally with Stephanie, I can *get
out of the house after dark*.

So, the next thing I know, I'm like actually talking
to Stephanie (and trying not to gag 'cause she like
waaay overdoes it with the perfume), asking about
the march, and saying I think she's got a point about
vamps. I totally cannot believe that this is coming out
of my mouth, but she's *buying* it. Her eyes go all
wide and she actually starts *bouncing*. She scribbles

her phone number on my notebook and says I should call her, 'cause her sister's gonna drive her to the rally and I can ride with them. Then she grabs my hand and she's saying how great it's gonna be and she's so glad I've seen the light.

She actually said that. "Seen the light." Could she *be* more lame?

Anyway. I knew it wasn't going to be anything like that easy with Mom. I couldn't just tell her I'd seen the light. She'd never buy it. I'd have to be a lot more . . . *subtle*.

So, I take the bogus leaflet and I hide it in my planner, but not all the way. Then, when I'm at the dining room table doing my homework, Mom gets a peek at it (it was hot pink, which helped).

So, Mom goes, "What's this?"

And I go, "Nothing," and try to push it down in the papers.

And she goes, "Let me see it."

And I go, "It's *nothing*."

And she gets this look on her face and she holds out her hand and she says, "*Now*, young lady." So I drag it out really slow, like it's the last thing I want to do. She takes it and she reads it and she looks at me over the rims of her glasses. "Why didn't you want me to see this?"

I look down at the table and give this little squirm and mumble, "'Cause I don't know if I'm going."

I'm all ready for one of her lectures about responsibility and safe choices and blah blah, but her whole scowl dissolves and her face goes all kind of misty (almost like Hannah's when she's talking about Damien, which is just *too* weird to contemplate).

She says, "Honey, if you're serious about this, I'll back you all the way. I know how hard it is to go against what everybody thinks is the right thing."

After that, it's a total piece of cake. She calls Stephanie's mom and gets the skinny on the carpool and everything. The only problem is I feel kind of sick to my stomach. I mean, here she is acting all proud of me and everything, and all I'm doing is trying to work out how to get away from the stupid rally *fast* so I can catch up with Hannah.

I feel so sick I almost tell her what's really going on, but I don't. 'Cause Hannah calls and she tells me she'd talked with Damien and he's going to encounter up with her Friday and he is *totally* cool with me being there. He said when he met up with Anastasia she always had a waiting lady with her, to keep lookout and stuff.

Hannah said it was a Sign about the Destiny and I was part of it.

So, how come she gets to be the reincarnated princess and I just get to be the stupid lookout? It's not *fair*.

But I have to go now. She is my BFF, after all. And who knows? Even ladies in waiting can have Destinies, right?

Friday

The ride to the Vampstinance march was the longest ride of my entire life.

Stephanie and her sister show up right after sundown. My mom shakes hands with Big Sister (whose name was Brittany or something, I don't know), and says how happy she is and when do we think we'll be home and blah blah blah. The whole time I'm standing there with my windbreaker zipped up to my neck so Mom doesn't see my Forever 21 shirt with the sweetheart neckline that shows the henna design I've got painted right where my cleavage starts. My right leg's going all pins and needles because I've got my stake taped under my peasant skirt (right below the leather mini I'm wearing *under* my peasant skirt). Worse, Stephanie gets all huggy again. I have to hold my breath when I hug her back because she's like wearing a total gallon of Abstract Patchouli #5 or something.

When we *finally* get in the car, Stephanie's squeeing like a fan girl—all about how she can't believe it's *finally* here and she can't believe she's *finally* getting to go, and how she didn't think Mom was ever going to let her go (which might show her mother's not a total lame-brain, but I can't decide), and maybe we should pull over and get a snack because it's going to be a long night, and on and on and *on*. Until finally her sister rolls her eyes and yells "Shut *up* already or I'm taking us all home! I *told* Mom you were too young for this!"

Which shut Stephanie right up. I looked out the window so she wouldn't see me smile.

By the time we get to Elizabeth Park, which was the rally point (it's the rally point for everything in Trenton, 'cause it's the only even semi-big park we've got), there's already a huge crowd. It's like every nerd girl in Wayne County is out. Somebody's on a podium making a speech under a big banner that says TAKE

BACK THE BITE! But nobody's listening to her because they're all singing and drumming and dancing. I'm trying to stick to the edges of the crowd, but Stephanie grabs my arm and pulls me *right* into the middle. Next thing I know, somebody's pinning this thing on me that looks like one of those squirting flowers clowns wear, except it's an open mouth and it says "The only wet kiss you'll get from me!"

"Holy water!" Pin Woman says. "Blessed fresh this morning." She makes this big deal out of showing me how to run the little pipe up my sleeve and put the little rubber squeezy-ball-thing in my pocket.

"Gosh. Thanks."

Pin Woman gives me this great big hug and runs off to pin somebody else, and I'm looking around, trying to figure out if there's anywhere I can sneak off and get rid of the totally lame thing. By now, my leg is really starting to itch from the tape holding the stake in place and I can't feel all my toes. I'm going deaf from all the cheering and drumming, and Stephanie's looking at me and her eyes are shining.

It takes me a minute to figure out the march is actually starting.

And I'm thinking, *Crap. How am I going to get out of here?* But right then, my cell goes off. I rip it out of my purse and check the number.

Hannah.

Stephanie's eyeing me. And I'm like *What? Were we supposed to turn our cells off so we wouldn't interrupt the chanting or something?* But, I just say, "One sec." I back off as far as I can and I whisper as soft as I can, "Hey, Hannah!"

"Where *are* you?"

She knows about the march, but I don't want to go into it. "Where are *you*?"

"I'm at the Fort Street bridge. Get over here!"

"Okay, okay!" I hang up and I give Stephanie this big grin. She's not grinning. She'd giving me this fish-eye and I know I've got to make this fast.

"That was Hannah. She totally wants to join us! I'm going to get her and we'll catch up, 'kay? 'Kay. Bye!"

I am *outta* there, moving as fast as I can. Which wasn't really fast. It's tough enough to run in spike heels, but with a stake taped to your leg... I think I deserve some kind of gold medal or something.

Hannah's right where she says she'd be. She is *not* wearing her Forever 21 ensemble. She must have been buying online, because she's in this *unbelievable* outfit. It's this long, poofy pink and gold skirt and this white poofy blouse that's so thin I can tell she's wearing a pink cami underneath (and she shouldn't be, because it is not her color). To top it off she's got this sparkly headband and these gold ballet flats.

"You like?" she twirls. "It's for Damien."

Like I didn't know *that*. "So, where is he?" Inside I'm going, *Is he going to bring a friend? Or take us to meet a friend?* 'Cause she can dress like Tinkerbell for all I care, as long as I finally get my chance to have a vamp of my own.

"We're going to meet him," she says. "He doesn't like crowds when he's trying not to feed."

"So what're we waiting for?"

Actually, we're waiting for me to get changed, which is when I discover what a big mistake my outfit was. For one thing, it's totally freezing, so I have to leave my windbreaker on or I'm going to be

a mass of totally non-hot goosepimples (but I do at
least stuff the stupid pin in the pocket). For another
I've got nowhere to stash my peasant skirt, so I have
to stuff it in the bushes (goodbye, forty-five dollars).
For another, I've got nowhere to stash my stake, so
I've got to stuff *it* up my sleeve, which, if anything,
is *less* comfortable than having it strapped to my leg.

And there's Hannah in her Pretty-Pretty Princess
outfit looking me over and saying "Well, you tried
anyway. Come on."

Inside I'm going, *This had better get me a vamp
or I swear I'm going to have to move, or kill Hannah
so there won't be any witnesses.*

Anyway.

We take off and I've got no idea where we're going,
but Hannah seems to, so I'm trying to find my strut
and not shiver. But we're definitely headed *down*town,
toward Preston's and the old factory. There's no sidewalks
here, just the shoulder of the road. There's not a whole
lot of streetlights either. The fence is pulled down in
half a dozen places so anybody can get into the old
buildings if they want. I'm pretty sure I'm hearing stuff
I don't want to know about. A guy in this pimp mobile
actually slows down to take a good look at us, and I
am starting to have second thoughts, vamp or no vamp.

But I can't say so, 'cause I can't look like a wuss,
but I kind of shimmy my arm so my stake slides down
into my palm. Fortunately, Hannah's walking on my
other side so she doesn't see. Having some kind of
weapon makes me feel just a little bit better.

Then, Hannah grabs my arm (*everybody* was grabbing my arm, what was *up* with that?) She squees,
"Damien!"

He's standing at the factory driveway, on the edge of the puddle of light from the one working streetlight beside the old guard shack. I can barely see him, but his shadow is tall and lean and in the streetlight his hair's almost white. He's wearing a long coat and a dark shirt and dark jeans and his eyes really do shine as he steps out into the light.

And he's alone. My heart sinks, but I rally. *This is just the first step,* I tell myself. *If I got out once, I can do it again.*

Hannah lets go and runs toward him, and he opens his arms, like in the old movies and I could scream, or spit, or something because I can barely stand to look at it.

But I look anyway, and I see this man's silhouette reach out and grab Damien and yank him into the guard shack. Hannah chokes and starts to scream.

Then she's gone too.

And like the idiot I am, I start running. Forward. "Hannah! Hannah!" I'm yelling and I'm thinking, *Oh shit, oh SHIT. Hunters, it's vamp hunters.*

I've got the stake in my hand because it's all I've got if I've got to fight, and I skid to a stop in front of the shack's open door.

Damien's sprawled on the ground and this guy's yanking his wallet out of his pocket, and this other guy's got a knife—a *knife*—and he's grabbing Hannah's purse, and she's hanging on and screaming for Damien. Part of me's thinking she's so dumb. She should just let the guy *have* it.

The rest of me is yelling "Hey! Assholes! Let her go!" And brandishing my stake.

One of the a-holes yells at the other. "It's a fucking

hunter, man!" And I run toward them, and they're shoving past me to get out the door, and I'm running after them across the broken asphalt and the weeds, and I feel like...I don't know, like I could take on the world. It feels so good I barely remember to stop running and turn around to get back to Hannah in the guard shack.

Hannah's on her knees beside Damien. She stares up at me, white as a ghost.

"He's...he's..." And she's on her feet and backing away. "He's..."

Next thing I know, she's out the door and running too.

He's dead, I'm thinking. *But the guys were just muggers. How could they have killed a vamp?*

Then Damien moans, and I kneel down next to him and shove him onto his back. And I'm thinking, *That's weird,* because he doesn't feel cold like vamps're supposed to.

Damien's chest heaves, and his eyes open and he sees me.

All at once, he's scrabbling backward, kind of one-handed, with his head under his arm. My fingers feel funny. I look down, and my whole hand's covered in this white stuff that in the bad light looks *exactly* like smeared makeup.

Next thing I know, I actually tackle Damien, and he starts yelling "Ah!" and "Get off me!" But I'm so mad I don't. Instead, I roll him over and I shove his arm away, and I see the big smear on his face, and the suntan underneath.

"Daytimer!" I yell, backing off, just like Hannah did. "You're a daytime boy! You lied!"

"Well what do you *expect!*" He yells back at me so loud I can see his two-tone fangs. "Girls won't look at you unless you're a vamp! I was never gonna get lai...a girlfriend!"

"What'd you do to your teeth?" I'm still on the trivialities because I cannot believe this. I can't believe Hannah, who knows more about vamps than anybody, was totally fooled!

"Caps," he says. "Come on, anybody can get them."

Yeah, but...yeah but... And I'm practically crying, because in the back of my head I'm going, *I'm never going to get a vamp. I'm never* ever *going to get a vamp.*

"You loser!" I whack him across the face leaving another big smear in the white makeup.

"Ow!" He pushes me back—hard—and I fall on my butt and he scrambles to his feet. "It's not my *fault!* If your *friend* was interested in something besides a big red hickey..."

I throw the stake at him and he ducks, and I leave him there.

I get out onto the empty, broken parking lot and don't feel much better. The whole night feels oily and I'm on my own. It's starting to sink in that Hannah and Daytime Boy had really almost been mugged and did I mention I was *alone* in my stupid leather mini and my stupid spike heel boots, and I threw my stake at "Damien." I'm about ready to haul out my phone and call Mom because the idea of being locked in my room until I'm thirty suddenly doesn't seem as bad as the idea of not living to *see* thirty when I see a flash of swirling skirt and sparkles back by this big, tin storage shed kind of building.

"Hannah!" And I'm running again. But my ankles are starting to wobble, and I'm starting to wheeze and I'm thinking if I can just get back home I'll never, *ever* go out after dark again, really. Daytime boys 4-me 4-ever.

This is all before I get around the corner and see Hannah, slumped against the tin wall. I shout her name again and run forward, but then I get a whiff of perfume and raw meat, and I turn, and see Stephanie.

Stephanie, with her hair messed up and her eyes shining and her fangs out.

Her *fangs*?!

"You're a... you're a..."

She laughs and it sounds exactly like a hyena in a nature film and all the hairs on the back of my neck stand up. "You daytimers are so pathetic!" She sashays forward and I back up, and hit the wall right beside Hannah and it goes *wham!* and wobbles under my back. Hannah's still standing up, but she's not moving, and I can't look at her. I can't take my eyes off Stephanie.

She goes, "And you're so stupid! You invent sunblock and polarized contacts and you still think we can't come out in the sunlight!" She smiles and I see how long and sharp her teeth are. They don't look sexy at all. Especially not because they're dark stained. She gets closer and all at once I know what's up with all the perfume. Vamps stink. They stink like blood and dirt from abandoned factories and old death left out in the heat.

"You're all soooo busy chasing after your pretty undead boys, you don't pay any attention to what we're doing, do you?"

"Vampstinance..." I gulp.

Her grin grows even wider. "Ever hear the term 'useful idiots'? It's so nice of them to organize a buffet night for us, don't you think?"

Beside me, Hannah slides down the wall. Her eyes are glazed over. There's a dark smear on her neck. My heart drops into my shoes. *It's real. It's really real. She's drained and she's gonna die, and I'm standing here with a freaking she-vamp...*

"Pathetic," sneers Stephanie.

Something hits me in the middle of the chest. The world spins and I slam against concrete and I can't breathe, and Stephanie—*with* her mouth open—is sitting on my chest. She hisses at me, and blood and spit drip on my face and and this little voice in the back of my head is screaming, *I'mgonnadieI'mgonnadieI'mgonnadieI'mgonnadie...*

"Get *off* her, mothersucker!"

Stephanie turns, and there's Damien towering over both of us, my stake raised up high over his head.

Stephanie laughs and shoves him one-handed and he goes flying and hits the wall next to Hannah and it wangs and it wobbles. It all takes maybe a second, but it's enough for my brain to quit screaming and start trying to keep itself alive. My hand dives into my pocket, and just as Stephanie turns back for another round of the whole bloody-drippy hissy fit thing, I cram her mouth with that stupid holy water pin thing that the totally lame Vampstinance woman pinned on me and if I ever see her again, I'm gonna like, have her baby or something (okay, maybe not have her baby, but you know what I'm saying).

Because Stephanie scrambles back and she's choking

and gagging and I grab up the stake and I'm sick and scared and furious all at the same time and I don't even know what I'm doing and my arms are swinging and I'm screaming and *WHAM!*

And there's Stephanie on the broken concrete, with my stake coming out of her chest. And it's so much less gross than the drippy-blood fangs, I don't even mind.

I'm panting and I'm staring at Damien with his smeared make-up, and he's suddenly the best, bravest, hottest thing I've ever seen.

At least he is until he says. "I thought you were Hannah."

And that was it.

Almost.

I had to call my mom, 'cause I'd staked our ride. Hannah had to go to the hospital. She's in there now, but they say she's getting out next week. But she's not going back to school. Her mom's sending her into a rehab program for vamp victims. I think she still doesn't know Hannah went out looking to get vamped.

Hannah's not talking to me, and she hasn't returned one of my texts. I think she doesn't want to deal with the fact she got vamp-scammed.

Mom's letting me stay home too, for as long as I want, which is great, because from the texts and stuff I was getting, the whole story was all over the school, and I don't want to face it. I just stayed in my room, trying to get my head around how I almost got myself killed just because I didn't want to be bored and how I might not have a best friend anymore and I'm feeling all weird and sad because I'm never going to have a vamp, even though I don't want to have a vamp anymore, but still...

Then, around four-thirty, just when it's starting to get dark she comes in with this leaflet for the Mina Harker School For Girls.

It's an alternative school.

For hunters.

Seems the hunter community heard about what happened and they called Mom. They told her they think I'm a Natural and she should really think about enrolling me so my Talents can be properly harnessed for the Good of Society. Or something.

Looks like I've got a Destiny after all.

An Air Force brat, **Linda Donahue** spent much of her childhood traveling. Having earned a pilot's certification and a SCUBA certification, she has been a threat by land, air or sea. For eighteen years she taught computer science and mathematics. When not writing, she teaches tai chi and belly dance. Linda has published twenty-some stories and coauthored a piece with Mike Resnick for *Future Americas*. Her stories also appear in *Sword & Sorceress 23* and *Strip Mauled*. She and her husband live in Texas with rabbits, sugar gliders and a cat for pets. You can visit her website at www.LindaLDonahue.com.

The Goth Girl Next Door

Linda L. Donahue

As Charles backed out of the driveway, his night-vision latched onto the SOLD sign next door.

Naturally, the *quiet* neighbors had moved away and not the Fergusons, whose son played in a garage band—or more aptly put, a maul band. If not for Charles's day job, he would've staked himself long ago to escape the noise.

Plus he needed the cash. Though he came from old blood, he wasn't from old money. And even vampires paid for rent and utilities.

Charles parked behind the Mosewell Funeral Parlor. Once inside, he wandered to the draining room where he poured himself a glass of blood from the fridge—one of his many job perks. He'd gotten an "irregular" coffin for half price, with velvet upholstery and a non-standard, interior latch thrown in.

Then he sat before the mirror, watching the cosmetologist work on what appeared an empty chair.

Though Marcie's graduation certificate said otherwise, rumor had it she'd honed her skills at a clown school. His fangs clenched, Charles prayed for a "natural" look, as opposed to what she called "Coffin Celebrity." Last week she'd given him a Liberace pompadour.

Marcie patted his shoulder. "You look just like George Hamilton."

Charles groaned, expecting she'd smeared him with a fake tan. Suddenly he was glad he couldn't see his reflection.

On the showroom floor, Charles climbed into a white display coffin with brass fittings. Sweet peace. No abused drums; no tortured guitar strings. No industrial-grunge racket. Just soft dirges and whispers.

Charles slept through people's comments, their words coming through like dreams—something he missed after his "mid-life crisis." In his family, one simply turned vampire between thirty-five and forty. As if one mid-life crisis wasn't enough.

A nasal voice intruded on Charles's solitude. "Whoa, there's a dude in the coffin. Is he, like, dead?"

The funeral director's resonate voice answered, "Charles is our coffin model."

"He's paid to lie there? Are you hiring?"

Charles slipped back into a restful stage . . . until someone shook him.

"Is that coffin comfortable?" a woman asked.

"I beg your pardon?"

"Are you comfortable? I'm looking at coffins for my aunt."

"I doubt she'll complain," Charles said.

"You don't know her. She claims her arthritis bothers her, but vampires don't have arthritis. Of course, we've never had a vampire in the family. Would glu-cosamine in her Bloody Marys help?"

Charles shook his head, mostly out of disbelief. "Are you sure your aunt's a vampire?"

"Let's see . . . came back from the dead and drinks blood. Yeah, I'm sure. And she's been hell to live with. I'm hoping a comfy coffin will improve her mood."

"That's . . . kind of you." Few families of Nuevo Vampires accepted their relatives' change. "I recommend extra thick lining. And if she smokes, go with fireproofing."

Charles hated Saturdays. Too many weekend shoppers.

Later, for the second time, someone shook him awake.

Doug leaned over and whispered, "Emergency meeting tonight. If something isn't done about that garage band, there's going to be hell to pay . . . figuratively speaking, since everyone's paid up on homeowner's dues."

That was all Charles needed . . . the neighborhood monsters going on a rampage. Yet a bloody, screaming rampage would be quieter than anything Rutabaga Riot ever played.

By the time Charles got home, after sundown, a moving van was pulling away from the neighbor's house. A slender woman with jet-black hair, pasty skin, and heavily lined eyes watched them leave. She wore red and black and had multiple piercings. She looked like a nice girl.

"I'm Charles, your neighbor," he said, wandering over.

"Andie." The woman thrust out her hand. A thick bracelet decorated with silver skulls adorned her wrist.

"Jazzed to meet you. The place is a mess, but who keeps house anymore? That's my way of inviting you inside—and maybe helping me with the unboxing."

Having enough of an invitation, he shrugged. "I've got a little time." But not much. Being late to the Special Homeowners' Meeting meant supplying snacks at the next one. And monsters were finicky eaters.

Heavy furniture stood where it'd likely remain. Stacked boxes and crates created a maze. Andie grabbed a cutter and sliced into box marked "Sharp."

"You must have a lot of knickknacks," Charles said.

"Nope." Andie pulled out an Indian tomahawk. "I don't keep things that break easy."

When she pulled out a wicked, curved axe, Charles asked, "Are you a collector?"

"I wish."

Charles laughed nervously. Normally—to a vampire—goth chicks looked all sweet and innocent, adorable girls in delicious black lipstick with pure white skin. But this chick made the schoolgirl goth getup seem like she was a wolf in sheep's clothing. "A serial killer?"

Andie gave the axe a one-handed swing. "That would make these my toy surprises." She laughed. "But no . . . *not* a serial killer. Try retired monster hunter."

Charles would've paled—but skin only went so white. Luckily, his George Hamilton tan covered his pasty fear. "Retired? Already? Did it pay that well?"

"It paid bupkus. Sure, it was exciting and came with spiffy accessories, but a girl gets tired of washing the 'ick' out of her clothes. Besides, I figured I'd stop the job before it stopped me, you know?"

Suddenly the Ferguson boy seemed a real prize. Once Andie discovered who lived on the block, she'd come out of retirement. But on the plus side, she might take out Rutabaga Riot.

Panic rising, Charles searched for an excuse to make like a bat and flap the hell out—but not literally, as it would give him away. Finally, he blurted, "I'd better feed the cat."

He cursed himself. Now he'd have to get a cat, in case she ever dropped by.

Charles hurried to the emergency meeting of the Special Homeowners Association. Bursting through Frankie's front door, he exploded, "Forget the band! We have a bigger problem."

Trying not to blather, Charles broke the news.

"This can't be happening," Goblin Glen murmured. "Sure, the neighborhood has a few cranks and too many teens, but it was always a safe place to live."

Frankie rubbed his black hand against his sallow cheek, his mismatched parts making him look like a badly made quilt. "Once she gets to know us, she'll see we aren't monsters. Okay, we *are* monsters, but we aren't *monsters*. After all, not everyone is put together the same way."

"Vhat you're forgetting," Vic said, "is ve didn't choose to be who ve are." Since chipping a tooth, Vic sounded like Count Chocula.

Gretta the ghoul nodded. "He's right. She *chose* to be a hunter."

"A *retired* hunter," Frankie argued. "So, let's not condemn her just yet. Let's throw a block party."

Doug scratched like he'd picked up fleas during the last full moon. "You think a hunter can live in the neighborhood and not notice us?"

"Retired hunter," Frankie repeated, his heart bigger

than his brain (an oversight, according to the mad doctor who'd made him).

Charles scoffed. "I've seen her arsenal. What you're proposing, Frankie, will be a block *massacre*."

"But after she gets to know us..." Frankie stressed.

"It'll make it easier for her to compile her 'to do' list," Charles finished.

"Say," Doug said, "suppose someone dates her? If she gets romantically interested in a monster—"

"Are you volunteering?" Goblin Glen asked. "Because I'm not dating a serial killer. Hunters and monsters mix like ammonia and bleach."

"What about you, Frankie?" Charles suggested. "You're big and rugged, held together by stitches and hardware bolts. A real goth chick magnet."

Frankie folded his mismatched arms. "Have you met my wife...*The Bride*? Her screaming all the time isn't just her way of communicating. She's a screaming loony!"

"So, she'd say 'no,'" Charles summed up. "Doug, would your wife let you take one for the gang?"

Doug snorted so hard a muzzle almost sprang out. "She'd turn me into a newt...or worse, a cat."

That meant a probable "no" from the witch.

Feeling the gazes turn on him, Charles waved his hands. "No way I'm ever going back inside her house, invitation or not."

So with reluctance, they voted in favor of the block party.

The week-long wait...planning the party...making final arrangements (just in case) wore Charles out. He couldn't even pretend to sleep on the job—which nearly got him fired. As the funeral director said, "Fidgety corpses remind our customers of zombies. And if zombification becomes popular, we'll go out of business."

Finally, the block party arrived...just as any apocalypse was destined to eventually arrive.

"In honor of your ex-profession," Charles told Andie, "everyone came dressed as a monster."

The Ferguson boy, with bloodshot and puffy eyes, staggered by. "You like my zombie look? We've renamed the band to Revolting Bloated Corpses."

"Catchy." Charles tried to hide his cringe, while hoping a new sound accompanied the new name. Yet he feared "revolting" said it all.

Andie appraised the costumes and non-costumes with a professional squint. "It looks like work followed me home."

"You mean," Charles said, smiling, "it looks like what *used* to be work."

"No...still looks like work."

"Heh, heh." Charles adjusted his ascot. "What exactly do you do?"

"A brain-sucking desk job." A wicked gleam flashed in Andie's dark eyes. "But it's worth it to put down monsters."

"Put down? I thought—"

"I don't kill them. But I can't leave 'em on the street or they'll come back to bite me in the ass—figuratively speaking. And sometimes literally."

Charles nodded, a glimmer of an idea forming. Unfortunately vampire etiquette required a lot of permission—permission to enter a dwelling, permission to turn someone and so on. Unconsented turning created enemies with really long memories. And no one held a grudge like the undead.

"You know," Charles said, "not all monsters are bad. I mean, there's no reason to 'put down' *all* monsters."

"Monsters . . . bad. That part's not changing."

"That's prejudiced. Not all humans are good, you know."

"Have you ever met a monster face-to-fang?" Andie asked.

"One or two." *Hundred.* Shuddering, Charles remembered Andie's tomahawk, axe, and other "trinkets."

"I'll bet you know loads of monsters, up close and personal." Andie's black lips curled. "What, you thought I couldn't spot the ringers? For instance, your teeth are too realistic. The plaque is a dead giveaway."

"You find a dentist who practices at night," Charles said defensively.

Doug, Vic, Frankie, Glen, and Gretta inched closer.

"She knows," Charles said.

Vic arched his angled brows. "Vhat? Did she come armed?"

Mimicking Vic, Andie raised her fine, blackened brows. "*Alvays.*" Her hand slipped inside her purse.

Doug jumped between Vic and Andie. "Before you do something we'll all regret—"

"Not really feeling the regret," she interrupted.

"But *we* will." Doug pressed his hands in prayer. "Please, just let us have our say."

"You think I'm going to go all mushy over a 'can't we overlook the fangs and claws and just get along' speech? But sure, sing out, little canary. The more you talk, the more I'll have to bury you with."

"You're being awfully closed-minded," Doug said.

"I'm a wolf three days out of twenty-eight—and then only at night. That makes me about ninety-five percent human."

Andie scoffed. "'I'm only sort of a monster' doesn't cut it."

"I don't see why I should be lumped in with them," said Gretta the ghoul. "Where's the harm in eating the dead? I'm just recycling. Green is good, right? Plus, formaldehyde keeps me young."

Charles, and the rest, looked away. Sure Gretta appeared youngish, but she was also corpse-pallor gray.

"Try to understand," Frankie said, "we just want what any other suburbanite wants, a quiet life."

"That's what you're going to get." Andie grabbed an iPhone from her purse. "Prison is a very quiet place."

"Prison!" they shouted in unison.

"I'm with the IRS—the Non-Human Taxation Department. Believe me, I can take you all down—but without the ick-factor." She smiled at Charles. "We got Al Capone . . . we'll get you." Andie tapped her iPhone screen and spun on Vic. "You're scheduled for Monday at nine. How's that work for you?"

Vic hissed. "You're vith the IRS and ve are the monsters? And is that nine A.M. or P.M.?"

"Really, Andie," Charles said, "a party is no place for business." He tried to sound jovial but couldn't shake the cold terror welling in his undead gut. Tax audit. Death by 1040E-Z. Charles flapped his arms, but in his panic, he couldn't poof into a bat.

Vic had no trouble and flew off before Andie could confirm his appointment.

"You're missing our point," Charles squeaked. "We're good people! Why persecute us?"

"Please." Andie waved her iPhone like a stake. "I've already started investigating you, neighbor. Not reporting your free blood 'perks'—naughty, naughty." She whirled on Goblin Glen. "Looks like I still have that slot open on Monday, if you want to spare yourself all that nasty waiting-in-suspense time."

Goblin Glen shrieked then ran behind Frankie. "Why *me* first? Take him!"

Frankie backed away, nearly trampling Glen. "I can't go to prison! Parts of me are too pretty!"

Glen screamed, then climbed onto Frankie's shoulder, screamed some more, and pointed . . . at the approaching mob.

People from two blocks over stormed the party armed with flashlights and garden implements. A man waving a leaf blower shouted, "Look! They're all together!"

"The monster scum is gathering to attack!" a woman shouted, shaking a lawn rake.

Andie mumbled, "Amateurs."

An old woman hobbled over then swung wildly at Frankie with a garden weasel.

"That's not nice. Let's be friends." Frankie reached out to shake hands when the garden weasel wacked him. Stitches around his wrist tore; his hand flopped loosely. Frankie wailed and that started Doug howling.

A man wielding a weed whacker shouted, "Did you see that? That monster tried to grab Mrs. MacDoon!"

"Kill them all!" The mob shook everything from a watering can to yard brooms. One man even carried a noose fashioned from a garden hose.

"We haven't done anything," Charles said.

"Not to any of you," Gretta added, not too helpfully.

"We only hurt bad people," Goblin Glen explained—again, probably not most helpful argument.

"Explain *him*." A woman waving a hand spade shoved a teenager forward.

Two bloody puncture marks stood out swollen and infected on his neck. Charles cringed, hoping Vic hadn't gone off the wagon.

"Nobody bit Taylor," the Ferguson boy said.

"That's not make-up," the woman said. "He's really bleeding!"

Taylor rolled his eyes. "I told you, Mom, I did it myself. Our fans would know if it was fake."

"He should put Neosporin on the wound," Charles said, certain neither Taylor nor any of the band members had "fans." At the woman's hard stare, he added meekly, "If it means anything...a vampire bite wouldn't get infected like that." Vampires generally kept a clean mouth. After all, having dirty fangs was like eating with dirty utensils. And Charles preferred a minty-fresh mouth.

"Listen," the Ferguson kid said, "these guy are cool. I've seen 'em going out and doing good things for the neighborhood."

"Like what?" Andie asked. "Picking up trash?"

"More like taking it out," Doug said. "We've formed our own neighbor watch."

"We're 'The Things that Go Bump in the Night,'" Frankie said.

"Why do you think our streets are so safe?" added the Ferguson kid. "It's why we have no graffiti or gangs hanging around."

"Leopards...spots, sound familiar?" Andie said. "It's your nature to hunt and *kill*."

"I don't hunt." Charles folded his arms. "You already know I get my blood at the parlor. I'm essentially a vampire vegetarian." At Andie's continued stare, he explained, "I get all my blood from people about to be *plant*ed."

"Hey, I mostly eat Alpo," Doug said. "And the occasional pedophile."

Goblin Glen nodded. "I only stalk burglars."

Andie grabbed Charles's neck. "Let me guess, Vic reads to the blind...then drains them dry?"

"Uh." Charles looked to his friends for help. Vic was a bit of a wild one, hanging out at the 7-11 all hours and driving up and down the main drag strip. "Vic has a diverse palate."

Goblin Glen piped up, "Some nights he hunts for car-jackers or armed robbers. But mostly he craves hot-blooded killers."

"Don't you mean *cold*-blooded?" Andie asked.

"No, he doesn't," Charles said. "To hear Vic tell it, most killings are in the heat of anger. He always says, there's not enough good, premeditated, revenge murders."

Andie's grip tightened around Charles's throat. "So Vic only 'vants to bite' bad guys?"

Charles coughed. Just because he didn't breathe didn't mean he didn't draw in air to speak. Besides, a crushed windpipe still hurt. He shut his eyes, flapped once, then poofed. Though he managed bat form, she still held him.

Andie snorted. "A *fruit* bat?"

Unable to hold his form, Charles shifted back. When Andie's hand fell from his throat, he felt a tiny bit relieved. "I told you, I'm a 'vegetarian' vampire."

"Hmm. You *are* embarrassingly not scary," she said. "But the rest of you—"

"Are why our streets are safer," the Ferguson kid repeated, his friend Taylor nodding.

Charles's faint tingle of relief swelled to near confidence that he would survive the night, and possibly his tax audit. "None of us are a threat."

Glen peered from behind Frankie's legs. "We disclose as much on our taxes as anybody else—and more than politicians!"

Andie sighed. "Seeing as you're already the community service lunch-bunch . . . and as long you aren't bloodsucking killers . . . I suppose I can overlook a few tax indiscretions."

Gretta let out a snort. "That's funny, *you* calling *us* bloodsuckers. And for the record, I much prefer bone marrow."

After glaring at Gretta, Charles drawled slowly, "Then we're okay? You're not lulling us into a false sense of security while planning to back-tax us out of our homes then throw us into prison?"

Andie smiled wickedly. "You can trust *me*. I'm with the government."

Esther M. Friesner dearly loves working in a field that has no trouble reconciling her role as the creator of the wildly popular *Chicks In Chainmail* series of anthologies, her Nebula Awards for some decidedly serious stories, and her latest vocation for YA novels (including *Nobody's Princess* and *Nobody's Prize* for Random House, *Temping Fate* for Penguin, and more on the horizon). Originally from New York until the siren song of Yale brought her to Ph.D.-land, she's been living in suburban Connecticut ever since and knows whereof she writes.

Long in the Tooth

Esther M. Friesner

This is a vampire story about (or more accurately, *around*) a young man named Billy Colfax who lived in the suburbs through no fault of his own.

Billy loved the ladies. Specifically, Billy loved older women—mature, ripe, experienced, what the French discreetly refer to as "ladies of a certain age." Clearly nobody had ever bothered to send Billy or the French a wake-up call to the fact that, in America, a woman must by law surrender her Object of Passionate Desire T-shirt the instant she hits the Big 3-5. It used to be the Big 4-0, but that's progress for you.

Billy was born in New York City, the only son and heir of a father whose stock portfolio would keep him irresistibly attractive as long as the Natural Male Enhancement products held out and the women didn't. As for Billy's mother, Dad traded her in for a newer model as soon as he could find a lawyer with chops worthy of Lizzie Borden. (The newer model *was* a model, and you betcha that little cupcake demanded a *lot* of icing.)

On his way out of his Dad's immediate life, Billy was swaddled in a comfortable trust fund accessible when he turned thirty. His poor mom got barely enough in alimony to manage the upkeep of the East 60s brownstone *and* the Paris *pied-à-terre* she cleared in the mingy divorce settlement. How could that fiend, her former husband, expect anyone to live like a human being on so piddling a yearly sum? Okay, most third world nations could do it in a walk, but still—she needed to cut expenses somehow. Something had to go.

She chose Billy.

Thus it was that Billy's mom shipped him off to her sister Francesca's tender care, in a town called Medad's Point, away in the coastal wilds of suburban Connecticut. In the years that followed, she saw her aesthetician more often than her only child, though perhaps if Billy had been willing to meet Mommy halfway and learn how to give Botox injections, things might have been different.

Billy came as a blessing to his childless Aunt Francesca and her husband Lewis, the proprietor of a fine local family restaurant, The Fish and Gravy. Billy helped out there part-time as soon as he was old enough to handle crockery without reducing it to shards. He loved his work, the relative peace of his seaside suburban home, his *restauranteur* uncle, but most of all, he loved his aunt with a deep devotion that knew no bounds.

Not in the creepy way! Not in the creepy way!

Aunt Francesca was a compendium of the best parts of every cherished maternal and para-maternal pop culture icon since the 1950s. She put Billy's needs first without putting her own into cold storage, provided unconditional love and an unassailable moral anchor, and pretty much ruined the boy for any hope of a career in politics or advertising.

Lucky for Billy, his idea of the perfect career was working at The Fish and Gravy. When the time came for Uncle Lewis and Aunt Francesca to think about retirement, they did so without qualm.

On the occasion of Billy's twenty-ninth birthday, they sat him down for a heart-to-heart concerning their separate futures. They did so at the kitchen table, where all truly important decisions must be made. There were brownies.

"Billy, dear," Aunt Francesca said, patting her darling's hand. "In a year you will come into your trust fund and be a man of means. You will be able to do whatever you like with your money and there will be so much of it that you won't have to work another day in your life. You could travel the globe, buy a mansion or two, dine on caviar—"

"Or you could take over The Fish and Gravy," said Uncle Lewis.

"Where do I sign up, Uncle Lewis?" Billy said.

"Don't make any hasty decisions," Aunt Francesca cautioned him. "A restaurant is a full-time job. Your life won't be your own, you'll have to deal with myriad daily crises, and you will develop a hollow, charnel-house laugh whenever anyone asks you what you do in your spare time."

"Plus it's not all that profitable," said Uncle Lewis.

Billy smiled. "Money's not going to be a problem for me, and I can't think of a better way to spend my time. It's the people that matter."

And really, that was the key truth behind The Fish

and Gravy: The people. Uncle Lewis's small restaurant had no delusions of *haute cuisine* nor aspirations to be an outpost of *la vie cosmopolitaine* in the land of strip malls. It served fish chowder, not *bouillabaise*, pickles instead of *cornichons*, and good old mayo straight out of the jar, *aioli* be damned. It didn't cater to its proprietor's ego, but to the good folk of Medad's Point and anyone else who wanted a *barista*-free cup of coffee to go with that burger and fries.

(All right, so the actual *name* of The Fish and Gravy did cater just a smidge to Uncle Lewis's ego. There is no greater expression of the human need to mark one's turf—before being compelled to sleep eternally beneath it—than the compulsion to slap cryptic names onto everything from your pets to your pickup truck to your progeny. But while The Fish and Gravy *did* serve fish and gravy—though, thank God, not in the same dish!—Uncle Lewis maintained that the *true* proximate cause for the name was "in memory of an unexpectedly delicious interlude spent with a highly open-minded economics major from Teaneck, New Jersey." No one ever *did* figure out what the hell he was talking about, and probably just as well.)

To resume:

Pursuant to the family discussion, a lawyer was consulted the very next day, papers were drawn up, and ownership transferred. Now at the helm of The Fish and Gravy, Billy Colfax steered with a discreet yet strong hand. Uncle Lewis and Aunt Francesca hung around just long enough to see that their nephew needed no guidance in his new role. The sunny Southwest beckoned and they departed, leaving him in charge of the family house as well. Billy felt that his life's dream was fulfilled.

Now if only he could meet a girl like Aunt Francesca, he'd be all set.

On a chill and dank day in late November, two months after his relatives' departure, Billy was hard at work supervising the smooth operation of The Fish and Gravy's kitchen when *they* came in with the dinner crowd. They were a group of curiously color-coordinated older women. They all wore dresses that some might deem purple and hats some might likewise deem red. But such a *serious* shade of red...

Because dinnertime customers expected an extra fillip of class, this was the only meal for which Billy tapped one of his waitresses to assume the role of hostess, as in: Please Wait To Be Seated By. That night, the cushy duty had fallen to a lass named Julie, a plump young morsel who had gone to high school with him.

Julie warmly welcomed the group of eight older women and seated them in one of the nicer tables. "Gosh, I *love* your hats!" she said as she handed out menus. "My mom just joined the local chapter of your organization, but she hasn't found the right hat yet. Would you mind if I asked where you got those?"

"What, these old things?" One woman touched the edge of her broad-brimmed felt *chapeau* with the tip of a milk-white finger and laughed. "We made them."

Julie was impressed. "I wish I were that handy."

"You would be surprised at the skills you can acquire, given enough time."

Julie sighed. "It'd be nice to have a spare day or two."

"Or century," said the woman. "Good millinery takes time."

"Lucy, stop teasing the nice young lady," said another of the group. She was a most striking woman, with a sharp face that was still richly sensual in spite of sags and wrinkles aplenty. Her eyes were the deep gold of Baltic amber, her hair a silver knot at the nape of her neck. She did not offer her comment as a gentle chiding. No, it emerged from her wine-red lips with the full, powerful, unmistakable intonation of a direct command.

"Oh!" Lucy was flustered. "I'm so sorry, Tina, I was only making conversation."

"Don't. You haven't got the knack for it." Tina opened the menu with a snap, putting paid to all further comment.

The ladies ordered Old Fashioneds and Caesar salads and steaks, blood rare. For some reason, this choice of entrée made some of them giggle and remark, "No pun intended" or "Oh my gracious, we should call ourselves the Crimson Cliché Club instead!" Julie was settling another group at a nearby table, so she heard all of the above. The ladies sat and ate and sat and drank and sat and *sat* at their places, conversing in genteel accents, and that might have been the end of the matter if not for the appearance of the Beswicks.

The Beswicks were one of the first families of Medad's Point, entrenched as a case of head lice. No one knew when the first one had arrived, but local historians and the Beswicks themselves agreed that said firstcomer was a woman. As to why the widow Abstinence Beswick arrived, nine children in tow, there were many catty theories uttered *sotto voce* about records from the Salem Village Witchcraft Trials filed under "The One That Got Away." Others suggested that somewhere in the annals of the Massachusetts

Bay Colony was a parchment with the Beswick family name in the header followed by the Puritan equivalent of OMG, KN U BLEEV THS BTCH? (Though it was arguable whether this canard were truly so or merely some people's only way of dealing with that alarming anomaly, a strong woman.)

Contemporary Beswick bitchery, however, was beyond debate. It manifested itself most in female family members. Strangely, one did not need to be born a Beswick to display their high-handed attitude. The moment a woman married into the clan, she contracted that attribute faster than you could say, "Bubonic plague? What's bu—? *Ack!*" (*thud*)

Which is not to say that the Beswick men were angels. Consider the scene that ensued at the hostess's podium of The Fish and Gravy when Jason Beswick, his wife Penny, and their four children showed up with no reservations. When Julie explained that there were no tables to be had, things went from zero to DoYouKnow-WhoWeARE?! in the blink of a rancor-bulging eyeball.

"What do you *mean* you haven't got any tables?" Jason pounded the podium so hard that the little lamp that lit the seating plan flickered.

"Jason, stop that, you're always too nice for your own good," Penny decreed, hip-checking him aside and thrusting their youngest into his arms. She leaned across the podium, full into Julie's face. "There's a table *right there*. Clear it."

And she pointed dramatically to where the be-hatted older women were lingering over crumbs and teacups long since drained of every last drop. The check lay on the table in their midst, untouched. They were having simply the *best* time!

"I'm sorry, Mrs. Beswick, but that table's not available yet," Julie said. "The previous party—"

"They're *done*. For God's sake, would you *look* at that table? It's totally obvious, unless you're blind as well as incompetent. Who are those old hens anyway? I don't recognize a one of them. Hmph. Nobodies. Go tell them to settle their bill and be on their way. I'm hungry."

Julie clung to her podium like Ishmael to Queequeg's coffin, and if you have no idea whence this simile derives, just go with it, okay? (Illiterate swine.) "Mrs. Beswick, Mr. Colfax's policy has always been that we're not supposed to rush our customers. I can't do that."

"Oh, you can't?" Penny Beswick's eyes narrowed. She strode across the dining room, snatched up the check from the ladies' table, sneered at the total, and slapped down her platinum-hued credit card with panache befitting a winning hand at poker.

"You poor things," she cooed gooily. "Let me help you along with that; my treat. No need to keep on pretending the bill's not there because you're afraid one of you's going to dither over it. I know how it is; I've got lots of old female relatives. It's always fuss, fuss, fuss about splitting the check, who had just the salad, who had the steak, and next thing you know, you've been parked for hours at a table that *other people want to use*." She surveyed the gape-mouthed faces regarding her and added, "Why don't I just run this over to the cashier, while I'm at it? No muss, no fuss, no worries about calculating the tip—it does get harder and harder to figure percentages in your head when you've been out of school as long as some of you girls, doesn't it?" She scooped up the check and her credit card, favoring the women with her most charming smile.

She never saw the hand that slapped both from her grasp. She *did* see the livid face of the lady named Tina. How could she help *but* see it, when Tina's patrician nose was no more than a fingernail's breadth away from her own?

"A word, young missy," Tina said coldly. "*Several* words: 'poor things,' 'dither,' 'fuss,' calling us 'girls,' plus any and all references to our age voiced as if we were backward children, mentally unfit, physically incapacitated, or otherwise in need of caretakers. Because—mark me well, you snippy hoyden—another such offense and *you* will be the one in need of a caretaker."

"Are you *threatening* me?" Penny could hardly contain her amusement.

"I'm doing better than that," said Tina, and she clouted Penny upside the head in a manner that the Victorians referred to as "boxing one's ears."

It was on.

It was subsequently off again, and in record time. Penny's howl of outrage and pain was followed by retribution—i.e. a wild swing at Tina. Tina simply grabbed Penny's incoming fist with the aplomb of a Major League outfielder playing catch with a kindergartener and squeezed it until something went *crunch* and some*one* went "Aaaaauuuuggggghhhhh!!!"

Three guesses who, and the first two don't count.

By the time Billy entered the dining room, Julie had phoned 911 and Mr. Beswick had phoned his lawyer.

Though relatively tender in years, Billy was seasoned

in the ways of restaurant crisis management, the nuances of Medad's Point pecking orders, Beswick hijinks, and lawyers. His first action was to provide Penny with a bucket of ice. His next was to ignore Jason Beswick's indignant, incoherent demands for the immediate and concurrent detention and expulsion of the woman responsible for his wife's injury. His third was to ask Julie what the hell had just happened. Armed with the necessary information, he finally turned to the alleged perp and her crimson be-hatted cronies and—

—crashed right through the guardrail of common sense, plunging headlong into the abyss of love.

What was it about Tina that had so precipitously pulled a Venus Flytrap maneuver on Billy's heart? It couldn't have been anything so shallow as appearances. Medad's Point teemed with women who were of the same age and the same degree of physical attractiveness. There was something different about Tina, though, something compelling, hypnotic, otherworldly.

Smitten, that's what he was. And being thus smitten, he swiftly used his authority as owner/manager of The Fish and Gravy to spin the situation in such a way that the Beswicks left the premises with a gift certificate for a hefty sum and the reminder that they did not want to be tagged as Permanent Do-Not-Seats at a long-established eatery in a fairly small town because people would Talk. Then he turned to Tina.

She declined his initial offer to comp the ladies' dinner, but she had no objections to his joining them for further socializing. They all occupied that contested table until closing time, when she deigned to swap e-mail addresses, but divulged no more of her personal information save that she and the rest of her group were from out of town. There was a certain fondness in her expression that gave the young man cause to hope that his attraction might be returned.

For so it was.

In the weeks that followed, the group of older women returned many times to dine at The Fish and Gravy, and eventually Tina herself showed up solo to pass an evening making goo-goo eyes at Billy. Julie witnessed the whole thing, for it was often her assigned task to wait on their table. Ever the romantic, she thought their courtship was kind of cute and she intuitively knew that there was much her old high school chum could be getting out of a relationship with an older woman that liaisons with younger fry could not provide. She could not but approve.

One mid-March morn, when Julie was on breakfast duty for change, a stunningly attractive young woman came into The Fish and Gravy. She was dressed in the height of Fashion Week, lean body and silicon-plumped bosoms sheathed in designer originals, feet stylishly warped by four-inch heels. She asked to see Billy. Julie fetched him from his office, only to stand appalled witness when the young woman threw herself into his arms with such force that she almost rebounded out of his arms again, thanks to the airbag action of her bespoke mammaries.

Between sobs that somehow lacked the tears to smear her eye makeup, the visitor wailed: "Oh Billy, I'm, like, sooooo sorry to have to tell you this, but your daddy is—is—is—"

"Dead? Injured?" Billy asked.

"Broke."

"I see," said Billy. "And, um, *who* in the hell are you?"

She blinked at him with glittering blue eyes. "I'm Gin-gin," she said. "Your daddy's personal assistant."

"I'll bet," said Billy, though he kept his cheap shot *sotto voce* because his Aunt Francesca had raised him to be a gentleman. In more audible tones he asked, "What happened?"

Gin-gin was pleased to elaborate. Apparently her employer's present state of insolvency was directly linked to having four ex-wives. It would have been a livable arrangement if Ex #3 had not recently gone on to marry a high-powered attorney with a nose for divorce settlement and pre-nup loopholes and the ability to flense former husbands like beached whales.

"So?" Billy asked testily once she was finished. "What do you want *me* to do about it?" He fully expected Gin-gin to turn on the waterworks, imploring him to dip into his now-available trust fund in order to help his poor, dear father back onto his custom-made Italian wingtip-shod feet.

But Gin-gin's actual answer was this: "Nothing. He's a big boy. I just figured you should know how broke he is in case you're thinking of hitting him up for money."

"Why would I want to do that?" Billy raised one eyebrow.

"Well, duh!" Gin-gin riposted. "You own a freakin' *restaurant*. Those things die faster than street-fair goldfish. Okay, I've done my good deed for the day; I'm outa here. When your daddy's finances tanked, he had to let me go, so I've got to get back to the city and find a new keep—job." She straightened her spine, showing off her assets to best advantage, and turned on her dainty heel to go.

It is said that history is often changed by a single word.

"Wait!" said Billy.

And Gin-gin waited.

By the time Tina and her group arrived that evening, Billy was ever so pleased to introduce his *d'une certain age* lady-love to his new chum. He and Gin-gin had gotten to talking and the day simply *flew* by! He was certain that Tina and Gin-gin would become fast friends, for despite the stranglehold of vile stereotype, Gin-gin was a young woman whose youth and beauty were mere enhancements to a keen intellect, more proper to someone nowhere near so young and beautiful. And did he happen to mention how young she was? And how beautiful? For such a young woman, that is.

Tina gave them both a tight-lipped grimace. It could have been a smile. She said, "So pleased to meet you." It could have been sincere.

And Julie, putting in overtime, observed it all and was supremely grateful to be a spectator, not a player. There was a strange tang in the air, as of freshly spilled blood.

But of course *that* was impossible.

Gin-gin became a frequent visitor to The Fish and Gravy. Oddly enough, she never mentioned her job search again. Not so oddly, Billy was too busy feasting his eyes on his dad's former employee to bother asking her for updates. When April rolled around, she let Billy know that Connecticut was not quite the toxic hellhole her Manhattan-centric lifestyle had conditioned her to believe. She was charmed by Medad's Point, and begged his help finding a suitable place to settle. He gave her the cards of any number of realtors and offered her his spare bedroom as a *pied-à-terre* for property-viewing sorties. It was the least he could do.

Gin-gin was grateful. So *very* grateful. Even on the kitchen table. And if you think this means she made Billy a home-cooked meal, you need to get out more.

Tina got out plenty, and she brought her crimson-hatted friends. The ladies showed up *en masse* at The Fish and Gravy one balmy May evening shortly after Billy called his erstwhile Romantic Interest to let her know that gosh, she really was a swell gal, and he'd never forget her, but maybe it would be better if they saw more of other people.

"God knows he's seeing more of that little trollop," Tina snarled while Julie seated the group at their usual table. "I don't mind being cast aside, but couldn't he have done it with a bit more originality? And for more quality goods than that—that—that *village bicycle*?"

"I don't think she's got wheels, dear," Lucy murmured.

"I mean that everyone's been on her," Tina snapped back. "Oh, I could make them both bleed for this!"

"Er, would you like a drink, ma'am?" Julie said. It was her diplomatic way of trying to make Tina aware that her plaints were audible. "Your usual Old Fashioned?"

"Accent on the *old*, no doubt," Tina said bitterly. She dumped the contents of her water glass into the floral centerpiece, slammed the empty tumbler on the table, and declared, "Fill 'er up with that loathsome little harlot's blood and you'll be able to *retire* on the tip I'll give you!"

"Uh..." Julie floundered in the shoals of server/diner

small talk. Her distress evoked a combination of pity and panic among Tina's cohorts.

"Oh, Tina, you did *not* just say that!" Lucy pressed her fingertips to her ruby-red mouth, distressed and a little embarrassed. "You mustn't mind her, dear," she told Julie. "She'll get over it, in time, but right now she's too freshly upset to know what she's saying."

"Upset?" Tina repeated haughtily. "After three and a half centuries of unnatural life, it takes more than a stripling's inconstancy to upset me. The point is, I expected better of Billy Colfax."

"You did?" Julie was boggled. Even though Billy was her employer, she never expected more than the occasional dinner-and-a-movie-or-maybe-a-beer-pong-grudge-match out of the lads who were her contemporaries "*Why?*"

"Do you think I brought my associates to this town by mere happenstance? I have connections to Medad's Point. I was once friends with Billy's aunt. The boy's actions did not betray merely me, but his entire upbringing, his *family*. It reflects badly on Francesca, whether or not she taught him better behavior. If he couldn't control his libidinous excesses for anyone else, at least he might have done so for her sake."

"But it's *his* life."

"And she is *his* family. All the *decent* family he's ever had, truth be told," Tina countered fiercely. "That might not mean a lot to you right now, young woman, but I assure you, wait three hundred years and you'll understand why family means *everything*; at least it does to me."

"Um, she seems nice," Julie said. "Billy's girlfriend, I mean." The words rang hollow. She was eying her customer uneasily. Normal people did not speak of glasses full of blood and centuries full of unnatural life, as a rule. Clearly this woman's crash-landing in Dump City had sent a collateral crack or two snaking up into the load-bearing walls of her sanity.

"Oh, *very* nice. Nice enough to share. Which is what I caught her doing more than once in a parked car with what's-his-name—the large, loud man whose wifey-poo tried to evict us from our table, that first night."

"Jason Beswick?" Julie's voice rose in a scandalized trill, though she managed to keep its volume to a whisper. Her doubts as to Tina's mental stability had flown. Who cared if the lady was nuts or not when she had gossip *this* juicy to dish!

"Beswick? His name is *Beswick*?" For an instant, Tina looked as if she'd been slapped. She froze in place, face a few shades paler than her norm. But she swiftly recaptured her aplomb and coolly added: "Isn't that interesting. From what *she* was saying at the time, I was under the impression that his parents had named him Yes-yes-oh-God-*yes*!"

"Well, I don't blame you for being mad," Julie said. A chance thought brightened her face. "You know what? You shouldn't be. You're a *much* classier lady than Billy ever deserved, *way* too classy to mess with some little skank he was dumb enough to drop you for." While Tina and her friends were still navigating the wide Sargasso Sea of Julie's grammar, the pert waitress added: "You can do *lots* better than him. Look, ladies, your first round tonight's on me; I insist. You just forget about him, drink up and smile. Okay?" She flew off to put in the bar order before anyone could say her nay.

"What a sweet young woman," Lucy remarked.

"Wise as well," a thoughtful Tina added. "She's quite correct on many counts. Drink up and smile... I think I will."

Later in the evening, when Julie came to clear the crimson-hatted coterie's table, she discovered a hundred dollar bill pinned under Tina's unused water glass, the money neatly folded inside an elegantly-scribed note that read simply: "*I* insist, too."

That night, while Billy slept the sleep of the clueless, Gin-gin quietly let herself into the house and tiptoed up the stairs. She was fresh from her latest backseat tryst with Jason Beswick. He'd parked at the back of the town's Revolutionary War-era burial ground again, with only the dead and the occasional bat to bear witness to their adulterous slitherings. Now, as Gin-gin flicked on the light in the upstairs bathroom and began running water to brush her teeth, she blithely contemplated how good it was to have *two* well-heeled men hooked on her trawling lines. What with the chancy nature of the stock market, a girl had to hedge her bets if not her funds. Raising her toothbrush to her lips, she took a moment to admire her image in the mirror and to give herself a smug look of triumph.

"Hello, dear."

The icy voice came from directly behind Gin-gin. Her toothbrush clattered into the basin as she whirled to confront Tina, standing nonchalantly in the bathtub. The mirror above the sink hadn't reflected so much as a hint of her presence.

"OhmyGod!" Gin-gin's arms crossed protectively over her size 38-D investments. "What do *you* want?"

"*Guess,*" Tina replied as she stepped out of the

tub. And then, because Julie had told her to do it, Tina smiled.

It was a marvelous smile. It could have given gloating lessons to a cat with a mouthful of stumble-footed chipmunk. It could have schooled Nero, Henry VIII, and Louis XIV in all the glorious possibilities of *I'm going to get my own way now because who's going to stop me?* Above all, it was a revelation, and what it revealed was a pair of fangs as pointy as you please.

Gin-gin gasped and collapsed onto the toilet. "You're a vampire," she whispered in terror.

"Well, *duh*," Tina said dryly.

Gin-gin screamed. There came the sound of drowsy confusion from the bedroom, followed by the irruption of a pajama-clad Billy. "What's going on in here?" he demanded.

Gin-gin cast herself into his arms, wailing and pointing wildly at the older woman. "She's a vampire and she's going to kill me and it's all your fault!"

"Gin-gin, are you crazy? None of that's true and you...know..." His voice trailed away as he got a good look at Tina, still smiling. "Are those *real*?" he demanded.

"More so than those," Tina countered, indicating Gin-gin's chest. "This little poppet stole your affections from me, but your lack of constancy is as much to blame for our parting as her lack of morals. I cannot in good conscience—if you understand the term—kill her for that. I'm a vampire, not a monster. My mission here tonight is something altogether different." She took the crimson hat from her head and proffered it to Gin-gin. "On behalf of myself and the other ladies, we'd like you to join us."

"*Join* you?" Gin-gin was taken aback, but her shock soon turned to scorn. She glared at the hat, her recent terror swept away on a spate of indignation. "I am *so* not old enough."

"Don't mistake this hat for the badge of some merely mortal organization," an unruffled Tina said. "*Our* official hats are white...at first."

Gin-gin squealed so loudly at this disclosure that Billy broke his protective embrace to clap his hands over his ears. Tina's lip curled.

"Stop that, you pusillanimous shoat," she snapped. "I've come to you tonight with a choice, not a death sentence: Join us and enjoy virtual immortality. Remain forever as lovely as you are at the moment you...join the club. As lovely, and as *rich*."

"Rich?" Gin-gin's ears perked up.

"Decandently. Filthily." Tina's smile was back. "Eternally. Our kind profit from the *really* long-term investments, and we've got a financial network in place with so many work-arounds, tax shelters, and double-blinds that we laugh at disclosure. Our only worry about money is where to spend it next. We're doing it in this jerkwater town at the moment because slumming it can be refreshing. Today, Medad's Point, but tomorrow, back to Paris, or perhaps Tokyo or Bali. Variety is the spice of unnatural life. How spicy is *yours*, these days?"

Gin-gin stepped away from Billy. She gave Tina a skeptical gaze. "What's the catch?"

"I have to drain your blood and you have to die— technically speaking—but I promise it won't hurt. It's really quite a quick and tidy operation." Her smile widened. "I won't even get my hands dirty, I promise."

"Why should I believe you?"

"Because I'm *asking your permission* when I could just tear out your throat and be done with it."

"You—you don't want to kill me?" Like many a practitioner of the deceitful and manipulative arts, Gin-gin had a hard time accepting good fortune at face value. "Why not?"

Tina made an impatient sound. "At this moment, I'm no longer sure. Your death would hardly affect the ecosphere. Dithery little butt-pains are not an endangered species. Let's forget the whole thing. You're clearly not interested." She popped her hat back on her head and started for the bathroom door.

"Wait!" Ah, that fateful word again! Gin-gin's hands clamped themselves to Tina's wrist and would not let go. It was all rather awkward. The upstairs bathroom *chez* Colfax was never designed with drama-rama in mind and the three occupants thereof staggered and jostled into one another in a dreadful manner until Tina stopped struggling and allowed Gin-gin to detain her. "Do you—will you—*can* you swear that you're really going to make me a vampire and not just kill me?"

"Yes, I can swear, and moreover I can do it in a manner more binding than any oath you have ever taken." Tina pointed majestically at the tube of toothpaste lying beside the sink. "Squoosh a cross on the countertop."

"Which a who the what now?" Gin-gin asked, blinking like a kitten.

"She wants you to squeeze out a cross made of toothpaste on the counter," Billy said, his helpful nature overcoming all else. "Like this." And he fulfilled Tina's directive as frugally as possible, for Aunt Francesca had raised him to be thrifty, and store brand dentifrices did not grow on trees.

Tina held one hand above the fluoride-enriched holy sign. "This do I swear," she intoned. "If ever I am the direct instrument of this woman's death, may my unnaturally extended days be cut short, and may my own flesh all suffer the same fate as that small portion thereof which I do herewith tender as my pledge!" She lowered her hand to the toothpaste cross, pausing only long enough to turn to Gin-gin and add: "That means if I kill you, this is what's going to happen to *all* of me." And with that, she slapped her palm down on the be-gooed countertop.

Then she screamed.

And well she should: She was in atrocious pain. The holy symbol seared her skin, as witness the threads of smoke rising from beneath her palm. And the smell—! The reek of burning flesh is not one of Mother Nature's more desirable perfumes. It was a relief to everyone when Tina finally raised her hand and displayed the scar that sealed her oath.

"Satisfied?" she asked Gin-gin.

"Oooooh!" said Gin-gin. And she bared her throat to Tina's promise of eternal life as readily as she'd bared other portions of her anatomy to so many, many others.

The whole operation did not take very long, in and of itself—half an hour at most. It would have taken less time, but there was the unavoidable delay of subduing Billy. When he saw Gin-gin had made up her mind to become a part of the nightlife, he actually had the gall to tell his bedmate that she was either stupid or insane to even *think* of following through on her avowed plans. Moreover, he declared that he was not going to stand idly by and watch her literally throw her life away.

He was quite right on that last count. He did not stand idly by. Tina and Gin-gin demonstrated the beauties of female solidarity by overpowering him, hustling him out of the bathroom, and locking him in the linen closet, whence his strident objections were duly noted and ignored.

He was released when it was all over. His first sight was his current girlfriend, bloodless and beautiful, grinning at him as fangily as his ex. It made him grumpy.

"I suppose you're pleased with yourself," he said sullenly.

"Oh *hell* yes," Gin-gin replied.

"You should be, too, darling Billy," Tina put in.

"I should?"

"Certainly. After all, you do love her. Don't you? What is true love if not eternal? Just think: She'll never change. She'll always look this young, this beautiful. And did I mention *young*?"

"Young..." Billy weighed the word. An odd expression wafted over his face. A fine line formed between his brows, then deepened. "That's—that's great. Really."

His patent lack of enthusiasm made Gin-gin frown. "What's the matter with you? Most men would kill to have someone like me! You won't even have to pay for plastic surgery when I get all old and saggy because that won't happen. *Ever!*"

"Yyyyyeah..." Billy rubbed the back of his head, his mouth twisted into a grimace that screamed, *Second thoughts! Getcher second thoughts right here!*

"Why don't I just leave you two lovebirds alone with your happiness?" Tina said pertly. "I know you have lots to discuss, including where she's going to spend her daylight hours. I'd suggest you settle that straightaway. Trust me, Gin-gin, you've just entered a life where 'sun damage' goes *far* beyond getting wrinkles. Ta-ta!"

Billy took Tina's arm firmly. "Allow me to show you out," he said, his voice grim.

"Always the gallant." Tina smiled and permitted him to steer her out of the bathroom. Gin-gin couldn't have cared less. She had dismissed Billy's attitude as his problem, not hers, and had just discovered her ability to turn into a bat. She was playing with her new "toy" giddily—SQUEAKgiggleSQUEAKgiggleSQUEAK!— while Billy and Tina left the room.

Downstairs, Tina asked, "So, where *are* you going to store your sweetheart from dawn 'til dusk? Until you can purchase her a *proper* coffin and tomb, that is? The trunk of your car? The deep freeze at The Fish and Gravy?"

"Probably the old cedar chest in the spare bedroom— hey! That is *not* what I want to talk to you about!" Billy exclaimed. "Is it true? She's *always* going to look like that?"

"I thought you'd be pleased." Tina smirked. "But you're not, are you? Poor Billy. A man can stray from anything except his own nature, and even though you jilted me to try a nibble of fresher fruit, *your* nature is to love older women. How lucky for you that—barring misfortune—all women become older women, in time." Her smirk grew smirkier. "All women except her."

Tina kissed him lightly on the cheek and turned to smoke, slipping away before he could say another word.

She rematerialized in front of the town post office. The rest of the ladies were waiting for her.

"How did it go?" Lucy asked.

"So far, so good. Now...do you have it?"

Lucy reached into her purse and produced two as-yet-unsealed, stamped envelopes the perfect size to accommodate a five-by-seven photograph. Tina opened one and slid out the picture within, an image of Gin-gin and Jason Beswick *in flagrante*. It had been taken earlier that night with a camera whose infrared bells and digital whistles were so easy to master, even a vampire in bat form could immortalize backseat shenanigans from mid-flight.

"One for him—" she said, as she sealed the first envelope and addressed it to Billy before popping it into the mailbox "—so he won't feel quite so dreadful when the inevitable happens."

She emptied the second envelope and wrote a brief-as-possible note on the back of the photo, giving an update on Gin-gin's recent transformation, the how-to basics of vampire slaying, and a friendly hint about what might be found sleeping inside the cedar chest in Billy Colfax's spare bedroom while that young man was conveniently out of the house, managing The Fish and Gravy.

"And one for her, so the inevitable *does* happen." She addressed this one to Penny Beswick.

Lucy looked uneasy. "I know you want revenge for being discarded, but arranging a *murder*?"

Tina sniffed haughtily. "Why do you think I went to the trouble of turning her into one of us first? Whether we like it or not, it's not murder to kill the undead. And this is *not* about the vengeance of a woman scorned. It's about something far more important: Honor. My *family* honor. If she'd cheated on Billy without besmirching *my* family name—"

"You and that family of yours!" Lucy rolled her eyes. "Even after all this time, you can't let it go. *Honestly*, Abstinence—!"

"That's my name," said the former Widow Beswick of Salem Village, Medad's Point, and numerous other abodes throughout the ages of her unnatural existence. "Don't wear it out. And don't blame me for what's to become of that consciousless little slut: I'm only obeying that wonderful old saying that goes, mmm—something before something . . ."

"Beer before whiskey? Pearls before swine? Death before dishonor?" the ever-helpful Lucy offered.

"No, I've got it now, dear," said Abstinence. Her special smile spread ear to ear. "Age before beauty."

Laura J. Underwood sometimes wonders if she was influenced by all those books she used to walk on as a child before she started reading them, or if it is just the plain fact that her entire family likes to tell stories, and she likes to write stories down. She is the author of *Hounds of Ardagh, Dragon's Tongue, Ard Magister* and *The City under the Bridge*. Her short fiction has been seen everywhere from *Marion Zimmer Bradley's Fantasy Magazine* to anthologies such as *Turn The Other Chick, Bubbas Of The Apocalypse, Sword And Sorceress* and a host of others. When not writing, she is a librarian who lives in East Tennessee with her folks and a cat that needs a brain transplant (because she has concluded that he doesn't have one—really). She is an active member of SFWA and a member of the SFWA Musketeers who likes to play with pointy steely objects from time to time.

Bella and the Flying Lugosi

Laura J. Underwood

Bella Van Helsing was standing at the garden window, watching the last pink rime of sunlight fading from the western sky and sipping her favorite vintage—a '67 Spaniard from Napa Valley—when she noticed there was a light in the house next door.

"Harker," she called. "Do we have new neighbors?"

Harker appeared at her side, holding a tray with the bottle, from which he proceeded to fill her glass once more. His gaunt features were serene. He straightened his collar slightly and bobbed his head. "Yes, Madam," he said. "They moved in just three days ago."

"And you didn't tell me?"

"I thought it best to give them time to settle before inviting them over, Madam," he said.

"True," she said and smiled. "It's always good to have new blood in the neighborhood, I will admit. Have you learned anything about them?"

"They are Romanian," Harker said.

"Really? What part?"

"From up near Tirgoviste in Walachia, as I recall."

"Really? Are they vampires, then?"

"Yes, Madam, I believe that they are."

Bella nodded.

"So you have spoken to them," Bella said. She looked back towards the gate that separated the yards of their suburbanite mansions. A structure rose that she was certain had not been there the night before—which might explain all the hammering that disturbed her beauty sleep. Two tall pairs of pillars with ropes suspended between them stood like sentries. "Is that a trapeze?" Bella asked, gesturing towards the back.

"Yes, Madam," Harker said. "They are the Flying Lugosi Family. And no, I have not spoken to them, but I met their servant as he was taking out the trash this morning, a strange little Englishman named Renfield who says he is their manager."

"Oh, circus performers as well as vampires," she said rather drably and frowned. "Figures. Well, we shall give them a few more days to get settled, and then you can invite them over for a late night dinner. And we will deal with them appropriately at that time if we must."

"Very good, Madam," Harker said, and slipped away just as quietly as he had come—one of the traits Bella appreciated in him.

She could not abide a noisy manservant.

Bella sat on her rooftop nursing a bit of a vintage Belgian—so hard to find anymore—and observed her new neighbors over the course of the next two evenings. It was clear to her that the Lugosi family were creatures of the night. Harker said they were never seen before the sun set, but once the last light faded, torches would brighten their back yard and they would be clambering up the tall poles with unnatural grace, and begin their practice. That they were excellent trapeze artists was clear. She counted six of them, from an elderly gentleman who seemed to have forgotten what it was like to be tanned down to a girl of seven whom Bella swore might be part monkey, the way she could go up and down the ropes and defied her parents. In fact, the child seemed to be the most feral of the bunch—and the messiest. At least once, Bella saw the little girl sucking on a dismembered arm, blood dribbling down her neck and chin.

Disgusting little creature, Bella thought. No one taught their children manners anymore.

The Lugosis would fly back and forth, looping and spinning through the air like wisps of milkweed until the few remaining hours before dawn. Bella found this annoying as well, for she liked her privacy to do her own work. The Lugosi family rarely took breaks from their strenuous exercise except to feed, and yet, she was quite certain, they were not the least bit tired. She saw their "manager" twice coming in the back way that first night with mysteriously large sacks that wriggled a bit as he carried them across his back. He giggled a lot more than seemed necessary, and on the second night, Bella watched him snagging the moths that flitted in and out of the soft torchlight and stuffing them into his mouth.

He's even more disgusting than the child. At least the child's manners could be partially excused because of her age, though Bella knew that was probably much older than appearances led one to believe. Indeed, she wondered if the entire family had been bitten and made at once. No True Blood descendant would have had such a lack of class. The True Bloods she had encountered before always had polite children—if they had them at all.

On the third evening, she chose to go turn out the lights and sit in the dark and listen with her window open as she read her papers and took notice of a report about a woman jogger and a man who went to walk his dog two evenings ago, and how neither of them had returned to their respective homes. Bella shook her head in dismay. This was not good. The Lugosi family were clearly hunting in their own neighborhood. Sooner or later, they would raise questions, the police would go door to door, and the neighbors would start wondering why they bothered with a neighborhood watch.

She turned towards the window when she saw Renfield returning once again with a large sack. This one did not move. Bella leaned a bit so she could get a better look.

The family members were up on their trapeze as usual when Renfield dragged his burden through the door and flung it down on the grass. At once, the Lugosis came scrambling down from their perches and leapt on the sack. But then, the senior Lugosi stood up and suddenly grabbed Renfield by the throat.

"This one is dead," she heard him snarl.

"I tried to find a live one, I swear!" Renfield protested, going to his knees. "Please, Master. The people are afraid to walk in the dark now. I had to steal this one from the morgue. It died just hours ago, I swear to you."

The elder Lugosi looked disgusted. "We must feed," he said and looked at the disappointment on the faces of his family. "Next time rob a blood bank if you must, but no more corpses. The body rotting taints the blood. My little Erica will keep us up all day with her puking."

Bella shook her head and went back to her paper and asked Harker to see if there was any of the new French-Canadian still available.

She gave the Lugosi family several more days before she sent Harker over with an invitation one evening. She watched from the window as he took the path to the gate separating their properties. He knocked with dignity, and then stepped on through. The previous owners had given him a key and *carte blanche* to move between the houses before they decided to leave several years ago.

At first, all the Lugosis tensed and went feral at the sight of a man wandering into their yard. Bella almost laughed aloud. She watched as the eldest dropped the distance to the ground like a panther and stalked up to Harker. Her manservant stood quiet and stoic, not showing the least bit of concern as the man practically lunged at him. But then, the eldest Lugosi drew up short and lowered his gaze and Bella smiled. Harker had been wise enough to prepare before going over. On the lapel of his meticulously pressed coat, he was wearing a bulb of garlic and a crucifix.

He is such a good man and he knows his place. The main reason she had kept him all those years.

Harker merely held out the invitation and she could see him turning affable and animated. The senior Lugosi cautiously took the envelope, keeping his distance. He opened it and read the contents—she had written it in Romanian, having learned to speak and write several old middle European languages in her day. She watched as the senior Lugosi's expression changed from feral to puzzled to delighted.

"Good, he took the bait," she said. "Now we shall find out if he is True Blood or New Blood."

Harker bowed and turned and headed back for the gate. The youngest Lugosi started to leap off her perch on the trapeze, but her mother wisely snatched her back and shook a long, red-nailed finger before her child.

Bella smiled and drew back from the window to plan the evening.

The doorbell rang at precisely 8:30 P.M., just as Bella was descending the stairs. She paused to glance around and make certain all the hall mirrors were covered—no use in making their guests nervous or suspicious—as Harker made his dignified way towards the door. She heard him say, "Enter through this doorway and be welcome," and smiled.

Wise move, Harker. Limit their entryway to only one access point in case things go wrong—or right.

It would make everything easier if anything went awry.

She waited on the stair, feeling a little like Norma Desmond from *Sunset Blvd* waiting for her cue. *Only I am certain that I look much more divine.* Age had been kind to Bella, she was wont to admit. Within moments, seven figured floated through the opening. Bella managed to smile. From a distance, they had seemed to have a bit of culture, but now that they were here in her foyer, she noticed that they were more than a little seedy and even crude. In fact, they reminded her a little of the Addams Family from those old *New Yorker* cartoons. The senior Lugosi had a bit of a John Astin swagger to him. His wife could have passed for Morticia. Their four children ranged from a goofy young man down to the little imp of a girl that had tried to leap on Harker several nights back.

Behind them all came Mr. Renfield, looking around with the curiosity of a frog seeking a fly.

Oh, dear, Bella thought. *They are such caricatures.*

That was not a pleasant thought, but it meant what she had to do would probably be easier.

Think of it as extermination, she told herself. Unless this Lugosi could claim to be a true blueblood and prove it—and she simply adored bluebloods for their taste—she had a feeling she would be doing the world a favor. She watched as Harker led them into the receiving hall. Only the youngest child seemed to notice Bella standing at the head of the stairs, and the creature had the audacity to stick out her tongue before being ushered on into the chamber by Renfield.

There is no room for such rude behavior. And no room for foolishness.

Bella shook the thoughts aside and descended the stairs.

She had told Harker to make them comfortable, and listened as he showed them the sideboard with its treats like steak tartar and a rather expensive Chardonnay that she kept for visitors. The eldest Lugosi thanked Harker and said, "I appreciate the gesture, but I don't drink wine..."

Can you not come up with anything more original than that? Bella thought and shook her head. *Have all these modern vampires seen the same old movies?* She stood at the door, waiting for her cue, knowing Harker would pick the appropriate moment.

And it came quite suddenly.

"Madam Bella Van Helsing," Harker announced as she stepped into the receiving hall to greet her guests and let the fun begin.

The senior Lugosi's eyes narrowed, but he bowed. His family followed his example, all save the little girl who sneered and wandered over to the sideboard.

"Thank you for indulging me on such short notice," Bella said, "but as soon as I learned you had moved into the old place, I knew I just had to meet my fascinating new neighbors."

Slurping sounds filled the pause. Bella glanced over and noticed that the youngest child was ravenously sucking on a piece of steak tartar. The mother frowned at her daughter and practically tore the meat from her grasp, giving her that, "Not until you've had dinner," look that only mothers can perfect.

The child sneered again and bared teeth that were unnaturally sharp for one so young.

"We thank you for inviting us over," the senior Lugosi replied. His accent rolled off his tongue. "I am Vladimir Lugosi, that is my lovely wife Sonja, my first son Eadric, my daughter Rulinska, my second son Frederick, and my youngest child Erica—you will have to forgive her manners, I am afraid."

Each of the children bobbed in turn—except for little Erica who stuck out her tongue and then hid her face in her mother's black silk dress that flowed like dirty cobwebs from the woman's otherwise stick-slender body.

"But of course," Bella said and looked hard at little Erica, resisting the temptation to bare her own teeth in response. *This is not the time to play alpha.* Bella certainly was not going to lower herself to doing so with this wild child. She was, after all, descended from a fine family herself, even if she was often tempted to curse her grandfather for the legacy he left her.

"Your name, Van Helsing," Vladimir said. "It is an ancient name, is it not?"

Bella smiled serenely. "Yes, I am from a fine old family, I will admit. And you?"

"We are but what you see. Humble circus performers," Vladimir said, "forced to leave the old country to seek a living elsewhere."

"Really?" Bella said. Harker was giving her the signal that all the preparations in the dining room were finished. "I would have thought the circuses were better attended in the old country than they are here in northern California."

"Alas, these are hard times, and what with the conflicts, we decided it was best to move someplace where we could start anew."

"Ah, a new country, new blood."

He smiled, and his canines revealed their extraordinary sharpness. "Indeed, you put it so quaintly, Missus Van Helsing."

"Miss Van Helsing," Bella said. "Because of my work, I never found time for a family. They would just burden me anyway." She gestured towards the dining room doorway before they could ask what she did. "I believe our meal is ready. Come."

"After you," Vladimir replied.

"Oh, but I must insist, after you," Bella said. "You are, after all, my guests."

Vladimir looked a little puzzled, but he bowed to her again, and taking his wife by the arm, he started for the door. Bella waited for all of them to enter the dining room before making her entrance.

Harker was holding a chair for the pesky little Erica as Bella entered the room. She glanced around, satisfied that everything was ready. This would be a short night's work, and timing was everything. Little Erica snapped at Harker's hand, but her mother snatched her back by the collar of her rather old-fashioned dress, nearly choking the child. Erica snarled and crossed her arms and sulked as only a small girl could.

Harker, meanwhile had gone to the head of the table and pulled back the tall, hooded chair there for Bella to sit in. It had thick velvet curtains drawn back. At one time, Bella learned from her grandfather, it has served as a Walachian throne to one of his greatest adversaries. He had taken it as a trophy, and Bella had inherited it.

She was pleased to see how the gentlemen had the courtesy to stand before she sat down. She nodded to them and then gestured for Harker to begin serving. More steak tartar was set all around, and she saw the eyes of the Lugosi family round in anticipation of the blood-soaked meat. Harker then brought out a carafe that was clearly not wine...

He poured it into everyone's glass save Bella's.

"You do not join us?" Vladimir asked as he lifted his glass.

"I prefer a different vintage," she said narrowing

her eyes. "You see, I know what you are, and I see no reason that we cannot be good neighbors, but you are going to have to learn that there are rules by which you must all abide."

Erica had drained her glass and burped. Renfield giggled, and Mrs. Lugosi shushed her rude daughter. Bella kept a serene smile on her face.

"Rules?" Vladimir repeated. "What rules?"

"Well, for instance, it is foolish of you to go out and snag just any old neighbor off the streets. People will notice. Questions will be asked."

Vladimir's eyes narrowed. "Then what do you suggest we do? Starve?"

"Well, your suggestion that your *manager* should try robbing a blood bank is a start—except you never know if you are getting a tainted vintage. Could be from any old street tramp—they all give blood these days."

"I am still not certain I understand," Vladimir said. "You know what we are, yet you make suggestions as to how we should live our lives? We left the old country because we were tired of being told how to live by the True Bloods who ruled our land."

"Really. Well, if you are going to stay in my neighborhood, you are going to abide by my rules. Elsewise, I will be forced to live up to my ancestor's name. Now are we agreed?"

Vladimir stood up, glaring at Bella. She noticed that Harker was moving discreetly towards the sideboard by the doorway.

"We live by our own rules, and you will not tell us how to live our lives," Vladimir snarled, and now he was showing his fangs. And as if that signaled his entire family that there was a bloodbath about to begin, the rest of them started leaning forward in anticipation of a feast beyond the one Bella had laid before them.

"Too bad," she said. She touched a switch on the side of her chair. The curtains disengaged and fell shut just as she shouted, "Now, Harker!"

In the cozy dark of the throne, Bella heard screams and sizzling and smelled the odor of meat burning. The screams died as rapidly as they started, and the sounds of a more human struggle ensued. "Madam, watch out!" Harker shouted. "I've killed the sun lights!"

Bella pushed the curtains aside in time to see a small child bursting out from under the table, looking a little toasted around the edges. Though the rest of her family had not been able to escape the tremendously hot sunlamps installed in Bella's ceilings—indeed, their crispy corpses were turning into ashes even as she watched—Erica had apparently managed to get under the huge dining room table before she could be fried. And now she was lunging at Bella like some small, rabid terrier, baring fangs.

Bella slipped out of her chair and backed away from it just moments before the angry child slammed into the back of it and sent it rocking precariously. She turned to see Harker engaged in a struggle against Renfield that neither seemed to be winning at the moment. But then there was a snarl that distracted Bella into remembering that one of her victims had escaped their elimination. Erica was on her feet, charging towards Bella so rapidly, the child was almost a blur. Bella grabbed the nearest chair and turned it so the legs were pointed at the small body flying across the room.

Either little Erica lacked experience in a battle, or her momentum was too great. She slammed into the chair, nearly knocking Bella back. Fortunately, Bella was made of sterner stuff—and she had over a century of practice in the family profession behind her. She used the chair like a sling and tossed little Erica over against the wall. The child hit it with a loud thud and tumbled to the floor just as Bella snapped one of the chair legs free.

Undaunted, little Erica snarled and pounced, and Bella stepped into the charge with a snarl of her own, ramming the sharp end of the chair leg through the small girl's long-dead heart. The child practically exploded into a pile of ashes that started Bella sneezing.

Bella heard a thunk—the sort of heavy candlestick against a skull thunk—and turned just as Renfield slid lifeless to the floor. Harker looked a bit ruffled as he straightened his collar and proceeded to clean the candlestick.

"Well, that was exciting," Bella said.

"Your grandfather Van Helsing would have been proud," Harker said.

"Yes, though it is unfortunate that I became that which he was sworn to destroy, all because he made enemies with the entire vampire nation..." Bella picked up a napkin and wiped the ashes from her hands. "Then again, it is not every day I get to kill an entire family of commoner vampires. The more of those cretins we eliminate, the better it is for the True Bloods who are smart enough to stay discreetly hidden, though I will admit I do wish they had been willing to negotiate. It would have been nice to have neighbors with whom I could share an evening without having to kill them."

"Alas they were clearly not True Bloods, Madam, or they would have accepted your kind offer of their blind obedience to your rules," Harker said. "Shall I finish cleaning up the mess?"

"Thank you, Harker. But before you do, is there any of that old Belgian left?"

Harker shook his head. "Sorry, Madam, but you finished him off the other night."

"Oh, well, I guess I shall have to find someone to replace him," she said with a sigh.

"Might I suggest a bit of Englishman?" he said, gesturing towards Renfield's corpse.

Bella shook her head and shuddered. "No, thank you, I've seen what he eats," she said. "I think I shall take a bit of night air while the night is still young and see if I can find another old Napa Valley Spaniard. The last one had quite a nice bouquet."

"Very good, Madam," Harker said.

Bella went to her chambers and changed out of her dinner clothes, selecting something darker and more aerodynamic before heading for the rooftop, turning into an old bat, and flapping off into the night.

Steven Piziks teaches high school English by day and returns home to a perfectly ordinary suburb by night. This is the third story he's written for the supernatural suburbia anthologies, and the third one he's set in the supernatural gated community Hidden Oaks Veneficus. (Look the last word up. It's Latin. Bad Latin.) He's currently working on a novel about Wanda Silver and Hidden Oaks.

Bait and Switch

Steven Piziks

Vampire Bait folded her arms across her little nubbin breasts and faced me down across the table. "Look, it doesn't matter how much Daddy paid you. Julian totally loves me. Our love is totally eternal, and we'll be together *forever*."

I shrugged, pulled a wad of bubble wrap from my purse, and popped a few plastic bomblettes. So satisfying. "Hey, I'm on your side, hon." Pop pop pop. "But like you said, Daddy is calling the shots. Once we finish up, I get a check and you get a Mazda. No strings." Pop pop pop.

Vampire Bait, whose real name was Aimee or Mimee or Pookee or something, looked longingly at the bubble wrap, but I don't share. The smell of sweetened coffee swirled around us as the baristas behind the counter tugged at their arcane machines. Customers perused laptops or flipped through newspapers with happy headlines like MISSING CHILD FOUND MURDERED and SUICIDE BOMBER KILLS TEN. Outside, the sun had already set on a spring strip mall evening. We sat at a tiny round table near the back of the coffee house, with the counter crowd between us and the front door. Vampire Bait had a double labradoodle with extra muggles, or something like that, and a chocolate muffin the size of a safe deposit box. I had tea. I turned thirty last week, and had noticed the difference in my waistline. Creamy coffee drinks were Out. No gray hair among the brown yet, at least.

When Vampire Bait wasn't looking, I gooshed my tea with the mega-sized flask of holy water I keep in my purse. "So Julian hangs outside your window and watches you sleep all night long," I prompted.

"Lots of times he slips into my room, too," she said. "He's totally there if I wake up to pee."

"And he tells you how good you smell?"

"Totally." Her brown eyes took on a dreamy cast. "He says I'm so beautiful he can barely keep from eating me *up*. But I let him munch on me a couple times because these leprechauns keep trying to attack my house, and fighting them takes a lot out of Julian, and he says my blood can heal him, but he's afraid he'll drink it all once he starts but I trust him so I've totally told him to take what he needs and he does and I'm totally cool with that."

I couldn't help asking, "How many leprechauns have actually attacked you?"

"None. Julian has totally kept them all away from me."

"Wow." Pop pop pop. "Let me know if he has a brother."

Vampire Bait picked at her muffin. "So tell the truth, Wanda. I thought Daddy was paying you to make me drop Julian. How can you be on my side?"

"Listen, hon, one thing I've learned after three years in this business is that nothing can stand in the way of eternal love. It always wins in the end, so I don't even try." Another thing I've learned after three years in this business is how to lie with a completely straight face. "That's why I don't make guarantees to my clients. Like I told your dad, we do one little thing when Julian shows up, and that's it. You get a new car out of it, and I collect my fee. No strings."

Bait sipped her labradoodle, leaving a whipped cream mustache. She was suspicious. The trouble was, she was suspicious of the wrong person. She was young, not quite pretty, and had a vampire boyfriend twenty times her age who told her she smelled like Twinkies. Every alarm bell she had should have been screaming ALERT! ALERT! I mean, look at it this way: if a guy from the social security set makes kissy noises at a sixteen year old, we rightly whip out a bucket of tar and open a goose feather pillow. But advance his age a couple centuries, mousse his hair into a haystack, and suddenly it's all cool? Right! So Vampire Bait becomes suspicious of me, and I pretend her boyfreak is the coolest thing since polar ice in order to develop rapport. Ah well. One day she'll look back on this and shudder. More importantly, she'll be alive to do so.

I was just extracting a silver-backed hand mirror from my industrial-sized purse when Vampire Bait grabbed my arm. "There he is!" she squeaked.

Into the coffee shop slouched an anemic-looking black-haired guy dressed in chinos and a black leather jacket. He was trying to look like a teenager, but it was clear to my practiced eye that he'd been closer to thirty when some passing vampire had slurped him dry. And if you went for the big-eyed, tousle-haired, lean-bodied, perfect-featured look, yeah—he was gorgeous.

"How old is he?" I asked.

Vampire Bait never took her eyes off him. "He was turned ninety-six years ago on his seventeenth birthday," she sighed. "It was a totally sad story. He was walking home from visiting his grandpa, who was dying of a totally incurable lung disease, and—"

"Wow, that's fascinating," I said before I had to sit through the entire romantic lie. Then I held the mirror so it reflected the coffee shop crowd. Julian scanned the tables, looking for Vampire Bait. "Okay, here's the deal. All you have to do is look at Julian's reflection in this mirror."

"His reflection?" Bait furrowed her brow, and two zits disappeared into the wrinkles. "But vampires don't have reflections."

"Actually, that's not true," I said. "They just avoid mirrors because some of them are enchanted like this one. It shows people the way they really are. Take a look."

She did. And all the blood drained from her face. I peeked, too. The coffee shop crowd looked much the same, but standing among them was an ancient, wrinkly man in a leather jacket and chinos. Liver spots dominated his bald skull, and his rheumy eyes bulged over a toothless mouth. A shiny bit of drool slid from slack lips, and his gaze darted hungrily around the shop. Vampire Bait squeaked in horror.

"That's what I'm kissing?" she blurted out.

"Totally."

Vampire Bait slid under the table. A moment later,

her hand appeared, groped for the chocolate muffin, found it, and yanked it out of sight. "Is there a back door to this place?" she whimpered. "I totally have to get out of here."

I pointed her toward it, covered her while she duck-walked away, and stuffed the mirror back into my purse. Then I caught up my tea and headed for Julian, who had his cell phone out, no doubt so he could text his dinner and ask her whereabouts. I tapped him on the shoulder.

"Hey, Julian," I said, ignoring the crowd. "I have a message from your girlfriend."

He turned just in time to catch my tea in his face. I walked away, ignoring the scream of pain. Holy water takes years—and layers—off the complexion.

Later that same evening, I deposited a fat check from Daddy and headed for my office, which is sand-wiched between a massage therapist and an upscale bead shop in yet another strip mall. The sign on the glass door says WANDA SILVER: FOR HIRE, and that's it. Although my clientele—worried parents whose kids fall in love with vampires—is rather specific, I stay surprisingly busy. Craigslist is my best friend, which says more about me than I'd like.

I opened the door, flipped on some lights, and scooped up the mail from its pile on the floor. Bills dominated, of course. Two were of the "we break legs" variety. They were, fittingly, from the hospital where Mom and Eric had gotten their treatments. I sat at my creaky old desk and forced myself to open the envelopes. A depressingly large number of zeroes followed the numbers. What were the odds that a mother and her son would end up with leukemia at the same time? Or that the daughter/sister would get stuck with the bills for three years running because no one had insurance and she was the only one with any kind of job? It was pay up or my mom would lose her house. And my brother Eric . . .

My front door opened, and a vampire edged inside. This one had the more textbook blond hair and green eyes, and his build went for broad-shouldered and tall. He wore a white T-shirt, jeans, and an acid-wash denim jacket that was almost out of style enough to be retro. His face was pale and perfect, of course, and he seemed to be nineteen or twenty. My jaw dropped, but not over his looks.

"You son of a bitch," I growled from behind my desk. He couldn't actually enter unless I invited him— that rule is true—so I wasn't worried he'd get close enough to treat me like a Big Gulp. Still, I rested my thumb lightly on the big red button labeled SPRINKLER. "What the hell are *you* doing here?"

"You have to help me, Wanda," he said. "Please. I'll give you anything."

"Anything?" My thumb quivered on the button. "Really? Can I have the pleasure of dumping a dozen gallons of holy water down your collar and watching you melt? Might I have the orgasmic joy I'll feel when I cut off your head, fill your mouth with holy wafers, and drive a stake through your heart? Will you give me that?"

Pause. ". . . No," the vampire said. "I was thinking more of cash under the table?"

"You're dead, Lucas. Again."

He held up his hands. "I'm desperate here. You have to know that. Why else would I come to you?"

"Because you're an evil creature of the night and you're trying to trick me like you tricked my brother," I snapped.

He ignored that remark. "Look, I want to hire you, and I'll pay ten times your usual fee."

Okay, here's the thing—I hated Lucas. For good reason. Loathing for him bubbled inside me like a tar cauldron. But he had my attention.

"My usual fee is twenty-five thousand," I lied. "You'd owe me a quarter of a million. Cash." That would clear up just about everything Mom and I owed.

"Done."

I forced myself not to blink in surprise, then moved my thumb a fraction of an inch away from the panic button. "I'm listening," I said guardedly. "But you're the reason I got into my current line of work. Why would you want to hire me?"

Lucas sighed. He was still standing in the doorway, and chilly air wafted inside with the smell of new leaves. "Look, can I come all the way in?"

"No." I paused, not wanting to ask but having to just the same. "How's Eric?"

"He's fine," Lucas said. "He sends his love."

"Yeah? So why does he never call? Or even e-mail? That your fault?"

Some heat hit Lucas's voice. "Listen, I never did anything he didn't want me to do—"

"—So you made him into an undead monster?" I finished. "You turned him into your eternal boytoy?"

Lucas sighed, an affectation, since I knew he didn't breathe. "Look, this isn't going to get us anywhere. Do you want the job or not?"

"My righteous anger says no, no, no, but my bill

collectors say yes, yes, yes," I admitted. "I'm still a little confused. Parents hire me because things like you come across as all cool and romantic and bad-boy sparkly, and they want me to put the kibosh on it before anyone gets slurped to the bloodsucking side of the force. Or maybe just killed. So what could *you* want me for?"

Lucas sighed again. "There's this . . . girl. Her name is Marissa Duncan, and she's convinced she's in love with me. She follows me everywhere I go. She leaves me black roses. She even writes me letters drawn in blood. I mean, they smell nice, but they're not my type, right?"

"Button, sprinkler system, holy water," I said, "if you throw me another pun."

"One evening I woke up and found her waiting outside my mausoleum. She said she'd been there all day, guarding me. It freaked me out. And she has this uncanny ability to track me while I'm . . . shopping."

"'Shopping'?" I took out a strip of bubble plastic. Lucas gave it an envious look—apparently even vampires like little bubbles—but I still don't share.

"If I even *look* at another human, she swoops down from the shadows and screams that I belong to her. I haven't drunk a drop in more than a week now, and I'm starving. You wouldn't believe what I had to go through just to sneak down to see you."

Pop pop pop. "Shop somewhere else. The world is wide."

"Hey, I have territory. I set one wing outside my boundaries, and I'm pulled into a blood match with another vampire or a werewolf or a banshee or worse."

"Then suck her dry." Poppity pop pop. "That's what your kind do, isn't it?"

"I would," he said in a dark voice, "but she came up from New Orleans."

"Ah. Vampire central."

"Yeah. The witch doctors down there really know how to deal. She paid big bucks for a juju tattoo that protects her from being harmed by undead. So I can't kill her. But I *can* turn her."

I blinked. "Breaking her neck—that's harm. But turning her into an undead human mosquito . . . that's angels and cotton candy."

"Hey, I didn't cast the spell. I'm just telling you how it works. And I'm *not* turning her." He shuddered. "That's what she wants. Eternity with me."

"You already have someone for that," I said acidly.

"Come on—you're the only one who can help." His eyes narrowed. "I know you need the money."

I set my jaw. I hated that he knew this. Probably as much as he hated having to crawl through my door. Pop pop pop.

"Fine," I said. "Toss me the full paywad up front, and I'll take care of her for you. Same rules apply—no timelines, no guarantees."

"Whatever happened to half now, half when the job is done?" he complained.

"Like I can send a collection agency after a dead guy with fangs," I scoffed. "Hand it over, bat-boy. Then meet me in the coffeehouse up the block at sunset tomorrow."

Like so many pieces of vampire bait, Marissa Duncan looked perfectly normal. Early twenties, hair dyed a bad black, brown eyes, a few freckles, shabby black clothes. But across the side of her neck looped an eye-twisting black tattoo the size of my hand—the spell that kept Lucas from killing her. Marissa was more mature than yesterday's case, but I still hoped to keep this quick. My supply of bubble wrap was almost completely popped out.

"So you're really a PI?" Marissa asked. We were already at the coffee house, my usual meeting place for this kind of thing.

"Yep," I said. This wasn't a lie—I have a license and everything. My practice is just a little . . . specialized. I popped some plastic. "Like I said on the phone, I was running a background check on your boyfriend Lucas for an unrelated case, and I learned a few things about him that I thought you might want to know."

"I already know he's a Lord of Darkness," she said, then looked at me, clearly expecting me to weird out. I just shook my head and gooshed my tea with my water flask. Lord of Darkness. Right. Lord of the Chicken Hawks was more like. Marissa seemed disappointed at my mastery of the blasé.

"That's not what this is about," I said.

"Well, whatever it is," Marissa said, "you won't shock me. He's a Shadow Lord, and I'm meant to be a Lady. These sheep—" She gestured at the other people in the coffee house. "—don't know what dances in the dark around them, but I do, and once my lord Lucas wraps me in shadow, I'll be one with—"

"That's great." I extracted the mirror from my purse. "And I wouldn't think of standing in your way. In fact, I want to help you."

That gave her pause. "You do?"

"Definitely." The patter was always similar. Gain the trust with lies, then break it with truth. "There's way more shadow in the universe than light. Anyone

who bothers to stop and think knows that. Most of
the sheep don't think, though, which is what gets
them through their dull, daily lives."

"Exactly!" Marissa said. "That's so true!"

In that moment, Lucas walked in the front door,
blond, handsome, and retro. I held up the mirror so it
caught his reflection. In ten seconds, my debts would
be paid and Lucas would be out of my life forever.
I was already feeling the relief.

"There he is," I said. "Take a look at him in this."

She did. A gasp inflated her chest. "Oh. My. God."

"I know," I said.

Her eyes stayed glued to the reflection. "This is . . .
it's just . . ."

"Yeah," I said. "I'm so sorry."

"Sorry?" she said. "Are you nuts? He's *gorgeous!*"

"What?" I snatched the mirror from her and aimed
it so I could see Lucas myself. My mouth dried up.
Marissa was right. Lucas was stunning. A little silver
streaked through the gold over his ears, and laugh
lines touched his eyes, but they only added maturity
and solidity to what had previously been ethereal
boyishness. Shit! My own hormones tried to squirt
into overdrive, and I hastily stuffed the mirror into
my bag. Marissa was already moving.

"My Dark Lord," she said huskily, sashaying toward
him across the coffee house. "Grant me your gift! I
am meant for shadow!"

Lucas shot her a glance of pure terror and fled
out the door.

"You suck," Lucas told me.

"From you, that's a compliment," I shot back. We

were in my office again, me at my desk, him at the door. "Exactly how old are you?"

"You mean in vampire years or human years?"

I covered my face with my hands. "Just the answer the question."

"I became a vampire twenty years ago," he said. "When I was nineteen. If I were alive, I wouldn't even be forty yet. Why does that matter?"

I wasn't about to tell him. The fewer vampires who knew about my mirror, the better. "Let's just say it alters my strategy. And remember, I said no guarantees. I keep your money no matter what."

Lucas smiled, wider than any human could. His fangs showed, and for the first time I felt a little chill. He frisbeed a manila envelope across the room to me. "Yeah? Check this out, Wanda."

I was suddenly scared of him. I didn't want to open the envelope, but I did. My chilly fingers found a photograph. Mom asleep on her bed, thin gray hair puffed out across the pillow. Her throat had two puncture marks on it. My hands turned to ice, and I couldn't breathe.

"You bastard," I whispered, knowing he could hear, even across the room. "How did you get into her house? Mom knows not to invite strangers in."

"I'm not a stranger. I'm a client looking for you. I can prove it. I can describe your office. I know you pop plastic. And I just need to use the phone for a second." Lucas blew me a kiss. "Screw the money. Get Marissa off my back or I'll make your dear, sweet mother into a lady of the night. Two generations of vampires in one family. Think of *that* when you're paying the bills, magic Wanda."

And he was gone before I could reply.

✧   ✧   ✧

I gave myself thirty seconds of rant and rave time. Lucas would be dead. I mean, *more* dead. Then I gulped down some holy water from my flask to calm myself. I swear the stuff is more addictive than Red Bull.

Next, I went over to my mother's house. It's a crackerbox from the fifties, surrounded by dozens of similar crackerboxes. Eric and I grew up there. The woods behind the subdivision has become a strip mall, and the local graveyard is a lot bigger, but everything else is the same.

The windows were dark, and I let myself in. Mom was asleep in her room, and I knew from experience only a bomb blast would wake her. I used my cell phone as a flashlight to check her. Good color, good breathing. No puncture wounds on her neck—they had apparently healed without even a scab. My stomach clenched in fear and anger all over again.

Out in the living room, I put on a light, sat on the sofa, and thought hard. How could I convince Marissa to leave Lucas alone? Idly, I glanced at Mom's telephone on the end table. The little screen listed recent calls. My heart jumped. I didn't recognize the third number, and it set off my PI instincts. Breathlessly, I entered it into my BlackBerry. I have access to reverse directories that give me addresses for most phone numbers, even unlisteds and cells.

The name on the listing was Eric Silver.

Questions crowded my mind as I drove across the darkened town, following my GPS. Why had Eric called Mom and not me? Why hadn't Mom told me? Was Eric all right?

Technically Eric was still a Missing Person, a high

school senior whose cancer ward bed had turned up empty three years ago. Witnesses had spoken of a blond man who had visited him more than once, always after dark. Mysteriously, the man didn't appear on any security cameras. The same security cameras didn't record Eric leaving the building, either. Today, even Mom didn't know the truth. But I did. It was the reason for my current profession.

I don't kill vampires. There's no good reason to. Stake one, and another just takes over the territory. Way easier to foil the bastards when you know who they are, where they hang out, and what their taste in bait is. Better the enemy you know, blah blah blah. But in Lucas's case, I would make an exception. If I could figure out how. Lucas wasn't stupid and had to know I would come after him.

My GPS took me to a condo complex. More than half of them were empty, thank you housing crunch and munch. My mind wouldn't stop moving. Three years since I had seen Eric. Three years since Lucas had made him a vampire. Mom thought he had decided to run off and commit suicide rather than let the cancer take him, and the thought of his body lying unburied somewhere caused her sorrow, though she said she understood what had driven him to it. I knew better because Lucas and Eric had showed up outside my bedroom window and told me not to worry. Then Lucas had called him beautiful and kissed him in a puddle of pale moonlight.

It had been a little much. In ten seconds, my baby brother had gone from terminal cancer patient missing from a hospital to gay vampire in a *really* long-term relationship. And there was only one person to blame.

I found Eric's place. My heart pounded, and I was raising my hand to knock when the door whipped open.

"Heard you," said Eric. "Vampire hearing."

"Oh." I couldn't think of anything better to say. "Hi. You look . . . good."

He just shrugged. It isn't fair. Vampires always look good. Eric's hair had come back in thick and autumn red. His blue eyes were clear and wide, and he had filled out from the wasted skeleton I'd last seen. The right liquid diet could do wonders. It was fantastic to see him. The only things that kept me from hugging him were the two little fangs that peeped from his mouth like baby walrus teeth.

"Why did you call Mom and not me?" I asked around the lump in my throat.

"I didn't call Mom," he said. "I chickened out and hung up after one ring. I guess I should have known that would be more than enough for the big time PI."

"Is *he* here?"

Eric caught my meaning. "No. Lucas bought this place for me. He likes tradition, but a stone slab mattress sucks on so many levels."

I privately decided that someone with fangs shouldn't say S that many times. "Can I come in?"

His condo was almost bare, with hardly enough furniture to sit on. I've noticed vampires tend to be either sybarites or Spartans. Just my luck my brother would be the latter. A little voice said that it made sense, considering Spartan tastes. I told my little voice to shut the hell up, but it was too late. I imagined him and Lucas here alone, with Lucas sliding his cold, dead hands over my baby brother's body. It made me sick.

"It's not much, but it's home," Eric said.

"Lucas isn't here," I blurted out. "I can get you away if we move fast, move now. Mom, too. Let's go!"

He stared at me with round eyes. It was a look I remembered from when we were younger and I babysat him. "I . . . can't do that," he whispered. "Wanda, you don't know what—"

The front door banged open and Lucas strode in. "Hey, kids. Catching up on old times?"

Vampire hearing. Eric had known Lucas was coming. Shit. I forced a smile to my face. "Not that old."

He leaned against a wall and crossed his arms, exuding sly power. "Marissa?"

"She still wants to walk on the dark side," I said shortly. "Give me another night or two."

"You hired my sister to get rid of Stalker Queen?" Eric asked. "Whoa. I didn't know you were that desperate, Luke."

"I've been trying not to worry you." He slid a possessive arm around Eric's shoulder as I set my jaw. "I know how upset you get."

Eric stared morosely down at the floor, and I wanted to snatch my baby brother away from the monster in the room. "Upset. Yeah."

"Don't let it bug you. Your big sister and I have it all under control." Lucas fixed me with a hard look. "Right?"

I stared back. "Absolutely."

"I was thinking," he continued softly into Eric's ear but without taking his eyes off me, "that maybe we should get your mom a Mother's Day present. Anonymously, of course."

My stomach clenched. "Don't trouble yourself."

"We'll have to see," Lucas said. "In any case, Wanda, don't you have work to do?"

I fled. Was I more angry or afraid? I couldn't tell, and it was really starting to piss me off. I swigged from my flask like a wino with the trembles and drove back to my office, even though it was almost two in the morning. No way I'd be able to sleep now, and I was used to all-nighters anyway.

I found the front door open, the window broken. Inside was worse. Papers flung around, chairs tipped over. The standard muss-and-toss. Spray-painted on the walls in sloppy red letters was HIS DARK GIFTS ARE MINE. Even more impressive was that Marissa Duncan was still spraying on the final E.

"What the great green hell are you doing?" I screeched, royally pissed now.

Marissa yowled like a cat and spun around. The can rolled away in a metallic-smelling cloud. Then she recovered herself. "Stay away from my Dark Lord. I won't let you steal his gift from me."

"Quit *calling* him that. Jesus, you sound like you're twelve."

Her face went hard as a gravestone, and her tattoo seemed to undulate in the dim light. "Don't talk to me that way. I've made the sacrifice. I've earned my place. He *has* to grant me the shadow gift."

The last sentence was cracker-barrel nuts, but my mind was highlighting the paragraph's main idea in pink neon marker. "Sacrifice? What sacrifice?"

"The blood of a child is required to summon the Dark Lord," she said fervently. "Even the sheep know that."

I remembered the headlines I had read in the

coffee shop. The letters she had sent to Lucas. Nausea sloshed through my stomach. "You killed a little kid because you thought it would summon Lucas? You filthy, monstrous—"

I was suddenly staring down the barrel of a pistol. "Maybe I'm not monstrous enough," Marissa said. "Maybe I need another sacrifice to get his attention."

Guns are amazing. They can send every thought flying from your head like a startled hummingbird or focus you like a magnifying glass on an ant. Lucky for me, I got the magnifying glass. I saw that I'd been stupid. Marissa wasn't obsessed with Lucas. She was obsessed with power. And that was the key.

"Put the gun down," I said in a low voice, "and I'll get your Dark Lord."

Marissa's eyes narrowed. "It's a trick."

"Nope. What do you think this office is for? I'm his chief minion."

"Then why has he been trying so hard to get rid of me?"

"Testing your devotion. Look, do you want his kiss or not?"

"His gift," she corrected.

I tossed my head, though my heart thudded hard enough to shake my shirt. "That's what the sheep call it. You have a lot to learn."

That broke her, though the gun never wavered. "Summon him, then. Do you have a dark ritual? Words of power?"

"Speed dial," I said, and whipped out my cell phone.

Lucas and Eric both arrived within ten minutes. I was forced to smile wide and invite Lucas in. Marissa's eyes went hot as steamed milk when she saw her

Dark Lord, and I forced myself to look properly min-ionesque amid my ruined office. Marissa and Lucas went through several *You!*s and *My Dark Lord*s before settling down enough to actually talk. I prayed this would work. Vampires are fast, but they can't outrace bullets, and Marissa had already killed a child. She wouldn't hesitate to turn me into chopped cheese.

"This one has earned your kiss, O Dark One," I said. "Your humble minion pleads with you to grant it to her."

Marissa, who was still pointing the pistol at me, exulted. Eric looked startled. Lucas's jaw dropped far enough to lick his belt buckle. But he recovered quickly. "A word with my . . . minion," he said, and drew me aside. His hand was cold on my wrist.

"What the hell are you—?"

"Just do it, bat-boy," I hissed. My fists were clenched, mostly in fear, truth be told. "Trust me."

"I'm not spending eternity with her," he hissed back. His fangs were showing now.

"No more talking," Marissa snapped, and I belat-edly realized she was standing at my desk. Little alarm demons jumped up and down inside my head. "Give me the kiss, or she dies."

"So?" Lucas snarled. "She's only a minion."

"Hey!" Eric said.

Before I could interject with my own reaction, Marissa upped the undead ante. "Oh? What about all that holy water above us? I can feel it in the pipes, thanks to my tattoo. And someone kindly labeled this button *sprinkler*." Marissa set her finger against it. "Doesn't take much to figure out what will happen if I give it a push. If I can't have your kiss, Dark Lord, no one can."

My heart tore in half. I would cheer if Lucas melted into sludge, but I couldn't watch Eric die again. My little brother swallowed and glanced at the ceiling, fear in his blue eyes, and all the air left the room. Lucas shot Eric a look, and I was forced to admit he seemed...concerned. Okay, he brimmed with full-blown distress. But probably more for himself than for Eric.

"Just do it, Lucas!" I said. "Now!"

Marissa made a move as if to push the button. In three strides, Lucas crossed the room and sank his fangs into her tattoo. She stiffened and the pistol fell to the floor, but her other hand never left the sprinkler button, and I had to give her brass points for that. Lucas, who hadn't eaten in days, gave himself over to feeding. Marissa moaned beneath him. I closed my eyes. Watching another woman's O-face has never been high on my list of fun times.

I heard a thud and opened my eyes. Marissa's body lay on the floor, paler than ever. Her mouth was open, and Lucas was holding his wrist over it, a strained look on his face. Blood from an open wound on his skin dripped over Marissa's tongue.

"Her spell tattoo is making me do this," he gasped. "And it won't take long. I hope you know what you're doing."

Marissa shuddered, then sat up. Her hair was wild, and her eyes were *hungry*. Fangs extended in her mouth, and she felt them with her tongue. She looked up at Lucas, then spread her hands before her and stared at them like a kid on pot.

"I feel it," she growled. "I'm transformed. I'm one with the dark." She looked at me. "And I *hunger*."

Lucas and Eric were both caught flat when she lunged for me. Me, I was ready. Though this meant I just stood there and let her take me. Dark world, here I come.

"Wanda!" Eric shouted, but he couldn't stop Marissa from sinking her fangs into my neck.

I felt the skin break with a pop louder than any bubble wrap, and it sent me into an paroxysm of both pleasure and pain. I heard sucking sounds as Marissa went to work. I heard feet scuffling as Eric and Lucas dashed forward. And then the screams began.

The pain and pleasure vanished. Eric hauled me upright with strong hands. Marissa writhed on the floor, hands clutching her throat and pain-filled screams wracked my ears. As the three of us watched, she dissolved from the inside out, hissing and bubbling, until there was nothing left but a noisome stain on the carpet. I doubted even a Sham-Wow would absorb it.

Relief, real relief, flooded my veins. I glanced at my office and at my little brother and at Lucas—the thing that had wrecked them both.

"We're done here," I said to him. "Get the hell out."

"How did you do that?" Eric asked in awe.

I slid my flask from my purse and held it up. "I titrate holy water. It gets into the blood. Wanda probably thought it was the pipes. Now get out, Lucas, before I throw some on you."

Lucas nodded. "I should tell you—the photo was a fake. I was afraid you wouldn't help me. I'm sorry."

He started to turn away, but Eric grabbed his arm. "Wait, Lucas. I can't keep this up. I can't watch the bad blood between you two. Wanda, you know that he loves—"

"No, he doesn't," I exploded. "He can't! He's an undead *thing*. He ate you alive and stole you away from us because he was *hungry*."

"Are you talking about Lucas," Eric said, "or the leukemia?"

That stopped me. I could only stare at my little brother. He wasn't so little, though. I hadn't noticed until now.

"When you say Lucas can't love because he's an undead thing," Eric continued softly, "you're saying the same thing about me. Is that what you believe?"

There was a long, long pause. "Shit," I managed.

Eric was relentless. "He saved me. I would be cold in a grave now if it weren't for him. Instead, we're standing here, having a nice family conversation."

"Shit," I said again.

"I think that's the closest we're going to get to an apology," Lucas put in.

"Don't push it, bat-boy," I croaked, but the insult was half-hearted.

In the end, I gave Eric a hug. I couldn't manage one for Lucas, though I did slug him on the shoulder, probably harder than I should have. And two days later, when I had finally finished cleaning up my office, I got a special delivery crate from him. It was a tiny flask of holy water. Surrounded by a three-foot cushion of bubble wrap.

Life is good.

The following is an excerpt from:

CRYOBURN

LOIS McMASTER BUJOLD

Available from Baen Books
November 2010
hardcover

He stumbled, and his hand banged against something hollow-sounding—had that bit of wall *shifted*? He snatched his arms in, wrapping them around himself, trembling. *I'm just cold, yeah, that's it.* Which had to be from the power of suggestion, since he was sweating.

Hesitantly, he stretched out again and felt along the corridor wall. He began to move forward more slowly, fingers lightly passing over the faint lines and ripples of drawer edges and handle-locks, rank after rank of them, stacked high beyond his reach. Behind each drawer-face, a frozen corpse: stiff, silent, waiting in mad hope. A hundred corpses to every thirty steps or so, thousands more around each corner, hundreds of thousands in this lost labyrinth. *No—millions.*

That part, unfortunately, was not a hallucination.

The Cryocombs, they called this place, rumored to wind for kilometers beneath the city. The tidy blocks of new mausoleums on the city's western fringe, zoned as the Cryopolis, did not account for all the older facilities scattered around and underneath the town going back as much as a hundred and fifty or two hundred years, some still operational, some cleared and abandoned. Some abandoned without being cleared? Miles's ears strained, trying to detect a reassuring hum of refrigeration machinery beyond the blood-surf and the angels' cries. Now, there was a nightmare for him—all those banks of drawers bumping under his fingertips concealing not frozen hope, but warm rotting death.

It would be stupid to run.

The angels kept sleeting. Miles refused to let what was left of his mind be diverted in an attempt to count them, even by a statistically valid sampling-and-multiplication method. Miles had done such a back-of-the-napkin rough calculation when he'd first arrived here on Kibou-daini, what, just five days ago? *Seems longer*. If the cryo-corpses were stacked up along the corridors at a density, on average, of a hundred per ten meters, that made for ten thousand along each kilometer of corridor. One hundred kilometers of corridors for every million frozen dead. Therefore, something between a hundred and fifty and two hundred kilometers of cryo-corridors tucked around this town somewhere.

I am so lost.

His hands were scraped and throbbing, his trouser knees torn and damp. With blood? There had been crawlspaces and ducts, hadn't there? Yes, what had seemed like kilometers of them, too. And more ordinary utility tunnels, lit by ceiling tubes and not lined with centuries of mortality. His weary legs stumbled, and he froze—um, *stopped*—once more, to be sure of his balance. He wished fiercely for his cane, gone astray in the scuffle earlier—how many hours ago, now?—he could be using it like a blind man on Old Earth or Barrayar's own Time of Isolation, tapping in front of his feet for those so-vividly-imagined gaps in the floor.

His would-be kidnappers hadn't roughed him up too badly in the botched snatch, relying instead on a hypospray of sedative to keep their captive under control. Too bad it had been in the same class of sedatives to which Miles was violently allergic—or even, judging by his present symptoms, the identical drug. Expecting a drowsy deadweight, they'd instead found themselves struggling with a maniacal little screaming man. This suggested his snatchers hadn't known everything about him, a somewhat reassuring thought.

Or even anything about him. *You bastards are on the top of Imperial Lord Auditor Miles Vorkosigan's very own shit list now, you bet.* But under what name? *Only five days on this benighted world, and already total strangers are trying to kill me.* Sadly, it wasn't even a record. He wished he knew who they'd been. He wished he were back home in the Barrayaran Empire, where the dread title of Imperial Auditor actually *meant* something to people. *I wish those wretched angels would stop shrieking at me.*

"Flights of angels," he muttered in experimental incantation, "sing me to my rest."

The angels declined to form up into a ball like a will-o'-the-wisp and lead him onward out of this place. So much for his dim hope that his subconscious had been keeping track of his direction while the rest of his mind was out, and would now produce some neat inspiration in dramatic form. Onward. One foot in front of the other, wasn't that the grownup way of solving problems? Surely he ought to be a grownup at his age.

He wondered if he was going in circles.

His trailing hand wavered through black air across a narrow cross-corridor, made for access to the banks' supporting machinery, which he ignored. Later, another. He'd been suckered into exploring down too many of those already, which was part of how he'd got so hideously turned around. Go straight or, if his corridor dead-ended, right, as much as possible, that was his new rule.

But then his bumping fingers crossed something that was not a bank of cryo-drawers, and he stopped abruptly. He felt around without turning, because turning, he'd discovered, destroyed what little orientation he still possessed. Yes, a door! If only it wasn't another utility closet. If only it was unlocked, for a change.

Unlocked, yes! Miles hissed through his teeth and pulled. Hinges creaked with corrosion. It seemed to weigh a ton, but the bloody thing moved! He stuck an experimental foot through the gap and felt around. A floor, not a drop—if his senses weren't lying, again. He had nothing with which to prop open the door; he hoped he might find it again if this proved another dead end. Carefully, he knelt on all fours and eased through, feeling in front of him.

Not another closet. Stairs, emergency stairs! He seemed to be on a landing in front of the door. To his right, steps went up, cool and gritty under his sore hand. To his left, down. Which way? He had to run out of up sooner, surely. It was probably a delusion, if a powerful one, that he might go down forever. This maze could not descend to the planet's magma, after all. The heat would thaw the dead.

There was a railing, not too wobbly, but he started up on all fours anyway, patting each riser to be sure the step was all there before trusting his weight to it. A reversal of direction, more painful climbing. Another turning at another landing—he tried its door, which was also unlocked, but did not enter it. Not unless or until he ran out of stairs would he let himself be forced back in there with those endless ranks of corpses. He tried to keep count of the flights, but lost track after a few turnings. He heard himself whimpering under his breath in time with the angel ululations, and forced himself to silence. Oh God, was that a faint gray glow overhead? Real light, or just another mirage?

He knew it for real light when he saw the pale glimmer of his hands, the white ghosts of his shirtsleeves. He hadn't become disembodied in the dark after all, huh.

On the next landing he found a door with a real window, a dirty square pane as wide as his two stretched hands. He craned his neck and peered out, blinking against the grayness that seemed bright as fire, making his dark-staring eyes water. *Oh gods and little fishes let it not be locked . . .*

He shoved, then gasped relief as the door moved. It didn't creak as loudly as the one below. *Could be a roof. Be careful.* He crawled again, out into free air at last.

Not a roof; a broad alley at ground level. One hand upon the rough stucco wall behind him, Miles clambered to his feet and squinted up at slate gray clouds, a spitting mist, and lowering dusk. All luminous beyond joy.

The structure from which he'd just emerged rose only one more storey, but opposite it another building rose higher. It seemed to have no doors on this side, nor lower windows, but above, dark panes gleamed silver in the diffuse light. None were broken, yet the windows had an empty, haunted look, like the eyes of an abandoned woman. It seemed a vaguely industrial block, no shops or houses in sight. No lights, security or otherwise. Warehouses, or a deserted factory? A chill wind blew a plastic flimsy skittering along the cracked pavement, a bit of bright trash more solid than all the wailing angels in the world. Or in his head. *Whichever.*

He was still, he judged, in the Territorial Prefecture

capital of Northbridge, or Kitahashi, as every place on this planet seemed to boast two interchangeable names, to ensure the confusion of tourists no doubt. Because to have arrived at any other urban area this size, he would have had to walk over a hundred kilometers underground in a straight line, and while he would buy the hundred kilometers, considering how his feet felt right now, the straight line part was right out. He might even be ironically close to his downtown starting point, but on the whole, he thought not.

With one hand trailing over the scabrous stucco, partly to hold himself upright and partly from what was by now grim superstitious habit, Miles turned—right—and stumbled up the alley to its first cross-corri—corner. The pavement was cold. His captors had taken away his shoes early on; his socks were in tatters, and possibly also his skin, but his feet were too numb to register pain.

His hand crossed a faded graffiti, sprayed in some red paint and then imperfectly rubbed out, *Burn The Dead*. It wasn't the first time he'd seen that slogan since he'd come downside: once on an underpass wall on the way from the shuttleport, where a cleaning crew was already at work effacing it; more frequently down in the utility tunnels, where no tourists were expected to venture. On Barrayar, people burned offerings *for* the dead, but Miles suspected that wasn't the meaning here. The mysterious phrase had been high on his list of items to investigate further, before it had all gone sideways...yesterday? This morning?

Turning the corner into another unlit street or access road, which was bounded on the opposite side by a dilapidated chain-link fence, Miles hesitated.

Looming out of the gathering gloom and angel-rain were two figures walking side-by-side. Miles blinked rapidly, trying to resolve them, then wished he hadn't.

The one on the right was a Tau Cetan beaded lizard, as tall, or short, as himself. Its skin rippled with variegated colored scales, maroon, yellow, black, ivory-white in the collar around its throat and down its belly, but rather than progressing in toad-like hops, it walked upright, which was a clue. A real Tau Cetan beaded lizard, squatting, might come up nearly to Miles's waist, so it wasn't *exceptionally* large for its species. But it also carried sacks swinging from its hands, definitely not real beaded lizard behavior.

Its taller companion...well. A six-foot-tall butter-bug was definitely a creature out of his own night-mares, and not anyone else's. Looking rather like a giant cockroach, with a pale pulsing abdomen, folded brown wing carapaces, and bobbing head, it nonethe-less strode along on two stick-like hind legs and also swung cloth sacks from its front claws. Its middle legs wavered in and out of existence uncertainly, as if Miles's brain could not decide exactly how to scale up the repulsive thing.

As the pair approached him and slowed, staring, Miles took a firmer grip on the nearest supporting wall, and essayed cautiously, "Hello?"

The butterbug turned its insectile head and studied him in turn. "Stay back, Jin," it advised its shorter companion. "He looks like some sort of druggie, stumbled in here. Lookit his eyes." Its mandibles and questing palps wiggled as it spoke, its male voice sounding aged and querulous

Miles wanted to explain that while he was certainly

drugged, he was no addict, but getting the distinction across seemed too much of a challenge. He tried a big reassuring smile, instead. His hallucinations recoiled.

"Hey," said Miles, annoyed. "I can't look nearly as bad to you as you look to me. Deal with it." Perhaps he had wandered into some talking animal story like the ones he'd read, over and over, in the nursery to Sasha and little Hellion. Except the creatures encountered in such tales were normally furrier, he thought. Why couldn't his chemically-enchanted neurons have spat out giant kittens?

He put on his most austere diplomat's tones, and said, "I beg your pardon, but I seem to have lost my way." *Also my wallet, my wristcom, half my clothes, my bodyguard, and my mind.* And—his hand felt around his neck—his Auditor's seal-ring on its chain. Not that any of its overrides or other tricks would work on this world's com-net, but Armsman Roic might at least have tracked him by its ping. If Roic was still alive. He'd been upright when Miles had last seen him, when they'd been separated by the panicking mob.

A fragment of broken stone pressed into his foot, and he shifted. If his eye could pick out the difference between pebbles and glass and plastic on the pavement, why couldn't it tell the difference between people and huge insects? "It was giant cicadas the last time I had a reaction this bad," he told the butterbug. "A giant butterbug is actually sort of reassuring. No one else's brain on this planet would generate butterbugs, except maybe Roic's, so I know exactly where you're coming from. Judging from the decor around here, the locals'd probably go for some jackal-headed fellow, or maybe a hawk-man. In a white lab coat." Miles realized he'd spoken aloud when the pair backed up another step. What, were his eyes flashing celestial light? Or glowing feral red?

"Just leave, Jin," the butterbug told its lizard companion, tugging on its arm. "Don't talk to him. Walk away slowly."

"Shouldn't we try to help him?" A much younger voice; Miles couldn't judge if it was a boy's or a girl's.

"Yes, you should!" said Miles. "With all these angels in my eyes I can't even tell where I'm stepping. And I lost my shoes. The bad guys took them away from me."

"Come on, Jin!" said the butterbug. "We got to get these bags of findings back to the secretaries before dark, or they'll be mad at us."

Miles tried to decide if that last remark would have made any more sense to his normal brain. Perhaps not.

"Where are you trying to get to?" asked the lizard with the young voice, resisting its companion's pull.

"I . . ." *don't know*, Miles realized. *Back* was not an option till the drug had cleared his system and he'd garnered some notion of who his enemies were—if he returned to the cryonics conference, assuming it was still going on after all the disruptions, he might just be rushing back into their arms. *Home* was definitely on the list, and up till yesterday at the top, but then things had grown . . . interesting. Still, if his enemies had just wanted him dead, they'd had plenty of chances. Some hope there . . ."I don't know yet," he confessed.

The elderly butterbug said in disgust, "Then we can't very well send you there, can we? Come *on*, Jin!"

Miles licked dry lips, or tried to. *No, don't leave me!* In a smaller voice, he said, "I'm very thirsty. Can you at least tell me where I might find the nearest drinking water?" How long had he been lost underground? The water-clock of his bladder was not reliable—he might well have pissed in a corner to relieve himself somewhere along his random route. His thirst suggested he'd been wandering something between ten hours and twenty, though. He almost hoped for the latter, as it meant the drug should start clearing soon.

The lizard, Jin, said slowly, "I could bring you some."

"No, Jin!"

The lizard jerked its arm back. "You can't tell me what to do, Yani! You're not my parents!" Its voice went jagged on that last.

"Come *along*. The custodian is waiting to close up!"

Reluctantly, with a backward glance over its brightly-patterned shoulder, the lizard allowed itself to be dragged away up the darkening street.

Miles sank down, spine against the building wall, and sighed in exhaustion and despair. He opened his mouth to the thickening mist, but it did not relieve his thirst. The chill of the pavement and the wall bit through his thin clothing—just his shirt and gray trousers, pockets emptied, his belt also taken. It was going to get colder as night fell. This access road was unlighted. But at least the urban sky would hold a steady apricot glow, better than the endless dark below ground. Miles wondered how cold he would have to grow before he crawled back inside the shelter of that last door. *A hell of a lot colder than this*. And he *hated* cold.

He sat there a long time, shivering, listening to the distant city sounds and the faint cries in his head. Was his plague of angels starting to melt back into formless streaks? He could hope. *I shouldn't have sat down*. His leg muscles were tightening and cramping, and he wasn't at all sure he could stand up again.

He'd thought himself too uncomfortable to doze, but he woke with a start, some unknown time later, to a shy touch on his shoulder. Jin was kneeling at his side, looking a bit less reptilian than before.

"If you want, mister," Jin whispered, "you can come along to my hide-out. I got some water bottles there. Yani won't see you, he's gone to bed."

"That's," Miles gasped, "that sounds great." He struggled to his feet; a firm young grip caught his stumble.

In a whining nimbus of whirling lights, Miles followed the friendly lizard.

Jin checked back over his shoulder to make sure the funny-looking little man, no taller than himself, was still following all right. Even in the dusk it was clear that the druggie was a grownup, and not another kid as Jin had hoped at first glance. He had a grownup voice, his words precise and complicated despite their tired slur and his strange accent, low and rumbly. He moved almost as stiff and slow as old Yani. But when his fleeting smiles lifted the strain from his face it looked oddly kind, in an accustomed way, as if smiles were at home there. Grouchy Yani never smiled.

Jin wondered if the little man had been beaten up, and why. Blood stained his torn trouser knees, and his white shirt bore browning smears. For a plain shirt, it looked pretty fancy, as if—before being rolled around in—it had been crisp and fine, but Jin couldn't figure out quite how that effect was done. Never mind. He had this novel creature all to himself, for now.

When they came to the metal ladder running up the outside of the exchanger building, Jin looked at the bloodstains and stiffness and thought to ask, "Can you climb?"

The little man stared upward. "It's not my favorite activity. How far up does this castle keep really go?"

"Just to the top."

"That would be, um, two stories?" He added in a low mutter, "Or twenty?"

Jin said, "Just three. My hideout's on the roof."

"The hideout part sounds good." The man licked at his cracked lips with a dry-looking tongue. He really did need water, Jin guessed. "Maybe you'd better go first. In case I slip."

"I have to go last to raise the ladder."

"Oh. All right." A small, square hand reached out to grip a rung. "Up. Up is good, right?" He paused, drew a breath, then lurched skyward.

Jin followed as lightly as a lizard. Three meters up, he stopped to crank the ratchet that raised the ladder out of reach of the unauthorized and latch it. Up another three meters, he came to the place where the rungs were replaced by broad steel staples, bolted to the building's side. The little man had managed them, but now seemed stuck on the ledge.

"Where am I now?" he called back to Jin in tense tones. "I can feel a drop, but I can't be sure how far down it really goes."

What, it wasn't *that* dark. "Just roll over and fall, if you can't lift yourself. The edge-wall's only about half a meter high."

"Ah." The sock feet swung out and disappeared. Jin heard a thump and a grunt. He popped over the parapet to find the little man sitting up on the flat rooftop, fingers scraping at the grit as if seeking a handhold on the surface.

"Oh, are you afraid of heights?" Jin asked, feeling dumb for not asking sooner.

"Not normally. Dizzy. Sorry."

Jin helped him up. The man did not shrug off his hand, so Jin led him on around the twin exchanger towers, set atop the roof like big blocks. Hearing Jin's familiar step, Galli, Twig, and Mrs. Speck, and Mrs. Speck's six surviving children, ran around the blocks to greet him, clucking and chuckling.

"Oh, God. Now I see chickens," said the man in a constricted voice, stopping short. "I suppose they could be related to the angels. Wings, after all."

"Quit that, Twig," said Jin sternly to the brown hen, who seemed inclined to peck at his guest's trouser leg. Jin shoved her aside with his foot. "I didn't bring you any food yet. Later."

"You see chickens, too?" the man inquired cautiously.

"Yah, they're mine. The white one is Galli, the brown one is Twig, and the black-and-white speckled one is Mrs. Speck. Those are all her babies, though I guess they're not really babies any more." Half-grown and molting, the brood didn't look too appetizing, a fact Jin almost apologized for as the man continued to peer down into the shadows at their greeting party. "I named her Galli because the scientific name of the chicken is *Gallus gallus*, you know." A cheerful name, sounding like *gallop-gallop*, which always made Jin smile.

"Makes . . . sense," the man said, and let Jin tug him onward.

As they rounded the corner Jin automatically checked

to be sure the roof of discarded tarps and drop cloths that he'd rigged on poles between the two exchanger towers was still holding firm, sheltering his animal family. The tent made a cozy space, bigger than his bedroom back before...he shied from that memory. He let go of the stranger long enough to jump up on the chair and switch on the hand light, hanging by a scrap of wire from the ridge-pole, which cast a bright circle of illumination over his secret kingdom as good as any ceiling fixture's. The man flung his arm up over his reddened eyes, and Jin dimmed the light to something softer.

As Jin stepped back down, Lucky rose from the bedroll atop the mattress of shredded flimsies, stretched, and hopped toward him, meowing, then rose on her hind legs to place her one front paw imploringly on Jin's knee, kneading her claws. Jin bent and scratched her fuzzy gray ears. "No dinner yet, Lucky."

"That cat does have three legs, right?" asked the man. He sounded nervous. Jin hoped he wasn't allergic to cats.

"Yah, she caught one in a door when she was a kitten. I didn't name her. She was my Mom's cat." Jin clenched his teeth. He didn't need to have added that last. "She's just a *Felis domesticus*."

Gyre the Falcon gave one ear-splitting shriek from his perch, and the black-and-white rats rustled in their cages. Jin called greetings to them all. When food was not immediately forthcoming, they all settled back in a disgruntled way. "Do you like rats?" Jin eagerly asked his guest. "I'll let you hold Jinni, if you want. She's the friendliest."

"Maybe later," said the man faintly, seemed to take in Jin's disappointed look, and after a squinting glance at the shelf of cages, added, "I like rats fine.

I'm just afraid I'd drop her. I'm still a bit shaky. I was lost in the Cryocombs for rather a long time, today." After another moment, he offered, "I used to know a spacer who kept hamsters."

This was encouraging; Jin brightened. "Oh, your water!"

"Yes, please," said the man. "This is a chair, right?" He was gripping the back of Jin's late stepstool, leaning on it. The scratched round table beside it, discarded from some cafe and the prize of an alley scavenge, had been a bit wobbly, but Custodian Tenbury had showed Jin how to fix it with a few shims and tacks.

"Yah, sit! I'm sorry there's only one, but usually I'm the only person who comes up here. You get it 'cause you're the guest." As the man dropped into the old plastic cafeteria chair, Jin rummaged on his shelves for his liter water bottle, uncapped it, and handed it over. "I'm sorry I don't have a cup. You don't mind drinking where my mouth was?"

"Not at all," said the man, raised the bottle, and gulped thirstily. He stopped suddenly when it was about three-fourths empty to ask, "Wait, is this all your water?"

"No, no. There's a tap on the outsides of each of these old heat exchanger towers. One's broken, but the custodian hooked up the other for me when I moved all my pets up here. He helped me rig my tent, too. The secretaries wouldn't let me keep my animals inside anymore, because the smell and noise bothered some folks. I like it better up here anyway. Drink all you want. I can just fill it up again."

The little man drained the bottle and, taking Jin at his word, handed it back. "More, please?"

Jin dashed out to the tap and refilled the bottle, taking a moment to rinse and top up the chickens' water pan at the same time. His guest drank another half-liter without stopping, then rested, his eyes sagging shut.

Jin tried to figure out how old the man was. His face was pale and furrowed, with sprays of fine lines at the corners of his eyes, and his chin was shadowed with a day's beard stubble, but that could be from being lost Below, which would unsettle anybody. His dark hair was neatly cut, a few gleams of gray showing in the light. His body seemed more scaled-down than distorted, sturdy enough, though his head, set on a short neck, was a bit big for it. Jin decided to work around to his curiosity more sideways, to be polite. "What's your name, mister?"

The man's eyes flew open; they were clear gray in color, and would probably be bright if they weren't so bloodshot. If the fellow had been bigger, his seedy looks might have alarmed Jin more. "Miles. Miles Vo— Well, the rest is a mouthful no one here seems able to pronounce. You can just call me Miles. And what's your name, young...person?"

"Jin Sato," said Jin.

"Do you live on this roof?"

Jin shrugged. "Pretty much. Nobody climbs up to bother me. The lift tubes inside don't work." He led on, "I'm almost twelve," and then, deciding he'd been polite enough, added, "How old are you?"

"I'm almost thirty-eight. From the other direction."

"Oh." Jin digested this. A disappointingly old person, therefore likely to be stodgy, if not so old as Yani, but then, it was hard to know how to count Yani's age. "You have a funny accent. Are you from around here?"

"By no means. I'm from Barrayar."

Jin's brow wrinkled. "Where's that? Is it a city?" It wasn't a Territorial Prefecture; Jin could name all twelve of those. "I never heard of it."

"Not a city. A planet. A triplanetary empire, technically."

"An off-worlder!" Jin's eyes widened with delight. "I never met an off-worlder before!" Tonight's scavenge suddenly seemed more fruitful. Though if the man was a tourist, he would likely leave as soon as he could call his hotel or his friends, which was a disheartening thought. "Did you get beaten up by robbers or something?" Robbers picked on druggies, drunks, and tourists, Jin had heard. He supposed they made easy targets.

"Something like that." Miles squinted at Jin. "You hear much news in the past day?"

Jin shook his head. "Only Suze the Secretary has a working comconsole, in here."

"In here?"

"This place. It was a cryofacility, but it was cleared out and abandoned, oh, way before I was born. A bunch of folks moved in who didn't have anywhere else to go. I suppose we're all sort of hiding out. Well, people living around here know there's people in here, but Suze-san says if we're all real careful not to bother anyone, they'll leave us be."

"That, um, person you were with earlier, Yani. Who is he? A relative of yours?"

Jin shook his head emphatically. "He just came here one day, the way most folks do. He's a revive." Jin gave the word its meaningful pronunciation, *re*-vive.

"He was cryo-revived, you mean?"

"Yah. He doesn't much like it, though. His contract with his corp was just for one hundred years—I guess he paid a lot for it, a long time ago. But he forgot to say he wasn't to be thawed out till folks had found a cure for being old. Since that's what his contract said, they brought him up, though I suppose his corp was sorry to lose his vote. This future wasn't what he was expecting, I guess—but he's too old and confused to work at anything and make enough money to get frozen again. He complains about it a lot."

"I . . . see. I think." The little man squeezed his eyes shut, and open again, and rubbed his brow, as if it ached. "God, I wish my head would clear."

"You could lie down in my bedroll, if you wanted," Jin suggested diffidently. "If you don't feel so good."

"Indeed, young Jin, I don't feel so good. Well put." Miles tilted up the water bottle and drained it. "The more I can drink the better—wash this damned poison out of my system. What do you do for a loo?" At Jin's blank look he added, "Latrine, bathroom, lavatory, pissoir? Is there one inside the building?"

"Oh! Not close, sorry. Usually when I'm up here for very long I sneak over and use the gutter in the corner, and slosh it down the drainpipe with a bucket of water. I don't tell the women, though. They'd complain, even though the chickens go all over the roof and nobody thinks anything of it. But it makes the grass down there really green."

"Ah ha," said Miles. "Congratulations—you have re-invented the garderobe, my lizard-squire. Appropriate, for a castle."

Jin didn't know what kind of clothes a *guarding-robe*

might be, but half the things this druggie said made no sense anyway, so he decided not to worry about it.

"And after your lie-down, I can come back with some food," Jin offered.

"After a lie-down, my stomach might well be settled enough to take you up on that, yes."

Jin smiled and jumped up. "Want any more water?"

"Please."

When Jin returned from the tap, he found the little man easing himself down in the bedroll, laid along the side wall of an exchanger tower. Lucky was helping him; he reached out and absently scritched her ears, then let his fingers massage expertly down either side of her spine, which arched under his hand. The cat deigned to emit a short purr, an unusual sign of approval. Miles grunted and lay back, accepting the water bottle and setting it beside his head. "Ah. God. That's so good." Lucky jumped up on his chest and sniffed his stubbly chin; he eyed her tolerantly.

A new concern crossed Jin's mind. "If heights make you dizzy, the gutter could be a problem." An awful picture arose of his guest falling head-first over the parapet while trying to pee in the dark. His *off-worlder* guest. "See, chickens don't fly as well as you'd think, and baby chicks can't fly at all. I lost two of Mrs. Speck's children over the parapet, when they got big enough to clamber up to the ledge but not big enough to flutter down safely if they fell over. So for the in-between time, I tied a long string to each one's leg, to keep them from going too far. Maybe I could, like . . . tie a line around your ankle or something?"

Miles stared up at him in a tilted fascination, and Jin was horribly afraid for a moment that he'd mortally offended the little man. But in a rusty voice, Miles finally said, "You know—under the circumstances—that might not be a bad idea, kid."

Jin grinned relief, and hurried to find a bit of rope in his cache of supplies. He hitched one end firmly to the metal rail beside the tower door, made sure it paid out all the way to the corner gutter, and returned to affix the other end to his guest's ankle. The little man was already asleep, the water bottle tucked under one arm and the gray cat under the other. Jin looped the rope around twice and made a good knot. After, he climbed back onto the chair and dimmed the hand light to a soft night-light glow, trying not to think about his mother.

Sleep tight, don't let the bedbugs bite.

If I ever find bedbugs, I'll catch them and put them in my jars. What do bedbugs look like, anyway?

I have no idea. It's just a silly rhyme for bedtimes. Go to sleep, Jin!

The words had used to make him feel warm, but now they made him feel cold. He hated cold.

Satisfied that he'd made all safe, and that the intriguing off-worlder could not now abandon him, Jin returned to the parapet, swung over, and started down the rungs. If he hurried, he would still get to the back door of Ayako's Cafe before all the good scraps were thrown out at closing time.

—end excerpt—

from *Cryoburn*
available in hardcover,
November 2010, from Baen Books

MERCEDES LACKEY:
MISTRESS OF FANTASY

Wen Spencer's Tinker:
A Heck of a Gal In a Whole Lot of Trouble

TINKER
0-7434-9871-2 • $6.99

Move over, Buffy! Tinker not only kicks supernatural elven butt—she's a techie genius, too! Armed with an intelligence the size of a planet, steel-toed boots, and a junkyard dog attitude, Tinker is ready for anything—except her first kiss. "Wit and intelligence inform this off-beat, tongue-in-cheek fantasy . . . Furious action . . . good characterization . . . Buffy fans should find a lot to like in the book's resourceful heroine."—*Publishers Weekly*

WOLF WHO RULES
1-4165-7381-X • $7.99

Tinker and her noble elven lover, Wolf Who Rules, find themselves stranded in the land of the elves—and half of human Pittsburgh with them. Wolf struggles to keep the peace between humans, oni dragons, the tengu trying to escape oni enslavement, and a horde of others, including his own elven brethren. For her part, Tinker strives to solve the mystery of the growing discontinuity that could unstabilize everybody's world—all the while trying to figure out just what being married means to an elven lord with a past hundreds of years long. . . .

Epic Urban Adventure by a New Star of Fantasy

DRAW ONE IN THE DARK

by Sarah A. Hoyt

Every one of us has a beast inside. But for Kyrie Smith, the beast is no metaphor. Thrust into an ever-changing world of shifters, where shape-shifting dragons, giant cats and other beasts wage a secret war behind humanity's back, Kyrie tries to control her inner animal and remain human as best she can....

"Analytically, it's a tour de force: logical, built from assumptions, with no contradictions, which is astonishing given the subject matter. It's also gripping enough that I finished it in one day."

—Jerry Pournelle

1-4165-2092-9 • $25.00